The Big Keep

Chris Grayling

Thank you!!

Chris Grayling

This book is a work of fiction. Names, characters, organisations, places and events are either the product of the author's imagination or are used fictitiously. Any resemblance to actual persons, living or dead, events or locales is entirely coincidental.

All rights reserved. No part of this publication may be reproduced or transmitted in any form or by any means without permission in writing from the author.

© Chris Grayling 2011

To
Theresa who edited the early versions of what follows
and pretended to like it and
Katie, Sophie and Lucie.

Thanks also
to Brian and Dick for taking the time to read it and also
pretending to like it.

And
Sarah Dickens and Sally Blackmore for their patience
and time.

1

'No!' Grace groaned quietly in the darkness. It seemed to sum up the situation perfectly.

Within a matter of seconds the lights in the room came on brightly and I heard Gilbert's voice. What the hell was he doing here? Grace gripped my arm so hard I had to grit my teeth to stop myself gasping. In other circumstances having her fingers around a bicep I had spent months honing at the Leisure Centre would have been pleasantly diverting but not at this particular moment.

'Put the bag on the chair by the desk.' Gilbert's voice came clearly from the other end of the room. It sounded as smooth and oily as I remembered it from the single time I had met him at a New Year's Eve do some weeks ago now. I hadn't liked the bastard back then - mostly if I'm honest because he had been shagging my ex girlfriend who wouldn't have been quite so ex if he hadn't swept her off her feet with his collection of expensive suits and whitened teeth. My boyish charm just couldn't compete with good looks and shed-loads of money.

The other person seemed to start doing as they were told judging by the sounds I could hear. I also realised the significance of the order - something was going to be put into or removed from the bag and I had a horrible feeling the safe might be involved in the exchange. If that was the case then the cat would be out of the bag big time. Fan-fucking-tastic.

'Easy on the death grip,' I whispered into Grace's ear.

'Sorry,' she whispered almost inaudibly and I felt her hand relax.

My mind carried on racing like Sky-Plus in forward times a lot, odd thoughts pushing and shoving their way into it like frantic bargain-hunters at a January sale. There seemed to be a surprising absence of fear but maybe that was just my usual lack of imagination saving me from myself. Instead I tried to remain calm by adopting the position of an interested observer, intrigued with the position Grace and I were in. How, for example, had my life gone from what can only be described as mundane to this in only a few months? Where life is concerned boring doesn't get enough credit for the good thing it actually is. Boring, for example, doesn't involve bad news from the doctor or being mugged. Bill Bush, a boyhood friend, had pointed that out to me a long time ago and back then I wasn't convinced. But from where I was standing, or rather lying now, he was looking more and more like Devon's answer to Confucius.

To state the blindingly obvious, life simply isn't exciting in the way it is on television is it? And that's okay because in our own way most of us enjoy just, well, living. We moan but as my mum once said when she was old and knew she had cancer 'no one wants to die Neil'. Before this year I was like most people I knew - too occupied with paying the mortgage until my ex kicked me out to have much energy left for anything else except pointing the television remote. All right, I'm exaggerating– there were the kids, a few friends and, oh yes, Wanderers Badminton Club and more of course, but hardly enough to make my bid for Mr Interesting of Kent 2009 a front-runner. Back then, as a distraction from my daily routine, I would have settled for a lottery win or England World Cup glory.

But now, hey presto, here I was - I had nearly succeeded in my first attempt at burglary. Big mansion near Sevenoaks, over the perimeter wall, across the grounds, past the security at the front door and upstairs to the study - safe opened and a large amount of cash removed and job done. Except for one thing – owner of said safe and contents – Gilbert - comes back and what's more he's not your regular country gent. No, he's probably the local criminal fraternity's Mr. Big and a genuinely nasty piece of work. Hearing his voice coming up the passage behind the study door had ensured Grace and I switched off the lamp on his desk and made it to behind the sofa in double quick time. As problems encountered during a burglary are concerned it was pretty obvious to me to be akin to the *Titanic* hitting that iceberg or England reaching a penalty shoot-out – not good.

Grace is next to me hiding behind an expensive leather couch. It is one of three arranged in a U shape at the other end of the large sumptuous study from where Gilbert and his associate are busy. She is dressed, as I am, all in black. We are sporting the same outfits - jeans, sweater, gloves and balaclava. She is nineteen and I was thirty seven last month so maybe I'm just having a mid-life crisis. You know what I mean – pretending you're cool enough for burglary in the hope it might impress a younger woman. Come on, could I really be that shallow? I hope not, but it's a sobering thought and I hurriedly postpone the debate with myself. I need to focus on the present and analyse my motives later in a safer environment.

After all, perhaps I'm being overly pessimistic and forgetting I'm usually a glass-half-full kind of guy. Maybe I'm grasping at straws, but the evening hasn't been a total disaster because we haven't actually been caught yet and there's no reason for Gilbert to suspect we're still in the study. On top of that we're both carrying back-packs stuffed with the twenty and fifty pound notes that were, up until a few minutes ago, crammed in the safe behind that painting of Venice. So in one respect the plan hasn't gone completely tits up – I just have to find a way out of the house without running into Gilbert or his hired help. How hard can that be?

Of course it really would be easier if I were a highly trained operative who could take a compromising situation such as this in his stride. Believe it or not, however, I'm a teacher – and before you ask, this isn't the time for a long explanation as to how a law abiding and risk-averse bloke like me ends up trapped like this. Suffice it to say that my usual routine at school is not the ideal preparation for my present predicament. Yes, Year Ten's last lesson on a Friday can be a bit of a bastard, but generally my profession is rarely noted for its thrills or danger. If I was a member of the SAS maybe all this wouldn't feel as nerve-wracking as taking part in a nude hundred metres race on Sports Day, but I should have thought of that when I agreed to help Grace.

From my position behind the couch I assume the safe has been opened because Gilbert suddenly goes stark staring mad. He's almost incoherent with rage and his voice has lost all of its smug self-confidence. There's no mistaking this would be a bad time to ask him for a trick or treat. Initially his shouting nearly makes me wince but once he is into his stride I make a conscious effort to let it wash over me. I assume he will soon realise that turning the air blue wasn't going to catch anybody and that he needed to start a search ASAP. Preferably a search outside the study!

For some bizarre reason I briefly wonder what Philip Marlowe would do in this situation. Yes Marlowe – outwardly tough and world-weary but incorruptible and moral nonetheless - a long-time hero of mine. I had been re-reading Raymond Chandler's novels so that probably accounts for such a random thought – it certainly wasn't going to help me come up with a plan of escape. Besides, I knew Marlowe would never have agreed to help a nineteen year old girl rob a gangster if it meant putting her life in danger. To help assuage the threat of imminent discovery he would also have a Luger nestling in its holster under his arm – something I am going to have to do without.

It is a warm evening and I notice sweat is trickling down my neck and that I'm feeling uncomfortably hot and damp. I hope my deodorant will last the evening because my position behind the couch has left me closer to Grace than would normally be acceptable. I reach for her hand and squeeze it anyway. Then I carry on waiting for Gilbert and his henchman to do something - something which would involve them leaving.

Eventually Gilbert sends the guy he came in with downstairs to find help and look for the intruders. Then there are noises suggesting he is examining what is left in the safe. I'm becoming more distracted by the thought that if anything happens to Grace I'll have a hard time forgiving myself. Her eyes are fixed on me and I try to look calm and reassuring. Okay, it's a tough one to pull off when you're wearing a balaclava and you're burning with self-reproach but I give it my best shot. Why couldn't I ever say no? It wasn't just my own children who could wrap me round their little fingers in the right circumstances, even at school it was routine for me to be eventually suckered into saying 'yes' to almost every request short of donating a testicle to one of the school's charity appeals. If I had acted like the responsible pillar of society teachers are supposed be I would be at home on a Friday night watching television and, who knows, horny and devoted girlfriend holding my hand.

So there's no one else to blame then. Not Gilbert even though he's an arrogant shit who deserves to be the love-slave of a sex-starved gorilla. Or Grace, who only wanted justice but should have been told to forget it - by yours truly. I could have made her see it was better to walk away, forget the money and get on with her own life. But no, Neil Mackenzie had to go and poke his nose in again, even though past experience should have taught him the opposite was almost always the more prudent option. That boring was good.

The seconds tick slowly by as Gilbert fiddles with his papers and I try to remember where it all began. At what moment did it become inevitable that I would end up like this – trapped and dressed up like a twat? God only knew but for some strange reason my mind wanders back to that football match last year when Grace scored the winner - when she gave me her bra to look after at half time.

2

Things had been going well. We were two one up, the sun was shining on a glorious April morning and the referee had just blown his whistle for the interval. The team trotted over to me by the half way line to grab their water bottles and gather round for the team talk I was expected to give. If I'm honest I was a little surprised that we were ahead - when we'd driven up in the minibus an hour or so earlier the school looked like it had a serious sporting ethos. The girls in their team looked well-drilled and tough and I suspected my team would be nursing a lot of sore shins by the end of the game. I had almost mistaken their goalkeeper for a member of the PE staff as she hung around outside waiting for her team-mates to appear from the changing rooms - she was huge and easily looked like she was in her mid-twenties. It was only a teacher telling her to collect some footballs from her office that had stopped me making small talk with her and instantly gaining a dodgy reputation. There were parents as well, more than a couple of dozen, whereas we had just me and Liz's mum and dad. We didn't even have a substitute.

It was the semi-final of the County Under Eighteen Girls' Football Tournament. I ran the football club at Mid Kent Grammar for Girls. On Fridays after school any girl who was interested came out to the practice games I organised. It wasn't really serious because our main sports were hockey and netball but I had been persuaded to start it seven or eight years ago by some Manchester United fans in Year Nine, even though they knew I was an Arsenal man. My eldest daughter, Rachel, was also keen and just about to start at the school so I had relented and kept it going ever since.

Sometimes it was a drag having to get changed when all I wanted to do was go home but I always ended up enjoying the kick-abouts with the girls. I was eventually cajoled by them into entering the various county tournaments and to my surprise we were reasonably successful.

'Well done everyone,' I said. 'You're all playing really well. Keep it going and we should be all right. Rachel, Michelle, keep the offside going; it's working okay. Midfield that's fine; keep tackling and try a few long balls over to Liz if you can. Let's make more noise as well; you're all too polite except for Michelle and Rachel.'

'Blah, blah, blah,' I continued. I'm not in Arsene Wenger's league when giving the half time pep talk so after a short exhortation I did what I preferred to do which was give individual encouragement or advice where I thought it was needed. For the remaining time members of the team would volunteer their ideas which I found useful as I often forgot at least half of what I intended to say.

We had about six good players in the team; the rest relied on enthusiasm and tactics. My job was to hide the inadequacies of the weaker players in a basic system they could follow - supporters of teams like Swindon Town will understand what I mean. Rachel and Michelle were excellent defenders. Rachel, my eldest, was one of only two Upper Sixth girls in the team and because of that, rather than a sneaky nepotism, was my captain. She was quick and intelligent and was almost never beaten in a one on one. Michelle brought two things to the team; cheerfulness and a dogged determination that always made me smile.

And then of course there was Grace in midfield and Liz up front. Grace was the other Upper Sixth; athletic, determined and drop dead gorgeous. Definitely the best legs I've ever seen in shorts and we needed her tireless running and tackling. Honest. Liz was just a genius. Curly-haired, quiet and seemingly pedestrian she could make a football do exactly as she pleased. She was our star player - a white, slow-motion version of Thierry Henry.

Standing there sucking their half time oranges they all looked red in the face and I hoped stamina or lack of it was not going to be an issue. I noticed Grace was fiddling underneath her shirt and only realised she was untangling herself from her sports bra when she handed it to me.

'Will you look after this Dr Mac? It's a bit tight'.

Some of the girls smirked and looked at their water bottles nervously. I passed it off as if I were looking after a watch; I had known her for years and I knew that all she was concerned about was playing better rather than flirting with me.

'Sure,' I said stuffing it, still warm, into the inside pocket of my raincoat. 'Okay, it's time,' I continued, watching the referee walking back to the centre. 'Concentrate and carry on from the whistle. We don't want to let them back into it.'

The start of the second half didn't go according to plan. The team ignored my instructions about concentrating and in their first attack the opposition winger hassled our full-back into a mistake, centred the ball and someone stuck out a foot and put it through our goalie's legs. From a neutral's perspective it must have looked funny; the parents on the other side certainly thought so.

'Try using your hands!' and other original bits of advice were flung in our goalie Annabel's direction.

Some other wags were having a go at her looks.

'Is that a boy in goal?'

'Thought this was a girls' competition.'

I wondered how long it had been since the ignorant sods had last looked in a mirror themselves. None of them were ever going to get a modelling contract unless being fat, ugly and stupid came into fashion. Annabel, looking embarrassed and self-conscious, stood hands on hips on her goal line gazing down the pitch. I called over to her.

'Annabel!'

She looked over towards me and I grinned and discreetly made a rude gesture in the direction of the far touchline, being careful that only she and not the rabid mob could see. She smiled at my juvenile show of solidarity which I hoped meant she felt better.

It was our full-back I was really annoyed with. How many times had I said 'Don't fiddle,' or 'When in doubt put it out'. I wondered how she had ever managed to pass the eleven plus and suppressed an urge to run on and throttle the cretin. Instead I contented myself by continuing to shout encouragement.

'Let's forget that one girls. Keep going…'

Apart from a few of the team and, of course, me, all of the noise was coming from the newly encouraged parents of the home school. As is usual at these matches most of the advice and support was pretty meaningless. All the dads seemed convinced that expressions like 'You need to want it more!' or 'We can do this!' or 'For fuck's sake!' would help rather than intimidate their kids. I stuck to bawling out specifics.

'Take your time Annabel! Don't kick yet! Edge of the area!'

For once Annabel got a good contact and the ball sailed over the halfway line and out of danger. As most girls are understandably nervous about putting their faces in the way of a fast moving muddy leather ball it bounced before anyone would have anything to do with it and Liz was on it like a flash As she turned with the ball their centre half slid in just a little too late; her shorts were still collecting mud and grass stains as Liz showed the ball to another defender before slipping it past her so there was only the goalie to beat. I've said the goalie was a big girl but that's doesn't count for much when the goal itself is so much wider and the striker you are facing directs it past you with slide rule precision. Thierry would have been proud. I clapped and resisted an impulse to raise two fingers vigorously towards the throng on the other touchline.

I wish I could say that was how it finished. If only. No, we had to let them equalise again so it went to extra time and first or 'golden' goal wins. My team were knackered and a home victory looked inevitable. Rachel made a few last ditch tackles when it looked odds-on we would concede and two or three times our offside trap went tits up, but somehow the ball never actually went in the goal. The parents on the other side of the pitch were almost beside themselves at the prospect of sending the grammar school lot packing and I was shattered. Watching was as draining, at least emotionally, as playing. I kept shouting but the frequency of my encouragements was falling off exponentially - I just became resigned to whichever way fate deemed the match would go.

After one of the opposition's breakaways on goal there was nearly a riot. Annabel came running out towards the ball and dived on it; nothing wrong with that except she was about ten yards outside the goal area. She should have been sent off, no argument, but as the referee ran over to the slightly overweight figure with the boyish haircut and mystified expression he must have experienced a rare emotion for such an official. He felt sorry for her! Shaking his head, he gave her a lecture through which Annabel nodded furiously, giving as good an impression of gratitude as I'd witnessed in fifteen years of teaching. He then only awarded a free kick.

The language on the other side of the pitch would have made a nun's ears bleed. I've refereed school matches that have turned ugly and if I had been in charge right now I think I would have been hoping none of the spectators had easy access to a noose or a shotgun. As it was, the referee must have been made of sterner stuff and seemed unaware of the blood vessels that were straining in the necks on the opposite touchline. The free kick sailed harmlessly over our goal and the match continued.

Maybe I was just drained but after that I became very calm. A part of me somehow knew we were going to win even though I was still stood helplessly on the half way line in my old blue raincoat trying to look confident for the team's sake. I had a great view of our winner. Rachel punted it to Liz on the right of their area who brought it down effortlessly as three or four of their defence converged on her. Out of the crowd of bodies she emerged with the ball just under control before toe-poking it across the six-yard line where Grace was running in. I was right in line and saw their goalie diving to palm away the side footer that had to be going to her right. Fortunately for us, however, the ball sliced off Grace's foot and instead of going where it should it skewed off the other way. It was comical seeing the giant goalie suspended briefly in mid air diving one way as the ball arced lazily in the other direction to her left. She flapped at it like a bird trying to execute a sharp turn in a cartoon but there was no defying gravity and basic A level Newtonian mechanics and the net ballooned gently.

I must have jumped four feet in the air. For that split second it was better than sex: actually it would be more accurate to say the *memory* of sex since I was going through a bit of a barren period, but I was still pretty damn sure Grace's winner shaded it in the pleasure department. As the referee finished blowing his whistle for full time Rachel eventually stopped hugging Michelle and came to her senses and led the team in giving three cheers to the outraged opposition. As they jogged off towards me I could see there was a broad smile on every pink face. I didn't hug them of course. Rachel was the only one I could embrace and be sure not to provoke a letter of complaint from a parent so I just I slapped a lot of shoulders and made a little speech about how well they had played. As we trudged back to the changing rooms I noticed the luckless referee being surrounded by the parents who obviously shared my view that Annabel should have been sent off for her excursion out of her penalty area. The noisy and bad-tempered protests just added to our enjoyment.

'Pikeys,' muttered Grace.

'Yes, language,' piped in Michelle, grinning from ear to ear.

'Well we were a bit lucky with the Annabel incident,' I smiled back. 'Thought it was rugby club for a second there did you?'

Annabel was striding along just in front and half turned and shrugged her shoulders.

'Slight miscalculation Dr Mac but no harm done,' she said jauntily.

'Lucky the ref fell for your girlish charms - or maybe he thought you were special needs and didn't want to ruin your day out,' I joked. Then I had to duck as Annabel threw one of her gloves at me.

The minibus ride back was a happy and noisy affair and there were a few cheers when I remembered I still had Grace's bra in my pocket and passed it back to her. They persuaded me to stop at McDonald's on the industrial estate outside town and as the happy bunch super-sized themselves I contented myself by chatting with a still grinning Rachel and Michelle. When we got back to school I parked the minibus and then dropped Rachel home. The house where she lived with her mum and my other daughter Alex was just around the corner and only took a minute.

Martine, my ex, and I had divorced three years ago and she tried not to have too much to do with me. It would probably make me look better if I mentioned that my marriage had ended because she had been a bitch and I had come home one day to find her screwing my best friend but that only happens in the movies doesn't it? No, it was me who took my eye off the ball; I deserved my reintroduction to bachelorhood and took it on the chin. Life goes on and you make the best of it. I've made plenty of mistakes, certainly ones Marlowe would have neatly side-stepped, but then again I never had Raymond Chandler writing my big scenes.

3

It took me twenty minutes to drive out of town into the Kent countryside to the village where I rented a cottage. Beechwood was off the usual commuter roads and only boasted a pub, a church and a bus stop as local amenities. The noisiest thing in the village was the occasional passing car and I always looked forward to coming home to the tranquillity of an empty house. When I was married I lived in Tunbridge Wells, a busy prosperous town but at the moment it suited me to live away from all that activity. Teaching is really just a daily maelstrom of interactions with students and colleagues so it is always bliss to escape into some silence - and the cottage had solitude in spades.

A short gravelled drive ran next to the house. I had to pass through a little wooden picket gate from the side of the drive and walk past the kitchen window at the rear to get to the back door. Through a glass-panelled door and I was into a sixties' style lobby with a blue and white tiled floor that continued into the small kitchen on the left. There was also a fairly basic bathroom to the right that had probably been built as an extension to the cottage back when even country folk caught on that outside toilets weren't the last word in bathing comfort. There was no shower in the bathroom, however, only a white bath, washbasin and toilet so there was clearly time to make up when the landlord eventually got around to modernising the place. Central heating would also have been a bonus; having a bath in the winter was like visiting my in-laws – it had to be done but I can't say I ever really enjoyed it.

The kitchen and bathroom each had a rear-facing window looking out onto an expanse of grass the size of a tennis court. It was a sort of communal area rather than my garden but nobody ever seemed to bother with it. Other rented cottages backed onto the grass to the right and at the far end from my place but they all had their own gardens so the occupants usually didn't feel the need to venture into my line of vision. Beyond that there were woods stretching up and over the surrounding hills.

In the kitchen was an old cooker and a stainless steel sink and drainer set on the top of one of three ancient beige kitchen units. Apart from that there was only enough room left for a small fridge and a melamine-topped table and chairs that were also verging on seventies retro.

On weekdays I usually got in after six depending on how much private tuition I had done after school. I would put the kettle on, pop a teabag in a mug and find my cigarettes. Once the teabag was immersed I would light up for the first time that day and sit down on one of the chairs. Then I would lean back against the wall opposite the window and enjoy the feeling of the smoke hitting my lungs. Like most smokers I was always trying to give up but at the moment I was in a phase where I simply acknowledged the futility of my predicament. Instead of trying to quit I contented myself with just attempting to control the quantity I got through. If I managed to keep it down to below ten a day I reckoned that was reasonable given I was always flogging myself in the gym or playing badminton.

Today I followed a similar ritual and I had just finished the tea when the phone rang from the front room. I put down the half-empty mug and walked into what I suppose could be described as the 'cosy' living room of the cottage. It was about twelve foot by nine with a fawn fitted carpet, cream walls and a fire place on the long wall opposite the door from the kitchen. In it there was a settee in front of the fireplace, an Ikea bookcase and a desk and chair in an alcove next to a door that hid the stairs up to the two bedrooms. I went to the desk and picked up the phone.

'Neil Mackenzie.'

'Morning Slick, or is it afternoon? Fuck it; anyway, just checking you're okay for tomorrow night.' It was Gere, as in Richard Gere, the film star, real name Andy, vice-captain of *The Wanderers*' badminton team. Andy had wavy grey hair which accounted for the nickname although his playing style was also reminiscent of the actor's lazy delivery. We had a match on Sunday at some god-forsaken village hall down in Sussex even though we played in the so-called 'West Kent' league. Slick? Long story.

'You know I never miss; are you picking me up or shall I meet you there?'

'No, Rocky's driving us so we'll be around at yours about six thirty.'

'I can hardly wait; pity about the venue though. It's going to be a late one.'

'Tell me about it,' groaned Gere. 'Give me a sports hall every time.' A sports centre meant two or three courts and a quick match whereas a village hall meant one court and a late bed-time.

'We'll be okay Gere. I'll bring some marking or maybe we could all try talking to each other; build up team spirit kind of thing.'

'Steady Slick these ideas of yours are way too advanced. I would bring your books.'

'Just trying to be constructive - anyway, see you tomorrow.'

'Sure thing sunshine, have a nice one.'

The weekend was beginning to look busy which on balance was a positive development when set in the context of the current lack of social engagements in my diary. As usual Rachel and Alex were spending Sunday afternoon with me when I cooked lunch. Today I was planning to do some weights at the gym before coming back and hoping there was something decent on the television. The gym was down in Edenbridge, the nearest reasonable sized town to where I lived. It had some shops, a large Co-op the locals called a superstore and a sports centre. It was ten minutes in the car and I did most of my shopping there as well as using the gym at the leisure centre.

After the gym I went back to the cottage, stopping off to buy food for Sunday lunch and the next few days. Rachel drove Alex over to the cottage the next day and we spent a relaxed afternoon preparing and eating a roast lunch, going for a quick walk on one of the routes around the village and watching television. Rachel helped me write a match report for Monday morning assembly and I made a fire to make the living room properly cosy. They got ready to leave at about six.

'See you tomorrow Dad,' Alex said, hugging me.

'Which lesson am I teaching your set?' I asked - the precise details of my timetable were never immediately accessible to me.

'First thing in the morning dumb-ass – just like it has been since September,' she said wearily.

'Oh yeah, course it is – and less of the 'dumb-ass' Alexis. Drive safely Rachel,' I advised, conscious that I always said it whenever she was driving anywhere.

'Yes Daddy,' she laughed.

I gave her a squeeze and watched them get in the old Saxo and disappear down the road. Kids – if only they knew the potential they had for breaking their parents' hearts. I think I did a pretty good job of not letting irrational fears get to me where they were concerned but it didn't stop me always feeling a pang of protectiveness whenever I said goodbye to them.

My watch told me Gere and Rocky would be calling in about half an hour. I groaned, but after retrieving my kitbag and rackets out of the spare bedroom and finding a towel and a couple of spare tee shirts from the un-ironed pile in the airing cupboard I was ready to go. After dropping my sports bag down by the settee I sat down to wait. Absently I reached over and prodded the CD player I kept on the bookcase. A Nat King Cole album continued from where I had switched off last night around midnight. Nat was half way through *Let There Be Love* so I pressed the replay button and enjoyed George Shearing's dazzling piano intro for the umpteenth time in my life.

Perched on the sofa I tried to rouse myself into a competitive frame of mind for the evening ahead - something I found more and more difficult after taking part in matches for nearly twenty years. I had started playing at school with my three best mates and then we had joined a club which had given us somewhere to go on a Saturday night. This was something of a result for sixteen year olds in a small Devon town in the eighties where nothing much went on during the winter. In fact sport and schoolwork didn't really leave me much time for anything else up until university - basically I was an extremely fit nerd. Don't get me wrong – I wanted a girlfriend all right, or at least my raging hormones kept letting it be known it was a priority but in my teens I never seemed to master the knack of being successful with the opposite sex.

So it was sport - badminton, football and karate that used up all of my spare time in Devon. At university I stopped playing football and concentrated on the other two until I got married when it seemed sensible to settle just for the racket sport as it was less dangerous and more sociable. After ten years of karate I'd just had enough of sparring with blokes who seemed to have more testosterone than me and didn't mind the occasional broken nose or mild dose of concussion.

When the girls were born I even stopped playing badminton so as to have more time to devote to being a dad. I would pop out for a run instead of spending whole evenings out at a time. After about five years, however, I found I was missing both the competition and the social side of the sport and with Martine's blessing I started playing again.

Men's badminton matches like the one tonight were usually long, hard fought affairs. We would start at about seven and sometimes still be playing well past midnight. I had even known matches end at three in the morning which made work the next day a bit of a challenge. I mostly knew everyone I played because the sport wasn't renowned for attracting young blood, so after a few years of matches it's usually a question of the same old faces on the other side of the net. The opposition tonight were pretty good and we would be lucky to win. Whatever the result, however, it wasn't going to be a fun night out unless you liked sitting in a church hall watching men past their prime running around in shorts.

I reached over and picked up my copy of *The Big Sleep* from the top of the television and found the dog-eared page that marked my place. I read a chapter slowly, grinning to myself at the cleverness of Marlowe's wise-cracks. He had one for every occasion. And what a constitution - the man seemed to live off cigarettes and pints of whisky rather than food! Keeping fit also appeared to be an alien concept to most men back then. Chandler never mentions what Marlowe does with his spare time but I was pretty sure he didn't belong to a badminton club or go to the gym.

I wondered what it would be like to be a private detective in Tunbridge Wells. I reckoned *The Big Snooze* would make a better title than *The Big Sleep* for a novel set in TW which, all things considered, was probably a good thing. LA might be more exciting but I thought TW shaded it in all the other categories of the dictionary definition of 'civilised'. Come to think of it, *The Big Snooze* would have also made a pretty accurate description of my own life recently. Apart from the match yesterday, a few dates and some nights on the town with Rocky and Gere my social life wasn't exactly buzzing. Yeah, my life was about as interesting as a rainy day in Hull and had been for months. What I needed was some excitement - but the chances of that seemed as likely as

Penelope Cruz calling me up and offering me Spanish lessons.

4

Rocky and Gere arrived on time and it took us about half an hour to drive over the Ashdown Forest and down into the village where we were playing. Rocky and Gere were easy to talk to and we were still laughing at one of Gere's jokes when we climbed out of the little Nissan in the car park at the rear of the village hall where the match was to be played. He told us that during his annual check up the nurse had told him that he would have to stop wanking.

'Why?' had been his understandable response.

'Because I'm trying to examine you!'

'Fuckin' 'ell Gere, they get worse,' chuckled Rocky, shaking his head as he opened the hatchback so that we could get out our gear.

Gere was tall and slim and his wavy grey hair often looked like it needed a cut. He was mid thirties so the hair colour was a result of genetics rather than stress. He worked in computers for a high-tech company in Sevenoaks but I wasn't very sure what he did exactly. If I'm honest I didn't really care – at a badminton club the conversation never really got around to what we actually did in real life. Nothing ever seemed to faze Gere - his face was usually creased in an amused smile, especially when a woman was around, and I had lost count of the girlfriends he had had since I met him. Gere's only other idiosyncrasy was his fanatical devotion to Swindon Town.

Rocky was late twenties and married to an understanding woman who didn't seem to mind him playing badminton most nights of the week and football at the weekend. He was loud, always up for anything and brimming with banter and enthusiasm. I could never work out who it was out of the pair that led the other astray but they always seemed to be planning something that involved mischief. Like Gere, Rocky also always had a grin on his face together with an ill-judged moustache and goatee. He was an engineer for BT but as far as I could tell spent most days sleeping at one of the exchanges most villages in the county seemed to boast, even if most of the inhabitants are unaware of their existence. Unlike Gere, however, badminton had revealed a certain - shall we say - volatility in his character and I tried to be a calming influence when I noticed signs that an *Incredible Hulk* moment might be approaching.

Rocky dished out all the nicknames which, I think, included his own, even though he didn't seem to have much in common with Sylvester Stallone. I guess he just preferred it to Will, his real name, unless there were some psychological issues I wasn't aware of. Despite all the sport, the copious amounts of lager Rocky could drink ensured any six-pack he might have had was well camouflaged by a generous layer of lard.

The rest of us were stuck with our aliases because Rocky had persuaded us to have them printed on the backs of our sports shirts. After the initial horror at the thought of being the laughing-stock of the badminton league we eventually accepted defeat in the face of Rocky's enthusiasm. There had been a fair amount of leg-pulling from opposition teams through the season but we tolerated the embarrassment for the sake of his concept of team spirit and a quiet life.

The other three in the team, Duncan, Rick and Mike; namely Whirler, Chunks and Ice Man respectively were already inside the hall. There was the usual exchange of gentle leg-pulling before Ice Man and Whirler went on to knock up in preparation for the first rubber. In a men's match there are three pairs on each side and each pair plays all three pairs on the other team once. That makes nine rubbers in total with each rubber the best of three games to fifteen points.

I hope you've watched some badminton on the television so I don't have to go into the ins and outs of the sport. Basically a shuttlecock is hit to and fro over the net until one side wins the rally by putting the shuttle on the floor in the opposition's court or forcing the other side to hit the shuttle out or into the net. The only difference between the rallies tonight and those at the Olympics is to think weaker, slower and less fit plus the language was worse. Don't dismiss the standard too easily though – most of us could smash shuttle faster than a men's tennis serve so it's not a game for pansies.

The four of us sat down on the steel chairs with saggy canvas seats and backs that were lined up against the wall next to the court. It was a typical old village hall circa nineteen thirties with a high enough roof for a good game but décor that must have been fresh and modern before I was born let alone when I picked up a racket for the first time. It would have been perfect for a 'Dads Army' platoon meeting.

'What do you think of our chances tonight then?' Rick asked me.

'Not a lot, especially if Rocky plays like he did last week,' I said so that Rocky could hear.

'Excuse me Slick,' Rocky interrupted, 'if I recall the captain, aka me, pretty much played like a hero and made up for the inadequacies of his ageing partner. I was wondering if you'd given up hitting it over the net for Lent or something,.'

'All right, all right. Just checking you were awake.'

'I couldn't be more focused if I were watching porn. Hey Slick, for God's sake let's not lose to that twat.' He nodded in the general direction of the other team who were sat further up the sideline but I knew immediately who he meant. Eddy, a stocky, miserable looking sod with a small bank manager's moustache was filling out what looked like a scorecard on his knee. Earlier in the season Rocky and I had just beaten him and his partner Richard but only after a few fruity exchanges across the net. Rocky had taken issue with Eddy's integrity over some line calls when the latter had called several of Rocky's shots out. At Wimbledon they have impartial line judges but here line calls were made by the team at the end where the shuttle dropped. Usually people are honest but it is an obvious area for tension to arise if a guy calls one of your shots out when you would have staked your pension that it was on the line. Rocky had complained to Eddy using his full vocabulary of expletives and if the match had been recorded for television the soundtrack would have sounded like a beginner's course in Morse code.

'Don't let him wind you up, you know he's a pillock,' I sighed resignedly.

'That's the understatement of the fuckin' year! Even Gere nearly lost it with him last time,' Rocky hissed so the other team couldn't overhear him.

'But Gere is a girl who has a tendency to overreact in stressful situations,' I grinned. 'Try and act like the leader you keep reminding us you are!'

Rocky grinned.

'Four, four Slick. Good advice, I will rise above it.'

Don't ask me where 'four, four' comes from but Rocky had been using the expression since I first got to know him. He used it to embellish his language in the most unexpected places like normal people might say 'okay', which was probably the closest equivalent in accepted speech.

'We're fucked,' said Rick. 'Just don't get us banned from the league when you hit him.'

It was three closely fought rubbers all and well past ten o' clock when Rocky and I went onto court to play Eddy and Richard. Richard was a young copper in real life and an arrogant little shit as well; you know the type - sweetness and light when they are winning and a pain in the arse when they aren't. It was a crucial game because the winner would put his team four three up with only one more rubber required for victory. I sensed Rocky was really up for it from the glint in his eye and the no-nonsense way he strutted around the court during the knock-up. I hoped I could bring a calming influence to our play to complement his impersonation of a shorter, overweight Basil Fawlty.

Richard and Eddy had beaten Rick and Gere earlier in the evening and during their match Eddy had made a questionable line call. It only happened once but Rocky was in the mood to make the most of it.

'For fuck's saake!' he said in a bit of a stage whisper. We were sat in a row next to the court watching the game and he turned his head sideways to look in our direction for support. Almost in unison we all shifted in our seats next to him and ignored his remark. In our defence it was only because Eddy and Richard were standing a few yards away on court looking pumped up and stony-faced but during the next rally Rocky said out of the side of his mouth.

'Thanks for the support lads.'

'Pleasure, but I think it slipped your mind that Mike, Whirler and I are all pacifists and find your overly aggressive approach a bit threatening,' I whispered back to avoid Eddy and Richard hearing. 'Besides, Richard might get his truncheon out.'

Rocky grinned as he nodded in grudging agreement.

'Fair point Slick. We wouldn't want to see that four, four.'

Anyway, Rocky and I went down narrowly fifteen-eleven in the first end in our rubber, but in the second game things started to look up and we won fifteen-eight, levelling the rubber at one all. In the final game we began to get on top and that's when it all kicked off. With the score at ten-eight to us Rocky hit a smash straight down the line which Eddy called out. It looked good to me and Rocky wasn't having it either.

'You're joking aren't you?' he exclaimed walking to the net and glaring at Eddy, his face red with exertion and anger.

'Sorry mate,' said Eddy with an insincere smile. 'Anyway it's our call Rocky - just out, service over.'

I immediately wanted to punch the annoying smirk off his face and I hoped no one noticed my knuckles whiten around my racket handle. He also placed an irritating emphasis on my partner's nickname as he spoke which didn't help either. I hoped Rocky would be mature.

'Fuck off. It was on the fucking line, do you need glasses or something?'

Ah well, maybe next time. Anyway, it was pretty obvious that Rocky was ready to explode so I tried to defuse the situation by saying reasonably.

'It looked good to me, anybody else see it?'

Richard immediately employed his policeman's wit.

'Who gives a shit what you think Slick. It's our call - the smash was out.'

I ignored him and looked over at the men sitting by the line in question.

'I wasn't speaking to you. Did any of you see it?'

In these situations the rest of the assembly prefers to keep out of it and as it landed at the end where Eddy's lot were sitting I knew there was no way they were going to get involved. As I suspected there was just some shrugging of shoulders and embarrassed blank looks. I walked over to Rocky.

'How about replaying the point?' I suggested to the other side of the net.

'Sorry mate it was out – my serve,' insisted Eddy moving to his service position.

He shaped up to serve and looked at Rocky and me, inviting us to get ready to receive. I took a very deep breath and caught Whirler's eye which had a thinly disguised look of mirth in it. I shrugged and looked at Rocky.

'Come on, forget it. We can still win this,' I said.

We didn't have much option really and shaking his head Rocky ambled over to his preferred spot to receive Eddy's serve.

But he wasn't finished yet. A few minutes later he left a high clear that landed near the back line. I thought it might have been in but I couldn't be sure.

'Out, twelve - ten second service.'

'What?' yelled Eddy, coming to the net himself. 'There's no way that was out.'

'Our call Eddy fella,' grinned Rocky, and flicked the shuttle to me to serve.

Eddy and Richard were not happy. There was a lot of muttering and pacing around but like us a minute ago there was nothing they could do about it. Before Richard got down to receive my service I looked over at our team and grinned. Gere and the others were gleefully enjoying proceedings and there were even a few smiles on the faces of the opposition. This was better than anything on the television that night - if you can call 'Midsomer Murders' or 'The Antiques Roadshow' entertainment.

In the next rally we were attacking until Eddy put up a short desperate lift. Rocky pounced on it and hit it full power, the shuttle arrowing into the back of Eddy's head as he turned in self-defence. It was so funny I nearly laughed out loud and there were a few stifled giggles from the audience up our end. Maybe that's what made Eddy snap. He dropped his racket and came over to our side of the net.

'What the fuck do you think you're doing?' he shouted at Rocky who was still standing by the net with a look on his face that was a million miles from being remorseful.

'Lucky shot…he was aiming for your arse.'

I could have bitten my tongue off but it was too late - why couldn't I ever resist playing to the crowd?

Eddy turned to me with an ugly look on his face which, to be honest, wasn't difficult and I sensed the audience tense in anticipation. We had switched from comedy to menace as effortlessly as my old history teacher Basil Crispin.

'You're a cocky twat,' he said which, to be honest again, wasn't that far from the truth either. 'Just shut the fuck up or maybe you'd like to come outside.'

There were a thousand clever answers to this and I sensed everyone was intrigued as to which I would pick but the excitement was inhibiting my creativity and I settled for: 'Get back to your own side and we'll try and aim for your dick next time.'

Someone at the side, probably Rick, said helpfully.

'You two could never be that accurate.'

Eddy ignored him and took a step towards me.

'What the fuck do you mean by that?' he said to me.

I grinned as annoyingly as I could.

'Is that a rhetorical question?'

He was just over an arm's length away and I could tell from his body language and the look in his eyes that he wasn't going to back down easily. I'd been in enough punch-ups back in my schooldays to know the time for exchanging insults was over unless one of us chose to lose some face quickly. I certainly didn't want a fight - the verbal exchanges were more than enough to keep me amused but I wasn't going to be bullied either. As I searched for a mood-lifting phrase he took another step towards me.

'Hey watch the personal space,' I said looking him right in the eye. 'Or do you just want a hug?'

I knew that a head butt was at hand and that I had probably asked for it but short of falling on my knees and begging Eddy's forgiveness I couldn't see a way out. I'd not personally been in a fight since I'd hit Michael Dauncey in the library back in the Sixth Form during a private study period. On the bright side I realised all the karate practice of my youth might just be about to pay off after twenty years of waiting! As he moved I bowed my own head quickly and his nose connected painfully with the top of my forehead and he staggered back clutching his face.

'My fucking nose,' he gasped, his voice rasping with the shock and pain from the impact of soft cartilage on hard bone.

I just stood there rubbing my head and looking at Eddy, the blood oozing between his fingers and around his moustache as he bent over cupping his nose in his hands. Marlowe would have treated everyone to a dry witticism but I was too busy wincing.

Everyone was up out of their seats now but there wasn't much danger of a brawl breaking out because even Eddy's lot could see that he'd had it coming and on top of that, of course, we were just too middle-class. Calm was eventually restored and a few of the opposition took Eddy out into the kitchen to help sort himself out. We agreed it would be better to get on with the next rubber to see if Eddy could recover enough to finish the match later. There was also a mutual consensus to leave the incident out of our match reports to the league committee in case the old buffers choked on their tea and biscuits and started issuing threats in both our teams' directions.

With Eddy safely in the kitchen both sets of players started to laugh coyly about what had happened but my lot were less successful in disguising their amusement and eventually gave up the pretence.

'He had that coming,' said Rocky' wiping the tears from his eyes.

'Yeah, you really got up his nose,' observed Mike dryly.

'Nice move Slick,' Whirler congratulated me. 'Bit of martial arts there I think.'

'More luck than judgement, but you would have been really impressed if all six of them had had a go.'

'You mean with your speed in the opposite direction?' Rocky was still finding it difficult to speak. He persevered 'at least one thing's for sure.'

'What's that?' Gere said obligingly.

'Eddy won't be picking his nose for a while.'

5

I handed in what I thought was an amusing notice about the football match which the Head read out in assembly on Monday morning. I was sitting near the front of the hall with my form and Rachel and Grace grinned at me from the stage where they were sitting behind the Head with the rest of the Upper Sixth. The Head liked reading out good news like they all do; even if, in the case of the football team winning, it meant I was involved in the success.

Delores and I loathed each other. On my side I thought she was pompous and brimming with a misguided self-confidence in her own abilities. You know the sort – a boss who probably looked in the mirror every morning and saw a born leader while the rest of the staff with any discernment thought 'prat'. If she had taken a moment every now and again to listen to advice or reflect on the effect she had on staff morale maybe there would have been some hope for her but she appeared, on the surface at least, to be condemned to a life of blissful ignorance of her own shortcomings.

Why she didn't like me I couldn't be sure. Yes, I probably came across as an arrogant bastard and I didn't exactly try hard to disguise my frustration with her methods so I'm guessing that made me less endearing than I might have been. On the plus side, however, she knew I was good at my job and did lots of extra-curricular as well so a decent head would have tolerated the fact we weren't best buddies and lived and let live.

I suppose it didn't help either when I began coming to school in open-necked polo shirts because I felt more comfortable teaching like that. When she challenged me I politely refused to go back to wearing a tie and pointed out I was still smarter than some of my female colleagues, several of whom looked like mobile sacks of potatoes. I don't think she envisaged staff ever saying 'no' to her and from then on my card was marked as a trouble-maker.

Anyway, I digress, it was coming up to Easter when a teacher doesn't do much else with his or her life except teach. I know teachers moan and I don't expect a mountain of sympathy but the classes and the marking kept coming at me with a depressing remorselessness. School was a blur of activity and I was so tired when I got home that cooking dinner and flopping in front of the telly was all I was fit for on most days. I was Head of Maths and I had examination classes coming out of my ears on top of keeping the whole departmental show on the road. Years ago when I was a student, revision had been a pretty lonely activity but these days teachers are much more proactive. Revision programmes are implemented at school, which involve practice, testing and timed questions - the works. I sometimes wonder if I'll be actually doing the exams for them one day. Even though I cut corners where I could there was still a shed-load of marking, preparation and organisation both for me as well as for the rest of the department.

Then there were the mostly pointless meetings: Tutor Teams, Heads of Departments and whole staff gatherings. I'd sit there irritated that I was wasting precious time and occasionally interjecting and asking verbose staff to stick to the point and spare the rest of us the personal anecdotes so we could all go home earlier. My interruptions went down well with the other staff who had lives outside school but they didn't amuse Delores and those with a tendency to be enthralled by the sound of their own voices. How bored must their classes have got? I personally didn't give a shit; I was past having my time wasted by colleagues who should have suspected hardly anyone was interested in what they had to say by the blank looks the rest of us had on our faces.

Endless administration was also persistently appearing in my pigeonhole. I binned whatever I could but there was frequently something I couldn't avoid attending to. Precious free lessons were often spent in my office along the corridor from my classroom filling a form out to keep somebody in the admin office happy.

On top of school work I did a lot of private tuition; too much actually but it was worth a fair amount of money and my life wasn't exactly full of exciting other stuff I could do after school. It meant I didn't get home until half six or seven Monday to Thursday and then it was football club on Friday. Most of the tutoring was interesting enough so long as the student concerned wasn't a complete introvert. They would appear outside my office after school and I would sometimes call at a house on the way home for another lesson.

Grace was one of the latter. After being let through the remotely controlled wrought iron electric gates of her house, I would drive up the fifty metre gravelled drive and park next to her little Ford or either of the parents' BMWs in front of the small mansion where she lived. When I say 'small' that is by way of distinguishing it from a National Trust property that takes a couple of hours to look round. It was built of grey stone and about forty metres long at the front with extras added on at one end which could have been stables or staff accommodation. It was probably Victorian, although I'm no expert, but I could see a lot of money had been spent on the house and gardens and their upkeep so that they both looked immaculate. I guess it was the sort of place Marlowe might have been summoned to at the start of an adventure. Some reclusive millionaire would need a man he could trust to sort out a delicate matter concerning a beautiful wife or daughter. Every time I walked across the gravel from the car to the broad oak front door I imagined Marlowe describing the house in that cynical and wearily lyrical way of his. Then the door would be opened by Grace or her mother and I would revert to teacher mode.

Grace should probably have never done A level maths; she had talent but not the work ethic one needed to be routinely successful in the subject. I had tutored her since she was a small Year Eight student up until the Sixth Form and my influence was just enough to keep maths as one of her best subjects. She had also been in my form and maths set for a couple of years so I knew her pretty well. I'd always had a soft spot for her even though most of the academic staff at school thought she was a pain in the neck. If she didn't like a member of staff or she thought they were crap she would give them an uncomfortable time. Grace had an acid wit and a particular way of smiling which made teachers want to punch her lights out. Once or twice in my own lessons at school I'd noticed how irritating she could be if she wanted, but somehow I'd managed to win her over to doing most of the work I set.

Sport was Grace's main interest and she played in virtually all the school teams. She also went to every sports club at the school until she got older when she narrowed it down to about four. A levels always came third after her sport and social life. She was even a talented badminton player and had been a member of *The Wanderers* for a couple of seasons, so she had seen me under pressure out of school as well as in the classroom.

    I always looked forward to seeing her because we got on so well. She liked to drink tea, eat biscuits and gossip as well as working. We'd sit in her suite of rooms on the top floor of the house looking out on gardens that stretched away in every direction working hard for a while and then relaxing into general chat. With our similar senses of humour it was easy to make her laugh with risqué comments and leg-pulling and sometimes she would complain that her face ached from laughing. Maybe I should have been more professional but as I mentioned before she was lovely to look at; rangy and athletic with straight dusky blonde hair, clear skin and neat attractive features and I am only human.

    I discovered soon after I began tutoring her that her parents had split up when she was in Year Seven. Then, a couple of years ago, her mother had moved in with a new man, Marc, taking Grace with her and our lessons had moved from her mother's semi in town to this grander venue. He was clearly loaded but Grace let me know soon after the move that he was someone she wasn't very keen on.

    I had actually hardly ever met the man as he always seemed to be out or busy somewhere else in the house when I was tutoring Grace. I assumed he was the dark good-looking chap who I had spotted leaving the house one evening as I was arriving in the car. He had on what looked like a very expensive suit and could have been Greek or Italian judging by the swarthy colour of his skin and his black well-groomed hair. I had just pulled up so he wasn't exactly being rude when he ignored me and walked to his car and driven off but he obviously wasn't the friendliest guy in the world either.

'What does he do for a living?' I asked during one lesson.

'Oh, Marc owns a hotel outside Sevenoaks.'

'Really, which one?'

'The Wealdon Manor Country Club – do you know it?'

'No, never heard of it. It sounds pretty posh though.'

'I've only been once or twice but yes it is pretty up market. It has a casino as well.'

I raised my eyebrows and grinned. 'How exciting, it obviously makes him a few bob.'

'Money's not everything Dr Mac,' she smiled.

'That's what I keep telling myself,' I said thoughtfully. 'Anyway, unless I win the lottery with the staff syndicate I'll probably never know. Come on, let's get on, we've nearly finished the paper and I'm not going until it's done.'

A week or so before the semi final he had come up again during a gossip break in a lesson. I had been commenting on the new Series 6 convertible I had seen in the drive which was apparently his. I asked if Grace's mum might be in line for a new car as well.

'I don't know,' she sighed, 'Actually I just wish he was a bit nicer to mum sometimes. I don't think she's that happy at the moment.'

This was the sort of revelation I normally don't want to hear about: being male I like to steer clear of discussions that might involve Kleenex although with Grace I could just about make an exception. Her mother's relationship with Marc interested me as much as the finer points of basket weaving but if it made Grace unhappy then I would overcome the Kleenex phobia for a for a few minutes.

Fiona, Grace's mum, was a stunner herself. Fairer than her daughter with shoulder length blond hair and a graceful willowy figure, she always struck me as shy and not as full of herself like some of the rich women are that I meet when I'm out teaching privately. If she opened the door to me before a lesson it was like being greeted by a reclusive Gwyneth Paltrow - she was always affable and yet I got the feeling that making conversation was not her favourite activity. I knew from Grace that she liked me and thought I was a good teacher so I never felt slighted by her reserved manner – it was just an unusual character trait in such an attractive woman. Sometimes I would make her smile by joking about Grace's lack of homework and spend a couple of minutes with her keeping my end of a dialogue up until Grace appeared, all the time trying to appear cool and not gush like an excited schoolboy.

'Er, what do you mean?' I asked, sipping my tea.

'I just think they aren't as happy as they used to be, that's all. Things were fine when we first moved in but lately there's been the odd row and she never wants to talk about it.'

Grace wasn't the sort to cry easily but I sensed she was a little wobbly so I smiled and tried to sound natural. I wanted to express my concern without making a big deal about it.

'Look kid, couples have rows. It's almost compulsory. Maybe they're just going through a bad patch?'

'Yeah, s'pose so,' she shrugged, without sounding very convinced by my inadequate platitudes.

'Look Grace, you know I'd be sorry about anything that upsets you,' I said candidly, 'but I'm a terrible psychotherapist. Have you mentioned it to anyone else?'

'Yes. She said about the same as you.'

'Well there's not much you can do really is there? They're two independent adults. You can't help worrying about your mum but you've got enough on your own plate - like A levels for example - to keep you occupied haven't you? The worse that can happen is you'll have to move out and live in a normal house. Your mum's gorgeous so she won't have any trouble finding a man, if that's what she wants, so there's no need to worry about her either.'

'Okay Neil.' Grace took a deep breath and nodded. 'Thanks for listening, I know you're right but it's difficult sometimes not to worry about her – you older people can really be a bit of a pain you know.'

'Yeah – age doesn't seem to bring much wisdom in most cases I agree,' I said. 'I've made plenty of mistakes myself but I bet I'd repeat them if the same circumstances came up tomorrow. Anyway, on that philosophical note let's get back to the maths, what about question five – what's the integral of two over x squared?'

Then it was Grace's turn to look confused.

After that I always took a minute to ask about Fiona's relationship with her boyfriend and, as the weeks passed, things settled down although it seemed as if Grace's dislike of him remained as constant as pi. I lent a sympathetic ear but I accepted my limitations as a councillor and concentrated on getting her through the A level which, after all, was what I was being paid for.

The week after the semi-final Grace and I indulged ourselves during the lesson by going over the victory.

'When's the final,' she asked.

'After Easter I should think so try and stay in one piece until then!' I threatened.

She played hockey for the county, a sport I considered both dangerous and pointless and was also going skiing at Easter.

'So do you think I should ease off on the badminton as well?' She was teasing me: without her the mixed team would be buggered.

'Badminton is hardly a dangerous sport,' I scoffed. 'Unless, that is, you count sleep deprivation or over-eating the refreshments.'

Grace sniggered. 'I hear matches can be a bit violent sometimes. Didn't someone get into a fight recently and break someone else's nose?'

I put my head in my hands and groaned. 'Okay, okay! It was just one of those things. He tried to head-butt me and used his nose instead. It was hardly a fight.'

'Now you're being modest Neil – funny, I never had you down as a hard man.'

'I have a darker side Grace so you'd better watch your step,' I said, in as deadpan a manner as I could muster before spoiling the effect with an inane grin. 'It might be a good idea not to spread the story around at school though, if you know what I mean.'

'Don't worry Neil; your secret is safe with me - although I can't rule out blackmailing you eventually.'

'That's fine - I'll do anything except tutor you for nothing,' I said absently - and promptly received a painful punch on the shoulder.

The Easter holidays came and went. The main highlight was the few days in Barcelona I spent with Rachel and Alex. The weather wasn't great but we saw the sights and it was fun to be away. Otherwise I didn't do a lot except play badminton, go to the gym and fit in as much tutoring as I could.

Back at school it was eyeballs out for a few weeks and then it was suddenly easier as the examination classes started to go on study leave. A week into term we played the U18 football final and, incredibly, won it 2-0. I was almost disbelieving as the final whistle blew - my teams always went down fighting against superior forces, they didn't cruise to victory and winners' medals and a cup!

This time we had quite a few supporters in the form of regular PE staff and some of the blokes from the staff room plus all the players' parents. My ex wasn't there because I did the football and she stuck to netball with Alex. I noticed Fiona standing with a few other parents and she waved across the pitch at me when the teams were doing their pre-match warm-up. She looked like a model on a photo shoot. Still, the girls were ecstatic and the win demanded another trip to McDonald's. I dropped Rachel off later.

'You were great,' I said in her ear as I reached across to kiss her goodbye. 'I can't believe that we actually won it.'

'Thanks Dad. I'm glad it's over. I'm so tired!'

'I'm not surprised. Anyway see you tomorrow - you'll have to get the cup off Delores in assembly. She'll love it!'

I drove home feeling pretty content with life. If I had not still been experiencing a drought in the girlfriend department it would have been dinner at a local restaurant and plenty of wine at my expense. As it was I went out to the gym and consoled myself by churning out half an hour on the running machine. When I got back to the cottage I really pushed the boat out and drank half a bottle of wine in front of the television.

I eventually picked up *The Big Sleep* which had sat untouched for weeks on top of the CD player and tried to remember where I was. I found my place near the end - Marlowe actually meets a woman who impresses him enough to suggest romance. Well, romance is probably too strong a word for Marlowe; it's difficult to imagine him ever remotely considering settling down or getting married. Let's face it - married men are just less interesting and dangerous – especially to their wives. I certainly didn't have any plans to swap my current independence even for regular sex, although if Ms Cruz moved into Beechwood I might be tempted.

6

The summer term drifted on uneventfully after my examination classes had left; even Year Twelve (Lower Sixth in old money) were off for nearly a month on study leave so I was on a refreshingly light timetable.

Badminton was over for the season but I still saw Gere and Rocky. They'd come over after school once a week and we'd play tennis on the school courts. Grace would make up the four and Gere and I usually managed to lose to her and Rocky in a best of three sets. Tennis was not really our game, except for Grace, whose strokes looked similar to the ones being produced by the players at Wimbledon. Gere was flash but made a lot of mistakes, Rocky was less flash but made fewer mistakes and I just concentrated on hitting the ball when it came in my direction. Some of our rallies were of a reasonable standard - 'that was almost like tennis' was Rocky's typical reaction to three or four consecutive good strokes but we were really more interested in relaxing rather than improving our tennis-playing prowess. Afterwards Gere, Rocky and I would find a pub with a garden and hang around until Rocky remembered he was married. Grace came for a drink occasionally and the three of us would keep her amused until she left for home and more revision. If I'm honest my summer term was pretty lacking in the social department so I guess I was grateful to Gere and Rocky for giving me something of a social life.

Leavers' Day came round again and it struck me afresh how quickly Rachel's time at school had come and gone. It only seemed like yesterday that she had been in Year Seven in her neat school uniform; serious, inscrutable and determined.

She had an offer from Oxford to do maths and I would have bet my mortgage, if I still had one, that she would get the grades she needed. I realised again school would be a little lonelier next term without her.

Grace also came to say goodbye and we exchanged mobile numbers. I felt privileged to have the number of a girl that half the sixth form of the neighbouring boys' school would have sacrificed a testicle to get hold of although I couldn't see myself ever calling her. She was about to go island hopping in Greece with a friend. After that they would be visiting her rich godfather on the mainland where the lucky girl had been going every summer since she was a toddler. He owned most of the resort where he lived apparently so it promised to be more fun than a couple of weeks at Butlin's. She promised to try and contact me when she was in Kefalonia where I was headed but I knew she wouldn't. Grace was always too busy and I didn't fool myself enough to think I rated high enough in her consciousness to merit a Greek island rendezvous.

I was returning to Kefalonia for the fourth time. Rachel and Alex would be with me for a week and then I would have a couple of weeks on my own, recharging my batteries and getting school out of my system. I had a friend on the island who rented me the villa he had built alongside the small hotel he owned. Angelos was okay; he could be a moody bastard but he was genuine and straightforward and I liked him. He had a sweet and indulgent wife called Karis who cut him the slack he obviously needed and also seemed to do most of the work around the hotel.

I had known Angelos ever since I had first come to the island when he was just a waiter at my hotel in Panos. We had run into each other late in the evenings at a few of the local bars and on one of those nights I promised to come back the following year to visit the hotel he planned to build. I kept my word and it started a trend that had continued ever since.

The Zephyrus was a small, quiet hotel with a bar and a swimming pool. It was brilliantly situated; there were mountains to the rear and from the pool at the front there was a fantastic view over the glittering waters of the Ionian Sea. The land round about was undeveloped and the beach was ten minutes away down a single-track road. The villa had a couple of bedrooms, a kitchen and a living room that opened out onto a veranda where evenings could be spent sipping drinks and reading. Now and again it was a relief to escape the heat and cool off in the air-conditioned comfort inside but I spent nearly all the time outside by the hotel pool lying prone under a sun shade either reading or day dreaming.

The flight was fairly uneventful although I can never quite get used to having to spend time with the morons who seem to inhabit airports and charter flights. It's hard to be patriotic when most travelling Brits are as annoying as men in Lycra shorts. Sharing a bus or a train compartment never seems quite as bad as sitting next to some fucking annoying half-wit on a plane. At least the new security arrangements at airports had limited the number of people clutching water bottles wherever they went; what's the point - it's not as if they are running a bloody marathon but these days every silly sod seems to think a regular supply of Evian is going to make up for the six pints they had the previous night or the exercise-free lifestyle they adopted since they left behind their compulsory games lessons at school. To save myself the mental strain of being adjacent to somebody with a holiday lobotomy I took a window seat and let my more easy-going daughters exercise tolerance.

The moment one steps out of the plane into hot Mediterranean air always raises a smile. We all grinned at each other in the realisation that this was going to be superior to a couple of weeks in Devon where we used to go. Even the perilous taxi ride to across the island to Panos, with the old boy driving the Mercedes making more overtaking manoeuvres than Paula Radcliff during a fun run, added to the excitement of coming back to a place where we could be sure of blue skies and Angelos's pool.

After about half an hour the taxi climbed the hill out of Panos and we saw the familiar yellow buildings of the hotel pop into view from behind some trees.

'Nearly there!' I observed chirpily.

'Thanks Dad but I think we spotted that,' Alex sighed from the back seat. Rachel laughed.

'Less of the sarcasm Alex or you'll be unloading the bags,' I cautioned. 'I wonder if Angelos is around?'

The taxi dropped us off and sped away, leaving us to pull our bags down the short drive to the bar area which overlooked the pool and the sea beyond. Angelos was talking to a guest from behind the bar but stopped and came over when he saw us. We shook hands and he kissed the girls.

'Mr *Malakas*!' he exclaimed grinning at me.

He looked as well as you would expect someone who lived in a Mediterranean paradise to appear although I noticed his black wavy hair had one or two grey streaks in it and a slight paunch was beginning to press gently against his shirt. He was mid-thirties, about my height, five ten, and had a long face I guess I would describe as open rather than handsome.

'That's no way to greet a guest you bastard.' I replied. *Malakas* roughly translates to wanker for those not fluent in Greek. 'Anyway, thanks I'll have a beer and I expect these two will want something cold.'

'I'll give you this,' said Angelos, moving a hand across his chest and unfolding his middle finger.

I glanced at his hand and laughed as dismissively as I could.

'No really, a beer and a couple of Sprites on the house will be fine and you could stop laughing at your own pitiful jokes as well if you like.'

Rachel and Alex were smiling as well, mostly at Angelos's laugh. It was the most recognisable thing about him - the staccato starter-motor sound he made when he was amused and which could be heard around the hotel whenever he was in the bar chatting up his guests.

After spending twenty minutes or so exchanging news with Angelos we eventually got to the villa. The girls took the twin room and I made myself at home in the double. It was late afternoon by now but Alex was determined to have a dip in the pool and disappeared outside as soon as she found her bikini. Rachel and I quickly got changed and followed her out.

We spent about an hour swimming and messing around in the pool or sun-bathing on one of the sun beds that were arranged around the water. When the sun began to edge behind the mountains we made our way back to the villa to get ready to go out.

Like most people on holiday in Greece we spent every evening eating out at a *taverna*. Dinner outside in England is possible but you have to pick your evening. In the Mediterranean it's different. If you're with a woman she's probably not wearing thermals and if you're lucky, displaying enough tanned flesh to make you look forward to the walk back to the hotel. The wine isn't going to double the bill either and you won't be getting up for work the next day. You can almost feel your batteries recharging as you sit there underneath the velvet black sky wondering why you went to Bognor for all those years. Even the lack of a woman didn't matter today because it was simply brilliant to be with Rachel and Alex.

We were soon showered and changed and set out down the steep asphalted lane from the hotel as night fell around us. The little road twisted through trees, rocky outcrops and bush before coming out on the coast road that led to the village. Stars peppered the sky overhead and the new moon shone on the sea. The air was soft and heavy with the heat and England seemed far, far away. At the bottom of the hill we turned right onto the road that separated the beach from the seafront villas, hotels and occasional restaurant. The gentle sounds of the sea drifted up across the beach and on the other side the restaurants were full of couples and families having their evening meals. The holidaymakers seemed mostly to be Brits but there were also plenty of Italians and, of course, Greeks. Every nationality was sporting a tan although it seemed that only some of my own countrymen and women had managed to perfect that painful medium rare look.

Soon we turned right again to walk a short distance back uphill to Panos's main thoroughfare and I wasn't surprised to find that the road was already crowded with people. It was just after eight and most Brits are ready to eat by then even if the locals prefer to leave dining for another couple of hours. We had eaten at most places on our previous visits but tonight there was only one place where I wanted to go.

Earlier in the afternoon, as we had sprawled reading beside the pool, Alex had teasingly asked where I wanted to eat that evening knowing full well I intended to take them to *The Secret Garden* whether they liked it or not. It served good food in surroundings where I unfailingly felt at ease. The tables were set well apart, everything was clean and even the chairs passed my own personal comfort test - I never eat at a place where the seats look unforgiving. If I'm being absolutely honest, however, the most compelling reason for returning to *The Secret Garden* was one particular member of staff. All the Greeks who worked there were friendly but you expect that and accept it as part of the methodology employed by restaurants to instil customer loyalty. No, *The Secret Garden's* secret weapon so far as I was concerned was a waitress called Renia.

'Don't tell me,' Alex had smirked. '*The Secret Garden!*'

'Could be,' I said, not looking up from my book 'the food's good and such excellent service. Any objections?'

Maybe it was just being on holiday in a foreign country or possibly the heat, but when I first saw Renia I was smitten. She had found us a table in the corner, fussed over us and had fixed me with green eyes that sent me back to an age where I sat in lessons rather than taught them. At the time I reminded myself that the days when I wore a school uniform were decades in the past and I ought to know better, but it didn't help much. Don't get me wrong – it wasn't love – there are limits to what even a holiday in Greece can do but I did enjoy seeing her. I might never ask her out and run the risk of humiliation either but it didn't stop me indulging in the odd day-dream involving the two of us and liberal amounts of baby oil.

Fortuitously, *The Secret Garden* had been the girls' favourite place to eat as well as mine and we had gone back many times that year and in the years after. She was always friendly and polite and tolerated my mild flirting even though I must have been giving her at least fifteen years. With an amused smile and a faint twinkle in her eyes she would stop at our table whenever we were in *The Secret Garden* and ask us what we had been doing and reply to my occasionally idiotic questions.

As we approached the steps at the front of the restaurant I spotted a couple of familiar faces; the curly haired owner with his moustache and his daughter Petra who was rushing into the kitchen with a pile of dirty dishes on a tray. He beamed when he saw us and we shook hands and exchanged pleasantries.

'Table for three?' he asked, and when I said that would be perfect he led us back into the walled garden at the rear.

The place was quite empty so we picked a table and made ourselves comfortable. It was just as I remembered it; about twenty tables enclosed on three sides by a six foot white wall that was mostly obscured by Mediterranean plants. The house bordered the front and the garden was reached down either side of the house by paved areas where there were also tables set out for dining. I wondered if the face that I most wanted to see was anywhere around but I needn't have worried - at that moment she appeared from around the corner at the other side of the garden and came walking elegantly towards us smiling. She had on a white open-necked blouse and a black skirt that came to three or four inches above the knee and showed off to good effect her slim, exercised figure and the smooth olive brown tan that only Mediterranean people seem to be able to achieve. She was blonder than I remembered but I didn't know if it that was the result of the sun or a bottle.

'Best behaviour dad,' whispered Alex, but I ignored her and stood up to kiss Renia on each cheek in the way that is customary in Greece. The girls did likewise.

'How are you?' she said, 'you came back again!' Her voice was as I remembered it - soft and intelligent and always hinting at humour.

'Dad loves you so we had to,' said Alex helpfully.

Renia gave me a resigned but mercifully friendly glance. I shrugged my shoulders and looked at Alex in an attempt to convey surprise and innocence while Rachel just laughed out loud at Alex's 'joke'. I was mentally rewriting my will when she saved their inheritances by saying cheerfully. 'Don't worry Renia, Alex likes to annoy Dad and we'll keep him under control for you anyway.'

'Yes ignore Alex,' I jumped in. 'She's had too much sun today…we're fine. How are you? How come you're still here? I thought you might have left by now - I'm pleased that you haven't of course.'

So we chatted for a bit and then we ordered and spent a very pleasant evening eating and drinking in the familiar surroundings. I tried not to watch Renia whenever she came into the garden but I wasn't really up to it. She moved with a unique unhurried grace as the rest of the staff scurried around and when she looked at me her expression seemed to say 'It's okay for you to love me - I understand and I won't spoil your fantasy' rather than the 'cute-aren't-I-but-dream-on-sucker' look that most attractive waitresses sport.

Later Mathius, the owner's handsome son and Petra came over to our table to say hello. Mathius made Rachel and Alex laugh even with his tentative English, but I sensed the majority of girls cut him a lot of slack where most things were concerned. Later on Renia visited us again when she was free and talked some more. It was probably only to make sure I left a decent tip, which of course I did, but I could forgive her for that as I could probably forgive her for anything.

I had brought another Marlowe story with me to Panos; *The Long Goodbye*, and over the next few days I re-read it by the pool. I tried to picture the detective on vacation, perhaps having dinner at *The Secret Garden*, but decided it was just too much of a leap of imagination. Marlowe did gin joints and bars, not restaurants with families enjoying quality time together.

And what would he have made of Renia? Most of the women Marlowe meets are either unpleasant or sex maniacs. Renia certainly wasn't unpleasant and there wasn't enough evidence to go on for me to be able to make a fair assessment of the other. I was, of course, prepared to do the necessary research but I couldn't see the opportunity to undertake such a study arising any time soon. Seriously though, Marlowe was, or appeared to be, as cynical about love as he was about most things and if I'm really honest I was only suspending a similar belief where Renia was concerned because I was on holiday and I wasn't used to the heat.

The rest of the week with Rachel and Alex was mostly centred around Angelos's pool by day and Panos in the evening. We visited *The Secret Garden* several more times and then it was suddenly time for me to take the girls back to the airport. They had both cultivated reasonable tans, despite the care they both took not to burn themselves, and they looked like bona fide holidaymakers as they disappeared through customs. They had been great company and it felt like a genuine long goodbye as I lost sight of them.

7

That left me with a couple of weeks on my own in Panos to relax. I mooched around by the pool or outside the villa reading, sunbathing and relaxing. It was lonely without the girls at first but I soon got used to the solitude. There was always Angelos or Karis to talk to at the bar and every evening I wandered into Panos at about ten and ate at *The Secret Garden*. There I would spend a convivial hour or so with a meal, a glass of wine and a few cigarettes. Renia or Petra would come and chat cheerfully to me as the restaurant quietened down after the evening rush and I enjoyed sitting at a table at the front watching the people passing up and down the town.

Near the end of the second week things got a lot more interesting. For a change I took a table back in the garden and Renia glided over smiling.

'Good evening Neil. How are you?' She smiled benignly like a goddess addressing one of her favourite slaves.

'*Kalispera* Renia,' I grinned back. 'Very well thank you. Are you working hard tonight?'

'Yes of course but tomorrow is my day off so I am happy.'

I wondered idly if she fancied sunbathing topless next to me by Angelos's pool as a way of relaxing. I would be only too happy to rub sun tan lotion onto her weary limbs or stand attentively waving a palm over her.

'What are your plans?' I said.

'Sleep!' She looked up longingly. 'Sunbathe. I need to rest!'

'It just so happens I'm free tomorrow,' I said. 'I could reserve a sun-lounger at *The Zephryus* if you like. My room is also very quiet.'

She gave me an amused 'silly boy' look and then deflected my suggestion by saying 'Would you like something to drink?'

I abandoned the verbal jousting which was getting me nowhere and settled for ordering my usual glass of white wine which she swayed languorously away to collect. As she was about to leave the garden to go down the side of the house to the kitchens she had to step aside to let past six Brits, talking loudly and all dressed in a less than beguiling uniform of cargo pants, replica football shirts and flip-flops.

'Look at the knockers on that!' said the one in front in a Lancastrian accent, turning to his mates behind him. The others laughed their approval after which one of the charmers belched appealingly. As usual I had been watching Renia depart and I saw her ignore the remark with a cold indifference that made me smile. I didn't want to excite the interest of the new arrivals by staring, however, so I returned my concentration to the cigarette I had just lit. It was also a relief when they wandered past my table towards the other side of the courtyard - as far as I was concerned the further away they were the better.

Mathius's dad must have alerted the staff to the arrival of the lads because he and his son appeared quickly and hastily shoved together a couple of tables and rearranged the cutlery so their new guests could sit down together. I'd never seen a group of single men on holiday in Panos before so maybe the guy who'd booked their stay had as much trouble reading travel brochures as appreciating football if he was one of the three in the Man United shirts?

They were all in their twenties and looked to a man like they had all seen too much of the sun. Foreheads and noses were flame-grilled to a colour matching their shirts and as they passed my table I caught an intoxicating whiff of lager mingled with deodorant. Thankfully for Mathius and the staff there were only about five other occupied tables at the relatively late hour but, even so, the diners concerned all looked like they had just been told their holidays had been cancelled.

I sipped my wine and lit another cigarette, drawing the smoke lazily into my lungs. I hadn't smoked much all year but in Greece my will to resist was powerless. As much as I tried I couldn't help observing the United table out of the corner of my eye. It was impossible not to hear what they were saying and I wondered if they knew the Arsenal score. Apparently United had won by four against Spurs, which, to be honest, isn't too much to get worked up about, but they were definitely intent on making the most of it. Predictably the first thing they ordered was more lager to complement what I suspect was the copious amounts they had already consumed during the match. After that it was mostly spag bol and other typical Greek cuisine. I wanted to go over and point out that *souvlaki* was in fact kebab which somehow seemed a more appropriate meal to go with lager but I didn't imagine they were much interested in my gastronomic input.

Live and let live I thought; stop being such a prejudiced bastard against your Northern cousins. For heaven's sake; I'd spent ten years in Liverpool as a student and then at my first teaching job. I'd had my car nicked or almost nicked half a dozen times but most of the scousers I'd got to know had been great. My next door neighbour, Alistair, for example, had driven me ten miles to work on a couple of occasions when the bloody Cortina wouldn't start in the morning and he couldn't ever let me work on it for more than five minutes before donning his overalls and coming out and giving me a hand.

Al and his wife Jean were, as they say, the salt of the earth. He seemed to have every tool known to man in his tiny backyard workroom. I often wondered if ever I'd needed a sonic screwdriver whether he would have whipped one out of one of the cupboards. As a newly married in his first home I was always in need of his advice on anything from changing a tap to a back axle and it almost always ended up with him on his hands and knees giving me a hand. When he found out I did karate at the university he took me along to his local club, where I discovered in astonishment that he was a fourth Dan black belt! The last neighbours I shared with Martine in Tunbridge Wells before she sent me packing had both worked in The City. One year I know they both received a Christmas bonus double what Al got working for a year at the council in Bootle but I know who I'd have rather had living next door to me.

The decibel levels were continuing to rise from the relocated Stretford End when Renia brought me my main course.

'Things are a bit lively tonight,' I observed, nodding over towards the noise. She frowned, slightly wrinkling the middle of her honey coloured forehead.

'Yes, we do not have men like this before. It makes me a little, er, nervous.'

'Don't worry, I'll look after you,' I grinned, trying to imitate a mock, heroic expression. 'Tell them your boyfriend is an origami expe-.'

I was interrupted by one of the dirty half dozen. 'Hey darling, why don't you come over to our table and leave that bastard alone before he drowns in his own dribble?'

I turned to face them and forced a smile.

'Sorry lads, I thought you were three happy couples from Gay Pride and would prefer a bloke to wait on you,' I said clearly across the courtyard.

I thought it was funny, although I say it myself, but hey, twenty years at the front of a classroom does at least prepare one for dealing with witticisms from the back row so I'm not claiming a wealth of natural talent. Then I wondered why the hell I was risking life and limb to get a laugh until I realised who was standing by my table. Disappointingly, the look on Renia's face seemed to be questioning my sanity rather than saluting my wit and it dawned on me that maybe I was the only one in earshot able to appreciate my own joke.

Thankfully, one or two men at other tables smiled despite the sudden tension in the air and the six singles looked momentarily gobsmacked. Now they had a decision to make - up the ante or accept what I'd said as banter. Normally in England I guess they would have started playing three a side with my head as a football but they were in a foreign country and there weren't enough of them for a riot. No disrespect to Marlowe but I felt like Clint Eastwood in a classic bar-room stand-off. Okay, I wasn't guaranteed the predetermined outcome where I would step over six prostrate bodies after beating them senseless single-handed and then off into the evening with Renia on my arm but what the hell, I hadn't had this much excitement since the badminton match with Eddy and Richard.

To my relief one of two of them started laughing until they all joined in, even the one who had called across. Amazing; United fans with a sense of humour - was there anything Greek air couldn't change?

'Nice one mate,' one of them grinned, raising his glass and then turning back to his pals.

Renia looked at me and just couldn't keep the admiration out of her eyes. I leant back in my chair and basked in its warming glow looking up at her enquiringly. This was the effect I remembered Marlowe having on women.

'Neil! I didn't know you could be so…'

'Attractive, brave, sexy…?' I inquired, smiling.

'No, stupid!' she corrected me. 'They may have come over and hit you, you silly man! Now, enjoy your meal!'

She turned and walked off, but as she was going back to the front down the courtyard at the side to the kitchen where no one could see, she looked over her shoulder and smiled back at me.

That wasn't the end of the excitement either. By the time I was onto my cappuccino the United fans were losing even more of their inhibitions as the glasses of lager were downed. If they had been younger they could have been on a school outing from Hogwarts' because I found their rate of consumption almost magical. They had forgotten me by now and were totally focused on the waitresses who were enduring upsetting and sexually explicit comments and suggestions. They seemed to believe that if it were demanded often enough then Petra or one of the others would eventually get their tits out. Most of the other diners had moved to the tables at the front or side of the restaurant and Mathius hovered angrily near their table looking as pissed off as I'd ever seen him.

Eventually it all kicked off when, after weaving their way back from a visit to the toilets two of them came upon Petra and Renia trying to clear a table of dirty dishes and attempted to make the girls dance with them along to the taped music coming though the restaurant's speaker system. The other four thought it was hilarious but Mathius had clearly had enough and walked over to his helpless sister and her unwanted partner.

'Please, dancing with the waitresses is not allowed,' he said, trying with all his power to be polite but firm and touching the bloke's arm to guide him away.

You can guess the rest; Petra's 'partner', a large shaven-headed bloke I would have normally crossed the street to avoid, took one look at Mathius's hand, let go of Petra and turned towards Mathius and head-butted him clumsily, catching Mathius on the side of his face as he turned away to avoid the blow. In unison, the other five of us still left sitting in the courtyard stood up. I was only a couple of steps away from a frightened looking Renia who was struggling to free herself from her own admirer. Petra screamed as Mathius staggered back. I walked over to Renia and her would-be partner.

'Sorry to butt in but the lady's allergic to wankers.'

As he turned it registered for a moment that he was at least ten years my junior and fitter looking than I would have liked but I was past the point of no return. I had a clear view of his throat and swung a short right hook using bent fingers instead of a fist and connected sweetly. It was enough to send him onto the floor, gasping and clutching his neck. One nil.

In passing I noted that Petra's knee must have made some sort of contact with her man's genitals because he had bent over slightly, giving Mathius enough time to recover and grab him. They grappled briefly like a couple of wrestlers in an outtake from WWE Bottom Line or Bottoms Up or whatever the fuck they call it before Mathius got a decent hold on his opponent and threw him clean over a vacant table for two onto another, scattering plates everywhere and making a strangely satisfying crashing sound of broken crockery and scattering cutlery. Mathius was a strong boy! I just kept going and pole-axed the nearest red shirt to me with a straight kick to his head using the sole of my sandal and enough force send him tottering backwards onto another table that collapsed under his weight. That made it three nil but before anyone could add to the scoring Mathius's dad arrived with two blokes who must have been working in the kitchen because they were each carrying knives the length of tennis rackets.

At this point the three Mancunians remaining vertical decided things were too one-sided to continue and raised their hands in a 'please don't butcher us' fashion. Always the businessman, Mathius's dad got their bill while the fans who had received their well-deserved slapping were each given an ice bucket of water over their heads to bring them to their senses. A crowd of diners from the front of The Secret Garden had left their meals and assembled in the courtyard and were taking in the carnage.

'Serves 'em right,' said a stocky middle-aged woman with a Yorkshire accent. I wished I knew if she disapproved of lager louts in general or United supporters in particular. Her husband and most of the others were nodding in agreement; I wondered if Mathius and I should pose for photographs like big game hunters so they could all have something concrete with which to embellish their holiday stories with when they returned to the UK.

'Nice throw,' I grinned at Mathius, motioning to his dancing partner of a few seconds who was sitting looking confused beside the upturned table that had broken his fall.

Mathius grinned back and flexed a bicep for us all to admire.

'But you hit two,' he exclaimed and doing some mock karate gestures. 'Are you James Bond in disguise?'

'I'm afraid not,' I shrugged with a smile. 'Besides, you know I prefer white wine to dry Martinis.' Mathius chuckled and nodded.

'Ah yes, Martinis, James Bond, good Neil.'

I turned to look at Petra and Renia to see how they were. Petra was standing by her dad and Renia was talking to the older of the two cooks and obviously telling him the whole story. She beckoned me over to them so I walked over trying not to look too pleased with myself.

'Neil, this is my father. You know that he works in the kitchen. He is very grateful that you helped me.'

We shook hands. He had grey curly hair and a wide moustache but apart from that I could see a certain family resemblance. I made a mental note that he would probably use the carving knife to relieve any bloke who mistreated his daughter of his main reason for living, so I was suitably respectful and focused on him rather than the beautiful woman standing by his side.

'What an evening,' sighed Renia, after he had departed back to the kitchen. 'I am sorry your meal was spoiled. Would you like something else on the house to say 'thank you'.

It crossed my mind to suggest she spend tomorrow on an empty beach with me but I settled for 'another cappuccino would be fine - as long as you have one as well and drink it with me.' She looked at me and smiled.

'Okay Neil but I choose another drink.'

So I finally got to speak to her face to face free from feeling that I was somehow keeping her from her work and the pressure that came with attempting to be witty but brief. Not unexpectedly she looked ravishing from this new angle and I had to work hard to keep up a semblance of relaxed normality. It had been a while since I had sat across a table from a beautiful woman and take it from me I mean beautiful. As I mentioned before her eyes were a striking amber green and they flashed hypnotically whenever I said something that amused her. I rationed myself to a few polite moments of eye contact but it required an iron will. I'm a long way from being romantic, at least if my ex was to be believed, so maybe it was the Greek air that was affecting my equilibrium. I didn't much care, however, as I was having so much fun.

Of course, talking to a woman in the circumstances I had found myself is always a delicate balancing act. You're not on a date or in a relationship so it is a bit like sky-diving with a parachute you're not entirely sure about. Even if the conversation flows as it was now and she laughs in most of the right places you can never be certain you'll land in one piece until you pull the rip-cord. Granted I wasn't exactly actually plummeting earthwards praying for a soft landing but at the back of my mind I knew a kind of rip-cord moment was inevitable - I was going to ask her out before the conversation was over. I hoped I hadn't picked up a rucksack by mistake before I got onto the plane.

I'd known all this a long time before she sat down with me of course but, up until now, I had managed to bury my intentions in a fog of indecision. Before she joined me for a drink my legs would have carried me out of *The Secret Garden* after paying my bill and not given me the opportunity to risk rejection. I wanted to spend time with her - no correction, I ached to spend time with her, but pride or whatever would have overridden any urge to satisfy that craving before she agreed to join me in a drink. Now we were together there was a chemistry between us, at least from where I was sitting, that I couldn't ignore anymore than a chocoholic could leave a Dairy Milk in its wrapper.

So I needed to make a decision. It was her day off tomorrow and I wanted to spend some of it with her. On the other hand, I would have rather faced all six of the United fans alone rather than hear her say something that could be summarised as 'no' if I asked her out. It was a big risk, because upsetting the status quo of waitress and guest might make future visits to *The Secret Garden* somewhat problematic. It would be embarrassing for everyone, especially me, unless I could pop the question using a degree of charm even Marlowe might struggle to achieve.

At last I got a grip of myself and decided to be honest with her. Hey, they couldn't take away my karate kid image now and if I didn't ask her now that would be my last chance done and dusted.

'Renia, may I ask you a question?' I began, trying not to look or sound like the jittery schoolboy I felt I was transforming into. She looked nervously quizzical herself but nodded.

'Would you spend some of your day off with me tomorrow?'

I took a sip of my coffee and looked at her with what I hoped was a relaxed and playful grin on my face. I could feel my heart battering the walls of my chest but there was nothing I do about that now - the words were out of my mouth and there was no going back.

Renia looked back at me across the table and I could see that she was making a few mental calculations herself. She smiled teasingly at me and I braced myself for the bad news. I really hoped I could pull off nonchalant in the face of devastating disappointment.

'Don't worry Neil, you are very sweet and I should like to see you tomorrow.' she said. 'What would you like to do?'

I hung my shoulders in mock relief and let out a long sigh and then laughed, only just managing to keep the hysteria out of my voice.

'Brilliant!' I exclaimed. 'What would you like to do? I haven't really planned anything I mean.'

She pondered for a moment or two.

'I have a car, my father's. I will drive us somewhere. Okay?'

It sounded fine by me. She could have suggested washing up in *The Secret Garden* kitchens all day and I would have jumped at the chance.

'I will meet you outside here at ten o clock. Is that okay Neil?'

It was better than satisfactory. I had a date at last and with the girl I would have walked naked across Trafalgar Square for. I was so excited the walk back to Angelos's place under the stars was over almost before it began. When I found him in the bar things got even better. He told me Arsenal had won 3-1.

8

The next morning I had breakfast at eight in Angelos's bar by the pool. The sea was shimmering in the distance and the air was so clear the undulating outline of mainland Greece on the horizon seemed the closest it had been for days. I showered and put on some calf length khaki cargo pants, an old training vest, a cap, sunglasses and sandals. I popped some cash, a pair of swimming trunks, sun tan lotion and a small towel in an old backpack and set off in the warming air towards Panos. I was a few minutes early reaching the restaurant and spotted Petra who was serving breakfasts. I waved and sat on a low wall under some old pine trees that grew next to the little square across the road from *The Secret Garden*. I waited nervously, watching the people passing by on their way down to the beach.

Just after ten an old Fiat with Renia at the wheel pulled up and she beckoned me to get in next to her. She was wearing a blue halter neck top and a little summer skirt resting on her hips so that there was a little of her midriff and just enough leg showing to be sexy without overdoing it. Her sunglasses were up on the top of her head holding back her hair. She looked a dream.

'Hi, you look even nicer without your waitressing clothes,' I said cheerily as I sank down into the ancient seat beside her.

'Of course,' she laughed, leaning over towards me so that I could kiss her hello Greek style.

'Where are you taking me?' I enquired. 'I am as excited a student on a school trip!' A more accurate description would have been 'on his first date' but I didn't want to spoil the day by allowing any of my adolescent urges to take over so I kept to the game plan of being manly and mature yet irresistibly amusing.

She smiled and raised her eyebrows in mock disappointment.

'So I remind you of your teacher?'

'Hardly, for a start none of them ever wore a skirt like that and most of them had beards. The men were even worse.'

'Very funny Neil – you are always joking. Do you have a serious, how you say – face?'

I laughed at her gently.

'Sometimes Renia but we say side – serious side. Anyway, let's forget about my sides – where are you taking me?'

She put the car in gear and we moved off slowly, talking as she glanced in her mirrors and turned the steering wheel.

'An old Venetian fort because I thought you would like to see something old like you and then perhaps Argostolli. We will see how it goes. In Greece we like to, how do you say - go with the flow?'

I nodded and went on to reassure her that I hadn't been around when the Venetians ruled the Mediterranean so it would be very interesting. Yes, a Venetian fort was fine, she was the boss and I would be happy whatever we did. In other words the usual bollocks we spout out on a first date although this of course wasn't technically a date. It just felt like one. I wanted her to like me and say nice things about me to, say, her children when she was telling them stories about Uncle Neil and how he saved her in *The Secret Garden* and then took her out and was the perfect gentleman. I daydreamed that she even might get a little misty eyed at the thought and feel compelled to call me up and brighten one of my days when I was even older than the decrepit age I felt now.

After about thirty is it me but does one always feel too old? I know it's a relative thing but I've always felt over the hill in some sense. In sport it's obvious but it's subtly there in so many other areas – too old to ever be a Head, too old to wear those Speedos and on and on. Okay, the Speedos aside, I knew it was all rubbish and was going to have to keep reminding myself about that for the rest of the day. On the other hand I didn't want to step into my own whacky Speedo-wearing universe. An eighty-five year old once told me that a pretty girl is always a pretty girl and I groaned inside as he said it – all those women out of bounds but still sexy – old age was bad enough without that! But thirty-seven wasn't eighty-five so think positive Mackenzie.

The half an hour's drive to the fort went swiftly. As Einstein observed, time passes more quickly when you're with a beautiful woman and it was no different for me. The spectacular Kefalonian scenery with its rugged hillsides and occasional glimpse of a blue sea would have been distracting usually but to be honest I hardly noticed.

She was a good driver but the last stretch of the journey up the steep approach to the fort was a little exhilarating. The straight sections where we were angling up the cliff weren't too bad but the hairpin bends required to get us onto each successive straight were a nightmare in the old car. First gear was needed each time and I hoped her clutch control was up to the job.

'Are you nervous?' She asked me as the car roared and lurched around one bend.

'It would be a shame to die so early in the day,' I said. 'In England we have engines in our cars.'

She raised an eyebrow at me, her eyes hinting at a smile.

'So you don't like my car?'

I shook my head and then nodded at the open windows.

'No, it's lovely, really. The air conditioning is especially efficient.' She slapped me playfully on my arm, which seemed like a good sign, and then we carried on up the mountain until we arrived in front of the fort and parked behind some other cars on a cobbled street running between a few white painted houses with walled gardens.

There was great view of what seemed like half of Kefalonia from the tumbling walls of the fort. We picked our way around, talking and occasionally stopped to look at the stunning vistas of the plain below us, the sea beyond and the mountains lying to the north. Renia pointed out the names of the distant settlements that she knew. It was already hot and afterwards we had a welcome drink in the garden of a little *taverna* outside the fort. We continued chatting and she told me that she lived with her mum and dad in Athens in the winter where her dad worked in various hotel kitchens as a chef. She had just finished University and was starting work in Athens in the autumn. Her boyfriend was a builder in Athens but she didn't want to get married until she was thirty; she wanted to spend at least five years starting her career, which, as far I could tell, was something to do with advertising.

She asked me whether I planned to get married again and I said I didn't think so.

'Do you have a girlfriend?' she asked, cutting to the chase.

'No, I'm a free agent. The past year has been a bit barren. Anyway, I think I'm too old to go falling in love again.' I looked at her to check she was smiling - she was.

'I am surprised Neil - you seem to me to be romantic. Perhaps you should live in Greece and meet Greek women. I think we are more, how you say, passionate?'

I laughed at her teasing but found myself replying more seriously.

'I don't know Renia. I like women, I fancy women but it's different to when I was young. Falling in love seems so adolescent somehow. Perhaps that's what divorce does to you or maybe I'm old enough to realise that I'm just not cut out for a life-long commitment now I know how fickle I can be?'

Renia wrinkled her brow at me.

'I'm sorry, what is this 'fickle' Neil?'

'Oh, sorry – er, changeable or maybe the potential to be unfaithful. Understand?'

She smiled as the light dawned.

'You mean like all men,' she said, her eyes glinting mischievously.

She had me there and I raised my hands in surrender.

'Ok, yes I'm just like all men but at least I'm trying to be honest about it. Don't I get some credit for that?'

'Perhaps,' she said, putting on a non-committal expression although the laughter was still in her eyes.

'Do you love your boyfriend?' I said, before she could carry on quizzing me about my commitment phobia.

'I think so, yes. Or why would I be with him?'

'Maybe you were desperate when he asked you out?' I said, shrugging my shoulders and shaking my head resignedly. Men can be sneaky sods. One minute you think he's completely un-sexy and the next he's convinced you to marry him.'

I got another gentle slap on the knee for that.

'So you think I am desperate Neil? Perhaps this is why I agree to go out with you!'

'You know I'm joking Renia. I expect half of Athens wanted you,' I laughed. 'He's a lucky boy but it's nice you decided to compare him with a grown up!'

She had to laugh at that. God, I could be entertaining when the girl was worth it. We carried on sipping our drinks and it vaguely crossed my mind that I hadn't smoked and didn't want too either. If paradise existed God would have his work cut out beating this. After a moment or two Renia spoke again.

'So why did you ask me out Neil? You knew I had a boyfriend. Is it the English way?!'

The short answer to that was probably 'yes' but I was hardly a spokesman for the rest of my countrymen, some of whom at least would have drawn the line way before I had. I tried to be honest again and almost managed it.

'No, it's exactly like I said last night. Yes I like you and want to spend time with you - I hope that's not wrong. A few times in my life I have had special feelings for a woman that I find difficult to analyse, and as soon as I met you at *The Secret Garden* I recognised an unusual attraction. Maybe you only wanted a good tip but I can only speak for myself. It doesn't mean I think we can get married or that I want to have sex with you.'

My God, what the fuck was I talking about? Of course I wanted to make love to her! Heck, give me a few months and I might propose marriage as well despite the fact I doubted my own ability to ever make a sensible decision where a woman was concerned. I hoped I wouldn't come to regret my lack of honesty. Mercifully, however, Renia just laughed at my remarks and seemed content to let the conversation take a lighter vein at last.

'Maybe we should not talk anymore about love or we will both be confused,' she smiled. 'Where would you like to go now on your school trip - how about Argostolli?'

'Argostolli sounds fine by me. There I shall buy you lunch if you can find a good restaurant '

After another short drive we arrived at the capital of the island, parked the car and wandered around the shops for a while until Renia found a *taverna* serving lunches in a shady garden terrace. My good form continued and the conversation flowed easily. After lunch I accompanied her while she did a little bit of shopping for things she couldn't get in Panos and then we headed back on the return journey. She suggested a swim as we approached a little resort a few miles from Panos and I readily agreed; I didn't want the date to end and a swim and some sun sounded just dandy.

She stopped the car at the rear of a few other cars parked in a line at the side of a little lane that she had turned into off the main road. She collected an old canvas beach bag from the boot, I grabbed my back-pack and we left the car and strolled down the lane which led to a beach after about fifty metres. The sun was taking no prisoners and I was sweating as much as I would in a gym session. I doubted if it was an attractive look and longed to get into the water.

The beach stretched for what seemed like a mile or so before us, sandy and quite narrow and arcing gently away to the headland beyond. I guessed Panos was the next resort along the coast. It was mid-afternoon and the sun was sparkling on the iridescent blue water as we walked onto the creamy coloured sand and paused to take it all in. There was the inevitable row of sun-loungers shaded by parasols that one could rent but Renia said that if we walked along the beach we would find some rocks that would give us some cover from the sun. There weren't many people around except for a few children splashing about in the water and about half a dozen adults either sprawled on their sun-beds or cooling off in the sea. It was beautiful but walking beside Renia it could have been Blackpool on a wet Monday in October and I wouldn't have much cared.

After a few hundred metres the sand dunes at the back of the beach gave way to rocky outcrops and we were walking around and between what looked like sandstone formations that formed secluded stretches of sand. There were fewer and fewer people until it all seemed satisfyingly deserted. We settled for a spot on a narrow bit of the beach where the sea lapped only about ten metres from a silver-grey outcrop of rocks that cast convenient shadows for shelter if the sun became too unbearable. Renia took out a towel and a bikini from her bag and disappeared behind a large rock to change. I just pulled on my trunks using my own towel for cover and then sat down on it and waited for her to return.

She looked good enough to give Ursula Andress a run for her money when she came back. Okay her bikini was black and there was no knife but you get the idea. In fact I would have chosen her over Miss Andress - for a start she was a better conversationalist - and Renia had sexier, fuller hips and that mesmerising skin tone. She flung out her towel next to mine and flopped down on it, resting her head on her hand. She was smiling as if I amused her. My own expression probably resembled a Labrador's expecting a walk - minus the drooling of course.

'You are very dark for someone from England,' she observed

'I've a Japanese grandfather.' I grinned and laid back and turned my face to look up at her. 'The muscles are all down to me though.'

'You have a good body for ... someone who is sixty,' she said, looking me up and down. 'I should congratulate you.'

'Ha, I see you are not so nice when you don't want a tip,' I sighed, still looking at her and enjoying every nanosecond.

'I'm sorry Neil - what do you mean. My English is not so good.'

'Ha, ha Miss Renia. How about getting me a cappuccino?'

'Later,' she said, slapping me on the hand. 'Come on Neil, let's go in the water.' With that she trotted down to the water's edge, beckoning me to follow.

'What, without my water wings!' I cried, chasing after her and following her into the sea until I was in up to my waist.

'Don't worry, I will look after you. If I lost *The Secret Garden's* best customer Petra's dad will keell me!'

The sea was cool and refreshing after our walk and the drive in the car. We larked about in it for about half an hour before returning to our towels.

'I'm going to wake up in a minute and realise this is just a dream,' I murmured, looking at her lying next to me.

'Me too,' she grinned mischievously. 'But for me it will be a nightmare!'

'Are all Greek women so cruel?' I said, closing my eyes contentedly as I rested my head back on the sand.

And then she kissed me: softly on the lips with one of her hands resting on my chest. It was a complete surprise but I must have sensed her intention because I didn't jump when her mouth first touched mine. Instead I was aware of her scent and her taste mixed with the fresh air and the salt from the sea and the realisation that it was better than, well, anything really. At least anything I could think of at that moment. After a few seconds she drew away and I raised myself up on an elbow as she resumed her place on her towel looking up at me, her eyes sparkling like the waves lapping a few feet away.

'Maybe I was wrong about Greek women.'

'It is to say 'thank you' for last night Mr Bond. But do not worry - you can kiss me now if you wish.'

'On a school trip! You'll be sacked!'

'I am giving up teaching to be a waitress. It is more interesting'

So I kissed her. As tenderly as I could; slowly, gently exploring her lips and her mouth and stroking the hair that framed her face with my fingers. I had waited a long time, never really expecting it to happen and here we were. Her mouth was soft and giving; it was like a kiss in a dream where all the senses are heightened and focused on the pleasure of the moment. Except it wasn't a dream and I didn't have to worry I was going to wake up. After a few minutes I slumped back again on my towel and took a deep breath.

'That was perfect,' I said, squinting up at her in the sunshine.

It was even easier from then on. As we lay there on the beach either kissing or holding hands or just touching arms we virtually exchanged life stories. The time flew by and soon the sun was sinking behind the hills and we wandered back hand in hand to the car. In Panos she dropped me at the bottom of the hill up to Angelos's and we agreed to meet at ten in *Corelli's Bar* and take it from there. Angelos was grinning when I got back to the hotel, sweating from the walk up the hill.

'How was Renia?' he smirked from behind the bar.

'Fuck me, news travels fast around here. How'd you know?'

Angelos laughed loudly.

'I have my finger on the pulse of Panos Mr *Malakas*. You look hot. Was Renia too much for you?'

'Fuck off you bastard. How about you take your finger out of you arse and off the pulse of Panos and get me a small beer,' I said, sitting on one of the stools by the bar.

'Ha, ha, ha.,' Angelos continued laughing.

'Do not worry Neil you will find an old lady to love you in England.'

I didn't really want to talk. All I wanted to do was sip my beer, smoke a cigarette, stare at the sea and relive the day in my head in peace. In the end Angelos had to answer the phone so I was left to do just that.

When she met me later Renia was in jeans and a simple black top. It was my last night in Panos and I would have liked to have gone to *The Secret Garden* to say goodbye but it seemed best to avoid it at least for dinner. As we sat nibbling on some water melon near the end of a pleasant meal at *The Aegean*, she asked me when my flight was due to leave.

'Angelos has ordered me a taxi for ten in the morning,' I informed her. 'You'll be working won't you?'

'Yes,' she sighed. 'You will come and say goodbye?'

'What do you think? Could I leave and not see you before I get on the plane? '

She smiled, and looking at her across the table I wanted to grab her and tell her how beautiful she was and how much I would miss her. For a few moments I began to suspect that falling in love wasn't totally beyond a man of my age - that it could be more than self-delusion and wishful thinking. She was funny, intelligent and sexy and I thought it would be easy to get used to sitting opposite her at dinner for the rest of my life. I almost convinced myself until I remembered that I was in Greece on a balmy evening and that things would look different on a cold November morning back in Blighty. There was also the age gap, the difference in culture and the fact that I didn't want to screw up again.

Just then her mobile rang. Glancing at who the caller was, she looked at me and put her finger to her lips, before answering. Naturally I was completely oblivious to the content of the conversation as it really was all Greek to me, but I could see she was looking less relaxed than before. When she had finished the call I looked at her questioningly.

'It is Petra,' she said quickly. My boyfriend has come from Athens to surprise me and has gone to *The Secret Garden* expecting me to be working. She told him I would be going there at midnight to go home with my father in the car. He thinks I am seeing friends and has decided to meet me at twelve at *The Secret Garden* to surprise me!'

'What a surprise that could have been!' I mused, leaning back and touching my temples. 'I am really sorry for making this problem. What do you want to do?'

She thought for a moment and looked at her watch. 'We will have to go,' she said.

Glancing at mine I saw that it was almost 11.45. Fuck, bollocks and buggery I didn't want the day to end like this. I wasn't planning on trying to make love to her but that was hardly an option now unless the rest of the late diners and the staff at our restaurant were prepared to look the other way for five minutes while we had it off on the table. I would have been happy with a walk on the beach and kissing her goodbye in the moonlight. A time machine to extend the evening was out of the question as well so I quickly paid the bill and we left.

Our restaurant was off the main thoroughfare and Renia guessed he would be in *Corelli's* so we found some shadows and I held her in my arms.

'I am so sorry,' I said again. 'Will you be all right making up a story?'

'Yes, don't worry, I will tell him that you took me to dinner and that you are old and ugly but you helped us all last night,' she giggled but there was a tear running down her cheek.

I pulled her close and kissed her hair as she pressed her face into my chest. I breathed in her scent and hoped I would be able to remember it.

'Thanks for a lovely day, I will never forget it.' I whispered.

'I also had a very nice day. Text me when you get home so I know you are back safe and I will send you e mails when I have started my job.'

She looked up and I kissed her on the lips for the last time.

'Do I look okay?' she asked as we parted.

'Horrible, but just say I bored you to tears.'

She smiled and shook her head.

'Goodbye Renia and take care,' I said. 'I will come back next year and see if you are single.'

As she turned and walked back towards *The Secret Garden* it was like being at the airport and saying goodbye to the girls again.

9

When I got back from Panos the rest of the holidays just drifted by as they do; the August weather was the climatic equivalent of musak in so far as it was never good enough for anywhere in Kent to require air-conditioning and merely provided an uninspiring back-drop to my equally dull life. It was great to be free of the routine of work but I have to admit to being a little bored. When I was married I had been busy for years. You know the stuff: young family, job, the garden, home improvements and badminton blah, blah. Now I could virtually please myself as to what I did but there is only so much shopping, going to the gym and surfing the internet a man can take. If Renia had been single I guess I would have gone back to Greece but that particular door had closed for now and I had real life to attend to.

On A level results day Rachel was all smiles as she discovered she would indeed be spending the next three years at Oxford. I never doubted it. Alex also managed to kick arse in most of her GCSE subjects so the kids weren't giving me any headaches. When I looked for Grace's results, however, there was little cause for celebration: two C's and a D weren't going to get her to either of her first two choices. I wondered whether or not to call her but decided settle for a text saying 'Does this mean you'll be wanting a refund?' She didn't reply so I guessed she was either still in Greece, too embarrassed to contact me or pissed-off with my attempt at humour.

I decided to use some of my free time to start going to a karate club again. There was one in Sevenoaks; that gave me something to do on Sunday mornings and Wednesday evenings other than running on the gym treadmill. I didn't intend to make a long term commitment but I thought that focusing on another aspect of my fitness for a while would be a change from the occasional tedium of the gym and also give me a chance of meeting women dressed in their pyjamas instead of Lycra. My old skills had come in useful in the past year and I wondered how much I could still do; it only took one session to show me how unsupple I had become and I reluctantly began doing the old stretching routines each day.

To put the last year in perspective, the day with Renia stood out like a red Ferrari in the staff car park. Nothing appeared from her in my e mail inbox for a couple of weeks, however, and it crossed my mind that she might be letting me down gently. I had to admit that as I usually only saw her once a year I didn't exactly qualify as urgent from her point of view and reminded myself again not to act like a moron. Apart from a sexy woman at the gym who didn't seem too averse to talking to me I hardly had a conversation with an adult female unless she happened to be checking out my groceries at the Co-op.

I used up a couple of days at the end of the month to drive down to Devon with Rachel and Alex to visit my younger brother Chris, similarly divorced and earning his living at a small country estate outside Exeter. It was good to breathe the familiar air of my home county and catch up with him. Rachel and Alex renewed contact with their cousins Emma, Rhiannon and Ben, the latter of whom made a gallant effort to mix with the girls considering he was a couple of years younger than Alex. Rhiannon was Rachel's age and Emma a year or so older and they always got on like a house on fire. I didn't know at the time what an unexpected and pivotal role Chris would play in the extraordinary year that lay ahead so my trip to see him was just an ordinary family get-together. There are always plenty of excuses for avoiding relations but I always tried to make it to Devon to see him every summer on the basis that he represented the only family I had left outside of Rachel and Alex.

If the best bit about teaching is the summer holidays then the worst is the end of the summer holidays. Meeting a teacher who is looking forward to going back in September is easier than finding a woman in a mini skirt working in an Oxfam shop. September means returning to the classroom and all those demanding and strength-sapping teenagers with their endless questions and energy. Education these days is full of the pressure to meet targets and satisfy criteria rather than imparting knowledge and inspiring children. Parental power and weak management mean that a classroom teacher always has to be continually on guard against upsetting anyone else with a stake in the school. I had been at Mid-Kent Grammar School for Girls for over ten years and during that time I had watched my profession lose more and more confidence while the job became noticeably less enjoyable. I had tried to carry on as normal but it was hard to ignore the atmosphere of anxiety that gripped my colleagues as they strained to observe every nuance of the profusion of policies and directives they were being constantly bombarded with.

This collective nervousness could have been easily assuaged if the staff had been confident of Delores's support and loyalty but there was as much chance of that as me developing X ray vision. Before the staffroom had been a convivial and disorganised collection of teachers where The

Head and her deputies kept a discrete distance - now they seemed to perceive the staff as a bunch of barely-competent halfwits who were to be monitored and managed to a fine degree. Those who expressed any criticism of the regime usually found themselves in Delores's office where she would deliver one of her pompous lectures about loyalty. She had a brilliant technique in a discussion of talking for the entire time - thus rendering her opponent impotent without the facility of reply. Trying to get a word in edgeways was harder than finding a seat on a commuter train to London in the rush hour. During one such monologue she provoked me enough to cut in on her diatribe. I said that as far as I was aware the right to freedom of speech in Britain didn't end at the staffroom door so if she didn't want to get upset about what staff thought about her she should stop listening to the obsequious little shits who gossiped to her. This, combined with my open-necked dress code, ensured my popularity rating with senior management would always hover on the part of the scale labelled 'detest'. I also presumed my career prospects weren't exactly enhanced either, although any sentence which included my name and the adjective 'career' would always guarantee a laugh in the staffroom.

We had a staff meeting on the first day back. Here we all assembled facing Delores who sat between Denis and Lynn, the Deputy Heads. They took it in turns to address the meeting while the rest of us grimly came to terms with the fact that we were facing another eleven months before the next summer holiday. The meeting lasted for about an hour during which the three of them told us about the results of last year's Year Eleven and Sixth Form and an endless list of issues to be borne in mind in the new term. After that we all escaped to our departments where my gang and I had a meeting before I sent them off to get themselves organised before the girls came back the next day.

Once the meeting was over I settled down in my office to analyse the summer's results and satisfy myself we were still actually teaching the girls stuff that they needed for their examinations. After I had convinced myself that mathematics exams were still being negotiated successfully, I set about clearing the list of jobs I had jotted down when I had first came in earlier that morning. I was just thinking it was time for lunch when I heard a familiar soft voice in the outer office 'Dr Mac, are you in there?'

'In here,' I called, swivelling around in my chair towards the door. A moment later Grace was standing there smiling, looking bronzed and beautiful in faded denim jeans and a yellow vest. She was carrying a couple of books in one hand and a bunch of car keys in the other.

'Hi Grace!' I grinned. 'How were the Greek Islands and your rich Greek Godfather? You look amazing!'

'Thanks…brilliant, I had a great time thank you. That is if you leave out the results part.'

I indicated for her to sit down and she perched on the edge of the easy chair next to the door.

'Yes I'm sorry. What are you going to do?'

'I'm not sure really - I thought maybe I would get a job and retake in January and next summer. What do you think? You will you carry on tutoring me won't you?'

I never really know what to say in these situations - it's not that I don't like being asked for advice - I'll do my best to spell out the options but I always hope something I say won't send a student down the wrong path. It was also difficult to be objective when Grace had already dangled the prospect of more tuition in front of me.

'Is that what you really want to do?' I ventured tentatively. 'What do your parents think?'

Grace leaned back in the chair

'Don't worry Dr Mac, I really do want to retake and get some decent grades and get to uni. I could have done more last year but I think I've learned my lesson.'

I could see her mind was made up despite what she had said when she sat down so I abandoned counselling mode.

'So you'll not be asking for a refund?'

'It's good to see you haven't changed,' she said, making an effort to look cross and laughing instead. 'I thought you might be mad with me.'

It was my turn to chuckle.

'I think I always knew that studying was never top of your list of priorities but I always try to teach the whole person rather than get too tied up with the academic.'

'You mean as long as you get paid you don't give a toss?'

'Er, something like that,' I admitted 'but I made an exception in your case.'

Grace looked at me with a half-amused and curious expression on her tanned face.

'Yes, Dr Mac, I'm sure,' she said in as unbelieving a tone as she could muster.

She stayed for twenty minutes or so and we exchanged holiday stories although hers seemed much more interesting than mine, mostly because I missed out any reference to Renia. I asked after her mum and it seemed things were much better on that front. We arranged for me to call at the usual time the following week and then I was alone in the office again.

Next day the girls were back in school so I was suddenly very busy once more. After less than a week the holidays seemed a long way away and I settled reluctantly into my normal term-time routine of work and tutoring until early evening. I soon gave up the Wednesday evening karate but thought I would try and keep Sunday going. Badminton matches started again and there I was - a year older and still doing virtually the same stuff I had been doing for years. Gradually the evenings began to draw in until I noticed in November that I was driving to work and back home again in darkness.

There was a little ray of light in the middle of the month, however, when one morning in my office I found an e mail from Renia in my inbox. I opened it, trying to imagine what she had written as I waited for the laptop to flash the message on the screen.

'Hello Neil, how are you? I am in my new job now but I am not sure if I will like it very much. Maybe I should stay being a waitress instead? The weather here in Athens is very cold and miserable - not like Panos!! Is it the same for you?

It was nice to see you this summer. I had a very good time with you which I remember with a smile. Petra told me that you came to the restaurant in the morning to say goodbye when I was collecting food from the supermarket. I am sorry I missed you and it all ended so suddenly.

I hope the girls are well and you too of course!

Love Renia'

Well, at least she hadn't forgotten me and I supposed I had done quite well to make it into her 'remember with a smile' memories. When I had a spare free period I composed a reply.

'Hi Renia, it was a lovely surprise to read your e mail. I am sorry the job is not much fun and Athens weather is getting like ours! I am working very hard at the moment so that I need another holiday.

Yes I called on the way to the airport – we were late and the taxi wanted to go so couldn't hang around and wait for you. Maybe I would have cried and embarrassed you so it was probably for the best!

I too smile when I remember our day together. I hope your boyfriend is well and he realises how lucky he is. Tell him there is an old Englishman who will marry you if he neglects you!

Please stay in touch and tell me how you are from time to time.
Much love
Neil'

I wondered whether 'much love' and the semi-serious offer of marriage was over-doing it, but what the hell; if it made her nervous I wasn't exactly within stalking range was I? It was about then I realised I needed some female company pronto. My last shag had been so long ago if I wasn't careful my next sexual partner would have to draw me diagrams. I was also pretty sure the long lay-off was affecting my brain as well. Renia was a case in point; I was in danger of turning into a character out of a Mills and Boon novel, except of course I wasn't particularly square-jawed or given to wearing riding breeches and white shirts open down to the navel. The fact was, and I knew it, that I had got as lucky as I ever was going to with Renia and that I needed to put her out of my mind and start concentrating on real life. She would always be special but I had to start playing the cards in the hand I was holding, not the ones I wished had been dealt.

Once I had decided to try and stop acting inwardly like a love-struck adolescent, by coincidence someone appeared on my radar. In late November things had become more friendly with the sexy woman from the gym; the one from the summer holidays whom I had chatted to on one or two occasions. I hadn't seen much of her after that, which is often the case at a place like a gym where people are always changing their schedules and visiting times, but around half term we seemed to be working out at a similar time a couple of days a week. I made more of an effort than in the summer and I seemed to be making progress.

She was certainly sexy. Most of the men who were around when she was building up a sweat on the treadmill or the cross-trainer usually took a moment to admire her toned and petite figure but it was me who actually made the effort to talk to her when the opportunity arose. She looked like she was in her mid-thirties, had a very attractive face, black hair almost to her shoulders and noteworthy breasts that contrasted nicely with her narrow waist and slim hips. Whenever we were working out at the same time she responded in a friendly enough manner to my casual conversation to suggest I wasn't entirely flogging a dead horse. So I persevered with the small talk and began to make progress. It turned out she was called Sasha but that seemed like the only odd thing about her and I eventually summoned up the nerve and suggested a coffee. Instead of laughing dismissively at the very idea she agreed and we spent a pleasant half an hour chatting in the centre's cafeteria. Even when I told her that I taught maths it didn't seem to be a problem and soon I was seeing her two or three times a week.

She had inherited a semi-detached three-storey townhouse in Edenbridge from a rich ex-husband and most of our dates centred on it. She had a couple of kids from the previous marriage but they spent half the time with their father so that left us enough freedom to have plenty of fun. I usually stayed the night if we were sharing a bottle of wine and watching a film or something and just interrupted my drive to work to pop into the cottage to change into my school clothes. I liked her a lot, but not enough to start getting ahead of myself. She seemed reasonably keen as well but maybe that was down to the legendary charm and prowess in bed we maths teachers are famous for. Actually 'keen' may be too strong a word as she always let me phone to arrange a date and seemed more relaxed about our relationship than other women I had been involved with.

If I'm honest I don't think I could have been committed to anyone at that stage. I had been married for a long time and apart from the lack of regular sex I was enjoying being single. The only people I felt properly committed to were Rachel and Alex and I still missed living with them in a way only fathers in my position will understand. In another way being a dad insulated me from loneliness so there wasn't the imperative to seek out another mate and settle down. At any rate Sasha wasn't forcing any issues and that suited me. She was witty and intelligent and liked to go to bed early so I wasn't complaining!

The first time I took her out was one of those evenings that couldn't have gone better if I'd written the script myself.

I had picked her up and taken her to a little Italian place near Croydon. When she opened the door of her house the dress she was wearing looked even better than the Lycra of the gym. Come to think of it Lycra probably had a part to play in the construction of the black halter-neck that seemed to follow every delicious toned contour of her body. It was just short enough to reveal a little bit of gently muscular thigh and low enough at the front to make looking her in the eye a bit of a challenge. Her dark hair almost reached the nape of her slender neck and her athletic shoulders and firm arms were those of a woman with the genes that made working out worthwhile.

'Nice car,' she observed as I opened the door of the black RX8 to let her in.

'Thanks, I blew some of the divorce settlement into it instead of topping up the pension,' I said, getting in beside her and starting the engine. 'Maybe it was a mid-life crisis or maybe I needed to compensate for some hidden inadequacy.'

She laughed,

'Perhaps I was too hasty in accepting your invitation out then?'

'Don't worry. My last car was a Ford Fiesta.'

And so it continued. I made her laugh and steered away from mathematical topics; a discussion of the finer points of calculus is not usually regarded as a winner with athletic looking women. The restaurant was just right; great food but informal and atmospheric enough to help put us at our ease. We shared a bottle of red although Sasha drank most of it as I was driving; I hoped it was true what they said and it lowered her inhibitions. The conversation flowed easily enough and I discovered with interest that she worked at

Wealdon Manor, the place near Sevenoaks that Fiona's partner Marc owned.

'That's incredible,' I exclaimed in genuine surprise. 'I tutor a girl whose, er, mother's partner owns it.'

'Oh, you mean Marc Gilbert.' Sasha took a sip of her wine and a strange look flickered across her face; her brow wrinkled slightly and her eyes looked momentarily distracted. I pretended not to notice but I was interested in her odd reaction and said casually.

'What's he like to work for? It sounds like a glamorous place to be according to my tutee.'

Sasha had instantly regained her composure and laughed.

'He's pretty ruthless but he's fine if he rates you. Luckily for me I've always been in his good books!'

'With looks like yours I imagine you'd be in most men's good books,' I said gallantly. 'What exactly do you do if you don't mind me asking?'

'I'm a duty manager but I only work four days a week. I started when the kids were younger and it suits me not to be completely full-time. Marc has tried a few times to persuade me to do more but I've resisted until now. Most attractive women are in Marc's good books if you know what I mean.'

I let the conversation move on even though I was intrigued to know more about Grace's family. I didn't want to appear too inquisitive on a first date when up to then things had been going so well.

Back at her place we had coffee and soon we were upstairs in her bedroom standing by her double bed pulling at each other's clothes. She had the simpler task because that dress really was tight. I managed to ease the halter over her head without causing serious injury, however, and then eased the rest of the outfit over her breasts and carefully work it down her torso. She deftly unbuttoned my shirt, unbuckled the belt of my jeans and with her thumbs removed my trousers and underwear in one move. She let me step out of the heap of material at my feet, I bent down and slipped off my socks and then she pushed me back onto the bed.

'Very impressive,' she smiled, getting onto the bed, kneeling upright and looking down at me, 'I'm glad to see you were being modest about the compensation with the car.'

'Thanks and you look pretty amazing yourself,' I replied, trying hard not to start foaming at the mouth. She did: kneeling there wearing nothing but that smile and a ring in one of the nipples of her beautifully rounded breasts. Everywhere on her body was firm and muscular - it was like going to bed with a porn star who did triathlons and gymnastics in her spare time.

'Will this go off if I touch it do you think?' she asked, reaching down towards me.

'Maybe, but not right away I hope,' I murmured.

'Good,' she said, bringing her lips to mine.

I was out of practice but I think I put up a reasonable show. Sasha elected to keep me on my back so I had an excellent view of her as she used me as her ride in the rarely run 'Shag-Me-Senseless' stakes. Everything worked despite first time nerves and I even managed to hold on with the help of mental arithmetic calculations until Sasha's rhythmic riding gained in urgency and she arched back and moaned exquisitely. I think I may have made some noise myself as well and we both laughed once the intensity of the moment had subsided. Sasha rolled off my chest and left an arm draped over it as she went to sleep after her exertions; I just lay on my back feeling relieved and relaxed. Heading inexorably towards unconsciousness, however, images of a hot afternoon on a beach near Panos percolated into my head again. Was this the way it worked; that great sex still wasn't a match for a kiss on a beach from a girl I wasn't likely to see again?

10

Those government adverts that try to persuade people to become teachers always make me wince. On the face of it, the holidays apart or maybe the pension, why would anyone want to teach? Most people think today's teenagers are, let's be fair, obnoxious and we've all experienced enough badly dressed and again, let's be fair, desperately ugly or useless teachers for the profession never to be high up the glamour league table. On reflection, however, the real reason I snort from the sofa is the implicit suggestion that standing up in front of a class is an easy gig that anyone could do. I also object to the suggestion that teaching is a rewarding joint venture with teenagers who will boost your self-esteem on a daily basis with their wide-eyed enthusiasm for learning and gentle joshing. You'll be a legend in your own lunchtime, the girls will adore you and the boys will have to grudgingly admit you're a cool dude. Okay, I'm overstating my case and most of the public understand that the adverts are all propaganda and basically bollocks; but, nevertheless, they do have a beguiling appeal to the idealist lurking in all of us that I'm sure is deliberate. And that's the point – teaching doesn't need idealists.

Teaching is either really hard or, if you haven't been born with the right gene, utterly impossible. The best teachers, the ones that succeed rather than survive, are the ones who are talented, amusing and interesting enough themselves to stimulate the mostly ill-disciplined, lazy, disinterested little shits into people worth teaching. On top of that you have to disguise any idealistic pretensions you might harbour behind a cool, don't-mess-with-me-you-little-bastards front because without respect they'll eat you up and spit you out for fun. If you can manage all of that *and* be hard-working and well-organised you'll get respect, and once you've got that it'll be fun.

When I say fun I should have probably added in a few provisos like annoying parents and so on, but more relevant as the end of term approached was exhaustion. The cumulative effect of six uninterrupted weeks of modern day teaching plus the extras like running the school's football teams I threw in every week for free had somewhat diminished my enthusiasm for getting up in the morning. There were only two weeks left but the prospect of those ten working days was as inviting as a night in a three-some with Delores and Denis. As I squinted at myself every morning in the icy chill of the bathroom my face didn't really look like it could cope with the rest of the day, let alone the lead up to Christmas.

It was far too cold to take a bath in the morning so I usually had one the night before when the electric heater on the wall had time enough bring the temperature up to the pre divorce levels I was accustomed to in a bathroom. Instead I got dressed up to the waist including my shoes so that only my torso had to endure the shock of the bracing bathroom air. Then I bent over the bath and used a rubber shower attachment I had to force onto the bath taps to wash my hair, face and, more trickily, under my arms. Then I would dry myself and clean my teeth, taking the opportunity to inspect the ageing process working on my face.

At school most of the staff were either fighting off viruses or saving them up for the holidays and the girls weren't in a much better state. For me it was the length of my extended days which had eventually worn me down, combined with the effort involved in entertaining my classes and, latterly, pretending that I actually cared if they learnt anything. I got up later and later and as the penultimate week began I was unlocking my office only ten minutes before registration was due to start, my mood not particularly enhanced by witty remarks such as, 'Cutting it fine today' that Alan, one of my maths colleagues, made as I entered Maths Resources.

As I drove into work on the Monday I booted up the part of my brain I deliberately keep switched off over the weekend. Lessons apart, there was still a lot of tutoring after school each day, a parents' evening on Wednesday and a badminton match on Thursday. The parents' evening meant a bit of re-jigging of my tutees to maximise my cash flow. I also had to pick an under-thirteens' team for Saturday morning, organise the transport to same and sort them out after school on Friday at Football Club. Not much on the face of it but probably a lot of buggering about passing messages around and chasing girls to play. At least then I could let off some steam at the Mens' A Christmas do on Friday night.

I had also agreed to help out with the Christmas pantomime. I hate being in it but I'd only managed the strength to say 'no' once in ten years. It ruins the last day of term because for all of the final week you have to live with the pressure of retaining your credibility in front of the whole school when you finally step out in front of them armed only with some ludicrous lines and your own personality for protection. If all goes well the Lower Sixth, who by tradition have to write and perform it, love you for helping and it is also satisfying to have succeeded in something that doesn't come naturally. Two of my favourite students, Rose and Carol, were in charge of this year and there was no way I could let them down. Anyway, Carol had convinced me I would look good with the part Rose had given me. There was probably going to be very little rehearsal, which was good because I had no spare time, but also bad because it made the performance even more luck than judgement.

As it turned out the week at school went okay. My junior forms got a lot of algebra which is the best topic I know for keeping students' heads down. An English teacher would just chuck on a DVD but algebra was even better because it gave you a silent classroom. Contrary to popular myth most students love algebra when it's well taught. Maybe it's a bit repetitive but they seem to find the application of concrete rules to short questions strangely satisfying and reassuring. More importantly, it is a doddle to teach and organise. A few choice examples mixed in with some fun questions and answers takes about twenty minutes. Then, off they go for the rest of the hour while you sit at the front and have them out to your desk for marking every now and again. You get to sit down and they get to feel they're good at something; the younger ones especially love coming out and collecting all those red ticks almost as much as I like giving them.

The sixth form were revising for their January exams so their lessons were a mixture of timed questions and yours truly going through the stuff they still had problems with. Any other lesson time was spent with them working on past papers which again involved me sitting down conserving energy for more important stuff like badminton and Sasha.

My Upper Sixth set had about twenty girls in it, nearly all of whom I'd taught since they'd come to the school when they were eleven, so lessons with them were as easy as eating biscuits. They knew my ways, trusted me as a half-decent teacher and seemed to enjoy my jokes although some or most of that might be self-delusion. Almost all of the girls were high achievers and hard-working to boot so I never had to agonise about their results, although the two who sat at the desks directly in front of mine, Lydia and Sarah, had been making me nervous recently.

Sarah was prim, petite and blonde; and she had smiled her way through six and a bit years of maths lessons with me. Sarah had always done well; until, that is, she acquired a boyfriend, the blessed Dan, last summer. Lydia meanwhile was almost the opposite of Sarah; utterly disorganised and seemingly perpetually on the cusp of a crisis. For most of the time I couldn't honestly say whether I wanted to strangle her or suggest marriage. She would prattle on about everything except my subject and yet I found it impossible not to be charmed by her self-deprecating and morbid sense of humour.

All of Sarah's gossip revolved around Dan and I had pulled her leg for weeks that the relationship wouldn't last. Back in September I had even bet her a pound she would be single by Christmas. At least I thought it had only been for a pound but she and Lydia had been winding me up for the past few weeks by claiming I had wagered a tenner, dismissing all of my protests with disdain. Lydia had also found a man a few months ago. He was in the army but had gone up to Scotland soon afterwards to help his grandparents with some kind of building project. Every week his return had been delayed and one morning during that week Sarah and I were pulling her leg about his non-appearance. The two of them were working on a past paper while I was trying unsuccessfully to focus on marking a set of books.

'Let's face it he's never coming back,' I said, looking up from the tedium that was a Year Eight equations homework. 'You're just going to have to accept a lonely Christmas.'

Sarah leant forward over her work nodded with a mock expression of sympathy and poorly disguised glee. Lydia glanced up from underneath a thick mop of curly brown hair and fixed me with her brown eyes.

'Bastard,' she whispered. 'Anyway, for your information he's back next Saturday.'

'Heard that before,' mused Sarah without looking up from her page.

'Army blokes are all the same,' I agreed, matter of factly but smiling at Lydia as I spoke. 'He's probably trying to let you down gently.'

'Okay, okay, we'll see,' she moaned as she shoved a sheet of untidy scrawl under my nose. 'But maybe now you could actually do some teaching and show me how to do this one here?'

Lydia was another one of my tutees and I had agreed to take her on immediately she asked. She was attractive in an old-fashioned, Moll Flanders kind of way and would have probably looked good in one of those seventeenth century dresses that show a lot of cleavage. As it was she usually treated me to a short skirt that confirmed my view that she had the best legs in the sixth form now that Grace had left and I grew to be quite fond of her disarming, direct approach and the hilarious way she fought a losing battle against her own inability to organise herself.

Anyway, as I said earlier, teaching was tough and energy levels were low but slowly the week progressed to Friday. I had managed to fit in most of the private lessons, bullshit my way through the parents evening and play badminton the night before. I'd played okay although the resulting aches and pains were still affecting me on Friday morning whenever I had a flight of stairs to climb. It was a mixed match at home and there was a club night taking place as well so there were plenty of people enjoying a few friendly games in addition to the serious match games. Grace was my partner and when we were both free we would sit on one of the benches that were placed against the walls of the four-court sports hall for the players to park themselves on between games. She seemed fine and we chatted and joked about the antics of the players who were playing on the courts around us. She was working at a large department store in town for the year and trying to fit in her studying in the evenings and on her days off. Her social life had taken a bit of a knock as most of her friends had gone off to university but, Sasha apart, it was still a long way ahead of mine.

'Rocky mentioned you're coming out to *The Palace* tomorrow.' I said at one point during a break. 'That's brave. I wouldn't have thought it was your scene.'

'Oh I like a bit of a booze-up and karaoke,' Grace laughed. 'Jenny and the others are coming and I'm looking forward to hearing you do a number Neil.'

'If I had my way I'd give the singing a miss but I don't think Rocky's going to take 'no' for an answer, I said in as resigned a tone as I could. 'And I thought it was just the

Men's' A going until he roped in the ladies for their Christmas do. I would have preferred fewer witnesses for what I've a feeling is going to be another rendition of 'Suspicious Minds' which, believe me, you should take as a cue to visit the ladies room.'

'Why 'Suspicious Minds?'' Grace asked, looking puzzled.

'God knows, but it's turned into a bit of a tradition. Every time I'm in a karaoke bar with Rocky I get to sing 'Suspicious Minds'. Maybe it's his favourite song or he's caught in a trap and he can't get out?'

'Ha, ha,' said Grace, looking a tiny bit amused at my wit. What about you Gere, do you have a favourite song?'

Gere was sitting on Grace's other side and turned to us, grinning like a Cheshire cat.

'Nah, I can't sing and Slick's the only one stupid enough to let Rocky bully him.'

'Come on.' I moaned. 'Be a sport – what about your signature tune 'I Can't Get No Satisfaction'?'

Grace giggled.

Gere's amused expression remained. 'Very funny, but you won't be laughing on Friday when you're dodging the empty beer bottles.'

'Well, you've been warned Grace,' I sighed.

Coincidentally, Sasha's works Christmas do was also taking place on Friday, so we would be both out at separate knees-ups. It was a little annoying that I was going to miss out on a posh do at her hotel but you can't have everything. She had said that she would be back before midnight anyway as her lift was not exactly a party animal so I made a mental note to make a detour and drive back past her house if I was feeling randy on the way home.

I had offered to pick Gere up from his flat in Edenbridge because I've never been much of a drinker and reckoned I could ration myself to a couple of drinks over the course of the evening and be okay to drive back. He accepted and dressed smart but casual in black suit and a navy open-necked polo shirt I collected him just after seven. He climbed into the car smelling of deodorant and aftershave wearing a red shirt and a black pair of slacks.

'Thanks Batman,' he said chirpily as he fastened himself in.

'No problem - like the shirt - does it come out every Christmas?' I said, trying to sound sincere.

'Nah, just feeling in the mood for some fun - I could do with a blast. Let's hope it's a good night.'

'Same here, two weeks in the Maldives are what I really need but that'll have to wait until my inheritance comes through.'

By the time we arrived at *The King's Palace* Chinese Restaurant in Tunbridge Wells half an hour later none of the Mens' A were in evidence. Gere and I were shown to our table and we sat down and ordered a bottle of house white. I paid the oriental waiter whose name I didn't know but whose face was a fixture and poured Gere and I a glass each. Gere told me he was planning either to crash at Rocky's place where I would have to join him if the lure of alcohol became too strong or come back with me if I managed to stay off the sauce and he couldn't face clubbing.

Gere, Rocky and I were familiar faces at *The Palace* and the other waiters and the English manageress came over while we were talking to say hello. While Gere worked his charm I glanced around at the familiar surroundings with amusement and something bordering on affection. It wasn't your normal Chinese restaurant; it was more like a club with its windowless black painted walls, karaoke stage and Elvis memorabilia which tonight had been decorated with tinsel and Christmas decorations. Every evening the owner, a Chinese guy with an obvious obsession with 'The King', would arrive and treat the diners to an extended session of famous Elvis hits. His Chinese accent and ridiculous Elvis jump suits usually made for a highly amusing half an hour or so because by then most of the clientele were well on the way to being pissed.

When I'd organised a couple of end of term dos for the staff from school at *The Palace* in the past some of my more staid colleagues had looked on in appalled consternation at 'Elvis's' performance. Delores's looked like her wine had been laced with cod liver oil and Denis like he had just been given the news that his penis would have to be amputated. But they were professional miseries. Most of us had a great time and I personally couldn't remember not enjoying myself when I spent an evening there. Okay, maybe the laughter usually turned out to be the prelude to some self inflicted karaoke horror later in the evening or a wretched alcohol plus Chinese food induced hang-over next day but it was always worth it.

Gere and I were soon joined by the others. Rocky ambled over from the lobby after pausing at the bar and glad-handing the waiters and kissing the manageress. He had on loose fitting jeans and a patterned XL Hawaiian shirt and when he got to the table he thrust out his hand and shook mine firmly followed by Gere's. He stood beside us looking around while Gere and I sat smiling up at him.

'Evening Squirrels, as you can see the captain has arrived so let the party commence!'

'I can hardly wait' I concurred. 'I've been looking forward to this all week.'

A waitress, a pretty waitress, brought Rocky a pint of lager which distracted him from making a reply so I tried again.

'We're ready to eat, drink and be merry all right. Where are the others?'

'They're just parking. Whirler picked Rick and Mike up and I saw them going up the road opposite *The Swan*,' said Rocky cheerily. 'Nice shirt Gere. You have the fur edging taken off?'

'Fuck off,' said Gere looking slightly peeved.

'Fuck off captain,' I corrected him.

Whirler, Rick and Mike soon followed and had their drinks ordered and placed in front of them in efficient style. The place was full with the usual mix of works dos, hen parties and the like. Grace and the other women from the club were on a table next to ours. I noticed there were three or four in their twenties and was relieved Grace would have some reasonable company. She came over when she arrived and said a cheery hello and we all raised a glass in her direction.

'Looking lovely Grace!' winked Rocky. 'Hope to see you on the dance floor later. As you can see this is the table with the Mens' A legends so look no further for entertainment and wit!'

'I'll try to remember,' she said, looking both amused and doubtful.

As she left Whirler muttered 'Ten out of ten!'

'Yes, I'd give her -' started Rocky

'One?' I interjected good-naturedly. 'You're so predictable. Yeah we agree she scrubs up very nicely Capt'n but I vote we just focus on slags and slappers like we normally do.'

'Er, sorry there Slick,' apologised Rocky. 'Yeah quite right, Whirler – she's ten out of ten all right but we'd all be batting way over our average with Grace.'

'The age gap would also be a bit embarrassing,' I chimed in. 'Well in my case anyway – let's stick to crumpet within ten years of our ages.'

'So for you that'd be, er say, anything from forty to sixty,' observed Rick.

'He'd accept anyone not attached to a life-support machine,' cut in Gere loyally.

We were all laughing now and Rocky raised his glass towards the centre of the table.

'Well gents, I hope you're all ready for a classic night out, four, four,' he grinned. 'It's nice to see all the 'Men's A' present I must say. To the best men's badminton team in the division!'

'So why are we only third in the table?' was Rick's highly understandable observation as we also raised our glasses.'

'Just drink Rick,' Gere grinned. 'In our case it's simple - we aren't, so he's talking through his arse as usual. On the other hand what other teams come out like this or, better still, have fucking ridiculous nicknames printed on their shirts? Are there other teams from The West Kent League out tonight getting mullahed and hoping against hope there are women out too who might actually be drunk enough to have sex with them?'

'Four, four Gere,' twinkled Rocky reaching over and shaking his hand again.

I looked at my empty glass. At this rate I wouldn't be driving anywhere later on so I called over the attractive waitress and ordered a coke.

'What's up Slick?' Rocky noticed straight away.

'Just keeping my options open that's all. I want to be able to decide between your sofa and Sasha's body before the alcohol takes it out of my hands.'

'Although none of us have met the lovely Sasha I think I that is a decision that shouldn't be that hard to make,' observed Whirler while the others, except Rocky, nodded sagely. He wouldn't be happy until we were all pissed and staggering home in the early hours.

The waitress came back with my drink. She was dark and Spanish looking with long hair and a slim figure.

'Thanks,' I grinned. 'I haven't seen you here before. Are you new?'

She smiled nervously.

'No, I just help out when we're busy. I'm Rhoda's daughter – the manager.'

'Oh right,' I grinned. 'Don't worry, I was just showing my friends here that it is possible to speak to a pretty girl without mumbling and going red.'

'Just humour him,' cut in Rick. 'He only gets out at Christmas and on birthdays.'

And so it went on. Rosie, the waitress, stayed for a bit and seemed reassured we weren't a threat and for the rest of the evening we insisted it was she who served us drinks.

After another half an hour of wise-cracking and gossip the first course arrived. The food, though acceptable, was a distraction rather than the focus of the evening and I didn't feel particularly hungry anyway. It was just good to be out with friends at the end of a long week. I was laughing at almost everything Rocky or the others said and there were a few pretty faces and interesting dresses dotted around the room helping to keep me alert and contented.

The 'cabaret', if I may use a loose definition of the expression, brought more pleasure: Elvis songs evoke a strange feeling of well-being no matter how badly they are sung. The Chinese 'Elvis' slurred, changed, erased and miss-timed familiar lyrics with a cavalier gusto but we were all singing along with him to his backing tracks as he moved among the tables dressed in a white Elvis outfit and an inscrutable oriental grin. 'It's Now or Never' flooded my relaxed senses and the pleasure continued through a dozen or so other songs including such favourites as 'Brue Suede Shoes' and 'Are You Ronery Tonight'. Some of the more daring and obviously drunken women lurched onto the floor near our table and treated us to what could also be loosely described as dancing. Mind you, I shouldn't really criticise, because there was no way I would have strutted my stuff in similar circumstances.

The second and third courses arrived during the singing and the wine and beer continued to flow liberally amongst the others. Rocky had brought a surprise along in the form of a few match reports he had compiled from our exploits since the start of the season back in September. He passed copies around and we perused them as we ate. His spelling was atrocious but that added to the report's humour. Apparently I had managed to say 'fuck' or 'fucking' over thirty times against a pair from Chelswood and Whirler's slanging match with a Scotsman from Invicta had almost been recorded verbatim until the moment when Mike, Whirler's partner, had stepped in and said 'That's enough Colin' at which the two protagonists had meekly stopped facing up to each other and got on with the game. Of course that was overshadowed by memories of my exploits with Eddy last season and by the end I was crying with laughter.

'You don't spell climax with a ck you pillock,' I spluttered, reading Rocky's description of the end of one of our best wins.

'He probably doesn't get much practice using that word,' suggested Rick.

'Unless it's in a self-abusing context,' I said quickly, looking at Rocky.

'Now, now chaps, I'm sure the Men's A is always ready to abuse itself,' he came back at us. 'For Slick and Chunks there can't be any other option! Four, four.'

'I think Wendy prefers it that way,' sighed Rick raising his glass for another mouthful of wine.

'Does that mean you would send a fax spelt f a c k s?' asked Whirler innocently.

'That's Irish for fuck isn't it?' Gere interjected.

'You'd better be careful if you tell someone you're going to send a fax off to them,' warned Whirler.

'Especially if it's to Ireland,' I said laughing at my own joke.

'Anyway, it was a good match to win,' said Mike.

'Four, four. Men's A!!' agreed Rocky and we raised our glasses again.

After the cabaret a list of songs available for karaoke were distributed throughout the restaurant. There was no holding us now and Rocky soon had us down for several old classics. He and I were one of the first up to do 'Suspicious Minds'. Most of the people were either pissed or high on the additives in the Chinese food so there was a lot of noise, and the little dance floor in front of the slightly raised platform from which we sang was crowded with dancers. Most of them were women, which was pleasant, although the average age could have been lower. Grace and the other women from *The Wanderers* were merrily joining in and I was relieved she was having a good time. There were even a few blokes around who were giving her the attention she deserved. After our rendition we joined the dancers and a forty-something female grabbed me and shouted in my ear 'hope you don't mind me being honest but that was crap!' I laughed and said I was under no illusions as to the quality of my duet with Rocky.

For the next couple of hours or so we carried on in the same vein. Grace came over to our table when I was taking a break and I made her laugh by showing her Rocky's attempts at match reports.

'Are you having a good time?' I half-shouted above the noise of the three women belting out a horrendous version of 'Girls Just Want to Have Fun'.

'Yes it's been great but I could do with going home now.'

'I thought you youngsters had more stamina,' I grinned, shaking my head.

'I've got a bit of a headache actually.'

'How are you getting back?'

'I came with Jo but I think she's up for clubbing so it could be a long night,' she shrugged resignedly.

'I'll take you if you like,' I offered. 'Rocky is bound to want to carry on but I'm happy to use you as an excuse.'

Grace looked relieved at my proposal so when Rocky came over at midnight and suggested going onto a club I told him I was wasted and was heading for home. Rick, Gere and Whirler were in no mood to end the evening out so Rocky didn't make too much fuss as he had enough of a gang to continue having fun with.

When *The King's Palace* started to clear we said our goodbyes. There were drunken handshakes and hugs all round and then we were outside the restaurant and Grace and I and the others went our separate ways. Mike had also made his apologies so a third of Men's A were heading for home and the rest for hangovers they would regret in the morning. There were still plenty of people around and the chilly winter air suddenly made me glad of the suit I was wearing. Grace had put on a long coat over her little black dress and we were soon in the car, electric seats warming our back-sides, and heading towards Sevenoaks. We talked for all of the way back, both of us relaxed and cheerful after an amiable evening. When we got to the house, Grace pressed something on her key ring and the electric gates edged out of the way. As I manoeuvred the car slowly up the drive, our arrival was greeted by the brightness of automatic lights that flashed on as we came into sensor range. I watched Grace let herself in through the wide oak front door before turning the car around and heading back down the drive.

I made it back to Edenbridge in less than fifteen minutes. Driving at night on country roads is so much quicker than in daylight as you can cut corners with impunity, knowing the road is clear in the absence of oncoming headlights. Without meaning to sound too much like Jeremy Clarkson and his petrol-head chums, the Mazda was also a very fast and a superbly balanced car and I liked to put it through its paces when I had a chance and was in the mood. When I turned into Sasha's road there was no parking outside her house so I left the car fifty yards down the road away from the double yellow lines.

With my hands deep in the pockets of my jacket I walked slowly back towards my destination, enjoying the unusual pleasure of being out late on my own. I hoped Sasha was back and feeling frisky after her do. I hadn't seen her since the weekend which was too long to go without enjoying her nubile body. It was about twelve thirty I guessed without looking at my watch so she probably wouldn't be too long if she hadn't already returned. About thirty or forty yards from the house I noticed a set of tail-lights lit up outside the Sasha's place. I wondered if it was her lift arriving virtually at the same time as me and stopped, thinking of some way I could surprise her without giving her a heart attack. It was me who got the surprise, however, when the car drove into her drive and Sasha and a bloke started to get out of the vehicle.

My mouth probably dropped open in that comical way mouths do when one is taken by surprise and without really thinking I stepped back quickly into the driveway I was standing next to. I was on the opposite side of the road to Sasha's place so either of them would have spotted me if they had looked back but why I hid myself I didn't quite know. Maybe it was just a reflex and even as I did it I felt a bit stupid. The most obvious and probably intelligent thing to have done would have been to keep walking and announce my arrival to them. On reflection I think I must have sensed the two of them weren't keen on seeing anyone else and that made me react in such a bizarre manner – I just didn't want to see two guilty faces as I strode up out of the night and, after all, I hadn't mentioned that I might call by.

Anyway, that was by the by now, I could hear their footsteps on the drive and two voices, one of whose was familiar while the other definitely was not. Sasha sounded a little the worse for wear and she seemed to be searching for the right key on the enormous bunch she always carried There was apologetic laughing and swearing alongside the metallic clinking of metal while the bloke was trying to be amusing and encouraging in a 'gosh you're cute when you can't find the right key' kind of way. If it had been his own partner he'd have probably told her that his bollocks were freezing off and why the fuck couldn't she carry fewer keys, unless of course he was aiming to get his leg over tonight and made a special effort to hide any irritation. It was clear to me, even from two houses away, that this guy was definitely hoping for more than the cup of coffee he professed to be looking forward to.

11

When they eventually negotiated the front door I crossed the road and made my way along to the house and waited to see which lights came on. When the hall light remained the only one in sight I guessed they had gone through to the kitchen at the back. I made a quick decision to hurry up the drive, sneak down the side of the house and find some vantage point from which I could observe the making of drinks.

It sounds like a cliché but I could feel my heart thumping like a drum in my chest and I considered my ridiculous behaviour again; fuck it Mackenzie, you weren't married to Sasha and you had told yourself enough times the relationship with her was only casual. Maybe that was the point – she had been growing on you so you needed the constant self-reminders to try and keep any romance out of the equation and that was why you were suddenly acting like a private detective with a speciality in divorce cases! Despite these self-recriminations, however, I still couldn't bring myself to exhibit mature and adult behaviour and knock on Sasha's front door like a normal person. Such a course of action might save a lot of trouble but I just wasn't in the mood to be sensible. I was intrigued by the whole situation. Up to a few minutes ago I had had complete confidence in Sasha but now I felt like a tit

If I thought that I was going to get a good look at the pair of them through the kitchen window I was thoroughly disappointed. Sasha appeared wearing a short, tight-fitting red dress, went to the fridge and took out a bottle of wine, grabbed some glasses and disappeared again. I was freezing by now and getting inside the warm house, whatever the consequences, seemed preferable to having my balls drop off outside in the cold. Thinking 'sod it' I tried the kitchen door to see if it was unlocked and when it opened I took a deep breath and slipped quietly into the kitchen.

I sneaked through the kitchen and tiptoed into the dining room and listened for their voices. Coming from the lounge at the front of the house I heard laughter accompanied by music from one of the Sinatra CDs I had lent her. I had to smile grimly to myself at Sasha's complete lack of decorum. This was rubbing salt in my wounded pride although, to be fair, I didn't suppose she expected me to be witnessing the inappropriate use of my CD. Still, if she was going to get up close and personal with some bloke after a party she could at least have used her own fucking music. Maybe I should have stormed in then and there and demanded she switch to one of her own albums, grabbed Frank's and the others I had left with her and pissed off.

I hesitated in the hallway outside the lounge and considered my options again. Obviously any confrontation over the CDs was a non-starter so that left me with two other options. The first and most sensible was to retrace my steps and bugger off. The second didn't really count as an option because even I could see that going outside, ringing the doorbell and suggesting a threesome when she tried to explain the company in the front room was as idiotic as the rest of my conduct since I parked the car.

My deliberations were brought to a sudden halt when the voices stopped and after a pregnant pause I heard Sasha say 'Is that how you treat all your staff?' in a way that intimated she didn't overly mind, to which Mister Hot Lips retorted 'no, only the really special ones'. I managed to suppress the urge to vomit as he followed up with 'is there somewhere more comfortable where I could show you how much I really appreciate you?'

I had to acknowledge that I was listening to a pretty smooth operator but I broke off from my reluctant admiration fest when Sasha replied.

'Hmmm, I think can arrange that,' she giggled. 'Do you think you're up to climbing two flights of stairs?'

I didn't bother to wait for his answer which I could guess the gist of, because I had only one option if I was to remain undiscovered. Going out the front door would be too noisy and retreating might take too long if Sasha visited the kitchen before going upstairs So I was left with taking the stairs myself, three at a time on tiptoe while the music covered the sounds of any creaking as I went. On the landing I chose the spare room because it was the only one with its door ajar and quickly slipped through into the darkness. Once inside I backed up against the door, trying to control my breathing after the rapid ascent.

A few moments later I heard them climbing up the stairs, pass my door and up the stairs to the top floor. The light pull in the en suite bathroom pinged and soon after that the toilet flushed followed by the sound of teeth being brushed. Then it was his turn and after that all I could hear was the sound of the water refilling the toilet cistern.

I waited about five minutes and then as quietly as I could I slipped back out of my hiding place. This was no time to be caught because I had clearly crossed the line separating acceptable and lunatic behaviour. I suppose I should have been angry but it felt that out of the three of us I was being the worst behaved. He was only doing what most blokes do naturally and I was guessing Sasha just wanted to shag whoever she had brought home which didn't seem entirely unreasonable. I'm no saint so I couldn't feel much righteous indignation; it was also Sasha's house for God's sake so technically I was probably breaking the law of the land as well as various tenants of commonsense and decency. Still, I couldn't help going to the foot of the stairs up to the top floor and pausing, straining to hear the sounds they were making.

I've never much been into porn; yes I'll watch it if the chance comes along but it's really not my cup of tea. Maybe I never got into the habit - when I was a lad the internet was as unimaginable as space travel was to The Romans so opportunities were rare. Now and again my friends and I might get hold of a glossy magazine with pictures of naked women to admire but that was about it. `Only recently has full-on sex only been a click or two away and I imagine today's male teenagers witness more action in an evening that me and my old school pals did in a decade. Anyway, once or twice in more intimate moments I had teased Sasha that she'd make a popular porn star and I had to admit that the sounds coming from upstairs seemed to be bestowing my remarks with a greater prophetic dimension than I had anticipated at the time. I was also becoming aroused myself which was disturbing given the circumstances, but the sensations emanating from my groin were definitely real enough. I half-crawled up to where the stairs reached the little landing at the top and paused.

'Shall I put that on for you?' I heard Sasha's voice coo and that was the moment I knew it was time to leave. The mental image that flashed into my mind drained any desire to hear any more and I retreated as quickly and as quietly as I could down the stairs, along the first floor landing and down to the ground floor. The front door obligingly opened without a sound and I crept back onto the street. The car in the drive sitting behind Sasha's Fiat was a black BMW with a personalised number plate and as I glanced at it the realisation hit me like a slap in the face with a wet flannel. The car was Marc Gilbert's - it had been outside the house several times when I had taught Grace! Fan-fucking-tastic, not only was I being two-timed tonight but I knew the other woman in this situation and the thought of Fiona being hurt somehow made it all ten times worse. Don't get me wrong – I didn't feel great but I would cope. I doubted if it would be so easy for Grace's mum if she found out about tonight.

I walked briskly back to the Mazda, fired the ignition and took off in the direction of Beechwood. I was home in five minutes, put the kettle on, lit a cigarette and sat back on the chair next to the kitchen table. Sasha was shagging someone else and I couldn't help smiling at the poetic justice of the situation - it was me who had a history of being seduced by the prospect of extra sex on the side and here I was smoking a cigarette while my lover was between the sheets with her horny boss. Feeling sorry for myself therefore seemed out of the question, although there was no denying it was a bit of a bummer. What I had to do now was cope with the disappointment and not be tempted to risk losing my dignity as well as the girl. I hoped that it wasn't going to be easier said than done – Sasha was hot and it would be simple to be weak and chase after her like a hormonal teenager.

There was much to consider and I played the situation through in my mind for a while until I realised there wasn't a lot I could do about anything that night. I also had the Under Thirteen's match to look after tomorrow morning so after a couple more cigarettes and a glass of single malt I gave up and wearily went to bed. It took a while to drift off to sleep, my brain addled with images and questions concerning Sasha and how I was going to take it from here. In the end I forced myself to think about Renia as I often did when sleep became elusive; I imagined flying over to Athens and knocking on her door on Christmas Eve with a bunch of flowers. She would smile and call me a silly boy just before I kissed her. Ah the power of the imagination!

The next day the football took up all of the morning. Afterwards I picked Alex up and we had lunch in town and did a bit of shopping. When I got home I was tempted to call Sasha to see what she was doing but didn't have the energy for the role of unsuspecting partner that I would have to perform on the phone. Despite my vow of the night before to play it cool I had to admit that I still wanted to see her and that it really was up to her who else she went to bed with. After more deliberation, however, I concluded that I really needed her to be keen if I were to retain some enthusiasm for the relationship. It clearly had no future in the long term but I had to be pragmatic; she was sexy and I reminded myself again there wasn't exactly a queue of shaggable women lining up in my appointments diary

There was also the not so small matter of Fiona and Marc Gilbert. I knew something that Fiona and Grace should know about which left me feeling uncomfortable. Should I keep quiet or mention in passing that Marc Gilbert was just like any other man but, like Rick's friend Captain Renault in *Casablanca*, more so? Now there was a poser and a fucking half! I didn't think there was any doubt that I would say nothing and let nature take its course but I did feel uneasy about keeping the truth from Grace. She was much more to me than just a student and I didn't want my friendship with her to be compromised by my silence. I doubted if Gilbert had ever been faithful but then I couldn't understand why he didn't just stay single and shag all the bimbos that came his way up at *The Wealdon*. Fiona was an extremely classy lady but she was a woman and that meant energy would have to be expended maintaining a relationship with her; why bother if you didn't need to? Perhaps Gilbert really did love her but needed some action on the side - I could understand that up to a point - I am a man after all - but I still didn't buy into it as a lifestyle option. He was going to find out that people were going to get hurt although I had a feeling he was pretty bullet-proof in that regard.

In spite of myself I typed *The Wealdon, Sevenoaks* into Google on my laptop later that afternoon. I found the website and had a look through it. Membership at *The Wealdon* was certainly out of my price range with the decimal points where they currently were but if I was looking to spend a few grand of a city bonus it looked like the ideal venue at which to act like a high-flying tosser. There was a photo of Gilbert hiding behind a series of links designed for those people who liked to know the background and history of where they were staying. He was smiling into the camera but the expression didn't seem to come naturally. With his smouldering Latin looks and dark floppy hair he reminded me of the C-Lister movie actors whose greatest achievements are the celebrity women they manage to date. Although I was clearly prejudiced I had to admit that if Sasha liked her men to be rich good-looking bastards then she had won the lottery.

Sasha didn't call; she sent a text, a bad sign in the circumstances. '*Hope you had a good night. Am working tonight but can see you in the week. Let me know xxx.*' Reading it I had a feeling that 'in the week' was code for 'shagging someone else tonight but you'll do if things don't work out'. It looked like my charms were not going to win out over money and good-looks especially if he had stamina on top. I thought about a pithy response over a cigarette and eventually settled for '*A bit hung over but no lasting damage. Don't work too hard! x.*'

I pressed the send button. It was the best I could do and I reckoned even Marlowe would have had a hard time coming up with something better in the circumstances.

'Suck on that,' I said to myself childishly and tossed the mobile onto the settee and lit another cigarette.

I managed to negotiate the last week at school and survived the pantomime on the final day. Rose and Carol gave me a bottle of wine and a funny card as a 'thank you' and I eventually staggered home late on Friday night after an end of term trip to several pubs with some of the younger staff from school. I had to get a taxi back so was car-less until Rachel, who was now back from Oxford, came and collected me on Saturday morning. I bought her and Alex lunch in town before they dropped me back in the school car park where I had left the car.

Sasha hadn't called in the week and I resisted several strong urges to text or call her. I had also suppressed any fleeting inclination to mention Gilbert's secret liaison to

Grace during her lesson. As things stood Christmas wasn't looking a very promising prospect and the New Year didn't appear to be offering much excitement either. As it turned out I was right about Christmas but dead wrong about everything else.

12

It was a quiet Christmas, at least for me. I spent the usual time tramping around the shops finding presents, often with either Alex or Rachel in tow to advise and keep me company. I made phone calls and sent e mails to the few friends around the country I was still in contact with and went out a couple of times with Gere and Rocky. There was another e mail from Renia telling me to have a Happy Christmas and giving me a brief account of how she had left her job and was now looking for something else. She didn't mention her boyfriend but I guessed he was still lurking around somewhere. It had been snowing in Athens.

In my reply I suggested that she come to England if she wanted to experience real weather. In fact, I said, she could stay with me but there was no room for her boyfriend. I hoped she understood the joke. I also mentioned the barren state of my love-life just so that she knew I was still available.

I spent Christmas Day on my own which was honestly no hardship. Fortunately there was plenty on the television and I had an abundant supply of food, wine and cigarettes. Outside the weather was the normal mundane grey that most Christmases seem to be. I went for a run for three or four miles in the afternoon along the lonely country lanes. There were a few families out walking but by the looks on the majority of their faces most were only really looking forward to getting back home to a warm fire. The empty fields and the bare trees waited patiently in the lifeless air with only the odd crow or other solitary bird giving movement to the Kent countryside. It might have been a dark day in the nineteenth century.

The cigarettes aside I was also in the middle of a real get fitter effort; hence the run. Perhaps I spent more time in the gym only on the off chance that I would bump into Sasha, but whatever the reason the muscles definition was improving a little and I could run faster for longer.

On Boxing Day I picked the girls up early and we spent the morning driving down to Chris's place in Devon. There was a steady stream of traffic but it took less than three and a half hours to reach the Hadley Estate north of Exeter where Chris was in charge of the gardens and woodland element of the enterprise. In essence his job was to make sure the estate owner, Sir Richard Ashcombe, had enough birds to shoot when the fancy took him and gardens pristine enough to impress any VIPs that might pop in for a visit. Chris had a cottage built along with various stables and agricultural buildings near the neo-gothic pile where Sir Richard lived with his family. We drove in the main gate but after a couple of hundred yards the drive forked off and swung around avoiding the ornamental gardens of the main house, eventually coming to a large yard off which Chris's cottage lay in its own garden and grounds. He must have been in the kitchen that looked out onto the wide gravelled area where his old Volvo was parked because he came out of the front door as we climbed out of the car.

Chris was taller and wirier than me, over six foot, and he was dressed in his customary jeans and a baggy checked shirt. His hair was very close cropped and his thin angular face was perpetually brown from his outdoor lifestyle. There was also the usual friendly and infectious grin on his face as he came over and gave us all a hug one by one. He had been a moody sod when we were boys but for the last twenty years we had grown closer and enjoyed the other's company. I didn't see a lot of him mind you, there were two hundred miles between our houses for a start, and I wouldn't say that either of us knew much about what the other was up to from day to day but all the same we both knew we could count on the other in a tight spot.

The four of us were soon sat around the hefty old wooden table in Chris's large comfortable kitchen drinking tea. There were knick-knacks and odds and ends everywhere but without giving the impression of untidiness or neglect. All the plates and fittings were modern and bright rather than old and weary and the positioning of the many pictures and photos on the walls betrayed an artistic disposition.

'They'll be here soon,' Chris told Alex when she asked him about the cousins who were due to appear that afternoon. 'They left Lorraine's place about ten minutes ago so it should only be a few minutes at the most.'

'You had Christmas Day to yourself as well then,' I observed.

'Yeah, nightmare,' said Chris shaking his head. He obviously didn't enjoy solitude as much as me. Maybe it was because I spent most of my life surrounded by teenagers whereas he spent long periods of time on his own in the gardens he had to run.

When we were younger Chris had always been the sociable one and was out so often with his friends my mother would almost forget what he looked like. He had adopted a hippy lifestyle for much of his late teens and early twenties based in Exeter before settling down here fifteen years ago. In Exeter he earned a living with seasonal and farm work. He could be a difficult bugger, like me, and usually pissed off his employers when he thought they were being unreasonable so the jobs were many and varied. When Emma came along he and his ex were lucky enough to be recommended to Sir Richard who had decided to give Chris a chance. Chris had knuckled down and now he was part of the furniture at Hadley. He still kept most of his old friends from his youth and during a stay with him there were always a lot of visits from people who all looked like fully paid up members of Friends of the Earth or the local Pagan Society.

Although we were worlds apart in terms of lifestyle Chris and I got on because I think we recognised something of ourselves in the other. He was a straight-talking fuck-off-if-you-don't-like-me sort of a guy. For Chris things were usually either black or white and people were either good guys or bad guys. Paradoxically, he could be charming and funny enough to merit the nickname 'Slick' if there had been a Rocky in his life, but that was a cross only I had to bear.

It wasn't long before my nieces and nephew arrived and Chris and I were left sitting alone at the kitchen table. I gave him a review of the past few months and he filled me in on life in Devon. Everything was fine as far as I could tell; Emma and Rhiannon had chosen to live with him and that gave him a focus apart from the job which he could do standing on his head and, of course, looking for a woman. He had so many contacts that meeting potential girlfriends wasn't a problem and he had one or two short-lived affairs but nothing more permanent. That sounded familiar.

When I ran through the night at Sasha's and my escapade as a peeping-tom Chris tried to look sympathetic until he realised I was playing it for laughs and relaxed.

'I wouldn't have minded but she put on my fucking CD while she was chatting him up in the front room!' I exclaimed with a grin.

'What if they'd heard you?' Chris began to snigger. 'That'd be more embarrassing than-'

'Yep, exactly - I might also have struggled to explain why I was inside the spare bedroom when they came upstairs! Thank God they were way too busy thinking out about how to impress each other once they got down to business.'

'So single again bro.'

'As a priest and with no choirboys to fall back on.'

Later on, out of the blue, he took a swig of his coffee and said casually.

'Ever thought of changing jobs Neil?'

I thought about the question for a second or two.

'I'd love to but what else is there that would give me the same money, not to mention the main reason for teaching - the holidays? I'll admit that I've done it for so long that I could do with a change but a man's got to live.'

Chris nodded but carried on nevertheless.

'You just seem a bit jaded to me. Apart from teaching itself and the students you can't stand the management. For God's sake Neil, you've no mortgage - why don't you bugger off somewhere and have a break?'

'You mean like a sabbatical?' I shook my head and flicked some ash off my cigarette into an ashtray. 'Sounds great but my boss wouldn't even consider it and I'm not the type to ask her just so that she can just say no. I'm like most teachers; I like what I do, it's just there's too much of it and management isn't in the business of cutting us any slack.'

'Sounds mad like you say,' nodded Chris.

'Yeah, then there's my old age to worry about and at least in teaching there's a pension at the end of it. Without that I would be fucked. I don't fancy ending up like mum did with hardly two pennies to rub together.'

'You're not exactly a risk-taker are you mate?' grinned Chris. 'Only seems like yesterday the whole idea of job security and pensions would have been the last things on our minds.'

'Yeah, maybe what I need is a rich widow,' I sighed, as Chris stood up and walked over to check the progress of the turkey in the Aga. He laughed.

'Yeah, preferably about twenty-five with big tits - it's a pity there aren't many of those around.'

'Yeah but it's nice to dream. Anyway, things could be worse - I've still got my health and good looks. I'm just going to have to put Sasha behind me and start again in the New Year. Can I do anything to help?'

'No, I did all the veg before you arrived,' Chris said over his shoulder as he carefully basted the back of the turkey in a baking tin he had manoeuvred onto the top of the range.

We stayed two nights at Chris's place. Rachel and Alex were happy spending time with their cousins and we all went on a couple of long walks around the estate in some bright winter weather. A shopping expedition to Exeter was squeezed in and Chris and I also had a chance to stay up to the early hours talking, playing his guitars and drinking too much. Before we knew it we were in the car making the journey back to real life.

That evening I surveyed my options for New Year's Eve. They weren't exactly enticing: either trawling around the pubs or staying in and watching some celebs see in the New

Year on the television. How is it that being a useless prat ensures an invite to a glamorous party at the BBC's expense?

The coming year itself looked even more uninspiring. What I needed was a complete change in lifestyle but there seemed as much chance of that happening as Hugh Grant taking a vow of celibacy. It looked like the next twelve months would be much the same as the past series - working my arse off at school, trying to be a reasonable father and engineering as much free time as I could. Giving up smoking was another perpetual theme to these end-of-year reflections but I was realistic enough to rate the chances of that on a similar level to Hugh entering a monastery.

I looked at the copy of *The Little Sister* that was perched on the arm of the sofa where I had left it before the trip to Devon. Yeah, my life wasn't entirely dissimilar to Marlowe's: while he sat in his office waiting for a new case, here I was festering on the sofa. Granted his office was in LA and I was in Beechwood – a big difference so far as potential thrills were concerned. Oh, there was also the small matter of Marlowe being a fictional character with all the possibilities of Raymond Chandler's imagination at his disposal! I was in a rut: it was an okay rut but it didn't offer the prospect of anything very exotic unless maybe I booked myself a weird holiday in the summer. Maybe I could swim with dolphins or, better still, tempt someone out of her leotard at a yogic retreat.

Just then the phone rang over on the desk in the corner. I raised my eyebrows – 'at last, a case' I muttered to myself as I hauled myself up off my arse. It was Grace.

'Hi, what a surprise! Don't tell me you need an extra lesson?' I said after she had announced herself.

'No Neil, as if. I'm actually inviting you to a New Year's Eve party at our place tomorrow. That is if you're not busy labelling your beer mat collection or polishing your badminton rackets or something.'

I laughed – how did she know?! No, this was silly, I had nothing planned but I wasn't in a mood for a party full of strangers either.

'I'm not normally one for turning down an invite to such a swell affair but I can't,' I said. 'Apart from you and your mum I won't know anyone.'

'Look Neil it doesn't matter in the least. There are over a hundred coming, mostly from *The Wealden*, so even you'll find someone to talk to. Besides, there are always plenty of attractive single women at Marc's parties. Haven't you been to a hotel or casino lately to check out the staff? Oh, forget I said that; I momentarily forgot your social life doesn't extend much beyond badminton matches.'

She had me there: the rackets could wait. Anyway, a moment ago I had been wishing for something exciting to happen. It would be free booze and possibly a lot of daring party dresses and maybe Sasha would be putting in an appearance? Hmm, Sasha, Gilbert, Fiona and me all in the same place at the same time – it could be an interesting party all right! But I still played it cool with Grace.

'You are tempting me Grace but are you sure your mum doesn't mind me coming? Oh, and what about Marvellous Marc?'

'Don't worry about him Neil,' she said dismissively. 'It was mum who suggested I invite you so you should be honoured! Most of the people are Marc's guests - it's a sort of office party - and Mum hasn't a lot of friends living near us now and most of mine have other stuff arranged, so we need you Neil!'

I thought of Sasha and Gilbert going upstairs at her place and I made up my mind. If Fiona needed a few friends along I was happy to be one of them.

'Okaay, okay I'll come! Maybe I'll find my perfect woman. I don't think I've gone so long without a steady girlfriend since I was at school. I'm going to need a refresher course in how to hold hands' Grace laughed down the phone.

'Yeah, I'm single right now. I think my standards are too high or I'm just too busy.'

'Or you're simply too unattractive?' I suggested. 'Anyway, when do we kick off?'

'Cheeky sod! Come around eight-thirty and wear your dinner jacket and all the trimmings.'

'I'll be there. Save a dance for me.'

'Right - in your dreams Neil.'

I put the phone down and went back to the sofa. So Mackenzie, a glamorous party beckoned. Perhaps I would be starting off the New Year with some excitement after all? At least I would be spared waking up with a hang-over by Rocky's snoring after an uncomfortable night on Gere's floor. Last year it had been very tempting to put a cushion over the bastard's face as he lay sprawled in a chair tenderly clutching an empty can of lager. Next to that memory I reckoned Grace's party could only be a step in the right direction.

13

When I arrived at Grace's house at about eight I was directed to park about half way down the drive behind a row of other cars. As I walked across the gravel towards the front door in my tuxedo I began to feel mildly excited at the prospect of a rare night out. A few yards from the front door I was greeted by a couple of smart looking bouncers standing outside in the chilly air. Most of the lights in the house were on and as I approached the men I could see people in party gear through the large downstairs windows. I smiled winningly, told them my name and was nodded through when they found it on their list.

The hallway on the other side of the door, familiar to me from my many tutoring visits, had some more hired help waiting. A couple of boys in uncomfortable looking waiter's outfits, each holding a tray of drinks, hovered just inside on the left. They looked like recruits from the Sixth Form of one of the local public schools and two similarly polished girls stood opposite the front door next to some clothes rails offering to take coats. I hadn't even owned an overcoat since my mother had relinquished responsibility for choosing my clothes so I settled for a glass of champagne.

I hesitated and had a look at my surroundings. As hallways went no estate agent alive would have bothered with a 'deceptively spacious' description because it was enormous. A grand oak-panelled affair, hung with a few oil paintings and liberally decorated for the occasion with silver balloons and sprigs of holly, it exuded class. The crimson-carpeted stairs were wide enough for three people to negotiate shoulder to shoulder and the girls were standing in front of the bottom step.

'Which way to all the fun?' I asked one of them. The question was pretty academic because the noise of music and voices was coming through some open double doors to the right of the front door on the other side of the entrance hall, but she seemed eager to be of service.

'That way sir,' she said, in a cut glass accent, nodding towards the double doors.

I thanked her and proceeded through the doors and into another room with the same oak panelling only this time it just went half way up the walls. The room was about the proportions of a decent sized classroom and there were sofas and chairs arranged around two glass coffee tables. It was almost like walking into the reception of an expensive hotel. A few dozen guests were in the room busy talking in groups and no one seemed to notice me as I strolled through in the direction of more double doors in the far wall. I could hear the sound of Van Morrison belting out 'Brown Eyed Girl' getting louder as I came up to the doors and stopped and had another look at my surroundings.

In height and size the room was so large it may have been possible to have a decent game of badminton in it. There must have been at least fifty people in attendance and most were dressed for an up-market bash. The men wore mostly tuxedos although there were the usual cretins dotted about who obviously thought that a shirt worn outside a cheap pair of chinos looked equally cool. At least they would be at the back of the night's 'who's getting laid' queue. The women were an eclectic mix in terms of age and size but most had been uniformly unimaginative in their choice of party wear: they all had on outfits that were either too tight or low-cut or short or all three - I mostly approved.

From the volume of the chatter and laughter I guessed that for most guests the glass of champagne they got at the door was not the first drink of the evening. Feeling very single I stood in the doorway and looked around to see if I could spot Grace. There was a tap on my shoulder.

'You're looking very smart Neil.'

I turned, grinning at the sound of her voice.

'Thanks. This is the closest I ever get to being James Bond. Looks like quite a party.'

She was wearing a long, dark, close-fitting dress that most women would have been popular in but in which she managed to pull off sensational. Her shoulders and arms were bare except for a black and silver heart-shaped necklace that sparkled nearly as much as her eyes.

'Come and say hello to Mum,' Grace said in a voice that betrayed the influence of more than one glass of wine and she led me over to one of the tables at the edge of the room. Fiona wouldn't have looked out of place at The Oscars either and gave me a bright and enthusiastic welcome. I guessed she must have finished off the bottle that Grace had started because she was certainly more animated than when I met her on my weekly visits. I sensed it was her version of the 'hostess with the mostest' routine but I think I preferred her thoughtful and enigmatic.

Grace led me over to an empty table at the end of the room nearest the entrance and we sat down with our drinks. Gilbert must have hired plenty of tables and chairs to put around the perimeter of the room as well as a temporary dance floor. There was a balding overweight guy and his disco equipment at the far end of the room. He looked like he wasn't going to see forty again so I guessed that explained the fact that I recognised most of the music he played. The lighting was dim enough to encourage people to dance without them feeling they weren't the focus of attention and a few had already started to try out a few well-worn routines even at this early hour.

'Who did all the hard work?' I asked looking around.

'Oh Marc's people from the hotel came and set it up. All the bouncers and waiters are his as well.'

'So all you and your mum have to do is turn up and be glamorous. I should have been a woman. Anyway how are you?'

Grace leaned over, pushing her hair from the side of her face with a slender hand.

'I've been doing a lot of socialising actually which was fun but mum insisted I be here tonight. I don't mind doing it for her but it's not exactly my scene.'

'What do you mean?' I asked. 'Doesn't feel like a party unless half the guests are being sick in the flower beds while the rest are trashing your parents' house?'

'I think you're fantasising about Year Eleven parties Neil - aren't you forgetting I'm nineteen now, not sixteen.' Grace frowned playfully. 'Besides, you forgot to mention the al fresco sex and blow jobs in the garden.'

'I knew I was a teenager in the wrong decade - mind you, some of the ladies here look like they might be up for more than a kiss under the mistletoe. How desperate do I look tonight?'

'Your pupils are a bit dilated but if you manage to control the nervous twitch you look reasonably normal,' Grace said, studying my face quizzically.

I decided to change the subject.

'Thanks - I'll try to remember. Anyway, how are your mum and Marc?'

'Not brilliant. She wasn't very impressed with her Christmas present and he's not made much of an effort this holiday. He's been out at *The Wealden* most days and at the casino as well in the evenings - she feels like she's hardly seen him.'

'What did he get her?' I asked, trying to be polite.

'A necklace but mum didn't think he'd tried very hard with the choice. Anyway she didn't like it.'

'Your mother sounds like a hard woman to please,' I joked, trying to keep things light. I looked around the room. 'Where is Mr Gilbert anyway?'

'Oh somewhere,' Grace shrugged. 'Don't worry you'll get to meet him.'

'Will I have to curtsey?'

'No, just be normal for my sake. I don't know why but I'd quite like it if he didn't think you were a sad moron.'

'Thanks for the advice Grace but relax, I'm on my best behaviour tonight - I'll even turn down sex in the garden if somebody offers.'

As we spoke I happened to be looking at the doors when who should appear and stand, drink in hand, scanning the room but the beautiful Sasha.

'Hello,' I exclaimed in surprise. 'Somebody I know at last; I wondered if she would come tonight. That's Sasha!'

Grace half-turned and followed my gaze.

'Gosh. Is she the one you went out with? I'm impressed Neil.'

'Try sounding impressed instead of surprised,' I said out of the corner of my mouth, because Sasha had turned and seen us. She hesitated but I was already grinning a 'hello' so that she couldn't make out she hadn't seen us and escape. Sasha walked the short distance to our table, returning my smile with a guarded one of her own, while I hoped Grace had banished the shocked look from her own face. She had on a short black sequined party dress that would have turned heads anywhere. As she strolled over on her lithe, muscular legs that were visible up to and including a generous proportion of thigh I found myself focusing on my breathing in order to maintain a regular pattern. I've always been a leg man so Sasha's pins were quite enough to keep me happy but I couldn't help noticing as well that her bare arms and shoulders also looked mouth-wateringly toned and that she was displaying a sporting amount of cleavage. I stood up to greet her and kissed her on both cheeks.

'Hi. Long time no see.' I said brightly. 'I don't know if you've met Grace. She lives here.' Sasha and Grace smiled at each other.

'Oh you must be Marc's, er, stepdaughter,' Sasha said tentatively.

'Not quite,' said Grace quickly. 'Maybe one day.' She didn't sound enthusiastic.

Grace stood up with her now empty glass and looked at me.

'Can I get you another drink Neil?'

'You'd better make it a tonic water for now,' I said. Grace disappeared. I looked at Sasha and offered her a chair

'Sit down for a few minutes. Tell me your news and let me look at your legs for a bit.'

Sasha seemed to relax and laughed, sitting down on a chair so that she was just around the table from me. She crossed her legs and as her chair was a couple of feet from the table I was aware of even more thigh, smooth and firm, screaming for my attention. Despite the distraction we had an amusing conversation for about five minutes before we were interrupted by Marc Gilbert.

I had noticed him come in and start circulating with his guests a few minutes after Sasha had sat down. He looked about middle thirties, medium build and about the same height as me. Even from a distance he looked like the boss; there was a subtle confidence in the way he moved and everyone he spoke to looked like they were trying extra hard when he was around. In the flesh I could see how his magnetism, tanned good looks and Al Pacino hair might turn a woman's head. As Sasha told me how her kids were doing I watched him stroll over out of the corner of my eye until he was standing next to her chair.

'Good evening. I'm Marc Gilbert. I don't think we've met.'

He was looking at me in a friendly enough way but he ignored Sasha.

'Neil Mackenzie. Grace's tutor. Pleased to meet you. Fantastic place you have here.'

That seemed to satisfy him and he turned to smile at Sasha. She looked up at him with an expression that was inviting as a cold beer in the Sahara. All of a sudden I felt like a gooseberry and he looked like he badly needed a drink.

'Sasha. Glad you could come,' purred Gilbert, and he bent over and kissed her cheek.

'Here's your drink Neil.' Grace had returned. She put my glass down on the table in front of me.

'Ah Grace,' said Gilbert. He sounded like he was trying hard to be charming but that's what it sounded like - hard work. 'Thank you for looking after Dr Mackenzie.'

Grace glanced at Sasha and then gave him a look I had seen a few times in class when she wasn't impressed. In school it had the instant effect of raising my blood pressure and only years of resisting similar urges to slap students managed to keep me calm. I looked at Gilbert to see if he had similar self-control. Not a flicker. He was obviously used to Grace's repertoire of disdainful glances.

'Well, very nice to meet you,' he said to me. 'Have a good evening.' Turning to Sasha he continued. 'There are some people I'd like you to meet Sasha.'

Sasha stood up.

'See you later,' she smiled. 'It was nice to see you again Neil.'

'Likewise,' I smiled, 'especially in that dress.'

A look flickered across Gilbert's face that wasn't exactly good-natured but I thought 'fuck you' as he led her off gently by the elbow.

'What a wanker!' exclaimed Grace.

'Who? Me or him?' I tried to look confused.

'Him, you idiot. He's always smarming over all the women he fancies. I don't know why mum doesn't notice.'

'Love is blind or at least partially sighted I guess. You're right though - he is a smarmy bastard *and* he's pinched the only woman I had an outside chance of snogging tonight. Hey, things are crowding up in here!'

The dance floor was half-full now and the party atmosphere was beginning to build. I did my best to keep Grace amused but I could see she was still irritated by Gilbert's behaviour with Sasha. I wasn't going to suggest a dance as I was only too aware of my limitations in that department but I would have made an effort if Grace had asked. Instead of that, however, she suddenly leaned over and whispered a rather different proposal into my ear.

'Would you like to see something interesting?'

I tried not to smirk; settling for raising an eyebrow in as casual manner as I could.

'Er, what exactly did you have in mind. We don't want to ruin a beautiful friendship and there's no way I'm looking at your maths on New Year's Eve.' She slapped my arm.

'Don't be an idiot Neil. Come with me. I'll tell you upstairs.'

I shrugged resignedly and stood up and followed her out of the room and back through the entrance hall and down a short passage to the kitchen. There were a few staff preparing nibbles for the party but Grace took me through and out of a door in the opposite wall, along a corridor and up some stairs I supposed had been for the servants years ago. On the first floor we went up another flight and eventually came to the room where I taught her each week. She left me standing by the desk where we had lessons and disappeared into what I supposed was her bedroom. She appeared a second or two later with a Yale type key in her hand.

'Wow, a key. I knew this would be a night out to remember,' I said, rubbing my hands together.

'I thought you agreed not to be a twat,' she smiled. 'Guess what this opens Mr Maths Teacher?' I leaned back so that my rump was resting against the desk and stroked my chin deliberately.

'I take it you're not wearing a chastity belt so that apart I haven't the faintest idea.' She ignored my weak attempt to be witty and came over and stood in front of me and waved the key between her fingers.

'It's the key to Marc's study!'

'So?' I shrugged my shoulders. 'Why do you think it's so cute to have his key?'

'It's cute because he doesn't know I have it - and I've used it a few times to get in and look around. He won't let the cleaners do his office so he got a key cut for mum so that she could do it. She was petrified that she'd lose it so she got an extra one cut and gave it to me to look after.' She stopped for a breath and carried on. 'I couldn't resist having a little check up on him.'

I had to smile. Marc Gilbert might be a rich deceitful bastard but he obviously hadn't counted on the resourcefulness of this feisty and determined young woman. When Grace didn't like someone changing her opinion was as difficult as moving the Earth's orbit around the Sun. I couldn't help wondering if she had discovered anything about Sasha or the probable other stuff Gilbert kept away from her mother.

'You did what?' It was difficult to keep the admiration out of my voice so I tried to disguise it with surprise. 'Correct me if I'm wrong but wouldn't you be in the sort of trouble that might involve a change of address if he found out?'

'Don't try and pretend you're not interested Neil,' Grace ignored what I had said which, to be fair, was the sensible option since I hadn't really meant it. 'You know I'm not stupid enough to get caught.' She paused for effect, her eyes fixing mine playfully. 'So, are you going to ask me what I found?'

'I've a feeling I'm going to get to know whether I like it or not.' It was difficult not to enjoy the look in her eyes. 'Go on then, tell me before I get too overwrought.'

Grace paused again. She was being more dramatic than an episode of Dr Who.

'I'll do better than that, I'll show you,' she said and, grinning, she turned to go. 'Come on, let's go and have a peep now.'

'Pardon me,' I laughed, trying to keep the mild panic out of my voice. 'What do you mean 'have a peep now'? Are you seriously suggesting we go into his study now while he's still in the house? I wouldn't even agree if he was in Antarctica. How much have you had to drink?'

'Four or five but that's irrelevant,' Grace grinned over her shoulder. She was nearly out the door so I had to start moving or be left behind. I caught her in the corridor and fell into step alongside her.

'Grace, hold on a second,' I pleaded. She stopped walking and I talked fast. 'What if Gilbert feels the urge to visit said study and finds us doing our burglary routine? You might get away with a tongue lashing but I'll be the stand-in for the punch-bag those bouncers out front use for training down at the gym. I really like my face the way it is - and no jokes please.'

'Don't be silly Neil, there's no way Marc will leave the party. Trust me, what I've found is worth the risk and if things go wrong I promise I'll visit you in hospital.'

Despite myself I smiled again at the joke. I had a really annoying habit of ignoring my own better judgement and giving myself away with a stupid grin. I think she knew me well enough to know that I would cave in; as I mentioned earlier I've never been any good at saying no to students and attractive women and Grace qualified on both counts. I let out a long resigned sigh.

'Okay, okay but this had better be good. I must be mad.'

'I knew I could count on you to liven up New Year's Eve,' grinned Grace. 'Follow me.'

We went down the same narrow stairs to the first floor where Grace led me along a wide half-panelled corridor that must have been above the large party-room downstairs. Music was seeping up through the carpet like a soundtrack to a film and the hairs on the back of my neck began to stir with excitement. Just before the corridor came to the end of the house there was a narrower passage leading off to the left towards the back of the house. Here carpet underfoot gave way to bare parquet flooring so that our footsteps suddenly became audible, causing us both to begin tiptoeing in unison. It was only about ten feet until the passage ended at a solid-looking oak door, the varnished wood gleaming softly in the low lighting of the corridor.

We stopped and listened at the door. I couldn't hear a thing and Grace must have heard nothing either because she put the key she had been holding into the lock and turned it slowly. With her other hand Grace turned the brass door handle by her hip and opened the door to Marc Gilbert's study.

14

Grace went in, flicked a light switch on the wall to her right and I followed, closing the door behind me. Grace locked us in. It was another room out of a National Trust brochure with a lot of polished wood, paintings hung in ornate, heavy frames and that sort of thing. The floor had the same parquet finish as in the corridor outside but now two large Turkish carpets left only a narrow strip of exposed wood around the edge of the room. Down to the left there were three shiny leather Chesterfields arranged in a U shape where I guessed Gilbert could entertain business associates if he wished. Failing that he could always watch the huge black flat-screen television that was fitted neatly into the bookcases that lined that end of the room.

The wall opposite the door was long enough to accommodate four large windows which were covered tonight by floor-length velvet crimson drapes. Gilbert's desk sat at a slight angle in front of the second from the right. It was about the size of four of my own desks at school but he didn't seem to need the extra space because there was nothing on it save for a sleek white Apple laptop and a phone. There were a couple of chairs in front of the desk but at that end of the study there were only a few other bits of gleaming antique furniture placed against the walls. Grace walked over towards the desk and turned and grinned at me. I said in a low voice

'I don't want to appear in a hurry or anything but what exactly is it you're showing me? I'll grant you that it's a very impressive office but I think Maths Resources at school still shades it.'

'Shut up Neil.' Grace said dismissively, and glided to the chimney breast nearest Gilbert's desk where there was no fireplace or mantelpiece, just a little chest of drawers below a large painting of what looked like Venice. She took hold of the right side of the painting, looked back at me and winked, and pulled the frame so that the painting swung open like a door to reveal a grey metal safe hiding in the wall.

I whistled softly and dug my hands into my trouser pockets and stared at it.

'Not bad Grace but doesn't every self-respecting millionaire have one? How did you know about it?'

'He doesn't keep it a secret, at least to Mum. I think he liked to impress her when they first got together. He opened it a few years ago when I was in here as well. We were going out for dinner and mum and I came to get him after he kept us waiting. He was all friendly and apologetic and said he just had to put some papers in the safe. I thought he was a tit because he obviously liked me to know how important he was.'

'It's a pity he didn't give you the combination while he was at it,' I said, walking over and looking at the LED display and the number pad in the centre of the impenetrable looking door.

Grace came over and stood next to me.

'This is where you're going to be very proud of me Dr M,' she said in a voice that sounded more than mildly pleased with itself. She leaned forward, her fingers contorted over the keypad and a green light instantly replaced the red one at the top of the pad. 'Stand back please,' she announced and she grabbed the handle of the safe and pulled open the heavy door.

'Is there any end to your talent?' I said in genuine admiration as she stood back so that I could see into the safe. 'Fuck me sideways, that *is* a lot of money!'

Grace and I stared at the three deep shelves that were tightly packed with bank notes. There was another shelf containing a neat pile of papers and documents but it was the money that was so impressive to a man for whom a few hundred in cash is heady stuff.

'I wonder where he gets it all from?' she said softly. 'It can't be legal.'

'Maybe he's just a very committed saver,' I ventured with a laugh. 'How did you get the code for fuck's sake?'

'Long story,' Grace closed the safe so that the red light came on again and swung the picture back into place. 'You take some of the credit though. Remember we were talking about security codes in a probability lesson last year I think and you said that most people used passwords or codes they could easily remember like names and birthdays?' I nodded.

'So, don't tell me, you reckoned a six figure code would probably be a date,' I ventured.

'Exactly, and being the nosy teenager I noticed the first two digits he put in when I was there and he opened the safe - two and five.'

'What's so special about twenty five - don't tell me it's his birthday or something?'

Grace walked away from the safe towards me in the centre of the study grinning broadly.

'The twenty fifth of August to be precise. I didn't put two and two together until after your lesson and I came in here and had a look at the safe again. He's so vain I just knew it had to be. Once I found out how old he was I came back and tried it out and hey presto!'

I returned her smile and patted her cheek gently.

'Genius - and at last I've taught a lesson that turned out to be useful. Ever thought of helping yourself to a loan?'

'Course not. What do you take me for? I just wanted to find out his secrets. Anyway we ought to be off Neil - come on, let's get back to the party.'

We turned towards the study door. At that split second the muffled sounds of footsteps on parquet flooring in the corridor outside demolished the moment like brake failure on a wet road. Grace's face drained faster than a whiskey at an Irish funeral and God knows what new expression my face must have invented. I managed to recover quickly enough to reach across with one hand to flick off the light switch and grab Grace's wrist with the other. Just as the room went dark I glanced at the Chesterfields so that we stood a reasonable chance of reaching them without demolishing other furniture in the process of reaching them. We ran down the room and skipped around the nearest sofa side onto the door and behind the middle of the three that faced up towards the door and the rest of the study. A moment later there was the sound of a key scraping into a lock and the lights came on.

Grace and I had managed to fall into uncomfortable semi-foetal positions behind the couch. My face was close to the back off her neck and my right arm was resting on hers but the potential embarrassment of this unaccustomed close proximity was lost in the panic of the situation. She was shaking but it was difficult to combine a reassuring grip while my own mind was racing coming to terms with our predicament. It was immediately obvious from their voices that it was Gilbert and surprise, surprise, Sasha who were taking time out from the merry-making downstairs. Sasha sounded like she hadn't skimped on the champagne since she had arrived.

'So this is where you do all your thinking,' her voice sparkled from the other end of the room.

'That wasn't what I was planning to do here tonight,' Gilbert laughed confidently. Then there were a few moments of quiet when, judging by the faint rustling of clothing, I assumed they were eating each other's faces. Gilbert sounded faintly breathless and hoarse when he eventually came up for air.

'You look amazing,' he purred. 'I've missed you.'

'Good. I've missed your visits, I've done nothing but be a good mother this holiday - which can be a bit tedious.' She made a few soft sighing noises which probably meant Gilbert had moved on from kissing her lips.

Grace had stopped shaking now and I was getting uncomfortable so I gently released her and rolled onto my back and lay there waiting for Gilbert and Sasha to get on with whatever they had in mind. I hoped it didn't involve going anywhere near the chesterfields. Grace moved onto her back as well, turning her face towards me. I mouthed 'okay?' and she nodded, although her eyes were moist and her expression strained. I didn't know whether she was angry or upset or both but I knew any combination of the two was pretty understandable in the circumstances and I reached over and held her hand.

Sasha's sighs had developed into encouraging moans now and I could hear Gilbert's breathing increasing in volume. This was becoming a habit for me; I needed them to keep me informed of their shagging intentions so I could arrange to be elsewhere. I raised my head slowly so that I was almost level with the arm of the couch placed at right angles to the one that was hiding us and inched it up. Gilbert had his back turned at a slight angle towards me because he had manoeuvred Sasha onto that large desk of his so that her backside was conveniently next to its edge. The only naked flesh I registered was his arse and Sasha's very attractive left leg and most of her torso. They both seemed to be having fun; Sasha was looking up over her shoulder at him and he was busy thrusting whilst holding her thighs for purchase. Out of decorum I rested my head back down until they eventually finished. Gilbert didn't make much noise but I thought Sasha made a passable attempt at faking an orgasm although that might have been sour grapes on my part.

When they had gathered themselves the two sex buddies didn't hang around for long. They spent a few minutes engaged in some playful post-coital exchanges before Sasha pointed out that they shouldn't be away from the party for too long. Gilbert agreed – he had got he wanted although I thought he made a reasonable effort not to sound too keen to get back downstairs. Sasha left first and a couple of minutes later Gilbert went out and locked the door. When the sounds of his footsteps had subsided I let go of Grace's hand and whispered to her in the darkness.

'I'm sorry you had to be here for that, he really is a bastard.'

'I always knew that,' Grace's voice was calm and resigned. 'Once I was old enough I could tell he had an eye for the ladies. Whenever we went out it was so obvious to me - why doesn't mum realise?'

'She's probably aware of it but he's not much different to a lot of blokes really. He just has more opportunity and talent.'

'The bastard - what am I going to do?' Grace let out a big sigh.

'Tonight nothing,' I said. 'Wait until the morning at least. There's no hurry. Come on let's get out of here while we can.'

Inside I felt numb and sick with worry for Grace but I couldn't be sure what to say in case I made things even worse than they were. I wondered how I would have reacted if I had seen my mother's boyfriend having it off with someone else but I didn't have the imagination for that to give me any extra insight so I kept myself in check and tried to project sympathy and solidarity without turning into Gok Wan.

Grace and I picked ourselves up from our hiding place and I felt my way over to the light switch so that we could see what we were doing and tidy ourselves up. Grace's blue eyes were a little red and there were tear stains running down the sides of her face. I looked at her and took out a clean white hanky and put it in her hand.

'I think you need to dry those eyes or someone will think I've been slapping you around again.'

Grace half-smiled and dabbed her eyes and face.

'Thanks,' she said quietly and passed the hanky back.

'Do you think you're okay to go downstairs now?' I asked, looking into her eyes. She nodded so I opened the door and led the way back to the party by the way we had come. I needed a drink and while Grace went to the bar for the alcohol I found an empty table back in the main hall and sat down. I looked around for Gilbert, Sasha and Fiona and spotted them chatting at three different tables in the room. I hoped Grace would be able to cope with what she had witnessed upstairs and wondered what I would do if she provoked some kind of scene. She quickly rejoined me from the bar and we looked at each other.

'How do you feel,' I asked. 'Not much like partying I expect?'

She shrugged her shoulders.

'Hardly, but like you say it would be sensible if I didn't do anything tonight so I'll try to pretend nothing has happened until I get a chance to think tomorrow.'

'I'm glad you said that - I was afraid you might start something which would end up with me stopping you inserting an item of cutlery into Gilbert's chest cavity. Does that mean I can stand down from red alert?'

Grace smiled weakly at me.

'Yes Neil, I won't need restraining tonight - but don't let me too near him just in case.'

'I promise - wow that was an exciting hour I don't ever want to repeat,' I said with feeling. 'If you have anything similar planned in the future please leave me out of it.' I took a generous mouthful of my Becks and placed the bottle back on the table.

Grace shook her head and a steely look came into her eyes.

'No, I'm glad we found out about Sasha and Marc - at least I feel like I know what's going on now. Forewarned is forearmed and all that. I just hope Mum isn't going to be too upset.'

'I think you'd better count on her being devastated but in the long run she'll definitely be better off without the bastard so there is a faint silver lining. It's just going to be a horrible few months for her.'

Grace took a while to respond. She sat for several seconds looking lost in thought and when she did speak the words came out in slowly.

'You're right I suppose Neil - thanks. You should take up counselling – for a maths teacher some of what you say makes surprisingly good sense.'

'I'm just multi-talented,' I smiled deprecatingly. 'It's a pity I can't think of a way to pay Gilbert back in some way.'

'So robbing the safe is out of the question,' Grace said in a matter of fact kind of way. She raised a bare, elegant arm in order to run her left hand like a comb through her hair at the same time as she spoke.

I raised an eyebrow at her.

'Ha, ha – nice try, though I admit it would be a great way of getting revenge,' I nodded. 'But don't even go there please – one of my new year's resolutions is to give up my part-time burglary business.'

'Why Neil, I thought you liked to live dangerously?'

'There's danger and there's danger young lady. Gilbert is no ordinary bloke as far as I can see so please forget it.'

She reached out and touched my arm.

'Okay, Neil, stay cool - I was only a thought. God I feel awful - some party this turned out to be! I'm sorry I've ruined your evening.'

'Forget it,' I smiled. 'I'm glad I'm around to keep you from doing something more stupid.'

Grace looked around the room and took a deep breath.

'You're right Neil, I need to pull myself together and try to act normally. Come on, let's dance to this one - just try not to embarrass me too much.'

15

I didn't hear from Grace until after I had been back at school for a couple of days. New Year's Eve had been on a Friday and our lessons were on Thursdays; I wondered if anything would happen before I was due to teach her again. Sure enough, on Thursday morning there was a text alert on my mobile when I got back to the office at break: *Hi Neil, mum has left Gilbert so do you mind if we miss this week? I'll tell you everything when I see you. He has been a real bastard. Men!* xxx

I replied straight away: *Hi Angel, no problem. Take care and don't leave it too long.*

I leant back in my chair and watched the little picture of an envelope disappear over the horizon on my mobile display. So Fiona had left the bastard - that had to be good news for her. It probably didn't feel that way at the moment but it wouldn't be long before she realised that ditching Gilbert had a lot going for it. Naturally I was keen to find out what Fiona knew about Sasha and, more precisely, the goings on in Gilbert's study on New Year's Eve. I hoped Grace had not got too involved in the break-up so I was keeping my fingers crossed that Sasha hadn't crossed Fiona's radar yet. I also wondered where they were living and so on until I remembered I still had lessons to teach and marking to get done.

The next Monday it was club night at *The Wanderers* and I drove over for a few games and some banter with Gere and Rocky and the others. I was one of the first to arrive at about seven-thirty and was playing in a men's doubles when Grace came through the doors just after eight with her sports bag slung over her shoulder. She grinned and waved a greeting and when I was finished I went over to where she was sitting and said hello.

'This is a nice surprise,' I said sitting down on the bench next to her. 'I hoped you would come tonight. How are you?'

She shrugged and smiled faintly. 'It's been a bit hairy but we've got somewhere to live now which is the main thing. I'm just glad we're free of him.'

'It's none of my business I know,' I said, trying to keep my tone light, 'but I'm really interested. How about I buy you a beer afterwards and you fill me in on all the gory details? I expect Rocky and the others will be there as well but I'm sure they'll leave us alone for ten minutes.'

Club nights for some of the men usually ended with a beer up at *The Primrose*, a quiet little pub about two minutes away in the car. There were generally about half a dozen of us who ended up there having a joke and a laugh for about half an hour before going home. Gere, Rocky and I always went but the other members of the party varied from week to week. That night Rocky persuaded a newly arrived and attractive brunette from New Zealand, Sandy, plus Whirler and Rick. Once we had parked our cars and were inside the otherwise empty oak-beamed bar I bought Grace a coke and sat with her several tables away from the others.

'We'll be with you in a second,' I called across to them. 'Grace just needs some advice on a few A level questions and you guys will disturb my concentration.'

'Don't make it too long Slick,' Rocky said cheerily, 'I'm out of cash tonight, four, four!'

'Alright honey,' I reassured him. 'Let me know when it's your round and I'll give you an advance on your pocket money.'

I turned back towards Grace. She had on a white tracksuit top with the collar turned up. Her hair was loose, falling around over her shoulders and she had her elbows resting on the table as she held her drink in both hands at chin level. Her blue eyes were looking steadily at me from over the rim of the glass. I took a mouthful of my lager which was just what I needed after the evening's exertions and returned her gaze.

'I'm all ears,' I said expectantly.

She collected her thoughts for a moment and then spoke softly to avoid the others overhearing. After the party she couldn't make up her mind how or even if she should tell her mother about Sasha and Gilbert. Relating the scene in his study was obviously out of the question. She also fretted over Gilbert's reaction if he knew it was she who had given away his infidelity with Sasha. As it turned out she needn't have worried because Gilbert made the first move by telling Grace's mother last Tuesday that he wanted her and her daughter out of his house.

'Wow, that must have been a shock for her,' I said, stating the blindingly obvious. 'How is she?'

'Surprisingly okay,' Grace shrugged. 'Yes she was upset but I've a feeling she knew it was coming. Christmas wasn't that great as I was telling you at the party. I don't think it will take her long to bounce back.'

'Maybe I could catch her on the rebound?' I said, narrowing my eyes thoughtfully and looking teasingly at Grace.

'And maybe I could shoot you in the head if you ever consider the possibility,' Grace said deliberately.

I changed the subject.

'Okay, only joking. How long did he give you to get out?'

'By the next day - he said he was going away for a couple of days but wanted us gone when he came back. She had to give the key to his study back there and then and the bastard even had one of his staff come down to the house to make sure we didn't take anything that wasn't ours. I don't know why he bothered as we had hardly anything except for clothes and stuff - when we moved in we left most of our furniture in our old house or gave it to friends.'

'Hang on a minute,' I said, raising my hands a little off the table towards her. 'So where are you staying? How the hell did he expect you to find anywhere in a day for God's sake?'

Grace told me briefly that her dad owned his own estate agency and lettings business and he had sorted out a pleasant little semi-detached place in Tunbridge Wells for them. He was fine about paying the rent for a couple of months until his ex wife could take back her own property from the people she was currently renting it out too. Grace paused to take a sip of her coke.

'It sounds to me that you and your mum are a couple of lucky ladies. Her especially - she's rid of Gilbert and she has a rich ex to fall back on when she's made homeless. If that had been me I would have been sleeping in the car or, worse still, staying at Gere's or Rocky's!'

Grace smiled and then carried on.

'That's not quite the end of the story Neil. There's something else that will make you realise what a true prick Gilbert is.'

'I don't need much convincing on that score,' I reassured her. 'Go on.'

'When mum moved in with him he persuaded her to let him invest her divorce settlement for her. Dad gave her enough to buy our house plus fifty thousand and she gave the money to Gilbert to invest for her. When she asked for it back he said he was sorry but the investment went bad and there's only a few thousand left.'

'Please say you're kidding me,' I exclaimed, leaning back in my chair and scratching my head in irritation. 'What a creep! Surely Fiona can take some sort of legal action or at least check out if he's telling the truth.'

'Not according to dad. Mum just handed the money over so there's no proof that it's actually hers anymore. He also told her that Gilbert has a bit of a dodgy reputation around Sevenoaks - apparently *The Wealden* is famous for attracting dangerous clientele.'

'Pity he didn't mention it when you were living with Gilbert,' I said, trying to keep the disdain out of my voice.

'He says he did warn mum years ago but she was so love-struck she wouldn't listen. Anyway he said he would talk to Gilbert and see what he could do.' said Grace coming to her father's defence.

'Come on Slick - time for another!'

It was Rocky's voice and I looked across to see him laughing and raising an empty pint glass in the air towards me.

'Okay, okay keep your hair on,' I stood up and looked at Grace. 'Let's finish this conversation another time,' I suggested. 'I think I've heard enough for one session. We ought to join the others - we'll carry on in the lesson on Thursday if you're still okay for tutoring.'

'That's fine,' she grinned. 'Can I have another coke!'

Grace kept me up to date on the saga of her mother's money over the next few lessons. Her dad was by all accounts a pretty hot shot businessman himself – there were half a dozen branches in his property business - but he didn't have much good news about Fiona's fifty thousand. Gilbert had apparently been charming but firm - the investment, a gold mine in Ecuador according to Gilbert, had gone wrong. He hadn't come up with any documentation to validate his story and Grace's dad didn't think he was likely to either. I was aware that I was only getting Grace's version of events so I tried to reserve judgement even though had a pretty strong feeling that Gilbert had essentially stolen Fiona's money and would never return it.

Once or twice we joked that we should have taken the fifty grand when we had the safe open on New Year's Eve but I didn't seriously think for a moment that we would ever see Gilbert or his safe again. Grace assured me she knew how to get into the house, having refined her route during the Sixth Form. After being dropped off late on Fridays or Saturdays following a night out drinking and clubbing she had apparently perfected the art of gaining surreptitious entry to the Gilbert residence.

'There's a way over the wall near the main gate and then it's all plain sailing up to the front door,' she told me during a coffee break in the dining room of her new house. Paper and books were set out in front of us on the table and she drew a neat map on a piece of scrap paper showing how she sneaked from the fence to the house without activating the security lights.

'Why not have the lights come on so you could see?' I suggested naively.

'And run the risk of the housekeeper or mum or Gilbert knowing how late I was? No chance. Besides, I didn't want to be caught on the security cameras at the front either in case they noticed me on the tapes.'

'What about the front door? Don't tell me you only need a key!' I said facetiously.

'Just that and the burglar alarm code - piece of cake!'

'You're almost tempting me,' I said, enjoying a sip of my coffee.

16

Let's be honest, most of the time our lives are as predictable as a Barbara Cartland novel minus the romance. Once in a blue moon something good happens that you didn't see coming but usually surprises are of the unpleasant variety. For every unexpected offer of sex from the colleague you always fancied there are dozens of stock market crashes, accidents that came out of nowhere or people dying when you least expect it. You get up on Monday morning as normal and by Friday or sooner your life has changed. Sometimes dramatically, sometimes hardly at all, but every time it happens I find myself marvelling at how flimsy and delicately balanced life is and how suddenly it can be changed forever.

I considered myself a pretty run of the mill bloke with a life to match. When you're young maybe you think you're special - that the world was devised only to serve as a backdrop to the epic story of your life, but usually the effects of bad parenting and megalomania wear off. You learn to live with your own mortality and commonness and get on with it.

So back then in late January I was blissfully unaware of all the surprises that were about to come my way. I had started the New Year without much idea of what it would bring and didn't know that within eight months nearly everything about my life would be different. I had slogged my way through a tedious Tuesday at work; the classes and teaching had been fine - it was just that I wasn't interested anymore. My colleagues were generally a great bunch of characters and I hoped the girls thought I was a good teacher but I was just bored with the same old routine. I dragged myself back to the cottage at around six thirty badly needing a cigarette and those two weeks in The Maldives I was always dreaming about. At about eight, just before I was going to pop out to the gym, my mobile rang. I squinted at the display.

'Grace, what's up?' I said, trying to sound unsurprised at her call.

'It's Dad, he's been in an accident.' Her voice was calm but I could tell it was taking an effort. I searched for something sensible to say.

'What sort of accident? Is he all right?'

'Oh he was in his car. He's pretty shaken up but I think he'll be okay. It's not so much that he crashed Neil but the fact that he was forced off the road by another car.'

'He was what? Forced off the road - are you sure?'

'That's right and Dad says he's sure it was deliberate. I couldn't help thinking that Gilbert may have had something to do with it. Neil, he would have died if he'd hit a tree or something!'

'Okay, okay, I understand what you're saying,' I said slowly. 'There's no way of knowing right now though is there? The police will be able to deal with that anyway. The main thing is that your dad is all right.'

'I suppose so,' she admitted. 'I just had to call you to let you know. I hope you don't mind.'

'Course not you idiot,' I said.

We talked for another five minutes or so. Her father had crashed on a country road near Edenbridge on his way home from work after, he claimed, a dark coloured Vectra had come quickly up behind him and rammed him on a corner. His momentum had carried him across the road into a hedge.

The Vectra had driven off without stopping. I was seeing Grace for a lesson in two days and she agreed to tell me about any fresh developments then.

We hung up and I had another cigarette and let Grace's news sink in. I needed to think but I also needed to get out of the house so I found a towel and left for the gym. There were only a couple of diehards churning out cardio work when I arrived and after a warm up I settled down to some weights while my mind went over the latest developments in Grace's life. If Gilbert had organised some kind of accident for her father he was clearly more than just an ordinary businessman. Even before this revelation I had some appreciation of the huge gulf between his lifestyle and my own but now I suspected there was even more of a gap between my humdrum nine to five existence and the world in which he moved.

The whole mess was, I observed rather wryly, not a million miles from something out of a Chandler novel. Except, that is, I didn't feel much like Marlowe — yeah I was only a few years away from being forty and about as single as I'd ever been but apart from that I didn't have a clue what to do. Grace certainly fitted the bill as the feisty young heroine and Fiona and Sasha would also fit nicely into some pot-boiler of a story. All I seemed cut out for was helping Grace get her A level grade and providing a sympathetic ear when she needed one.

Despite the distraction of my thoughts I managed a new personal best on the chest press and I drove home feeling I had achieved something. While the heater worked on the temperature in the bathroom I smoked a cigarette before running the bath and stripping off my kit and stepping gingerly into the water. I soaked my body in the hot water, watching the steam condense on the peeling magnolia walls, sitting up occasionally to reach for the hot tap to up the temperature of the water. It was the best I had felt all day.

An hour or so later I climbed wearily into bed wishing I didn't have to go to work in the morning. Lying under the duvet I thought about resigning from teaching and trying something else. Chris was right - I had no mortgage so there was nothing to stop me leaving for Greece and working out there as an aging holiday representative for a travel firm of some kind. There would be women, sun and little responsibility as well as the outside chance of engineering my way into Renia's life. Being in the same country would certainly increase my chances of convincing her that I was worth taking a chance on. I groaned out loud in the darkness when I finally ran out of the will required to continue believing in such bollocks.

On Thursday I left school around five after a lesson with Lydia. Twenty minutes later I was pulling into the cul de sac where Fiona and Grace were now living. It was a far cry from Gilbert's place – a seventies semi in a development in Tunbridge Wells south of the Pantiles. If I had been house-hunting I wouldn't have given it a second glance because I don't go in for open-plan front gardens and houses that look like they were designed in Legoland. As it was in a desirable part of Tunbridge Wells it was probably worth the best part of three hundred thousand quid but that just went to show how absurd the housing market can be.

Grace answered the glass-panelled front door and ushered me in out of the cold evening air and into the narrow hallway in which there were stairs and doors leading to the kitchen, lounge and dining room. The walls had been painted white and an inoffensive beige fitted carpet covered the floor. Grace's face was more drawn than normal which I assumed had something to do with her father's recent misfortune and I gave her a reassuring smile as I stepped inside. The house seemed quieter than usual and as we walked through the hallway into the dining room on the left Grace announced that her mother was up in London visiting a friend. We sat down at the dining table and I wriggled out of my jacket.

'I can see from your face that things could be better. Is there any more news?' I said, turning towards her.

Grace's voice was measured and she spoke slowly.

'It was Gilbert - Dad got an anonymous phone call yesterday.'

I wrinkled up my forehead in genuine astonishment.

'Excuse me?' I said, managing to sound calm. 'An anonymous phone call? This is bizarre Grace - anyway, how do you know it was Gilbert if the call was anonymous?'

'This man - Dad didn't know who it was - said that the roads were very dangerous and he should mind his own business if he wanted to stay safe. When dad asked him what he was talking about the guy just rang off.'

I could see that Grace had been genuinely shaken up by the concern and worry showing in her eyes. I had a mad impulse to give her a hug but settled for moving my hand from my bag and squeezing the hand she was resting on the table. I let out an exaggerated breath.

'What, this is surreal. I thought things like this only happened in the movies - certainly not around Tunbridge Wells of all places! When did you find out?'

'I visited Dad today. I think he was worried about me or else he might have not let on. I'm sorry Neil, I didn't want Gilbert to get to me but I can't help feeling so angry.'

'Trust you,' I grinned, withdrawing my hand 'Most people would be scared witless and you're sitting here wanting to punch Gilbert's lights out - calm down girl, he's not worth it. Anyway, what about the police? Did your father let them know what happened?'

'Yeah, he told the police but they were pretty useless. They called into his office this morning and interviewed him and said they'd look into it - I don't know what that means but dad said they didn't seem very hopeful about catching whoever made the call. Apparently it was probably made from an unregistered mobile or something.'

I shook my head wearily.

'Typical,' I scoffed. 'They're pretty good at dishing out speeding fines but that's about as far as it goes. If it was an episode of *Spooks* they'd have found out who the drivers of the Vectra were plus what they had for breakfast by now. What's your Dad going to do now?'

'What about?'

'Well, there's your mum's money for a start. Don't tell me that bastard Gilbert is going to get away with that as well!'

'He doesn't think there's much chance as of getting it back as mum doesn't have any documents to prove she gave it to him. It was all done on trust which was probably a bit naïve to put it mildly.' Grace said grimly, doodling with a pen she had picked up from the table.

'Yeah, I wouldn't trust Gilbert if he told me it was Thursday. I guess your dad is a bit nervous as well. What's he going to do?'

'Leave it I think,' she said, shrugging her shoulders. 'He's got a wife and the two young kids to worry about so I can't blame him.'

'So that's it?' I said. 'Gilbert gets away with your mum's money and nearly knocking off your father. This is getting to be a bit difficult to swallow, even on a very empty stomach.'

I leant forward and rested my chin on my hands, elbows on the table. I heard Grace's voice almost whisper, as if she were afraid of being overheard.

'Unless, of course, we robbed Gilbert's safe and get the money back that way.'

I turned to look at her, letting my left hand drop so that my right cheek was creased against my other hand. I gave her an affectionate smile.

'Are you being serious or is this a pitiful effort to distract me from doing some work with you?' I said wearily. 'Besides, your mother would be thrilled if she ever got wind of what we, sorry you, were planning.'

'Come on Neil,' she said, fixing her eyes on mine. 'He deserves it, nobody would ever know and we'd be rich. Mum wouldn't need to know – I could get Dad to give her the money and pretend it was from him or something.'

'You make it sound so easy,' I chuckled, returning her stare. 'Like recent GCSE maths papers - it's a pity you left out the bit about prison or Gilbert chopping our hands off. There's also the slight problem that I was brought up to obey the law and I'm at an age where all I worry about is where Arsenal are going to get their next three points from.'

I had never looked into her eyes properly before but it was one of those moments when normal etiquette is temporarily suspended. I needed to know exactly where

Grace was coming from and I guessed she felt the same about me. Almost subconsciously I noticed how blue they were – two crystal-clear pools of Mediterranean lapis lazuli but, uncharacteristically for me, that wasn't what struck me the most. No, I could see instantly that Grace was deadly serious and that the expression she was fixing me with was completely unguarded. I would remember that look in her eyes for a long time. She continued to speak as I re-evaluated my previous light-hearted attitude to the conversation.

'For a start I bet the money's dodgy so the police aren't going to get involved,' she said, holding out a hand and pressing one finger to emphasise a point in favour of her argument.

'Well, yes. And..?'

She tapped a second finger.

'As for Gilbert - how will he ever know who did it? He doesn't know I have the combination and I'm betting a nineteen year old girl and an ageing maths teacher are down at the bottom of the list of suspects.'

'Less of the ageing - good point, well made. I can see you've been thinking about this.'

I broke eye contact so that I had a better chance of thinking straight without the distraction of the reminders of the Mediterranean. I had to admit that what she said made sense even if her speech sounded like it had been rehearsed a few times. At the same time, however, I also knew that deep down there wasn't a chance I could ever agree to what Grace was proposing. Yes, I'd always liked a challenge and was a pain in the arse at school but my life-long struggle with authority had never led me into outright criminal activity - the risks are too great – prison and humiliation being among the first that spring to mind. Even so, I couldn't bring myself to admit to my lack of appetite there and then so I prevaricated.

'I hear what you're saying Grace and I can see that emptying his safe is a possibility but it's a crazy idea - you know that don't you? Anyway, suppose we did it - I'm not sure I could trust you. Love you as I do, how could I be sure that you won't give the game away at some point in the future so that we both end up dead. I've watched *The Sopranos* - people who take a gangster's money don't usually live to spend it.'

'Of course I wouldn't tell anyone. Do you think I'm mad? I thought you trusted me,' she exclaimed, giving me the benefit of a convincingly sincere look of exasperation.

'I do,' I sighed in frustration. 'You know I think you're great. It's just a fantastic burden to put on someone - you I mean. I need to think it all through without you sitting there putting the pressure on.'

Grace clapped her hands softly and I realised I had inadvertently made some sort of commitment to consider her daft plan. There was a huge grin her face and I laughed despite my inner conflict.

'Promise you'll think about it,' she said, reaching out and touching my arm.

'That doesn't mean I'll say yes – far from it.' I cautioned her. 'It's a crazy idea but I just need to think it through before I totally dismiss it - give me a week.'

'All right I'll give you 'til next lesson.'

'Very gracious but don't get your hopes up – I'm serious Grace, this isn't me deciding where to go on my holidays.

Now you can make me a coffee and we can get on with some work.'

Grace was all smiles now and made the coffee. She even let me make her work through a statistics paper for the hour after that so I could at least feel I had accomplished what I had come to the house for.

So that was it. I had raised her hopes even though I hadn't really the slightest intention of agreeing to her scheme. I just found it tough saying 'no' – always had done - at least straight away. Kids had been playing me for years by taking advantage of that character flaw. The little swines always seemed to sense I was all mush underneath and generally managed to push back any lines I had metaphorically drawn in the sand. But not this time – yes Gilbert was probably as pleasant as a tarantula under a pillow and deserved retribution but that was even more reason to keep Grace from pulling such a mad stunt. As for me, I just had too many responsibilities to fulfil; Rachel and Alex for starters and some nebulous but nonetheless real regard for my reputation.

Don't get me wrong – I was tempted by the money and the excitement that promised to be part of the scenario proposed by Grace. Besides, I was a rule-breaker – no question m'lord, but there was a limit. The risks were too dangerous, deadly even, if we failed and Grace's youth probably blinded her to those consequences. Even if we managed to empty the safe it would only be the beginning of the adventure. There would be the problem of laundering the money and trusting in Grace's silence for the rest of time; the first of which I knew nothing about and the other I only had a gut feeling for.

When we were finished she surprised me by inviting me to stay for some pasta. To be honest my glass of wine and cigarette were calling me and I wasn't sure what her mum would say if she came back from London to find me alone in the house with her daughter. In the end I agreed to stay as long as she was sure her mum wouldn't mind and if she didn't try to make me plan any robberies over my spaghetti. I could see that Grace could probably do with some company - even mine - and it did mean I wouldn't have to cook myself.

'I promise,' she smiled. 'I've already mentioned it to mum as well so you don't have to worry. I think she was a bit nervous after what happened to dad so she was glad I'm not going to be alone in the house. Look, you go into the front room and watch the telly or something while I get it together in the kitchen. Would you like a glass of wine while you're waiting?'

'No thanks,' I said, thinking of my driving licence. 'I'll save it for the meal so I can get away with driving home.'

'Very responsible Neil,' she nodded, 'I'll try and work fast so you don't have to wait too long,' and with that she stood up from the table and headed for the kitchen.

I wandered into the front room, found the television remote and a few minutes later was sitting back in a comfortable old sofa with an episode of an American hospital comedy series playing on the screen in front of my tired eyes. It had been a long day, the room was pleasantly warm and I could feel my senses drifting away from me. I rubbed my eyes and focused my thoughts on Grace's news about her dad and our pact concerning Gilbert and his safe full of money. It must have distracted me long enough to make Grace's appearance with a tray holding a plate of spaghetti bolognaise a genuine surprise. I hauled myself into a more upright position and took it from her gratefully.

She returned to the kitchen and appeared a few seconds later with her own dinner and a bottle of red wine and some glasses. She sat down next to me on the sofa and we ate in virtual silence in front of the television. When I had finished I slumped back contentedly on the sofa. I felt good - I had even managed to keep the sauce off my shirt.

'Very nice Grace,' I said as appreciatively as I could. 'That was an unexpected treat - and there I was thinking you'd have trouble boiling an egg.'

'Thanks,' she said, setting down her own tray on the floor. 'And you look like you need a nap but I guess that's normal at your age.'

'Only after I've smoked my pipe but I'll skip it tonight and do the washing up.'

'No you won't,' she said with a reassuring tone of finality, 'just relax and I'll shove it in the dishwasher when you've gone.'

'You're an angel - thanks. You just keep going up in my estimation or is it all part of the plan to get me to agree to your plan?'

Grace tossed back her hair and laughed. She clicked the fingers of one hand in mock frustration.

'Damn it, you've seen through me Dr M. I thought one spag bol and he'll be putty in my hands.'

'Okay, only joking,' I conceded. 'You know I expect you to be much more devious than that! Anyway, changing the subject, do you like *Scrubs*?'

Grace looked at the television.

'Course I do! JD's really quite cute,' she said matter of factly. She was watching the screen where the young doctor John Dorian in the comedy was being mercilessly chastised and tormented by his mentor Dr Cox. 'And you probably won't like it but you used to remind some of us at school of Dr Cox.'

'Thanks – you mean the self-absorbed narcissist bastard with bad hair and an inability to make proper relationships?' I protested, although I knew the show myself and guessed what she was driving at and wasn't going to stop her massaging my ego.

'Come on, he may not look like you but lots of the other stuff fits - he doesn't seem to give a shit about authority, he's mean to all the young doctors even though it's obvious he's the only one they can rely on when things go wrong - face it Neil, you're not the most popular man at school but at least we all respected you.'

'Thanks,' I grinned, finishing my wine with a swallow. 'I've obviously been over-doing the sarcasm and wise-cracks if that's what you lot used to think of me but I suppose it's better than nothing.'

'Don't get carried away, there were a few girls who absolutely hated you. I know you can't get many accolades but try to stay humble.' Grace heaved her feet off the floor and swung around to face me on the sofa, holding her knees in front of her chest looking at me teasingly.

'Maybe you should spend more time studying your A levels rather than TV characters that remind you of me,' I said, turning to face her.

Grace kicked me in rebuke but not hard enough to distract me from the smile on her face. I looked at her and took a deep breath - with her blonde hair framing her beautiful lean face I had to admit she was one of the loveliest women who had ever cooked me dinner. In another life I might have imagined kissing her. With an effort I pulled myself together before it became too obvious that my eyes were glazing over embarrassingly and rubbed my thigh where her foot had landed.

'Steady girl, you could have fractured by brittle old hip with those big sporty feet of yours,' I grimaced, 'anyway you've always been a rebel yourself - maybe that's why we get on so well - if we discount my obvious sexual appeal and charisma of course.'

She ignored my repartee and looked genuinely surprised and raised her delicate eyebrows.

'A rebel - have I?' she exclaimed slowly, 'how do you mean?'

'Maybe rebel is the wrong word – let's say single-minded, a free spirit or something. You never seemed to care much what anyone thought of you.' I said, bracing myself for another kick before continuing. 'Don't get me wrong - I always liked you even though you could be a difficult sod – besides I needed you for the football team!'

'Or maybe you just fancied me?' said Grace thoughtfully, looking at me from under her eyelashes so that I could feel myself beginning to blush. 'Anyway, I don't mind admitting I was a bit of a bitch back then so perhaps that does come across as rebellious.'

'No, 'bitch' probably sums it up better,' I grinned, using my fingers to put quotes around the word. 'Okay – joking - let's leave it that you were just moody and I only picked you for the team on account of that and your legs looking good in shorts. I needed you as a kindred rebellious spirit and being blonde was a bonus.'

'I'll take that as a compliment,' she said. 'It's funny to think of you needing moral support though.'

'Maybe because I've been offending people I think need offending all my life and sometimes it just gets a bit lonely. Meeting someone else who's on your side can give you a lift that's all. I've never had any time for arse-lickers and bull-shitters but the trouble is most people are exactly that – frightened to stand up for what's right and only really worried about their salaries and climbing the greasy pole.'

I paused for a moment, realising I had let my guard drop to reveal thoughts that I usually kept to myself.

'Sorry about that,' I said. 'One glass of wine doesn't usually make me so aggressive!'

Grace looked knowingly at me.

'You don't need a glass of wine to be aggressive Neil - it just comes naturally. Perhaps you should be in another job where people don't tell you what to do?'

'You're probably right.' I let my head drop back on the back of the sofa, 'I've tried to bite my tongue and keep a low profile but I just can't help myself; it's a character flaw I don't seem to be able to master. Anyway, that's enough analysis of my personality - let's talk about something else. You for example - why were you so difficult when you were at school?'

Grace put her head on one side and let it rest against the back of the settee while I hoped I wasn't being too personal with my question. After a moment or two she just shrugged and smiled.

'I honestly don't know Neil. Perhaps I just didn't want to be like all the others – either goody-two-shoes or out and out slappers. Besides I loved sport and there are only so many hours in a day.'

'Sorry, it was a stupid question but I think we can safely say you succeeded in avoiding being classed as a boffin or a slapper. Anyway, I'm going to drive home now and continue with my nicotine habit.'

I didn't go straight away because I was enjoying myself and Grace didn't seem in any hurry to kick me out. She was good company and there was a shortage of that back at Beechwood. We talked some more about Gilbert and the whole sorry mess with her mother and the strain it was putting on Fiona. When I finally shoved myself onto my feet to leave my watch said it was after nine. Graced hugged me as I got to the front door and thanked me for staying. I pointed out that the pleasure was all mine and tried to look cool as I turned and walked to the Mazda which flashed as I unlocked it from the remote. She waved from the door as I pulled out of the cul de sac and I gently beeped the horn in acknowledgement.

The cottage was freezing when I got back so I switched on the cheap electric convection heater in the front room and smoked a cigarette in my outdoor jacket while the temperature climbed to a comfortable level. I flicked on the television for company and poured myself a glass of white from an already opened bottle waiting in the fridge. By the time I had started my second glass I felt warm enough to ease myself out of my jacket. The cigarette count slowly rose as I thought about the situation and what I should do.

I wondered if I should see Sasha and tell her about Grace's dad's 'accident'; I didn't want to poke my nose into her business but she had to be unaware of how potentially dangerous Gilbert was. Maybe she knew enough already and that was part of the attraction - when a girl is seventeen a teddy-bear makes a passable love offering but when she reaches Sasha's age men who think a cuddly toy makes a hit as a present are going to be viewed as coming up short in the testosterone department. I couldn't imagine Gilbert ever surprising her with something soft and furry to cuddle – no, he would be a cool, confident bastard and who could blame her for fancying him? If I kept on totting up his plus points like this I might even end up being tempted myself.

Then I found myself planning the robbery and the aftermath which I knew was crazy but kept me amused nevertheless. I did a lot of thinking as the wine bottle emptied and the clock on the mantelpiece ticked around to midnight. I remembered a sunny day in Kefalonia and a waitress who kissed me on the beach. One thing was for sure; unless I did something drastic she would never do that again.

17

The next day at work I typed 'money laundering' into Google and after about five minutes research found a couple of books that looked interesting and cheap enough to buy. I was just being curious but it didn't stop me tapping in my credit card details and placing an order. As soon as I'd done it I cursed my own idiocy – I never had any time to read stuff I liked let alone crap about money laundering. Another sparkling investment decision.

To distract myself from further self-recrimination I checked my e mail account. A good decision this time – there was a message from Renia, the Greek characters of her name standing out on the screen like a naked pair of breasts at a WI meeting.

'Hello Neil,' I read nervously. 'How are you and the girls? I hope you are all very good. Thank you for your message that you sent at Christmas. I have only just received it because of my complicated life!!

I have little news to tell you I am afraid. I still have the same job which is very boring. I think maybe I have chosen the wrong career. I hope to go to Panos again this summer so I hope to see you then if you come.

If you have news I would like to hear it so please write to me. I like to get messages from England!

Love Renia'

It wasn't much but it put me in a good mood nevertheless. In the cold light of day maybe Renia was just a romantic ideal, but I wasn't ready to face up to it now. After all, there wasn't much else going on to get excited about. Maybe when a woman who was more attainable and well-suited came along I would turn the page, but until then I settled for living in hope. I wasn't completely deluded – even for me this had to count as the most protracted attempt at courtship I had ever managed. At the present rate of progress she would only be marrying me for my pension.

Then there was Sasha, the thought of whom still aroused certain passions in me. Okay, she was obviously a nymphomaniac but that was a plus point wasn't it? Her bad taste in men was more of a problem, even if it included me, but nobody's perfect. For some reason I felt I had to tell her what I knew about Gilbert behaviour towards Grace's mother and father - but how? In the end I girded up my loins and rang her at home that evening. She seemed friendly enough and after a bit of polite banter I asked if I could pop around to see her. Before she could panic I assured her it would just be a quick visit and that I had something to tell her that wasn't remotely connected to us having sex. She laughed - Sasha had a good sense of humour; it was a pity her choice of a current boyfriend wasn't as discerning as her appreciation of irony. We arranged for me to call by on Saturday after my morning visit to the gym and I made a mental note to wear my best kit for the occasion. I doubted if I could pull off 'sexy' but I wanted to avoid my customary un-ironed look.

When I called she was dressed in jeans and a vest that better befitted the description sexy. I was glad I had settled for a tee shirt in the interests of subtlety; I guess she knew that if she wanted to inspect my biceps then she only had to ask. We sat in her front room over a cup of tea on two cream-coloured sofas at right angles to each other; she was perched with her feet under her on the one in the window while I sank back into the one set against the adjacent wall. We made small talk about training and work until it came to the point when she asked me why I wanted to see her.

'Look, I hope you're not going to chuck me out when I tell you what I came over for,' I said slowly, choosing my words as carefully as I could and leaning forward into a less relaxed position. 'It's really not any of my business and I debated long and hard with myself as to what to do, but in the end I came to the conclusion that it wouldn't be fair of me not to tell you.'

Sasha frowned slightly behind her mug of tea.

'How intriguing,' she said. 'You'd better spill the beans Neil.'

I took a deep breath.

'Okay I'll make it as brief as I can. I'm afraid it's about Marc Gilbert - your boss and my successor as the subject of your affections.'

Sasha raised her eyebrows and I thought her fingers were a little tighter on her mug. I smiled again and shrugged my shoulders.

'No problem there - except for the odd pang of jealousy maybe but the counselling has helped a lot. Anyway, to be serious, I tutor his ex's daughter and I've known Grace and her mum for years. When Gilbert moved her out he apparently kept fifty grand of Fiona's money that he was supposed to have invested for her back when love was new and unsullied. Gilbert now says the money has gone - it was a bad investment. Who knows, he may be telling the truth, but I still think he owes her.'

Sasha didn't interrupt me so I carried on.

'There's more - Grace's dad approached Gilbert about the money. A few days later he's been run off the road by another car and ends up in casualty. Later there's a phone call telling him to mind his own business. You're an adult so you can draw your own conclusions but I thought you should know the Gilbert might be more dangerous than he appears.'

I finished talking and looked for a reaction in her face. She thought for a moment before saying in a genuinely surprised voice.

'How did you know Marc and I were involved? I didn't know anyone around here knew.'

Typical woman! Never mind about the fraud or the attempted murder, let's focus on the love angle. Mind you, she had a good point - how did I know? Clearly I had to leave out New Year's Eve.

'I, er, came back here after my King's Palace do before Christmas. Gilbert's car was outside and the light was on up in your bedroom. I put two and two together. You seemed pretty friendly on New Year's Eve as well and then he moved Grace's mother out,' I said.

Sasha didn't smile but she didn't look angry either.

'I'm sorry,' she said softy. 'I should have told you but you weren't exactly beating down my door before Christmas so I let things drift.'

'No problem,' I grinned wryly. 'It was fun while it lasted but we weren't exactly engaged. I'm no angel myself so I can't condemn a woman who plays a bit fast and loose. Anyway, I've told you what I intended to so let's forget it.'

I stayed another fifteen minutes or so. She thanked me for coming but I could see she wasn't convinced about my assessment of Gilbert's character. She pointed out that he had a lot of enemies and that she had found him to be a nice guy when he didn't have to be the boss at work. I skipped running the alternative view of his character past her and when I left we were still on friendly terms.

The rest of the weekend went quietly. Rachel, Alex and I went out to a film on Saturday night and we spent Sunday morning shopping for a new mobile for Alex. When they left after lunch I tidied up and made sure I had enough clean clothes to get me through the week. There wasn't much on the television and I didn't feel like reading so I went to bed early. I slept like a baby and woke up on Monday morning feeling ready for anything which, in retrospect, shows just how self-deluded I can be sometimes.

There was another parents evening on the Wednesday so I didn't leave school until after seven thirty. The weather was still cold so I was glad of the suit I had worn for the occasion as I hurried around to the back car park where the Mazda flashed welcomingly at me as I unlocked it. I started the car up and picked my way through the parents' and staff cars that were parked around the grounds in the darkness. Fortunately the main road out of town was relatively empty and after five minutes I was breaking the forty speed limit in the first suburb and the temperature inside the car had risen to a comfortable level.

I scanned in the mirror to check for stray patrol cars but the only set of headlights I could see were so far behind that they didn't need worrying about. As soon as the forty limit finished I pushed the speed up past sixty and enjoyed the poise and grip of the coupé as it ate up the road for the mile or so to the next village. At the end of the long straight before the road meanders down to the river at Penshurst, I happened to glance in the mirror again. I was surprised and a little concerned to see that there was a set of lights only a couple of hundred metres back and evidently going at least as fast as I was. I was always in the mood for a race but still wary that the boys in blue might be in the car behind so I settled myself down in my seat and concentrated hard. I knew the route like the back of my hand, from every overtaking spot to the position of every pothole and I was in a car that could take it all in its confident stride.

As the road began to slope down to the river I used its full width to take each increasingly tight turn as rapidly as I dared, keeping the car smooth and staying alert for the lights of any oncoming cars. When the road straightened I raced down the hill to the hump back bridge over the river and around a sharp left hander into the village. Just before the corner the lights of the car following appeared at the top of the hill behind me which reassured me that it wasn't making any progress in catching me. Things were looking good - once I was through Penshurst I would take the road up past the vineyard and that would be *adios amigos*.

Well it would have been if I there hadn't been two cars queuing to turn right and blocking my progress fifty metres past the corner in the centre of the village. The idiot at the front also saw fit to let an Astra turn right in front of him before he and the car following him made their manoeuvre. I always find this aggravating but it was particularly frustrating now and I let off a few exasperated expletives to myself. Didn't the stupid fucker know I was in a race with a possible police car? Of course he didn't – why would he - but it didn't stop me from wanting to rip the bastard's head off. I lost a few seconds waiting for the jokers to sort themselves and then I was stuck behind the Astra doing thirty heading out of the village.

The headlights of my pursuer came rapidly up from behind and parked themselves about ten metres from my exhausts. I relaxed a little when I realised it wasn't a patrol car until Grace's dad's accident popped into my mind out of nowhere. I heard myself groan 'shit' and, if you'll forgive the pun, my brain kicked into overdrive. With my heart rate increasing enough so that I started to notice, I checked my mirror and the street lights were enough to show the familiar outline of a Vectra. That was all the confirmation I needed to tell me the next few minutes were going to be potentially lively.

One thing was for sure - I had to get some distance between me and the Vectra, and I hoped I could use the Astra to help. There was a short overtaking stretch after the last house before the countryside resumed followed by sharp bends to the right and left before my right turn up past the vineyard. I put the Mazda gently into second and screamed past the Astra, timing it so the bastard at the back would have to wait until the Astra had negotiated the corners before he could do the same.

'Suck on that arsehole,' I muttered to myself, simultaneously ignoring the loud blast of the Astra's horn as its outraged driver fumed at my apparent disregard for road safety. I ignored the idiot and took a deep breath to try and ease the tension in my arms and shoulders as I accelerated away from him. I needed to drive fast now and take advantage of my knowledge of the twists and turns on the road up into the woods.

As I swung the Mazda into the right turn up to the vineyard I heard another muffled blast of the Astra's horn – presumably the Vectra was executing a similar overtaking manoeuvre to mine while the Astra driver was spontaneously combusting with fury. A few seconds later lights on full beam lit up my mirrors from about eighty yards back as the Vectra turned to follow me up the hill. I was now into the woods, the trees flashing by on either side to the soundtrack of the whine of the rotary engine. I kept the car revving mostly in third and fourth gear and blood was pounding in my head as I tried to focus on driving fast and keeping the car on the narrow strip of tarmacadam. I prayed the road was empty and the deer one sometimes encountered at night on these back lanes wouldn't decide to do any roadside wandering.

Soon the road began to twist and turn like an angry rattlesnake through trees and hedgerows and I lost the glare of the Vectra's lights in the cabin. A faint acrid smell began to make itself felt in the cabin, presumably from the brakes or the engine or both but this didn't seem like a time to be worrying about flogging the car. The adrenalin was still burning in my chest and head but it began to become more manageable as it slowly dawned on me that, barring some unforeseen disaster, I wasn't going to be caught; the Mazda was just too good on these roads and I knew them too well. I was guessing my tail had probably never been on this out of the way country road or at least didn't know it as well as me. At the top of the climb the road was still deserted so I shot right at the T junction hardly lifting my foot and accelerated away at the start of the two miles or so of essentially straight country road towards Beechwood. My pursuer eventually appeared from the junction over a couple of hundred yards down the road and soon disappeared again as the road took a slight curve to the left.

There were a number of side turns coming up that I could escape down or I could just make it to the cottage and phone the police. On rapid reflection, however, I didn't think the police would be very interested in someone following me on a public road so what else? I thought about driving onto Gere's place but I had no idea if he would be in and it did feel a bit lame. And that's when it dawned on me – why was I running away like a cat from the neighbour's dog?

If it was Gilbert's boys in the car behind what gave them the right to ruin my journey home to my much deserved cigarette and glass on wine? Didn't they know there was a pissed off karate black belt in the Mazda up ahead? Well they soon would; suddenly I stopped being nervous and a cold, calculating anger began to wash through my veins replacing fear with a determined ruthlessness. I started to analyse my situation and a plan came to me almost at once. As the hedgerows rushed by I weighed the probabilities of success and failure. Yep, it might work and, if it did, we would see which car had the meanest occupants.

At the end of the curving straight the road split into two; one branch continued on with a slight break to the left while the way to my cottage was around the ninety degree right hand turn where, if it was dark, I sometimes practised my own private game of 'chicken'. The lane was at least three car widths at the turn and I had got around it at forty five but that would have been higher save for my consideration for my tyres and fear of an expensive mistake.

I eased off the accelerator a touch and watched for the Vauxhall to appear. Within a couple of seconds the lights behind me flashed in the distance and gradually grew brighter. This was good - I wanted us to be doing at least sixty as we approached the right-hander so I needed him behind me pretty soon. About two hundred yards from the corner that was still hidden from view by the curve of the road and the high hedgerows, the Vectra's lights grew triumphantly in my mirrors so that the inside of the car began to resemble the interior of a sun bed salon. I had sneaked the Mazda into second and at forty the engine was whining for me to change up but I needed the gear to accelerate away from the Vauxhall if it tried to ram me. Sure enough, he came up to within a few metres of my rear bumper and for a moment I thought I had left it too late. My mirrors were engulfed by dazzling light and I floored the accelerator to escape the impact.

In the space of a couple of seconds the corner materialised out of the night. I had no time for the mirrors now as getting around the right-hander at sixty was a more of a priority but I must have avoided contact by only a whisker. Meanwhile I hoped the driver of the Vectra was enjoying the nasty surprise I had prepared for him – having to brake to get around the corner almost as soon as he had accelerated in response to my surge in speed. If he had any sense he should have ignored the turn and carried on down the smaller road ahead but it's easy to have twenty-twenty vision after you've put your motor into a hedge backwards.

The Mazda only just stayed on the road. As I wrestled with the wheel the dynamic stability control vibrated alarmingly as it fought to keep the back end from overtaking the front and the car lurched frighteningly from side to side. The driver of the Vectra must have been too distracted in his aim of sending me off the road to get around the corner himself because the glare in my cabin disappeared abruptly. I heard the muffled sound of exploding glass and metal and when I looked in my mirror I was just in time to see the car pirouette across the road and smash into the hedgerow on the opposite side of the road to the one it must have hit first when it failed to make the turn. It was a surreal moment watching the Vectra spin out of control until it finally came to rest half in and half out in the hedgerow facing back the way it had come.

I hesitated for a moment and then braked and quickly reversed the fifty yards or so back to where it's red rear lights glowed brightly in the darkness. I stopped about a car length away from stricken vehicle, got out of the Mazda and ran to look in at the driver's window, the smell of burnt oil and brake linings assaulting my senses. There were two of them; a guy who looked unconscious slumped in the passenger seat and a driver, groaning loudly, wearing a light coloured New York baseball cap. I opened the driver's door sharply.

'Fuck me, looks like you took that last corner a touch on the fast side,' I said cheerily to the driver who looked up at me in surprise. He grunted and amusingly tried to get out of his seat - amusingly since he still had his seat belt fastened. I punched him hard in the face just below the eye, and I mean hard - I was severely pissed-off and he looked like a mean bastard. His head snapped back and I hit him again more cleanly in the throat. He gasped and heaved in the seat trying to catch his breath.

'You should have said you wanted to get out,' I said sympathetically and leaning over him I released his seat belt and hauled him out of the car. It was an effort because he was verging on the obese but I managed to disengage him from the Vectra without falling over myself and leaned him against the side of the car. I sensed he was recovering from the first two cuffs so as I was getting him upright I put my knee up into his stomach, stepped back and kicked him in the face. He collapsed like a sack of potatoes on the road beside his car.

I quickly found a mobile in his jeans' pocket and called for an ambulance without bothering to leave my own name and address. I searched through his other pockets and found nothing except for a wallet containing a couple of plastic cards and plenty of cash; his name was Ben Day if the cards were to be believed. I looked at his face and there was just enough light to make out the face of a bloke in his late twenties sporting a shaven head and an eyebrow piercing. So stereotypical; he looked like a guest on the Jerry Springer show who'd just found out his wife has been shagging the pet dog for years.

That wasn't all either; under his left arm I found a nasty looking black gun resting in a shoulder holster. I don't think I'd ever seen a gun in the flesh, so to speak, but I thought it would be better if I confiscated it for now in case Benny came to and suddenly remembered what was under his armpit. I pulled him out of his jacket by tugging at the one of the cuffs until his arm fell loose and then I was able to disengage the gun and its holster from around his back.

I leant in the open door of the Vectra, feeling for the pulse of the guy in the passenger seat. It seemed to be there and a feel inside his jacket didn't reveal another weapon so I drew myself back out of the car and looked around. There was nobody else out on the road tonight - all I could hear was the rustling of the branches of the trees in the breeze until an owl hooted somewhere far away. I walked over to where Ben Day was beginning to stir and bent over and grabbed him by the front of his jacket, pulling him up to a sitting position.

'Come near me again and you're dead,' I said in his ear and then stood up and kicked him again so that he slumped back with his head half in a pile of leaves lying next to the road.

I took his phone and gun and walked back to the Mazda and drove the mile or so home. As I pulled into the drive a police car roared by on its way to Ben and his pal. I went in and chucked the gun, still in its holster, and the mobile on the kitchen table, pulled off my jacket and lit my first cigarette of the day. After a welcome drag I opened the fridge and pulled out a bottle of beer and found the bottle opener. For the next five minutes I sat back by the table waiting for my heart rate to subside. I looked at the gun and realised I had been lucky to put it mildly. If Benny and pal had got me out of the car it wouldn't have been Queensbury rules and I don't think the karate would have cut much ice either. I reached over and removed the gun from the holster and looked for the safety catch, making sure the bloody thing was pointing away from me all the time. I eventually got the hang of its workings without actually firing off a round and then put it carefully in a built-in cupboard in the corner of the kitchen.

It was an effort but I made myself rustle up some food, eat it, cleared up the kitchen and ran a bath. I sat in the steamy atmosphere and began to feel a little more normal. My right hand was sore from its impact with Ben's face but only enough to enhance the soothing effect of the hot water. My legs, which had ached after the tension of the previous couple of hours, began to feel relaxed again as I reviewed the evening's events. My first impulse was to call Sasha and ask her if she had told Gilbert about our chat but on reflection I thought that was a bit lame; like telling your mother your brother has farted in the bath, so I rejected that course of action.

I had found Gilbert's name in the contacts list on Ben's phone so I was pretty sure who had decreed that my drive home should involve an off-road experience and yet I couldn't understand his motives. Assuming Sasha had told him about the not so glowing character reference I had given her about him I supposed he could have been pissed off with me; but enough to send in the cavalry? Perhaps he was the jealous sort and thought I wanted to get Sasha back into bed - fair comment there I guess. Maybe my involvement with Grace and her mum had played a part and convinced him that I needed scaring off. And how bad was my accident supposed to be? At the speeds we were going I could easily have been killed if the delightful Ben had rammed me as he had attempted to.

In the end I decided that Gilbert must have big time anger or jealousy management issues because tonight showed an alarming lack of judgement. Perhaps it is the territory that goes with always getting your own way - I had certainly seen head teachers with the same personality disorder! If it had been me in his position I would have left Sasha's ex alone in case his 'accident' scared Sasha off but there you go - I tend to be more careful than your average gangster.

I wondered what Gilbert would do now that it was Ben and his friend who were in hospital rather than me. The thought didn't thrill me but I was fucked if I was going to let it paralyse me. If he had any sense he would just move on and hope I had got the message and if he didn't I would just have to be more careful. My neighbour Maureen was in most of the time and would keep an eye on the cottage for me if I asked her and the rest of the time I was either at school, in the car or at home. Whatever happened, one thing was for sure - I was going to help Grace empty the bastard's safe.

18

The next day the Vectra was gone when I drove past the crash scene on the way to work. As I neared the spot I slowed the Mazda to have a look but except for some scars in the hedgerow there was little sign of the excitement of the evening before. I assumed it had been towed away by a recovery truck because Ben and his pal were in no state to drive when I had left them and the Vectra itself was probably knackered as well. I hoped they had endured an uncomfortable night in A and E. As I pulled away I wondered if there had been any feedback given to Gilbert yet and I allowed myself a smile at the thought of the meeting. It was obvious Ben and whoever the other one was would massage the truth to their own advantage but there would be no getting away from the fact that rather than hit their targets their target had hit them.

Gilbert's face would be a picture when he realised life wasn't always guaranteed to go his way. Welcome to the real world Marc, the one the rest of us inhabit – and if I have anything to do with it you'll have to put up with another major disappointment as soon as I can organise it. Maybe I was crazy but after last night a switch had been tripped in my head. Now it seemed absolutely right that Gilbert deserved retribution for acting like a knob and that I should be part of the getting even process. How hard could it be? or *'Quanta Fiat Difficultus?'*. I had pinned that notice on the door of my office at school years ago and it had served me well as a conversation starter and a motto for the department. But now I would be applying it to a criminal enterprise - overnight I had grown a backbone and it felt strangely liberating. Okay, Gilbert was rich and dangerous and I respected that but before last night I had forgotten that I had a few aces to play myself - like brains. They had never made me rich but I told myself that was a lifestyle choice and during my deliberations the night before I thought there was a fair chance I could successfully apply my analytical skills, if only once, to burglary instead of equation solving.

I was tempted fleetingly to text Grace and tell her my decision but I resisted the impulse and decided to leave it to her lesson that evening. It would be more fun to tease her for a bit before hitting her with the revelation that underneath my teacher's persona I was in fact up for a real life *Mission Impossible*.

School was the same as usual - I managed to teach my lessons without giving too much of an impression that I really couldn't be arsed and the girls succeeded for the most part in returning the compliment. After school Lydia kept me amused with her pitiful attempts to master vectors and a skirt that most of my colleagues would have said, though not me, needed its hem a few inches longer. We walked out to the car park together and I waved her off in her old green Beetle before driving over to Grace's place for her lesson.

When she opened the front door she did a good job of hiding any expectancy from her face and I just said hello in a way I hoped gave nothing away except that I was pleased to see her. Fiona was in the kitchen talking on the phone and gave me a friendly wave as I followed Grace into the dining room.

'What do you want to do today?' I said, once we were sat down in the dining room. 'Another paper or have you got something else you would like to go over?'

I studied her face as I spoke but annoyingly it betrayed no sign of expectancy or excitement. How long, I wondered, would it take for her to ask me if I had decided to take up a life of crime?

'Let's do a paper,' she said, taking a pen out of her pencil case while I got a folder out of my bag and found a past paper.

After about twenty minutes of Grace making reasonable progress with the paper Fiona came in with a coffee and a few biscuits on a plate for me. When she had left the room I took a sip of my coffee. Grace could obviously stand it no longer but still managed to sound casual when she said.

'So Neil, have you come to a decision?'

I looked at her questioningly – as if I didn't have the faintest idea what she was talking about. It was cruel but it was too much fun not to. I took another sip of the coffee and put the cup slowly back on the table. I looked at her as innocently as I could.

'I'm sorry, you've lost me – what decision?'

Grace rolled her eyes in frustration.

'Stop being an idiot Neil, you know very well what I'm talking about. Are you going to help me with Gilbert's money or aren't you?'

It was no use – I've never been any good at keeping a straight face in a stressful situation and I began to crack under the scrutiny of her exasperated expression. With more than a hint of a smile forming on my cheeks I said.

'So you're going solo if I say no?'

'I don't know. If I have the guts I think I will but I suppose I was relying on you believe it or not,' she said, doodling on her work as she spoke, sketching out a design that was as confused as her face. I couldn't be cruel any longer and said gently.

'Okay, you can leave out the emotional blackmail. Yes I'll help – I've been contemplating a career change for a while now so why not a spot of burglary? It certainly sounds more interesting than teaching.'

Grace looked at me with a disbelieving expression that turned slowly into an excited grin when she saw that I wasn't joking.

'Oh God you're serious. That's brilliant, I can hardly believe it!' she gushed in a most un-Grace-like way.

'Okay, okay, don't get carried away,' I said, 'This is a big deal Grace. If we mess up it could get nasty. Are you sure you're really up for this?'

She didn't hesitate.

'Yes Neil I am. I know it's a long shot but I want to try.'

'Even though we can't tell anyone – not even Fiona?'

She nodded again.

'Even though you'll have to sleep with me?'

'Stop being disgusting.'

Despite the joke I don't think I had ever seen Grace so animated. She didn't jump onto the table and treat me to a tap dance but her cheeks did turn a little red and her eyes were as bright as a four-year-old's on Christmas morning. I tried to look cool and help maintain her loose grip of reality.

'You know I'm going to have to do the planning don't you? I've always been a control-freak and I'm hoping my huge intellect will come in handy in my new hobby.'

Ignoring the quizzical look and raised eyebrows I continued.

'And as the brains of this outfit I'll have a think and we'll get together at the weekend and talk some more. Whatever you do don't tell a soul or that's the end of it. It's dangerous enough as it is so you must promise me that before we even start or the whole thing is off. Okay?'

'Of course I won't tell anyone, do I look like I have a death wish? What made you change your mind? I thought that you were only palming me off last week.'

'I was, but one or two things have happened since then to convince me to break my law-abiding habit of a lifetime. It may be just a manifestation of a mid-life crisis but I've had it with Gilbert. There's also a chance we might find an empty safe so no harm will be done anyway - if you're sure we can get in and out without being detected.'

I then gave her a shortened version of the previous evening although modesty made me play down my exchange with Ben. Grace's mouth actually opened and shut in surprise as I talked and I realised I had never seen her like this before with her cool exterior so inoperative. When I had finished she looked at me.

'Isn't Gilbert going to be even madder with you after this? Why do you think he sent those men anyway?'

'God knows to both questions. I guess he probably took offence at what I said to Sasha but it does seem over the top. He must be an impetuous bastard to have a go at me like that. Perhaps he's jealous that Sasha might be tempted by my obvious charms so he had two reasons to scare me?'

'No Neil,' Grace said slowly. 'He was always a bastard. He loved telling us how no one ever got the better of him - not in an obviously boasting way - but I could see by reading between the lines that he could be very vindictive.'

'So he is going to be planning his next surprise for me?'

'Probably - unless you can do something to make him change his mind quickly. It's lucky you have that huge intellect to work out what to do.'

'Yeah,' I nodded. 'As a matter of fact I do have an idea but I'll let you know what it is after I've tried it. As for you Miss I think it's about time we got back to what I was paid to do while I'm here.'

'If we get the money,' said Grace, 'you won't have to tutor anymore.'

'If we get the money I won't even teach anymore,' I said emphatically, looking at the next question on the paper.

When I got back to the cottage I found my old pay as you go mobile and the Sim card that went with it while the curry I intended for my dinner was simmering. I put the phone on charge and by the time I had eaten, cleared up and changed for club-night there was enough juice in it for my purposes. On the way to club I dropped into a garage in Tonbridge and bought some credit for the phone.

In between games I suggested our usual excursion to *The Primrose* to Rocky and Gere and, as I expected, they were easily suggestible. Rocky had a habit of bringing anybody else along that he had any sort of conversation with during the evening but I told them to keep it exclusive because I had something important to tell them. I ignored Rocky's repertoire of questioning expressions and chin stroking and just told him to do me the favour 'just this once'. After a couple of hours we'd had enough practice and the first round was sitting in front of us soon after ten.

'Do you remember that time you bastards phoned me up pretending to be the Inland Revenue?' I said, putting my glass down after about my second mouthful.

Rocky's eyes lit up with glee.

'Yeah, and you fell for it like Gere's ex when he told her he was working late?!' he guffawed. 'Hey Gere, how long did you string him along for?'

'Couldn't help laughing or you would have had a serious brown trouser problem. All those secret tax free private lessons,' Gere chuckled over his pint.

'All right, all right. I admit I was a little naïve but I need you to make a similar call for me to someone else. That's if you don't think you've lost any of your, er, magic.'

'Blimey Slick,' Rocky said, still twinkling, 'who do ya want us to have some fun with? It's not a lady is it, what, what?'

'Even you two in the wildest of your infantile dreams can't imagine I'd let either of you set me up on a date,' I said, grimacing at the suggestion. 'I might be desperate right now but I'm not insane.'

'So what's the story?' Gere was grinning and looking at me good-humouredly.

'Top secret. Not a word to anyone - not even pillow talk,' I looked at Rocky. 'Assuming Michelle does still let you sleep with her.'

'Fuck off. Come on - out with it.' Rocky's voice dropped as he spoke and Gere and I both smirked at Rocky's impatient expression.

I leant forward towards them conspiratorially and they involuntarily followed suit. I looked at them and glanced around the pub to check no one was listening.

'For fuck's sake Slick,' hissed Rocky. 'What's all this nudge, nudge, wink, wink stuff?'

'Somebody tried to kill me last night.'

The two of them suddenly became two wide-eyed statues, paralysed over their drinks like two actors in a quirky television advertisement. Gere reacted first.

'Thank god for that, for a minute I thought it was serious,' he said, looking deadpan at Rocky who seemed unsure whether to laugh or try to look serious. Before he came to a decision I butted in.

'Don't confuse him Gere - yes some bastards tried to run me off the road - and no it's not funny. If you fucking laugh Rocky remember you'll have to play with this girl in the Men's A if I'm lying in the fucking cemetery.'

'Good point fella,' said Rocky, nodding and scratching his goatee. 'That would seriously affect my average.' I gave him a look that I hoped conveyed something like disgust to which he laughed in my face.

'Thank god you've got your priorities sorted. Anyway, as I was saying before your fucking average suddenly became more important than my mere existence, I'm in a delicate situation which I was hoping you Gere might be able to help me out with.'

'You're fucking dead Slick!' exclaimed Rocky with a laugh. 'If you wanted him to help you out with some housework you might get lucky but save your life? You are joking aren't you?'

'Hey, listen to my plan first you moron,' I said, straining to keep a serious demeanour at the sight of the incredulous look that had fixed itself on Rocky's face. I then gave them both a brief résumé of the events of the previous evening and my dealings with Gilbert, Sasha and Grace et al. I left out the parts about Gilbert's safe stash and my plans for it but I had to admit that it wasn't the sort of story you usually hear when you're down the pub with some mates. Gere and Rocky looked suitably impressed as I filled them in, interrupting me when they wanted more details about a particular part of the story. We had finished our drinks by the time I had brought them up to date and Rocky got up to get us some refills.

'Don't go saying anything else I should know Slick,' he told me as he eased himself out of his seat.

'Don't fret darling - just get the drinks.'

'See if they've got any crisps will you?' Gere chipped in helpfully as Rocky departed with a less than amused expression forming on his face.

'Okay, what's the plan Batman?' Gere said, ignoring Rocky's request to be in on all the details.

I leant back in my chair and looked at him, at the same time weighing up the right choice of words with which to make my request.

'How'd feel about warning Gilbert off for me? Over the phone I mean - you act like a hard bastard who's pissed off that he's turning the screw on a pal of yours.'

Gere's face creased into the dubious look that I was anticipating.

'You call that a plan?' he laughed. 'Sounds more like suicide to me.'

'I know it sounds a little desperate but I've thought about it and I think it's worth a shot if you can reprise your telephonic acting skills,' I said in what I thought was my most reasonable voice. 'I've got his number from the mobile I confiscated off the muppet last night and an untraceable pay as you go mobile on which I hope you will weave your magic.'

Gere was still chuckling and shaking his head.

'Is there a plan B?' he asked in a resigned voice.

'What's this about a plan B?' Rocky had returned with a drink in each hand and a furrowed brow that gave away his curiosity and impatience with us.

'Keep your hair on,' I reassured him. 'I was just outlining a possible way of getting me out of the shit which involves our smooth-talking associate here making a phone call on my behalf. He just has to pretend to Gilbert that he's a hard case who is looking out for yours truly so that it would be in Gilbert's best interests to leave me well alone.'

'Say nothing until I've got my drink and the crisps,' he said, holding his hand up to me like a copper in the street directing traffic. When he came back he was wearing a rare serious expression.

'Couple of flaws Slick,' he said, sitting down again. 'Well one really - the whole fucking idea! This Gilbert is obviously a kosher serious criminal besides which he's barking mad, while Gere here couldn't knock the skin off a rice pudding. Call me old-fashioned but that looks like a serious mismatch from where I am.'

'Thanks for the vote of confidence,' grinned Gere, taking a swig of his cider.

'But Gilbert isn't going to know what a girl Gere is,' I said. 'To him it's just a voice on a phone. All you need to do is *ab lib* - get into the role and convince Gilbert that it's pointless and against his best interests to carry on persecuting me. If he ignores you I've lost nothing but if he doesn't its problem solved!'

'Yeah easy,' said Gere, his voice as ironic as I had ever heard it. 'As you say there's nothing to lose unless I manage to piss him off even more.'

Rocky was laughing as well now. The prospect of Gere trying to con Gilbert was even more amusing to him than the idea of me as an assassination target.

'I don't believe this,' he said, wiping his eyes with the back of a hand. 'I come out for a game of shuttles and a pint in the pub and now Gere is just about to go head to head with the local mafia. You couldn't make it up!'

'He's not mafia,' I said quickly, looking at Gere. 'He's just a jumped up son of a bitch with a big ego and a quick temper. Why else would he get heavy with me when all I can have done to annoy him is criticise his behaviour to his girlfriend?'

'Maybe he finds you as annoying as the rest of us and actually decided to do something about it,' suggested Gere innocently.

'Yeah, knowing you Slick he probably thought you were after his woman and that made him chuck the toys out of the pram.'

'Okay, okay,' I sighed. 'You're both right - it's probably no big deal but I'd still like you to make that call Gere - and preferably tonight.'

'What! You are joking again - I hope.' Rocky's face changed from highly amused to stunned surprised in a moment.

'Why wait?' I said. 'We're in the mood, Gere's character is supposed to keep unsocial hours so calling now is a plus and I want to get it over with.'

I took the mobile out of my tracksuit and placed it on the table in front of Gere. He looked at it and then back to me; he was still smiling but there was a look in his eyes that had been absent before.

'You're up for it aren't you,' I exclaimed. 'You are a lifesaver mate! Thank God you didn't listen to Mr Shitting Myself Slowly here - maybe we should find a new Men's A captain next year and make bollocks a job requirement.'

'Fuck off Slick, I was just trying to be the voice of reason and sanity in the situation. Anyway fella, after Underarm here has phoned your Mr Gilbert he'll probably want you dead for sure so don't start handing out the bouquets yet.'

'So how do you want me to play it?' Gere asked, ignoring Rocky's jousting.

'I see you as some tough criminal operator with an unspecified connection to yours truly that means you want me left alone. You need to be vague on the one hand and menacing on the other.'

'Vague certainly won't be a problem but menacing - are you serious Slick?'

I looked at Rocky, half grinning and half scowling. He raised his left hand in a conciliatory gesture as he finished a swig of the pint of lager that was in his right.

'Sorry, sorry - just slipped out what, what. Carry on with your instructions and I'll keep quiet,' he chuckled, almost apologetically. I shook my head slowly and turned back to Gere.

'Your first problem is going to be actually getting him to talk to you. He won't be admitting anything in case you're somebody official. Do you think you can get round that one?'

'Who knows?' laughed Gere. 'But I'll give it a go sunshine.'

We kicked the subject around for a few more inches of lager. Even Rocky made a few sensible suggestions and I hoped that it was helping Gere get a game-plan into his head. When a suitable pause came in the conversation I proposed Gere make the call.

'What's the number?' Gere reached out for the phone and picked it off the table. Apart from a couple of locals sitting on stools at the bar keeping the barman from an evening of loneliness and replacing it with one of arse-clenching tedium, we were the only ones in the pub. Our table in the corner was far enough from the other three life forms at the bar for a heated argument to go unnoticed so I didn't see why Gere couldn't get it over with now.

'It's in the phonebook under Gilbert - I copied it off last night's hit man's mobile.'

'Four, four, we'll be calling you 007 before long,' observed Rocky, lifting his glass in mock salute.

'Thank you Miss Moneypenny. Steady Gere, are you sure you're ready for this? No pressure but it's my balls dangling by the thread of your wit and ingenuity.'

'Relax Slick. He's a natural. Your tax office call is just one of many little pranks Gere and me have done. I usually can't stop pissing myself but he always sees it through to the end.'

Just like Rocky - take the piss and throw insults around like confetti before switching into a beacon of hope and positivity.

'Just checking, but remember - you mysterious friend, possible gangster etc. Want me alive etc. Point out to Gilbert he's overreacted without making him come over all alpha male again.'

Gere took a moment to compose himself and pressed the call button. As it was connecting Rocky seemed calm enough but I was beginning to sense a bout of the giggles approaching. Gere held the phone to his ear nonchalantly before raising an eyebrow and saying.

'Ah good evening - Mr Gilbert?'

Rocky and I looked at each other: a mistake. My face must have had the same effect on him - the need to laugh hysterically that rose unbidden but uncontrollably to my lips. I clutched my mouth hard and in my agony as I heard Gere say 'Let's say I'm a interested party in one of your current, er, enterprises,' before I grabbed Rocky's arm and dragged him across the room and away from Gere. That calmed us both down but I decided to stay distanced from Gere while he was on the phone in case Rocky or I lost control again. Gere seemed to be doing well - he was sitting back in his chair with his left ankle resting on his right knee as if he were making a call to find out the time of the next train to Victoria. I was still too nervous to listen properly to his side of the conversation in case I didn't like what I was hearing but I relaxed a little when he laughed once or twice. I was just beginning to wonder how long he could keep up his act when there was some nodding followed by another laugh.

'Gilbert's just told him what a tit you are,' whispered Rocky in my ear.

'Fuck off, can't you see I'm trying to hear what's going on.'

As soon as I had spoken Gere said 'Goodnight, I'm glad we could find some common ground.'

'You can ask him fella, looks like he's finished,' said Rocky perceptively.

We walked back to Gere who had an annoyingly deadpan expression on his face. He was obviously going to play us along until his own physical safety was in danger of being compromised.

'So? What happened?' Rocky could be so diplomatic when he had a mind.

'Sorted,' grinned Gere. 'I don't think he's gonna be looking for you anymore Slick - unless you do anything fresh to piss him off.'

'I think I should get the last round in before he owns up to not pressing the call button,' I said. 'If you're serious Gere I owe you big time.'

'Pleasure,' said Gere. 'Now get me a drink and some crisps and I'll tell you how I did it.'

'Fucking hell,' groaned Rocky. 'I don't think I can stand you being smug after Slick's James Bond impersonation. Hurry up with those drinks mate before I lose the will to carry on breathing.'

I bought the drinks and went back to the table. I wanted to believe Gere had somehow talked Gilbert round but I needed to hear some reassuring evidence before I tried out a few cartwheels. Gere was sitting quietly, sipping the dregs of his last drink and making Rocky wait like a puppy for a dog biscuit.

'Okay, impress us - take us through the call step by step. No long words either - it'll waste time explaining them to Squishy,' I said as I sat down, trying not to sound too eager.

'Yeah it was tough going at first. Said he didn't know what I was on about until I told him nicely to shut the fuck up and listen to me because if I couldn't sort this over the phone he'd have to suck on the end of a sawn-off while I said my piece in person - that seemed to loosen the arrogant bastard up a bit.'

'You told him what?!' Rocky gasped. I think if he had been drinking it would have been a case of an impromptu and forceful recycling of lager from mouth back into glass and surrounding surfaces but unfortunately his mouth was empty at the magic moment. 'My God Gere, you really know how to make an impression I'll give you that!'

I couldn't help laughing both at Gere's nerve and Rocky's reaction.

'So he didn't call your bluff - bugger me, he can't be that big a noise in criminal circles after all. That's a relief; in weaker moments I had visions of contracts being dished out on me.'

'This is real life Slick,' Rocky said in an irritating voice. 'He may be mad but it sounds like you only pissed him off so he just wanted to give you a spanking. He didn't know you're Kent's answer to Jason Bourne who wouldn't do the decent thing and take a well-deserved beating.'

'Anyway back to me,' said Gere, with a sigh. 'In a reasonable way I told him that I understood how aggravating you could be but that I had an obligation to look after you for 'family reasons'. I said that I had spelt out to you the importance of minding your own business and that you had promised to keep well away from his affairs from now on.'

'And he bought it?' I couldn't keep the incredulity out of my voice.

'Well...yes I think he did. I think it helped that I said you were scared shitless last night and that he didn't need to concern himself anymore with such a snivelling little twat.'

'Nice one! Four, four.' Rocky raised his glass in salute. 'Snivelling little twat sounds pretty reasonable to me – result Mr Gere!'

'Yeah, okay,' I sighed resignedly. 'I don't mind being called anything if it spares me physical pain. Hey Gere, you really are a genius - even I didn't think it would work but somehow you've pulled it off.'

'As opposed to himself, four, four.'

I laughed at Rocky's attempt at wit but I was feeling so relieved I would have probably found anything amusing. Suddenly there seemed a good chance that I could forget about Gilbert's boys coming for a social call and concentrate on the rest of my life. It also meant I could start planning my first safe-cracking gig without the added complication of Gilbert's interest in me. After all, the whole point of robbing Gilbert was the security of him never suspecting that a maths teacher and a nineteen year old girl could ever be involved. Without that anonymity there was no point in even attempting the robbery. Yes, if he had succeeded, I owed Gere big-time.

We stayed in the pub until we were kicked out well after eleven. I thanked Gere again when we stopped in the car park by the cars ready to drive home. It was drizzling so after arranging the lifts to the next match on Monday we said our goodbyes and I headed for Beechwood. It was still raining when I got to the cottage but as far as I was concerned it could chuck it down for a week – I had a robbery to organise and I didn't need the sun to be shining for that.

19

It was comforting, to put it mildly, knowing that if Gere was right and I had dropped off Gilbert's 'to do' list then I could go about my usual routines without constantly looking over my shoulder. Nevertheless, I was still more careful than normal; I varied my route to and from work and bought a couple of bolts for the back door of the cottage. I wiped Ben's gun clean of my fingerprints and put it up in the loft. I could reach it there if I needed it at night and also deny knowledge of its existence if by some quirk of fate the police discovered it – I had only rented the cottage for about a year and kept nothing else up there.

I also had a word with my neighbour Maureen about keeping an eye on the cottage. From her kitchen window she could see my back door from across her garden and I asked her to let me know if any strangers took an interest in the cottage. Maureen must have been well into her seventies and, not unsurprisingly, didn't seem to do much else except potter around with her plants and watch day-time television. Since I started renting the cottage I always stopped to have a natter with her if I was coming in or leaving the house and saw her outside in her garden on the other side of the driveway. Every time I said hello I knew I was kissing goodbye to at least ten minutes of my life I would never see again but I've always been a sucker for old ladies and feigned as much interest as I could in whatever was on her mind at the time.

When I saw her on Saturday morning I slipped into the conversation some cock and bull story about my ex wife and her violent new boyfriend. I painted a picture of a paranoid and insanely jealous body-builder – the boyfriend that is -

who felt intimidated by my good looks and charm and had made threats against me that included finding out where I lived and paying me a visit. Maureen missed the irony as to why my ex's boyfriend regarded me as a hazard to his love life but she looked outraged on my behalf and said it would be a pleasure. I was grateful for her predicable response to my white lies and congratulated myself for enlisting her as a lookout - why I'd even brought some excitement into her life.

I also began to take other precautions. Instead of using the cottage's drive I parked the car every evening in a little communal car-park on the far side of the green. There was plenty of space and it couldn't be seen from the road as it was up a short drive between two cottages - all I had to do was walk through a gate set in the hedge around the car-park and across the grass to my back door. It was a bit of a pain but at least I didn't have to fret about the car being messed with while I was asleep.

At night I locked and bolted the back door and pulled the door at the foot of the stairs closed using some nylon rope which I tied to the foot of my bed upstairs. If someone tried to open the door the rope would make it difficult and also alert me to my visitors.

It seemed like my life and a Phillip Marlowe story were taking on more features in common than they had previously. A car chase, some fisticuffs, a villain and a beautiful heroine to name but four – if I wasn't careful I would be treating my classes to a Humphrey Bogart leer and a 'well done kid' every time a girl answered a question right. Anyway, I spent the next few evenings trying to come up with some sort of plan to relieve Gilbert's safe of its contents. After I had something to eat I would spend an hour or so sitting on the sofa in front of a fire with an A4 notepad on my lap. I lit the fire to make the cottage feel a bit cosier and to try and induce the relaxed ambience that creative thinking requires. I left the television off and put on the CD player quietly in the background.

Of course, mathematicians aren't renowned on the street for their creative thinking, more a general lack of fashion sense, but it should be said that this is to do us a genuine injustice. Mathematical or any kind of scientific research requires imagination and inspiration as well as a dogged tenacity in the face of often impenetrable problems. For a mathematician being right is everything, a quality that can have those closest to us running for the nearest baseball bat but, and take a moment here, who would you rather have planning your burglary – one of us or a team player with good interpersonal skills?

It seemed obvious to me that I had essentially two problems; stealing the money and then laundering it. The first part of the problem seemed reasonably straightforward in principle although I guessed in practice it would be anything but. Sneaking about in someone else's house in the middle of the night would probably induce the kind of nerves that usually results in incomprehensibly idiotic behaviour and ineptitude. Bearing this in mind I sketched out a plan together with a list of the stuff we would need to get to support the operation. I hoped that careful and thorough rehearsal and, modestly, intelligence would make up for lack of experience of the clandestine and keep *Dad's Army* type 'don't panic' situations from arising. I didn't have any worries about Grace suffering under pressure - I had stood watching her from the touchline too many times to doubt her ability to cope with a bit of excitement.

The second part of the problem - how to launder any money we stole looked like a more challenging concern. The books I had ordered weren't a great deal of use and the internet yielded fuck all whatever I Googled. I had a vague idea of taking the money across to Switzerland in a car and walking into a bank with it but I had no idea if that were a sensible plan or not (in fact I had a niggling suspicion that it was actually quite a stupid idea). I decided I would look into this but in the meantime go ahead with planning the burglary. I was pretty sure that if we got away with a substantial amount of cash then it would be the perfect motivator to coming up with a means of disposal.

Of course, it was exciting to be involved in a Marlowe-type escapade. All in all I thought I had done pretty well for a beginner – the car chase had ended satisfactorily and I had been equal to the confrontation with Ben. Alright, I couldn't see Marlowe requiring Gere to make the phone call to Gilbert for him but hey, I had used my initiative hadn't I?

Grace was also the perfect damsel in distress, although I had a strong feeling Marlowe wouldn't have agreed to help her steal Gilbert's money. The guy was just too honest for that – a man of scruples in a dirty world. But I wasn't Marlowe and this wasn't a neat plot where all the decisions I made had obvious right or wrong answers. As far as I was concerned Gilbert was a bastard and, given the circumstances, deserved to be robbed and I was prepared to argue that with anyone, even Marlowe himself. Trouble was there was no one around I could discuss it with and, since

Marlowe was a fictional character, that talk would have to wait indefinitely as well.

I picked up *The Big Sleep* where it lay on the floor by the sofa and found my favourite chapter near the end where Marlowe charms Silver Wig into untying him. Some great lines – "You know what Canino will do – beat my teeth out and then kick me in the stomach for mumbling". Then Marlowe goes outside and waits for Canino. Silver Wig distracts Canino when he follows Marlowe out into the night – "He fell for it like a bucket of lead" - and Marlowe shoots the bastard four times in the belly. I finished the book and tossed it back on the floor and lit a cigarette. No Mackenzie, there was a fair way to go before your life turns into a Marlowe story. Firstly, you've not been beaten and tied up yet and second there's not been the need to convince a gangster's moll to risk her life and save you. That would always be problematic anyway - given the chance most of the women I knew would probably have shot me themselves and saved the assassin the bother. I couldn't imagine shooting anyone myself either – even a gangster – no, this was not quite the full Monty as far as a Marlowe investigation was concerned even if it showed some promise.

Easter was only a few weeks away and seemed the best time to do the deed; I was just too tied up with school and my private lessons to cope with anything before then. Yep, that's right; I was too busy to fit a burglary into my schedule. There was also the problem of getting to and from Gilbert's house and I couldn't see any way around bringing someone else into the scheme to provide transport. The question was - who? It didn't take me long to eliminate all of my friends simply because I couldn't trust them in the long run to stay quiet or in the short term to agree to risking their liberty or their health. Besides, the thought of Rocky in a tight-fitting cat-burglar's outfit just brought tears to my eyes. No, I desperately needed secrecy and someone who would trust me to plan the thing properly - it had to be Chris.

On Thursday evening I called Grace and told her I was thinking of Easter and could she work on the best night for the jaunt? She immediately said that Fridays were good because Gilbert always spent the evening at *The Wealden* then so we pencilled in the first Friday in April. I also gave her my view about a driver and who it should be and why. She wasn't hard to convince and I said I aimed to go and visit Chris in Devon at the weekend to put forward our proposal.

'What if he says no?' Grace had said. 'Will we still be able to do it?'

'It'll be harder but don't worry, we'll find a way,' I had reassured her, although I couldn't think of one at that moment. 'I thought I'd offer him twenty per cent if that's okay with you. You and I can split the rest or did you have something else in mind?'

'No, no that sounds fine,' she had said breezily. 'Are you sure that's alright for you Neil?'

'No that's great. I just wanted us all to be happy about the split - with our luck the safe'll probably be empty when we open it anyway.'

'Yeah,' Grace laughed down the phone. 'Then I really will have to do well in my A levels!'

'You'd better do well whatever - I don't want your mother getting angry with me.'

'She'd never do that Neil. Anyway, will you let me know what Chris says when you see him?'

'Course I will. I'm going to go now and carry on with my master-planning. Try and get some work done before the next lesson.'

'Yes Neil! Don't plan too hard!'

'Night Grace. Take care.'

'You too, see you soon.'

I phoned Chris that night and he said I was welcome to come down. I told him I would aim to be there late Saturday afternoon and be off again the following morning. He was intrigued when I said I had something I wanted to tell him that I'd rather do face to face instead of over the phone but he didn't press me and we both hung up after a few minutes.

The M25 and A303 were mercifully quieter than I expected on Saturday and I got to Chris's place without the frustration of any hold-ups. The only nerve-wracking element of the drive was Ben's gun which I had brought with me on an impulse. If the police found it I would probably go to prison which would be inconvenient in any circumstances but especially at the moment.

Emma and Rhiannon were at their mum's when I arrived and Chris was without a date so it was an easy decision to go out to the local pub for dinner. Over a couple of pints of Guinness I filled him in on the last few weeks and told him what I was thinking about getting up to next. All the crucial conversations in my life seemed to be taking place in bars at the moment which didn't seem entirely healthy but I reassured myself that this was a phase rather than the beginning of a life-long theme. Chris was suitably surprised and impressed in most of the right places and interrupted me several times to check that I had really meant the last section of the tale he was hearing. When I had finished he started rolling a cigarette from his tin of tobacco and the packet of *Rizlas* I always associated with him.

'Now I know why you wanted to tell me face to face,' he said, lighting his cigarette with a battered old lighter. 'Are you sure you know what you're doing Neil? This Gilbert guy sounds dangerous to me. I knew teaching was losing its sheen but isn't robbery a bit of a drastic career change?'

'I know, I know,' I shrugged my shoulders. 'I'm not sure myself how I've managed it but here I am. I said I would help Grace and I like to think I usually keep my word if I say I'll do something - so one way or another I'm going to try and open that safe.'

'You always were a sucker for a sob story,' he said reasonably. 'Anyway, why come down and tell me? I can't see how I can give you any fresh insights and you know I'm not the guy to come to for sensible advice.'

I took a deep breath and said slowly.

'Actually I was going to ask you to drive the getaway car for a twenty per cent cut. It should be pretty risk free and who knows what twenty per cent will amount to? I can't trust anyone else so the job's yours if you want it.'

Chris chuckled and took a drag of his cigarette. He shifted in his seat as he struggled to compose an answer.

'Fuck me Neil, you really know how to slip in a conversation-stopper, I'll give you that. Now I see why you've made the flying visit you sneaky bastard.'

'Sorry mate,' I acknowledged with a sheepish look. 'I know it's a big thing to ask. It's just that when it came to the crunch you were the only one that ticked all the boxes if you know what I mean.'

Chris took a last drag of his cigarette and stubbed the inch out in the glass ashtray that sat on the table between us. I could see that he still wasn't convinced but I wanted it to be his decision so I resisted the urge to apply more pressure. I hadn't a clue what I would do without him and an image of Rocky dressed to burgle flashed disturbingly across my mind again. After a moment's more thought he finally pushed the ashtray away from him and fixed his eyes on me.

'Thanks for the vote of confidence but are you sure you haven't let this mid-life crisis thing of yours get out of control,' he said reasonably. 'For a start what about my car - for Christ's sake Neil it's a fifteen year old Volvo. If Gilbert has a push bike handy he could probably catch us on that if we got into a car chase!'

I had to admit he had a point but I had a ready answer.

'That's the clever bit – no one will ever suspect we're up to no good in your old crate and it isn't going to come to that anyway. It's not like Grace and I are going to walk into a branch of Barclays with a couple of sawn-offs while you wait outside with the engine running. You'll be out of sight waiting for my call when we've got the money and we're ready to leave. No one will ever know.'

I ran him through my initial thoughts on the choreography of the burglary and this seemed to reassure him a little more. We had another pint and I continued to answer his questions as best I could. I also reminded him of the potential reward.

'Look Chris, there was a shed-load of money in that safe when I saw it on New Year's Eve. Maybe it will be empty when we open it next time but if it isn't your cut will run into tens of thousands. That's not bad for giving me a lift and a late night.'

I took a swig of my Guinness and lent back in my chair. I was finished – I had said all I could without turning into a nag. It was up to him – so I waited as he started to roll himself his umpteenth cigarette.

'Okay I'm in,' he said cautiously moulding the thin tube of tobacco delicately between his fingers. 'But only if you're pretty damn sure you know what you're doing. We've both got kids and I'm not letting them suffer the consequences of any numbskull behaviour on our part - divorce is one thing but I don't see an easy way back from prison or, worse case scenario, a couple of bullets.'

As the meaning of his words registered I grinned and exhaled with relief.

'Thanks mate,' I said, with genuine conviction. 'Don't worry - I know I can be impetuous but where this job is concerned I'll run it all by you when I've finalised the plans and you can be sure I won't leave anything to chance - as far as is humanly possible that is.'

It was a weight off my mind having Chris on board and we used the rest of the evening by talking through a few feasible plans and, more notably, getting as pissed as a couple of newts. We walked the two or three miles back to Chris's place under a starry moon-lit sky but it may as well have been a short stroll to the end of the street because of the dulled nature of my senses. I hadn't staggered home from a pub for years and it was like being a student again back in Liverpool, except there were fewer bottles flying around than on Smithdown Road in the early hours.

I woke up the next morning in Chris's spare bed but I was buggered if I could remember ever finding the room I was in, let alone summoning up the coordination to undress and find my way under the duvet. An hour later I felt marginally better after a shower and breakfast and a couple of paracetamol. Chris was looking a bit rough as well but, like me, he began to perk up once he had demolished his bacon and eggs and was sitting opposite me at the old kitchen table with a cup of tea and a roll-up. We talked some more about my proposal of the previous evening and I was relieved to hear that he hadn't changed his mind and was still up for doing the driving.

Before I left I went out to the car and collected the pistol from the glove-compartment and took it back into the kitchen and put it on the table in front of Chris.

'Look I know you mostly work with shotguns when you're out shooting innocent little squirrels in the woods but do you know how the fuck one of these works?' I said, watching the look of interest on his face as he stared at the new table ornament.

'I think you'll find you just point and shoot Neil,' he said, gingerly picking up the gun by the end of its handle and resting it in his other hand as he examined it. 'You do know you need a licence for this and if the old bill catch you with it you could be looking at five years inside don't you?'

'Yeah I know it's illegal but self-preservation seemed a more attractive option when I took it off Benny boy. I'll dump it as soon as I can but right now all I want to know is would you know how to fire it?'

'Well, we could go for a quick stroll and find out,' he offered, 'no one will take any notice around here if I take you to the right place. How much ammo have you got?'

'What's in it. I was going to get some more but my local Tesco doesn't stock them.'

Chris shook his head and, after finding our jackets, he shoved the gun into a pocket and I followed him out into the trees behind his house. Ten minutes later we came to a bit of a clearing and Chris took the gun out of his pocket. He pushed what we assumed was the safety catch into the 'off' position and aimed the gun a tree about thirty yards away. He adopted the stance of a cop in a television show which for some reason set me off laughing so that he had to pause to retain his own composure. When he pulled the trigger the explosive crack was bloody deafening and I could see the power of the recoil as Chris's arms twitched upwards. There was a fair old thud as the bullet hit the tree as well and I whistled in admiration.

'Fucking hell, great shot Hutch! You're a natural,' I laughed. 'It's a shame my eardrums have been perforated.'

'Thanks, have a go yourself - but watch the recoil, it's surprisingly fierce if you're not used to firing a gun - just squeeze the trigger smoothly,' he said, offering me the weapon.

I limited myself to a couple of shots so I at least knew what it was like to fire the gun at a target. I managed to hit the tree as well so it seems that shooting people is not a particularly difficult art - not surprising I guess or Americans wouldn't be so keen on owning guns. The bullets were stored in a magazine that fitted neatly into the handle of the pistol and Chris and I counted seven when we released the magazine and the round in the firing chamber.

After walking back to Chris's place we had another brew and I succumbed to temptation and lit my first cigarette of the day. I agreed to keep him up to speed by calling him regularly and I finally left for home just before mid-day.

The next two weeks up to the holidays flew by as I juggled work, tutoring and badminton commitments along with the sorting out of the details of the burglary. Grace and I drove over to Gilbert's place a few times in the evenings so that I could have a thorough look at the roads around about the house and acquaint myself with the setting of the electric gates and the adjoining walls and laurel hedges. Grace pointed out to me the place where she had made her late-night entries when she lived with Gilbert and I found a spot nearby where Chris could wait for us while we were inside.

There was a pub on the Sevenoaks road a few hundred yards away from where the lane leading past Gilbert's house joined the main road. There were tables out front and I reckoned it might be a reasonable spot to watch and see when Gilbert's car drove past on the way to *The Wealden* on the night of the job. Less than a quarter of a mile away from the pub we found a church with a car-park that I also thought we could use.

I have to confess that it was fun driving around with Grace in her old car taking photos with her digital camera and discussing and formulating our plans. It was doing me good spending time with her and not doing maths for a change. Marlowe should have hired an attractive assistant – it would have made the sneaking around much more interesting.

We organised a rota for recording Gilbert's journeys to *The Wealden* in the evenings for the whole week before the proposed day of the job. According to Grace he usually left the house at around eight so we reckoned that popping into the pub for a quick drink at around that time would afford us the opportunity to check that his habits had remained the same since she and her mother had been sent packing. It would be the first week of the holidays so I volunteered to do most of the shifts so that Grace wouldn't arouse her mum's suspicions by going out at uncharacteristic times. I was fairly relaxed about the date we had pencilled in anyway because if Gilbert didn't show we would just have to postpone despite the inconvenience to Chris who would have had a wasted two hundred mile journey.

In the end my decision to remain fatalistic about the first Friday in April was a fortuitous one because Chris called me up over the weekend beforehand to let me know he couldn't make it on that date after all. His boss had organised a shoot of some kind for the Saturday so Chris's presence was required on the Friday. I must admit to a pang of disappointment but there was nothing I could do about it but reschedule. Grace was more openly frustrated when I called her to break the news but eventually her common sense kicked in and she accepted the situation with good humour.

The first Friday when all three of us were available was a further three weeks off when I would be back at school. Not really having a social life outside of the gym and *The Wanderers* I could have done any Friday between then and Christmas but the other two seemed to have more going on in their lives. Easter was late that year and it was a busy time for Chris on the estate and Grace was already booked on a holiday in the Canaries with her dad and his new family. I told Chris to tell Sir Richard that he was coming to my wedding if he needed an excuse next time and wondered as I said it whether I should have suggested funeral instead.

By the end of the holidays I was as ready as I was ever going to be to have a go at Gilbert's place. All the shopping for the outfits and accessories for the big day had been done and laid out on the bed in the spare room at the cottage. I had talked through the plan with Chris several times on the phone and satisfied myself he knew what was required. With Grace I left nothing to chance - I gave her a list of the items she needed for the operation and checked when she had bought them. During the first week back at school I sat and watched Gilbert drive past me soon after eight from Monday through to Wednesday while Grace covered Thursday. It was heartening that his routine seemed pretty set and as predicted.

On Thursday, after she had checked on Gilbert, Grace drove around to the cottage for a final meeting. It was usually the evening for her lesson but we had decided that it would be a waste of Fiona's money to try and do anything maths related the night before the robbery. I was in the kitchen when she arrived and spying me through the window she waved and let herself in at the back door. She was wearing a heavy, loose pink woollen sweater over her faded Levis and trainers and a happy excited smile. I threw the tea-towel I had been drying-up with onto the draining-board, took her through into the front room and sat her down on the sofa in front of the fire. She agreed to a cup of coffee while I continued with the glass of white left over from my dinner.

I took her through the plan step by step for the last time and checked she had bought everything she needed. I was as excited as a bride on her wedding day and having Grace sitting next to me by the fire was the icing on the cake.

'So that's it - we're all set at last,' I said after about an hour's discussion. 'It's probably tempting fate but I can hardly wait to get started.'

'Same here,' she sighed almost wistfully. 'I hope it all goes well - can you imagine what would happen if we're caught?'

'I'm hoping it won't come to that – and it's unlikely too so relax.' I said in a calm voice and took a sip of my drink. 'If we're reasonably lucky the worse that can happen is we find the safe empty or he's changed the code and we leave empty handed.'

I wasn't trying to sell Grace anything I wasn't already confident about – what's the point of making plans and then having second thoughts every five minutes? The best laid schemes of mice and men etc – and, after all, this was a tricky and delicate operation we were going to undertake. Still, it was a surprise when she said in a low voice. 'If I'm honest I'm a bit scared Neil.'

She was leaning forward over her knees and staring at the fire. Her expression was suddenly as severe and anxious as it had been on the evening she had told me about her father's accident.

If she had just announced she was contemplating going into a nunnery I don't imagine I would have been more surprised or disappointed. My mouth drained miraculously of saliva in an instant and a heaviness swept over me as any immediate meaning for my life was summarily erased. If she was serious - and it looked like she was - then all bets were off. I needed her commitment and without it Gilbert could keep his money. Maybe for the first time I realised how much I wanted to execute the plan if only to see if it worked. I took another sip of my wine, a larger one this time, and leant forward and put my hand on her knee.

'Grace, don't tell me you've charmed me into planning Kent's burglary of the year and now you're having second thoughts?' I said as casually as I could in the circumstances. 'We can easily call it off if that's what you want. I'm definitely not going through with it unless you're sure.'

Grace turned her head and faced me. She had crinkled her forehead and there was teasing look of amusement in her blue eyes.

'You're so easy to wind up Neil,' she chuckled in a soft voice. 'What do you take me for – a wimp?'

I took my hand back, smiling with reluctant admiration at the ease with which she had taken me in.

'No not exactly,' I said. 'But I'm pretty sure I could come up with some better words to describe you if you give me a minute.'

She laughed and leant forward towards me, fixing me with a steady, penetrating gaze. I felt a little like an exhibit on my own sofa, vulnerable but vaguely aware that the worse that could happen might be rather pleasant. In a level voice she said.

'Are you going to kiss me?'

Of course I wanted to - it was difficult to imagine a more kissable face than hers at that moment but I settled for forcing a crooked grin and putting a hand to her face and patting her cheek gently.

'Love to, but you're not catching me twice. Anyway, you're not my type – I only go for women who don't try and give me a heart attack whenever they feel like a bit of sport.'

It was a strange sensation hearing myself saying one thing while inside my head I could distinctly hear a voice saying something along the lines of, 'sure, but be gentle with me and I wouldn't say no to a shag either'. Those thoughts were extinguished quickly, however, when she laughed and put her arms around my neck and hugged me. I squeezed her with my free arm holding the wine up out of harm's way with the other.

'Ha, ha Neil. If I wanted to give you a heart attack I could do a bit better than that,' she purred into my ear.

'Promises, promises,' I said evenly. 'But right now you ought to be going home and getting a good night's sleep, we've a got a big day tomorrow.'

In fact she stayed for another hour. I prefer to think it was because I can be such diverting company on the night before a big robbery but it was probably more a matter of inertia. It was warm by the fire and we were both too excited to contemplate an early night. Besides, it wasn't every evening a beautiful woman popped in to see me so I wasn't in much of a hurry to show her the door. Eventually, however, as the clock ticked around to past eleven I escorted her out to her car. Before she got in she turned and gave me a hug which I was only too happy to return: I'm not much of a touchy-feely type but with Grace I was prepared to make an effort. She drove off, leaving me staring after her tail lights until they disappeared into the night. I took a deep breath of the cool evening air and went back in and lit a cigarette.

I sat in the kitchen staring at the ceiling. This time tomorrow if things were going to plan I would be in Gilbert's house with Grace and a considerably higher pulse rate. I wondered how I would cope – it would be embarrassing to have a panic attack with Grace as a witness but not quite so awkward I reasoned as being discovered or something worse. Then I realised there was nothing worse and mentally changed the subject. I thought about going to bed but it seemed pointless so I did some mindless household chores and tidying up. It was a battle to keep the doubts about my own sanity at the back of my mind but I just about managed and finally made it to bed well after midnight.

20

The radio alarm woke me at six-thirty after a disturbed night where I seemed to spend more time rearranging my pillows than sleeping. I couldn't remember most of the dreams I had staggered through but a few images still survived as I lay there contemplating the trip downstairs to the kitchen. I had a vivid recollection of an attempt to escape Gilbert and his men where I was hindered by an alarming lack of muscle strength in my legs. It was like running in treacle. Grace had also, not surprisingly, made a nocturnal appearance or two, mostly dressed in black and looking achingly sexy.

I thought about the day ahead and a brief tingle of excitement filtered up through my body although perhaps that's putting it too strongly because I'm past tingling at my age. It was a pleasurable sensation, however, like the anticipation I felt before meeting a girl on a first date back in my schooldays. Maybe that was it - the impending attempt at high stakes burglary was just an excuse to recapture a long lost youth? Or was it a really convoluted way of getting out on a date with Grace?! Or maybe I should quit the attempts at self-analysis and get my arse out of bed? With an effort I swung my legs out from under the duvet and padded across the bedroom and downstairs. I washed, had breakfast and left for work.

It was a beautiful May morning. Mist still nestled in the low-lying fields giving the countryside a medieval feel and it and the early sunshine and blue sky enhanced my expectant mood. As the hedgerows slipped by I couldn't help myself thinking about the night ahead and the possibilities of disaster. Now and again Terry Wogan would catch my attention with an amusing anecdote from one of his conspiritorial listeners and then my mind would wander back to the coming evening's activities.

The day's lessons rushed by giving me no time to do any further speculating and at about four and with my office tidied I wandered up to the staff room for a cup of tea. Being Friday it was pretty empty although there were three or four people still pottering around including Jan and Anna, a couple of chemistry teachers who I counted as mates.

Jan was in her forties, perpetually cheerful and terminally nosy. She wore clothes and a haircut most women seem to settle for out of boredom once they reach a certain time of life. Anna was a similar age and outlook but still, in my humble opinion, managed to pull off sexy. Jan had a constant and, let's not beat about the bush, losing battle with her weight, whereas Anna had a figure that often brought interest to the staffroom especially when she wore tops that revealed the compelling outline of her nipples. She was also attractive in one of those difficult to pin down kind of ways with her dark hair and friendly demeanour. I sat down and joined them at the large table in the middle of the room. It was just to kill some time really; it had been non-stop all day and I needed to unwind. A friendly chat about the weekend would suffice.

'What have you two got lined up for the next few days?' I ventured, looking at the pair of them.

'Nothing very exciting,' sighed Anna. 'What about you - anything daring?'

I resisted the urge to sail too close to the wind and settled for: 'I'm seeing an old student tonight but I doubt if we'll be doing anything too demanding.'

'Getting a bit old for that sort of thing aren't we?' chimed in Jan, shaking her head and eyeing me doubtfully.

'Is that a challenge?' I said smartly, to which Jan gave a disgusted look and Anna's eyes twinkled with amusement. I could always make Anna laugh and it crossed my mind that she would make an interesting date herself.

It carried on like that for a while until one by one we realised that going home needed to be negotiated. That still left me with over an hour to kill before Chris arrived but I was ready to get back and sort myself out so I made a move to go as Anna finished packing up her stuff. I offered to carry one of her bags of exercise books and we wandered down to the car park together chatting about this and that. As we parted we exchanged friendly goodbyes and I found the Mazda and started the engine.

As I joined the traffic outside school it struck me again that it was almost time for action now and I felt another mini surge of adrenaline. On the way home I took a detour through Edenbridge and stopped at an off-licence and bought some bubbly in case I really had something to celebrate later. Maybe I was tempting fate but I reasoned I would need a drink whatever happened.

Once I was home I had a long relaxing bath and thought through the plan one last time. I hoped Grace's information about Gilbert's place was accurate. If it was there was a good chance we would get away with the loot and, just as important, stay off Gilbert's radar. How much money was there in that safe? Okay, let's not get carried away: the most important thing was to remain undetected. Gilbert had already proved to be a nasty and unpredictable piece of work and there was no way I wanted to be the focus of his attention again.

Chris had texted me to say that he would be arriving around six and when I heard the sound of his car on the gravel in the drive from the kitchen I went out to meet him.

'Good journey?' I called as he climbed out of the old Volvo.

'The M25 was a nightmare but I allowed plenty of time so no worries,' he grinned. 'Are we all set?'

'As far as I know - hey come in, I'm just starting dinner.'

He followed me into the kitchen and sat down behind the Formica topped table and started to roll himself a cigarette. He was wearing a pair of Levis and an old check shirt mum had bought him years ago.

'Beer?' I asked as I chucked some chicken into a wok and it started to hiss and sizzle.

'Cup of coffee if you don't mind Neil. I need to keep my wits about me tonight seeing as I'm a virgin so far as getaway driving is concerned.'

'Coming up,' I said, flicking on the kettle. 'Let's hope we don't need to call upon the undoubted speed of your motor.'

'Well if we do we're fucked so try not to get chased out of the scene of the crime,' Chris grinned, taking his first drag from his freshly manufactured roll-up.

The stir-fry I cooked for dinner was passable but if I'm honest I shouldn't have bothered. Neither of us was very hungry and I had to scrape most of it off our plates into the bin when we were finished. While I washed up Chris fiddled with my guitar in the front room and then afterwards we went through the plan again over a cup of tea and another cigarette.

'Are you sure you don't want to stay tonight?' I asked him I as stood up from the settee where we had been sitting. 'What's the big rush to get back to Devon?'

'Just paranoid I guess – if I can make it back before first light no one will know I've been up here. The kids think I'm out on the piss down in Torquay,' he shrugged.

'Suit yourself - anyway, I'm going to go upstairs and get myself organised.'

'Yeah, okay; I'll be fine down here.'

The clothes and equipment for the night's escapade were laid out on the bed in the spare bedroom where I had been accumulating them over the past month or so. There were new jeans and trainers both in black and for on top I'd chosen a new long-sleeved cotton tee-shirt in the same colour. I was going to look rather gay although I would be wearing a less eye-catching blue shirt over the tee-shirt and casual shoes before I started being illegal. Stored in Chris's car would be a bin-liner in which was squeezed everything else we had figured we would need; two balaclavas with holes only for mouth and eyes, back-packs, also in regulation black and two pairs of gloves each; a fingerless pair of padded gloves used for lifting weights in the gym and ultra thin medical ones to wear underneath. In the back-packs were stored a new pay as you go mobile, a couple of narrow-beam torches, a length of high-tech rope, light and incredibly strong plus a Swiss army knife if the rope needed cutting or I came across a horse needing a stone removed from its hoof.

There was also the gun and the shoulder holster I had relieved Ben of all those weeks ago sitting in the loft. I was in two minds whether to take it or not - I certainly wasn't planning to shoot anyone but I was nervous about Gilbert's men who obviously did carry firearms, one of whom might be at the house looking after the ranch so to speak. In the end I left it where it was because I couldn't imagine using it whatever the circumstances. I would dump it somewhere once all the excitement was over.

At eight Chris and I left the cottage. While I locked up he shoved the bin-liner in the boot of the Volvo and gunned the engine. I took a deep breath of the evening air and took in appreciatively the tranquil scene of the village, wondering if the feeling in my stomach was down to nerves or whether I should have chewed the stir-fry more thoroughly.

Chris and I didn't speak much on the drive over towards Sevenoaks. We had run through the choreography of the evening back at the cottage, concentrating on the arrangements for the pick-up after the job was done and ensuring he understood the layout of the roads in the vicinity of Gilbert's place. I had to act as navigator for the journey as the roads were as unfamiliar to him as the North-West Passage but there was little other conversation. It had crossed my mind that a get-away driver should perhaps have spent a few hours getting himself clued-up on the crime-scene but it was too late now and I couldn't see Chris's lack of knowledge being a critical factor in our endeavours.

Grace was supposed to be waiting for us in the pub just across from the entrance to the lane on which the Gilbert residence was situated. There were tables out front about ten yards from the main road and she would be there watching to make sure Gilbert made his usual trip to his club in Sevenoaks. She had convinced me that she should wear a disguise in order to eliminate any chance of recognition from the road and as Gilbert had to be out for the burglary to go ahead I had little option but to agree. She would be arriving at the pub at eight and I was supposed to get there by eight-thirty.

Chris dropped me off outside *The Foresters' Arms* and then drove on, heading towards the church hall car park where we had arranged to meet in ten minutes. As I walked up the little incline towards the primrose-coloured building that had been decorated with several impressive hanging baskets I looked out for Grace. The pub was surrounded at the front and one side by more than a dozen garden tables occupied by people enjoying the double whammy of a lovely spring evening on a Friday. Only one table, however, had a lone female sitting at it nursing a Coke so I angled my approach towards her. As I drew nearer to her table I almost began to have doubts about the identity of the dark-haired, chunky looking female staring at me from behind a pair of unflattering sunglasses, but the shape of the nose was the clincher and I sat down opposite her.

'You remind me of a girl I once taught,' I said quietly, looking at her with an almost straight face. Grace's forehead wrinkled but her eyes were invisible behind the glasses.

'I'm sorry, do I know you?' she said, her voice not much more than a whisper.

The voice was definitely Grace's: Ingrid Bergman without the Swedish accent; I almost felt like Humphrey Bogart myself.

'Ha, ha very funny – those glasses hide your squint brilliantly but the missing teeth are a giveaway. Has Gilbert gone by yet?'

'Bastard! You just missed him. Shall we go?'

'Sounds good - how are you feeling? It's difficult to tell when you look like Dawn French from the neck down with Ozzy Osborne's head stuck on the top.'

'Pretty good eh Neil! It's amazing what you can do with some cushions, a size 16 dress and a black wig. Bit sweaty though.'

'What about your face. You look like someone's shoved it in a bowl of flour.'

'Yeah, a bit disappointing to lose the tan but don't worry it'll soon be off and you can carry on with your crush.'

'Fuck off Grace,' I grinned. 'Let's go or my brother will be having a nervous breakdown.'

Grace and I left our table and I followed her around to the rear of the pub to the car park. From behind she really did look like an overweight woman walking slowly to ease the chaffing of her inner thighs and hardly any of the male drinkers paid her any attention. None of them had the faintest suspicion that if Grace had been wearing a mini skirt her thighs would have been the highlight of their trip to the pub that night.

She unlocked her car and squeezed behind the wheel, leaning across to let me in.

'Thanks,' I said. 'That's some arse you have in that disguise – I thought I was back in the staffroom for a moment.'

She sniggered and manoeuvred the car out of the car park to the main road. In a few minutes we were turning into the church car park where Chris was waiting for us, sat behind the wheel of the Volvo. It was behind the church and out of sight of the road which meant we should be unobserved unless the vicar had a nasty surprise in store for me. The church had certainly been empty on a Friday for the last four weeks so barring an impromptu choir practice or something I hoped we would be all right.

'Give me a minute to get out of this outfit,' said Grace as she cut the engine.

'Okay, I'll be over with Chris.'

I walked over to the Volvo and got in the back, sliding myself over so I was behind the passenger seat.

'She's getting changed,' I told him as I started to unbutton my shirt.

'What about Gilbert?'

'He left about ten minutes ago so we're on.'

Chris had retrieved the bin-liner from the boot so I stuffed my shirt into it. I then took off my shoes, found the black trainers and put them on

We could see Grace sitting behind the wheel of her car wrestling the black dress over her head. It was flung onto the back seats followed by what I guessed was the cushions that had helped to redefine her figure. Finally, the hair came off, after which she appeared to be wiping her face with a cloth or two.

'Must look your best on a robbery,' I murmured.

When she got out of her car it was the familiar Grace. Slim, athletic, the dusky blonde hair restored. She was in black jeans and trainers with a matching top like me. This was our idea of a burglar's uniform but it certainly looked better on her. She trotted over to us smiling.

'All set,' I asked as she came up to the car and got in beside me. She grinned even more broadly.

'Sure am. Hi, you must be Chris.'

'Hello Grace', said Chris, turning around to smile and shake her hand 'I've heard a lot about you.'

Grace momentarily looked a little embarrassed.

'Don't worry - I missed out all the annoying stuff,' I broke in. 'Chris is under the impression you're okay.'

'Which I am so shut up Neil - don't listen to him Chris.' She sounded relaxed - I felt like a footballer an hour before playing in the Champions League Final while she was just off for a kick-about in the park.

'Don't worry - I've learnt to ignore him over the years,' laughed Chris.

'Time to go I think,' I said, checking my watch. Chris started the engine and took us out of the car park and back towards *The Foresters' Arms*. Just past the pub he made a left turn into Harkness Lane; the light was fading now and he had the headlights on and they lit up the hedgerows and occasional sets of gates in the lane. We were getting close to Gilbert's place so I pulled on the balaclava and tucked it in inside the neck of my T, strapped my back-pack on and carefully put on the two pairs of gloves.

'Looking good Neil,' muttered Grace from beside me as she started to pull on her own head-gear.

'Very funny but how about you get all your gear on asap,' I hissed, wriggling into the straps of my back-pack.

'Coming up now Chris,' I continued, noticing a familiar stone wall coming up on the left. 'By that telegraph pole.'

'Yes, under control.' The car came to a halt.

'See you later,' I said opening my door. We had to be quick; if a random car went past now and saw us posing like extras in *Mission Impossible IV* we were fucked. As soon as

Grace was out of the car Chris was in first gear and the car's tail-lights moved rapidly away from us up the lane.

'Over to you,' I said softly.

'This way,' she said, moving towards the familiar iron gates some thirty yards up the lane, keeping close to the eight foot wall that separated Gilbert's grounds from the road. Where the wall adjoined the brick pillar holding the nearest gate she stopped and pointed at the indentations in the brickwork we were to use as foot and hand holds to get over.

'It's easy Neil. If I can do it drunk after a Friday night on the town you'll be fine.'

There was a high laurel hedge behind the wall and we were to use that to climb down on the other side. It would also shield us from the CCTV camera that was continuously trained on the gates from a perch on a tree about ten yards up the drive past the gates. I hoped she was right about how easy it was going to be – okay I wasn't drunk but it was a long time since I had done any climbing.

She put a foot on the wall about waist high and pulled herself up with her arms while I tried to see exactly how to do it. In a few seconds she was almost at the top. The sound of a car approaching up the lane spurred me into action and I reached out, found a gap in the brickwork for my fingers and pulled myself up so my head came over the top of the wall and against the laurel branches. With another effort I swung my right leg over the top of the wall and wrestled myself into the hedge on the other side of the wall. Grace had already disappeared down the other side and was waiting for me hidden in the generous cover offered by the laurel trees. The car passed beneath me on the lane but I had made it just in time to avoid the sweep of its headlights and I felt my muscles relax in relief as I realised this was not going to be the moment of discovery. When the car had gone I clambered down the remainder of the hedge. Grace was crouching as I landed gently beside her, slightly out of breath but more from nerves rather than the exertion of the climb.

'That wasn't too bad,' I said quietly. 'Take me to the house partner.'

'Follow me,' she whispered, and she turned and pushed her way out of the laurels and to the right away from the gates.

She began to run slowly, keeping low and skirting the laurels until we came to a waist-high hedge and a few trees some thirty metres from the drive and running parallel to it. The shadows were almost impenetrable now and I didn't feel as exposed as I expected to be. We soon arrived at the side of the house; all of the windows I could see were in darkness but that made two sides and a couple of outbuildings still unaccounted for. The corner we were crouching by was about twenty five yards from the front door porch. Only a porch-light shone; but no doubt a security light would bathe the gravel and the two cars parked over on the far side in a sea of unfriendly bright light if we approached without care.

'Do we just stay close to the wall?' I asked, as quietly as I could.

'Yeah, do you want to hold my hand?'

'Just lead the bloody way,' I whispered.

'Ok,' was all she said, but she took my hand anyway and advanced slowly along next to the brickwork bringing me behind her like some naughty toddler. We soon came to the porch which jutted out from the front wall by about six feet and edged around it until we were standing inside it in front of the large, polished oak door. I remembered the last time I had stood here was on New Year's Eve feeling a great deal less apprehensive. Grace let me go and we stood straining our senses for any signs of activity on the other side of the door. All seemed quiet and after a moment's pause Grace squeezed her hand into her jeans pocket and found a small set of two keys.

'Let's hope he hasn't changed the locks,' I murmured. Grace crossed her fingers in front of my face and turned to insert one of the keys in the deadlock next to her shoulder. Pleasingly it turned in the lock and Grace slowly pushed the door open. As we slipped inside the high-pitched sounds of alarm beeps warning that a code needed to be inputted rang out at a level which I hoped wasn't too loud to disturb anyone else in the large house. Grace walked over to the little keypad on the wall next to a door on the left leading to the corridor to the kitchen and carefully pressed four numbers in succession. Silence – the code had not been changed!

The hall was lit by some tasteful wall-lights protruding from the dark oak panelling. We paused, waiting to see if the noise of the beeps would bring anyone down to the entrance hall to investigate. Nothing happened, so if the house were occupied, presumably by staff, at least they had been too busy elsewhere to notice our arrival. I put my mouth close to Grace's right ear.

'It all seems pretty dead. Are you okay to go ahead but with minimal sound effects?'

'Course I am. I'll just reset the alarm and we'll go.'

I felt the same but her enthusiasm was a fillip. I didn't want to be in a situation like this with a reluctant partner. After resetting the alarm she motioned me to follow and we tiptoed away from the door, up the stairs and onto the first-floor landing. The lights were off up here so we took our torches out of our back-packs before Grace set off along a corridor with me bringing up the rear. Even by torchlight I recognised the passageway that led to Gilbert's study when we came to it and we turned and tip-toed forward, straining our ears for noises that might mean we had company. We paused outside the door and I put my ear to the wood - nothing. Grace found her keys, selected one and inserted it into the lock. She took the door-handle and turned it slowly, swinging the door open to reveal a dark empty study.

'Lights?' asked Grace quietly.

'The curtains are drawn - yeah, but only the one on the desk.'

She went to the lamp on the large imposing desk that sat in front of the painting of Venice and switched it on while I closed the study door behind us. The low lighting revealed the same long room from New Year's Eve with the desk facing our door and the three leather sofas down to the left at the far end of the room.

'Okay, let's get the safe open,' I said in a matter-of-fact sounding way. God, I sounded cooler than I felt; my chest was a little tight and my face was damp under the balaclava.

Grace obeyed and swung back the painting so we could see the dull impassive metal of the safe and its keypad.

'This is it Grace,' I said rather melodramatically. 'Ready with the code?'

She moved closer to the safe. Carefully and methodically she pressed the six numbers that were required and stood back. As she finished I realised that I was holding my breath and exhaled suddenly. Almost immediately the array turned green and after a quiet beep we heard the click as the locking mechanism released itself.

'The dozy sod didn't bother to change this code either!' I exclaimed, stating the blindingly obvious and grabbing Grace's arm and giving it a squeeze.

'Let's have a look and see what's in it first'

She voiced what had just leapt into both our minds and she was also the first to move towards the steel door. I followed; as thrilled as an Irishman in a free bar but trying hard to keep my mind calm and in neutral - we were still in the middle of a burglary after all. Grace grabbed the door-handle, twisted it and pulled. It looked heavy but swung out smoothly until we could see inside.

'Bugger me!' I heard myself gasp.

'Thanks Marc,' laughed Grace quietly. 'That'll do nicely you bastard!'

21

'Very nicely,' I said, failing to keep the amusement out of my voice. 'But let's not get carried away - there's still a way to go yet,'

There was a lot of money in the safe. More than that – shed loads of money stacked neatly on three shelves. The notes I could see were fifties and twenties and there looked to be enough of them to severely stretch our carrying capacity of two slim-line back packs.

'Okay, let's fill the bags carefully,' I ordered, sounding too much like the teacher I was.

'Yes sir!' Grace laughed quietly again, already unzipping her pack.

Hers was empty so we filled that one first; stuffing as much of the money in as we possibly could so that I had to compress the pack with both hands while Grace zipped it back up. There was still the rope, mobile and knife in my pack so I jammed the latter into my jeans pocket and discarded the rope and phone on the floor while we filled the pack with the rest of the bank notes and then squeezed them back in on top.

Once the packs were full and the safe empty of money Grace closed the door and swung the view of the Grand Canal back into place. I walked over to the study entrance while Grace switched off the light, using her torch to guide her way back to me. This was certainly easier than teaching I thought as we closed the study door behind us and began to tiptoe back to the front door.

That's when things started to stop going according to plan. We'd only gone a few paces when I heard the faint sound of voices somewhere up ahead. I stopped and froze, straining to hear what was being said and whether or not the source of the noise was coming our way. It didn't take long for me to answer the second question – the voices were getting louder.

'Back into the study!' I whispered, turning towards Grace who was just behind me. She was already reaching into her jeans for the keys and shoved one into the Yale, switching her torch off simultaneously. She dived into the darkness and I followed, closing the door as rapidly and as quietly as I could.

It goes without saying that I felt sicker than the proverbial parrot - we had been so close and now this! I flashed on my torch and pointed at the sofas.

'Quick, behind the couches!'

Grace's eyes opened wider and seemed to say 'what, again?' and I almost smiled myself underneath my balaclava. Actually I felt more like crying but there wasn't any time for embarrassing displays of emotion.

We scampered down the study and dived out of sight. All I could hear for a while was my own heart threatening to break the two hundred barrier and then the ominous sounds of voices outside the study door. I switched off the torch.

'No!' Grace sighed quietly in the darkness. It seemed to sum up the situation perfectly

Within a matter of seconds the lights in the room came on brightly and I heard Gilbert's voice. What the fuck was he doing here? Grace gripped my arm so hard I had to grit my teeth to stop myself gasping; in other circumstances having her fingers around a bicep I had spent long hours honing at the Leisure Centre would have been pleasantly distracting but not at that moment.

'Put the bag on the chair by the desk,' Gilbert instructed whoever he was with.

The other person seemed to do as they were told judging by the sounds I could hear. I also realised the significance of the order - something was going to be put into or removed from the bag and I had a horrible feeling the safe might be involved in the exchange. If that were the case then the cat would be out of the bag and the fur would be flying. Fan-fucking-tastic.

'Easy on the death grip,' I whispered into Grace's ear.

If it hadn't been for her balaclava my lips would have been against her flesh which is an odd thing to think about in such a delicate situation. I wondered what I should do - about our situation that is - not my close proximity to Grace's ear and as I did I noticed that sweat was trickling down the back of my neck. How the hell had I ever let myself get into this situation? I squeezed Grace's hand and at the same time attempted to weigh up my options. Violence would seem to be a possibility if things turned ugly - the gun would have come in handy on that front but I tried not to dwell on another wrong decision. Naturally it would be best to avoid a confrontation in which I might suffer physical harm but if needs must I hoped my karate would be up to the task. I cursed the fact I had no easy access to a weapon except for the Swiss army knife that would probably only give Gilbert and his mate a couple of a hernias from laughing so much if I attempted to threaten them with it.

We waited for the noise of the opening safe and the sounds of disbelief and spontaneous combustion that would announce the discovery of empty shelves. Toys were going to leave pram big time I suspected and I hoped they wouldn't land anywhere near us.

'What the fuck - where's the fucking money?' was Gilbert's predictable reaction to what must have been a major disappointment pretty much guaranteed to ruin his evening. Of course it also meant that our crime had been discovered and our own evening had also taken a decided turn for the worse.

For some reason I had a repeat of the almost uncontrollable urge to giggle that I seemed to have experienced regularly over the past few months. Surprisingly, I could feel from the sudden tensing in Grace's body against mine that she had seen the funny side of it too. Of course that made it worse but the shear desperation of our precarious position behind the couch did stop me from going from silent mode into a scene-stealing burst of loud guffaws. I waited for the next move from in front of the safe, hoping rather naively Gilbert and his pal would bugger off and allow us to make our escape. Not surprisingly it wasn't going to be that easy.

'Some cunt's been in here while I was at the club,' went on Gilbert, still shouting. 'I should have taken it myself earlier instead of bringing you two back to handle the delivery. What the fuck am I going to do? Don't just stand there with your fucking mouth open - get Barry and have a look around, whoever it is can't have been gone long. Oh send Sasha up here as well - she might have heard something. No, on second thoughts I'll find the silly bitch myself.'

There followed the sounds of closing the safe, some movement and then the room went dark as Gilbert left the study. After a few seconds, I got up, switched on my torch and tip-toed over to the door. What was I going to do next? Grace was standing up as well waiting for me to make a decision.

'Okay, it looks like leaving sharpish would be a sensible option,' I announced as calmly as I could. I felt like someone had kicked me in the stomach but I had to get my act together rather than feel sorry for myself. 'Can you find us a way out that gives us a fighting chance of avoiding an embarrassing scene with the natives?'

Grace nodded.

'I'll do my best, we could use a back door or a window - I'll play it by ear when we're down there' she said bravely, making me feel even worse for putting her in this much danger. I went over to her and put my hands on her shoulders.

'I'm sorry,' I said. 'I should never have agreed to this but I'll do my best to get you home safe.'

'Fuck, it's not your fault, but thanks for saying - I didn't know you had such a sense of the dramatic.'

Typical, always the smart-arsed reply - I slapped my balaclava-covered forehead in feigned exasperation and went back to the study door, unlocked it, edged it open and stood listening. There were voices coming from a long way off but certainly not from the corridor so I ushered her in front of me and followed her down the short passage and right into the main corridor. We passed the main stairs and I realised we were headed towards the back stairs we had used on the night of the party. With my ears straining for sounds of Gilbert and his minions I stayed close behind Grace until we came to the stairs and, after pausing at the top, we crept as quickly and as quietly as we could down to ground level.

There were two directions to choose from now. We were standing in a low-ceilinged, windowless room about ten feet square which had passages heading off from it to the right and left. I could hear raised voices off to the left where I had an idea the kitchen was situated so it seemed like a no-brainer as to the way we would be going. That was until we heard the sound of a woman scream in pain or shock coming loudly down the passage leading to the kitchen. I guessed it must have been Sasha although I'd never heard her scream before and the balaclava and the intervening brickwork wasn't helping on the hearing front.

'The bastard's murdering her.' Grace sounded horrified which I thought was pretty commendable seeing as Sasha couldn't have been one of her favourite people.

'Where are they?' I asked quietly, 'Is that the kitchen down there?'

'Yes. Gilbert sounds like he's lost it - what shall we do?'

Grace was right; I could hear Gilbert's raised voice, threatening and unpleasant and Sasha's shrill cries in reply. It also sounded as if the kitchen utensils were being rearranged judging by the crashing sounds that were now coming our way. Shit, what was I going to do? It really wasn't my problem; we ought to be off while we had the chance but the woman sounded desperate.

'Look, hang onto this a minute,' I said quickly, letting the back-pack slip off my shoulders. 'I'll just make sure he's not murdering her? Wait for me, I won't be a minute. Get the mobile out ready to call Chris while you're waiting.'

'Okay.' Grace whispered. 'But don't be long, for God's sake.'

I didn't bother to answer; I just squeezed her shoulders and turned and tip-toed as quickly as I could towards the kitchen. The door was about ten feet away and pushed almost closed but I could hear their voices long before I reached it. Sasha was shouting.

'I told you for the last time - I don't know what happened Marc. I was down here waiting for you to pick me up like you said. If you come near me again I'll stick this in you, you fucking bastard.'

I came up to the door and peeped around into the kitchen keeping as far back as I could. Gilbert and Sasha had taken the genre of the domestic row into territory I wasn't familiar with. My ex had probably been tempted to grab a kitchen knife and disembowel me on several occasions but had always resisted the temptation; but then again I had never given her a shiny red cheek which was what Sasha was sporting after what I guessed was a slap from her lover. She was pointing a nasty-looking carving knife in his direction and standing behind a large pine kitchen table which was keeping Gilbert a safe distance away from her. I was almost side-on to the confrontation - they could have both spotted me if either had turned their heads about ninety degrees but neither seemed interested in anything other than each other.

'You're telling me that some cunts break in and you don't notice,' spat Gilbert. 'You stupid bitch; the alarm was on when I left for the club and when I get back it's off - you must think I'm fucking stupid. How do you explain that?'

'Fuck off, I told you' shouted Sasha. 'I've been in here having something to eat and watching the TV. I popped out to the car to fetch my make-up bag – I'm sorry about the alarm but it was only ten or fifteen minutes ago – I didn't think it was worth resetting with you coming back. Now piss off and leave me alone!'

Sasha was game all right but I didn't think it was going to do her much good. She had also done me a bit of a favour by cancelling the alarm for the sake of looking her best for Gilbert. Was that ironic? Gilbert himself looked out of control and he started edging around the table towards me but with his eyes fixed on her. All of a sudden he heaved the whole table towards her, rotating it so that she was trapped between a wall, the cupboards behind her and the table on her left. At the same instant he stepped in front of her so that only the knife was keeping him at bay.

It was obvious to me in that Gilbert would try to get the knife and that Sasha was going to be sorry if he succeeded. He was just a thug - the dinner jacket he was wearing was the only civilised thing about him – and for a thug winning the physical battle is all that matters. As these half-formed thoughts flashed across my mind Gilbert reached out with his right hand even more quickly and made a grab for the knife. He just missed and the blade caught him on the hand but Sasha was too slow to stop his left reaching her wrist and twisting it sharply so that it fell to the quarry-tiled floor with a clatter.

'You cut me!' he roared, taking her by both wrists. Sasha cried out and tried to kick him in the crutch. She must have caught him a glancing blow because his arse went backwards slightly in that amusing way footballers' do when they intercept a ball with their testicles but it wasn't enough to make him release his grip. He let go of one of her wrists and slapped her hard around the temple and which left me no choice.

I pulled back the door and took two steps into the room, coming up from behind Gilbert's left shoulder. He must have seen something out of the corner of his eye because he began to turn his head to check but by that time an arcing right hook was already on its way. Instead of catching him on the side of the face, his movement meant that my fist landed just above his mouth on his left cheek. It was a hard punch - not full power in case I ended up with a broken hand but I knew I'd really stung the bastard and my hand certainly felt it through the padding on the knuckle. He staggered back his hands falling almost down at his sides but I didn't get in too close. Instead I turned sideways and kicked him in the face with the heel of my right foot with as much controlled force as I could. He tumbled backwards over the table and then toppled sideways onto the floor, his head finally meeting the tiles with dull thud.

I glanced over at Sasha who, not unsurprisingly, was crying and rubbing her reddened face. Keeping my eye on her, I went over to Gilbert and checked his breathing. His lungs seemed to be operational which I hoped meant he would be okay except for a sore head. I turned to Sasha and put a finger to my lips before placing my palms together as if in a prayer of supplication. She didn't smile but just stared blankly at me through her tears, searching for an expression that never materialised. I was momentarily torn but I knew I had to leave before Gilbert's reinforcements appeared so I backed out of the kitchen and then raced down the passageway to Grace – there were too many other people relying on me not getting caught to worry about Sasha now.

At least Gilbert would know she wasn't involved in the robbery. Shit - would he? And what would Sasha do now? Fuck, bollocks and buggery; I couldn't leave her in the kitchen!

Grace was standing at the far end of the passage, a slim, black silhouette holding my back-pack. As I reached her I was just about to say we needed to get back to the kitchen when Sasha started screaming. My mind made up for me – she was on her own now. I grabbed my pack from Grace who turned and began running down the passage towards fuck knows where. I followed as fast as I could, slinging my pack into position on my back as I ran. It was only a few strides before Grace turned left into a darkened utility room which led out through a door into the night. We were at the far end of the house away from the front gates, a hundred metres away. We stopped in the shadow of the corner of the house and listened. I noticed with a frisson of trepidation that the whole of the front of the house was lit up like Buckingham Palace for the tourists, revealing Gilbert's BMW and the two other cars that had been there when we arrived..

'What next?' breathed Grace, looking at me through the holes in her balaclava.

'Call Chris, tell him to park as close as he can without being seen. We're going to run for it.'

Grace made the call while I waited to see if Gilbert's two goons, or however many there were, appeared. I hoped they had both been attracted by Sasha's screams for help leaving the coast clear but I could only just hear her myself now we was outside so my expectations might have been more properly classified as wishful thinking. Maybe they were looking for us over near the gate and couldn't hear her which would be bad news so far as our escape route was concerned. Suddenly, however, Sasha went quiet so I hoped at least one heavy was with her for a moment although it wouldn't be long before he would be directed out towards us. Grace finished whispering into the mobile to Chris so I made up my mind we should leave while we could.

'Can you take us to the gates via the back of the house,' I asked quietly.

'Think so - now?'

'Yeah, and as fast as you can.'

Grace wheeled around to her right and began to trot down the side of the main house and away from the floodlit front area. We were on a generous paved pathway that went between the house and the outbuildings which I had always assumed were stables and garages or suchlike. It was pretty dark but my eyes had grown accustomed to the low light levels so I had no problem following Grace's back and watching where I was putting my feet.

At the corner of the house Grace didn't turn right and stay close to the rear of the building as I expected her to but carried straight on down the path away from the house keeping a large grass lawn on our right. After thirty or forty yards we came to a path running across our own and now Grace turned right. She was moving faster now so I tried to concentrate on running efficiently and staying alert, straining my ears for any sounds of pursuit or discovery. I guessed we were behind the lawn at the back of the house on one of the paths running through the ornamental trees and shrubs I had looked out at all those months ago when tutoring Grace up in her rooms.

At the next corner we left the main gardens and half-sprinted, keeping low, over the grass that extended as far as the property boundary and the gate. There were mid-sized trees dotted about and it was a relief that we were partially shielded from the driveway by the neat, waist-high hedge, even though the route up to the house was lit up by two rows of lights set into the ground on either side of the gravelled surface. I hoped we were far enough away from the drive to be invisible in the dark of the night even though it felt the opposite because I could clearly see the main gates up ahead and the lit-up area around the drive. As I ran I scanned around looking for company but as far as I could tell there was no one about so with any luck Sasha was keeping everyone occupied.

As Grace neared the gates and our way over the laurels she slowed which was a relief because I wasn't accustomed to sprinting in a balaclava and a back-pack for over two hundred metres. She chose a route that kept us about twenty yards from the drive until we reached the hedge and then she stooped even lower as she ran along to the gates where the lights banished any chance of staying completely unseen. She stopped a few yards from our exit point and stepped into the cover of the laurels. I followed her into the greenery and bent over, hands on my knees beside her, breathing deeply; I would have preferred to pant but I didn't want her worrying about me having a seizure on top of all the other excitement. Grace pulled out the mobile and rang Chris again, halting the call after three rings as arranged; the Volvo should be passing us in one minute. Security lights were now illuminating the road in front of the gates so I whispered.

'Over you go, be careful and try to keep out of the light.'

Grace gave me a thumbs-up to signal that she understood and then turned and took a grip of a laurel branch beside the pillar. She lifted herself into the hedge and once she was at the top I followed. A few seconds later I landed beside her in the road. All seemed quiet and still but nevertheless I stepped out a little into the road to see if the Volvo was coming and it was then I heard a man's voice say:

'Freeze arsehole! Both of you - get away from the side and into the road, now!'

It probably goes without saying that it was one of the most sickening moments in my life, making even our adventures in Gilbert's study seem hardly worth a chuckle over a cup of tea. Success was almost ours; we had lived the dream so to speak and now I was waking up to an unpleasant reality. We were into injury time with a one goal advantage to clinch the title and the referee had awarded an undeserved penalty against us. On top of all that it was embarrassing because of the way I jumped in surprise at the man's order and managed to let out an un-masculine gasp of shock. I took a deep breath and took a few seconds before replying, trying to regain some composure and think clearly.

'Make your mind up - what is it to be, freeze or get into the road,' I said in my best Irish accent.

'Just do as you're fucking told Paddy - and you.'

He was standing next to the pillar on the other side of the gates where he must have been waiting for us. The lights of the drive showed us he was another thickset bouncer type in a tuxedo with a pistol like Ben's held up in front of him in both hands. I stepped out as ordered and Grace followed behind me. I wanted to scream in frustration and then I saw he had a friend which just about put the tin lid on the situation.

Or did it? The 'friend' was standing in the road about ten metres behind the guy with the pistol and it was then I recognised the shape of the shaved head and the old donkey jacket outlined by the glow of the driveway lighting. It was Chris, and forgive me but there's no other way to say this, he had something long and shiny in his hands.

'Freeze yourself arse-hole - or you'll be getting both barrels and trust me, you'll remember what a poor choice you made every time you sit down for the rest of your life. Now, just let the gun drop without you moving anything except your little pinkies.'

Chris's attempt at a Southern Irish was even worse than mine but what he was saying amounted to probably the most welcome words I think I had ever heard - well from a man anyway.

Tuxedo-guy hesitated so Chris obligingly cocked both barrels to encourage him to do as he was being advised. The gun slipped out of our party-pooper's fingers and landed on the tarmac with a clatter - the football analogy was the last thing on my mind but it looked as if the keeper had saved the penalty after all.

'Oops – looks like you're fucked,' I said, stepping forward towards the pissed-off looking heavy. 'Right, you two keep away from the camera and you face down on the road and no peeping.'

As he did as he was told I looked back at Grace in the shadows and put my fingers to my lips to warn her not to speak and then I stepped over into the light to pick up the latest addition to my gun collection. I figured it didn't matter if I was on tape but Chris's face was uncovered and even in her outfit Grace was definitely a woman so they had to stay out of sight of the camera I could see in the tree a few metres away. I rested my wrist on a cross beam and aimed the gun through the gates at the camera on the tree. It took two shots to smash it to pieces, which was less embarrassing than it might have been. Now we had to be quick. I turned to Grace again.

'Get the rope out of my bag and then go and get the car, Mick and I will restrain Mr Sneaky.'

Grace nodded and pulled the rope out the top of my pack, took the car keys from Chris's out-stretched hand and sprinted off down the road into the darkness

'Hands behind you,' I hissed at Tuxedo-guy. 'And don't look round or I'll forget my vow of non-violence.'

While Chris stood by with his shotgun at the ready I cut off a length of rope with the finally-useful Swiss army knife and started to tie our prisoner's hands behind his back. Just as I did I spotted another figure come running out of the house towards us. Even at a distance of fifty metres or so I could see from the security lights he was carrying a gun.

'Mick, remind them how dangerous it is to play with guns,' I ordered and Chris stepped up to the gates and fired off both barrels towards the house. At that range a shotgun isn't going to kill anyone but it had the desired effect of making the guy hit the ground hurriedly. The rope tied, I slipped off my balaclava and shoved it on my victim's head back to front so that he couldn't see and dragged him out of the road into the gateway. In the meantime Chris had reloaded and fired off another salvo and then the Volvo arrived and drew up past the gates out of sight of the house.

'Get in!' I shouted at Chris and as he ran to the car I stepped forward and emptied the gatekeeper's gun through the bars of the gate over the head of the still prone figure on the gravel. Then it was my turn to run to the Volvo and wrench open the back door and dive in.

We accelerated away towards the main road.

'Straight to the church and don't spare the horses, I said urgently towards Grace as I sat up. 'If the idiot I fired at starts a car and comes after us we're in trouble.'

'No sweat Neil,' Chris said from the front seat. 'It's only a few minutes away and they'll have to avoid running over the bloke you left in the gateway.'

I guessed he was probably right and relaxed a little and let out a sigh.

'Bugger me, what a night', I gasped, pulling off the backpack and sinking back in the seat. 'Am I dreaming or are we really driving away from that house of fucking horrors? Fuck me Grace, I'm never going in that study again whatever you say. I'm also never going to go running around in the dark like that again either - dressed like a tit trying to keep up with Paula fucking Radcliff out for a quarter mile sprint in backpacks just to make it interesting - God, I'm sweating like a pig. Then to top it all off I have some muppet point a gun at me which is a very sobering experience to put it mildly.'

'But we did get the money,' said Grace, glancing over her shoulder and grinning at me. She had taken off her balaclava and could see her cheeks were flushed and her fair hair was matted with the sweat and exhilaration of the evening.

'Hey yeah we did!' I said emphatically. 'We got Gilbert's money - in the end we got the bastard's money – maybe you should keep your eyes on the road for now though – it would be a shame to die now when we're so rich!'

'What happened?' said Chris, sounding more than a little interested. 'You were a bit longer than I thought you'd be.'

'Complications, to put it mildly but I think we're all right. We'll fill you in over a drink.'

'Is Sasha okay?' asked Grace, as we drew up to the junction with the Sevenoaks road.

'Sasha, not -?!' I thought Chris was going to bring up my history with the aforementioned lady so I quickly started to explain what had transpired in the study and kitchen while Grace made the right turn towards the church where we had left her car.

'Anyway,' I said, 'you never said you were bringing along your gamekeeper's equipment although it's a fucking good job that you did!'

'Had it in the boot under a blanket for emergencies; Gilbert sounded like a serious piece of bad news so I brought it along. When you called me first time I parked the car close and crept up to the gates to have a look and there was our friend waiting for you. I went back and got the gun from the boot just as you sent the one minute warning. You know the rest.'

We were almost at the church now and Grace turned into the narrow entrance to the car park that stretched around to the side of the church away from the road and where her car was parked.

'Coming back to Sasha - do you think she'll be alright now,' Grace asked in a concerned voice.

'God knows but I hope she doesn't stick that knife in Gilbert and claim it was the burglar,' I grinned nervously.

'That would make it too complicated if the police get involved.'

'Can't see it myself,' said Chris. 'Gilbert is the only one who sounds like a likely murderer.'

'I thought of calling the police now actually,' I said. 'A quick call to send them over to Gilbert's just to make sure Sasha gets out.'

'Good idea,' nodded Chris. 'We don't want someone getting grief because of us. Okay with you Grace?'

'Course - she's a bitch but no one deserves to die for that. You could use the mobile before we ditch it.'

That made me feel better; I had been concerned about Sasha's fate since I ran with Grace from the house. The Volvo stopped and Grace and I got out.

'See you in half an hour then,' she said brightly as I opened the front passenger door to let myself in while Chris heaved himself across behind the steering wheel. 'I hope you've got the drinks in Neil.'

'What do you think? Now drive carefully.'

She smiled at me and then turned and strode confidently over to her car, got inside and drove off slowly.

I sat down in the front seat next to Chris who was ready to drive again. Adrenalin was still keeping me firing so the trip back seemed over very quickly. On the way I made the call and told the police there had been shots fired at Gilbert's house and hoped that would get them access. That done I settled back in the comfortable leather seat in the Volvo and grinned to myself - it looked like we had actually done it!

22

When Chris and I arrived back at the cottage Grace's car was already outside in the drive and the light was on in the kitchen. I got out of the Volvo, pulled open the car's back door and yanked the two heavy packs off the back seat. I looked at my watch: just past eleven thirty - it wasn't even that late!

'God I need a piss,' I announced following Chris to the back door. 'Take these will you and chuck 'em in the front room or something?'

I went into the bathroom and had a very necessary pee and an equally welcome face wash. Then, resting my hands on the washbasin, I leant forward and studied my reflection grinning back at me. I felt good - not many blokes of my or any other age for that matter got to pull off the stunt we had managed tonight. On top of that I had enjoyed nearly every minute. Okay, the unwelcome surprise near the end at the front gates was a little hairy, but in the end we had made it. I could see how adrenalin might become as addictive as nicotine. Eat your heart out Marlowe.

And the face didn't look too bad either did it? There weren't many grey hairs in the perpetual stubble and the number three haircut and I reckoned it would only need a day or two in the sun to bring my tan back up to scratch. Maybe Renia might be worth another try once the holidays came - oops, I was losing track of reality again.

After a moment or two of the pointless but admittedly congenial day-dreaming I dragged myself away from my own reflection and went through to the front room where Chris and Grace had lit a fire and were sitting waiting for me.

Grace had removed her trainers and was sitting on the sofa, arms wrapped around her knees and chin tucked in against the chill of the room. Chris was perched next to her rolling a cigarette, his tin of tobacco and *Rizlas* on the carpet between his feet.

'So have you counted it yet?' I said, smiling and standing in the doorway.

'You're the bloody maths teacher Neil so we thought you'd want to supervise,' grinned Chris, looking up at me.

'Sod the money for a minute, let's have a drink. I've got some bubbly in the fridge and I need alcohol and a fag before anything else.'

I retrieved the champagne and three glasses and poured the three of us a drink.

'To a night I'll never forget.' I said, raising my glass.

'Yeah,' said Grace with a conviction that made Chris and I laugh. 'We did it, we actually did it!'

We sipped the wine in silence for a few moments before Grace, obviously unable to contain her enthusiasm, got off the sofa and slid over to the bags on her knees.

'Shall we?' she asked.

'Give us old-timers a minute sugar,' I sighed. 'How about you make a start and we'll join you in a mo' I'm going to savour this cigarette if you don't mind.'

Grace unzipped the packs and emptied the money onto the floor into a pile. Chris whistled in surprise when he saw the size of the stash for the first time.

'Bugger me, it really was worth the effort of coming up to visit.'

Rather conveniently the money came in uniformly sized wads held together by elastic bands. It didn't take long for

Grace to realise that each wad was worth ten thousand or five thousand quid, depending on whether it consisted of fifty or twenty pound notes. It was then just a question of counting the wads and doing some simple arithmetic. Chris and I had hardly finished our cigarettes before she had finished sorting the wads into two piles and counting the number in each. After ten minutes or so we all agreed there were ninety wads of fifties and thirty wads of twenties.

'Okay, Grace, how much?' I asked mischievously.

'God knows,' she smiled gleefully, 'but I bet you're going to tell me.'

'Go on,' I said encouragingly. 'After all those lessons surely you can make a reasonable estimate.'

She considered the neatly stacked wads.

'Okay, I'd say about a quarter of a million.'

'No, it's more than that,' chipped in Chris shaking his head. 'There's about half a million I reckon. Mind you I didn't even get O level so I'm not feeling that confident.'

'You two are rubbish,' I groaned, looking as shocked as I could. 'I'll think you'll find we're sitting in front of over a million. A million and fifty thousand give or take.'

'What?!'

'Is it?'

They looked satisfyingly stunned.

'That's right – you're both so rich it doesn't matter you can't count!' I looked at Chris. 'What are you going to do with yours mate - two hundred thousand of that is yours. Do you want me to launder it into a bank account for you or can you do it yourself?'

Chris laughed.

'I'm buggered if I know Neil. I never really thought we'd make any money so I've nothing in mind. I only came along to keep you out of trouble! I know what you mean though - questions will be asked if we all start flashing the cash or trying to open a bank account with a couple of hundred thousand in readies. How are you going to do it?'

Grace looked at me with an enigmatic smile as if to say 'yes, please tell' as Chris spoke. I rubbed my face wearily and owned up straight away.

'Okay, good question to which I haven't the faintest bloody idea. You know what I'm like - there didn't seem any reason to go to all the trouble and research to find out about money-laundering when there was a chance the safe might be empty or we might never even make it into Gilbert's place. It seemed like an inefficient use of time, like tempting fate, and I've had a lot of balls in the air recently. Now it has to be done I'm sure we can sort something out. Come on, how hard can it be?!'

'Good old Dr Mac,' teased Grace, finishing her first glass and reaching for the bottle for a refill. 'I hope you're right.'

'I know, I know,' I said defensively. 'Should have sorted it out before but there you go. It's a couple of months until the summer holidays so that should be enough time to do some serious research and then I'll sort it out when I'm free. Whatever happens, Gilbert must never know so that means we have to be subtle with a capital s. I don't even want to do it in the UK because who knows how the criminal grapevine works?'

'So if I take mine tonight you don't want me popping into Barclay's tomorrow?' Chris grinned. 'It's funny - in all the films I've ever watched the only problem is stealing the money - it's just taken as read. For us that was the easy bit.'

'Ironic eh,' mused Grace, looking at me.

'Something like that Grace -'

'I've got it.' Interrupted Chris, with a snap of his fingers. 'I think I'll just open a few savings accounts and pay a little in at a time. Hey if I open ten different accounts that's only twenty grand in each and I could pay it in gradually over a couple of years.'

'Sounds good,' I agreed, 'but be careful - we've got the same name and you could lead them back to me.'

'You always worry too much,' my brother pointed out knowingly. 'Don't panic - I've got kids too and there's no way I'll take a risk with them involved.'

I felt relieved by his reassurances and left it at that. So far we had the perfect crime and it would stay that way so long as no one ever got wind of our new wealth.

'I still don't understand why Gilbert would keep so much money in his safe,' said Grace reasonably. 'It was lovely that he did of course, but why?'

'Maybe he was money-laundering himself,' I said. 'I've been thinking about it and I guess a casino is a great place for generating large amounts of cash. Maybe the money was from drugs or to buy drugs?'

'Or in other words you haven't a clue,' said Chris wryly.

'What will you two do with your shares,' asked Grace, changing the subject and grabbing the champagne bottle to refill her glass again. Chris declined another but I gratefully accepted. Getting drunk seemed like a reasonable and attractive option and the room was now pleasantly warm.

'It'll just be nice to have some money in the bank for a change,' said Chris.

'Steady Chris', I chuckled. 'We don't want to raise questions with our extravagant lifestyles. Is Devon so exciting there's no room in your life for a sports-car or something?'

'Alright, a new car maybe; I could even afford a bloody Land Rover now!'

'Okay then Neil, what about you,' said Grace, looking at me with an interested expression. 'What about a Thai bride?'

'Bollocks, I'm not that desperate. Alright then, one luxury; how about a blonde in her twenties with great legs whose only interested in me for my body - how's that?'

'You're not that rich Neil,' Grace observed sarcastically. 'Come on, seriously; one sensible thing.'

'A sobering thought…okay, one luxury; let me see. You know, I can't really think of anything. I like my car so no need to change there unless I get it tuned up, um, am I really that boring? Ha, got it - a season ticket at The Emirates - only about a grand so there'd be enough left to give up having to work every hour God made and do something else. Mind you the waiting list is probably four or five years so I'll have to be patient'

'Gosh you are easy to please,' said Grace dismissively.

'No need to scoff, what about you? A huge wardrobe of designer gear and a lifetime supply of 'Heat' magazine?'

'Very funny, no - I'd like to travel for a year and be able to hang out in nice hotels wherever I stayed. Then carry on as normal - you know, university etc.'

It went on like that for a while until, after a third or fourth glance at his watch Chris said he ought to be off. I tried to persuade him to stay, but he insisted; he wanted to get back to Devon. I told him he was mad but he'd always been stubborn and there really was no way of changing his mind. I packed two hundred thousand into one of the backpacks and then helped him check he had all his gear. Grace came with me to see him out to the Volvo.

'Be careful mate,' I said, giving him a manly hug and a few slaps on the back. 'Thank God you bought the fucking shotgun.'

'Yeah, you too Neil; and don't worry, I won't go flashing the cash around. It's going straight into the loft until I get organised.'

'Bye Chris,' grinned Grace, reaching out and giving him another hug. 'It was nice to meet you, even if it was only briefly!'

Chris chucked the back-pack in the boot and then started up the engine. We watched him reverse out and drive off into the night before we raced back inside out of the cold.

'I'm starving with all this excitement!' exclaimed Grace as we came into the kitchen. 'Have you anything edible in here?'

'There's cheese and odds and ends in the fridge,' I said, trying to remember what I had. Thinking was becoming more of an effort than usual. 'There's bread, biscuits and crisps and stuff in the cupboard in the corner as well. If you're doing toast I wouldn't say no myself - God is it me or do you feel completely wasted as well?'

'It's just your age Neil - you've probably had too much excitement. Why don't you have a lie down while I make us some supper?' Grace gave me an understanding look of mock sympathy as she popped a couple of slices of wholemeal in the toaster. 'Have you any more wine or would you prefer a cup of cocoa?'

'Fuck off Grace - there's another bottle of white at the top of the fridge but if you open that you'll be staying the night.'

She continued to grin at me from over by the toaster.

'So you've made up the spare bed then?'

'It's always made up - you never know who might pop in late at night,' I said truthfully. 'Look, you sort out the food and I'll open the wine and make sure the fire doesn't die. My brain may have stopped working but I'm not drunk enough yet and I think what we've done deserves a decent celebration.'

The next hour or so is, like recent champions league final parties, still a bit of a blur. We finished the champagne with the cheese, toast and crisps Grace found in the kitchen and moved seamlessly onto the white. I'm a light-weight at the best of times so I was soon laughing at anything remotely amusing that Grace said which seemed to be nearly everything. We talked the usual quasi-serious bollocks that drunks do with the chat mainly devoted to Grace filling me in on all the gossip that, as a teacher, I usually missed out on. By the time she was finished, if I could have actually remembered anything I was told, I think I would have had a definitive knowledge of the sexual habits of most of last year's Upper Sixth. I eventually sank into a prone position at one end of the sofa with my feet up because Grace elected to sit on the floor facing the fire with her head propped up near my knees.

Eventually the wine was finished and I found the combined effects of the long and, let's be fair, exhausting evening and the alcohol were making it difficult for me to keep my eyes open. I staggered to the bathroom and then returned and surveyed the pile of money and Grace's comical attempts to stuff it in the remaining backpack. Her lack of coordination seemed to indicate that I wasn't the only one who felt his reactions should be measured in minutes rather than micro-seconds and I laughed out loud.

'I'll get a bin liner and we'll put it all in that,' I said, stepping back into the kitchen and finding a black bag under the sink.

While Grace tottered out to use the loo I just about managed to get all of the bundles of bank notes into the bag and tie it at the top. When she came back she followed me up the stairs to the first floor.

'Watch yourself when you go downstairs,' I said at the top of the twisting flight. 'It would be embarrassing if you broke your neck after spending the night here. I'll chuck the money in my room.'

From the tiny landing it was possible to touch both bedroom doors simultaneously. I pushed open the door into my room, flicked on the light and dumped the sack in the middle of the floor while Grace propped herself against the door frame. She looked round and took in my quaint little sleeping quarters and the three pieces of furniture: double bed, chest of drawers and a bedside table.

'Very minimalist Neil,' she observed.

'I had to get rid of my cuddly toy collection to pay off some debts.'

'How sad.' She smiled and looked straight into my eyes. 'Do you want to make love?'

It would be disingenuous of me to say I was surprised by her question - for fuck's sake she was gorgeous and we had a connection as well. I had been fighting a rearguard action since Chris had left to keep my hands off her anyway and still wasn't sure what had stopped me making the same suggestion myself while we were downstairs. If I'm honest I'd rather she had just pushed me back on the bed and taken me there and then. I could have mumbled a few half-hearted protests while undoing her bra strap and argued afterwards I was too weak and drunk to resist.

'I keep telling you you're not my type,' I lied. 'Besides I'm drunk so I doubt if I could satisfy anyone tonight, not even myself. I admit you're gorgeous and absolutely out of my league but I'll only embarrass myself and why spoil a wonderful friendship?'

She looked so utterly beautiful standing there it was all I could do to stop myself grabbing her and feeling for that bra strap, but before I succumbed to the impulse Grace grinned in acceptance of my inane little speech.

'Mmm, I see you're not the romantic type,' she said. 'You're probably right I guess... so am I in here?'

'Oh - yeah,' I stepped back and leaned over and pushed her bedroom door open. I sounded chirpy but it was hard work. 'See - a bit more feminine for your ladyship.'

'But I only get a single bed and it's so cold,' she observed, looking first at the spare bed and then back at me with a wistful smile.

'Oh fuck it, come in with me and we'll shag ourselves senseless,' I relented. Well that's what the honest version of me in a parallel universe opted for but in the one I occupied I settled for. 'Yeah, as parties go we did pretty well with just the two of us – thanks, I really enjoyed myself - now get to bed and don't snore too loudly.'

Before she could protest I turned back to my room and stumbled through the doorway, closing the door behind me. I didn't even bother to undress properly - it was too chilly away from the fire so I slipped under the duvet minus only my jeans and pants. If Grace forced her way into my bed now she would find a man in T shirt and socks which would finally dispel any drunken ardour she still had.

Then, as I was drifting off, I heard the bedroom door creak open. As I twisted round on the pillow Grace arrived under the duvet. This time I didn't let my conscience stick its oar in and reached out and pulled her towards me.

23

'The time is nine minutes past nine - you may begin.'

Almost a hundred girls opened their examination papers and settled down to see what the next two and a half hours had in store for them. I turned from looking at the clock above the swing doors at the front of the hall and climbed the four steps onto the stage and over to a blackboard perched on an easel positioned in full view of the hall. On the board I chalked up the start and end times, so that every student could keep a check on how much longer they had left before another examination was over.

As far as the next hour was concerned that was my excitement over too. Until ten past ten and the next shift appeared I would be stuck invigilating with two other staff with nothing to do except give the impression of being reasonably awake. I usually sneaked something in to read but Lynn had taken to popping in to check that invigilating staff really were taking their roles seriously so it was going to be a huge challenge not to start dribbling before I was relieved. The seat behind the table in the middle of the stage was acceptably comfortable with arms and a padded seat and back so I sat myself down in it, folded my arms and looked around. I wasn't looking for suspicious behaviour amongst the girls - it was a fucking English exam for God's sake so cheating was about as likely as one of the girls ripping off her top and waving it above her head. No, I was condemned to an hour of day-dreaming and excruciating boredom.

I absently looked along the rows of desks and their occupants and inwardly laughed at something Barry, the Head of Politics, not Gilbert's heavy, had said in the staffroom yesterday. I had been sitting with him waiting for briefing to start and he had been moaning about all the invigilation he was doing.

'You know Neil, the only thing that keeps me awake is deciding which girls are worth being ship-wrecked on a desert island with,' he said with conviction.

'Whoa, steady there mate. If Delores hears you it could be the precursor to an uncomfortable interview in her office.'

'Fuck her,' he grunted. 'What else do they expect if they sit a man down in front of ninety eighteen year old girls, most of whom are sitting with their legs crossed in skirts short enough to see virtually up to their crutches!'

He had a point. Barry wasn't a pervert, just a bloke who, along with most of his sex, liked the look of the female form. He would have no more attempted to sleep with a student than dye his pubic hair pink. Barry himself was also about as attractive as a fresh dog turd so the opportunity wasn't likely to present itself to him in this lifetime either. As for me, the whole sexy schoolgirl thing just washed over me after years in the job so, as the minutes ticked by, I tried to distract myself with other thoughts. That was inevitably the cue for Grace to pop into my head.

Was it really two months since that night with her? She would always be the perfect desert island companion, whether it was witty banter that you wanted or just someone to curl up with by the camp fire. Thank God we were still friends.

I had woken up first and turned to see a mess of blonde hair spread out on the pillow next to me. With a tremendous effort, considering the force of the hang-over that seemed to be pressing on my forehead like a vice, I had slipped out of bed and staggered downstairs to the bathroom. After a shower in the bath I had found some jeans and a T shirt to hide my modesty and then rummaged around to find some extra-strength paracetamol. I made some tea and brought it up to her on a tray along with some toast and the packet of pills in case she was feeling as rough as I was. She stirred beneath the duvet as I came into the bedroom and sat down on my side of the bed with the tray.

'Sleep well?' I said, as her face emerged from under her hair and the top of the duvet. Grace groaned and reached up and dragged her hair back with a slender hand.

'Yeah, but I've felt better.'

'Here, I've brought you some tea and paracetamol for your head if you want it. If you feel anything like me you'll need something to numb the pain.'

Grace propped herself up, keeping the duvet wrapped around under her arms to spare me the sight of more than just her bare shoulders.

'Oh thanks Neil, you're an angel.' She reached out and manoeuvred a couple of pain-killers into her mouth with a sip of the tea. She sat up a little with her tea and looked at me, a hint of a smile on her pale face.

'So we did it,' she announced softly.

'Yeah, we did it. The robbery that is – plus a less well-planned episode as far as I can remember. I hope we're going to be all right after what happened at the end. I'm sorry, I should have known better.'

The smile on her face didn't waver.

'There's nothing to be sorry about Neil. That was probably the best bit apart from the money – it sort of finished off the evening perfectly.'

'Thank God,' I laughed with what must have been very obvious relief. 'I was worried downstairs that you would hate me forever – that I'd taken advantage of you.'

'I think it was both of us taking advantage, don't you. Anyway, there's no harm done if you can cope with a one night stand.'

'It was my first and probably last, believe it or not. Anyway, I hope we can carry on as before.'

'Of course we can. We both know last night was lust in the heat of the moment after a lot of wine. It wasn't my first time if that's what you're worried about - just try not to pine too much after my body and we'll be fine.'

'It'll be tough,' I confessed, standing up and grinning down at her. 'But self-discipline is my middle name so no problem. Anyway, I'm going to clear up and leave you to rejoin the world of the living at you own pace.'

So that was that. I had slept with Grace once and once was all it was going to be. Sex is usually the beginning of the end of most relationships unless you are as single-minded as an addict kicking that cigarette habit. If there's any compromise you'll be back up to your regular quota before you know it and it was the same with Grace – if we started indulging ourselves we would have ended up saying awkward goodbyes pretty soon. I knew it would be tough but it was just a question of getting on with it. Thankfully Grace was even more unwavering than me in putting the night at the cottage behind us and, as the days and weeks went by, it got easier to slip back into our old familiar routine of banter, gossip and maths lessons in Fiona's dining room.

Except it wasn't quite the same of course - it never could be completely. But what the hell, there was no point obsessing about it. Now and again I would beat myself up about what I had allowed to happen but if I'm honest I couldn't regret it completely. We probably both needed to be close that night and for me it wasn't simply an expression of lust.

Maybe a fictional hero like Marlowe would never take advantage of drunken women so I was going to have to let him have the moral high ground there. Anyway, there was a lot more to that night than the sex – we had shared the adventure of a life-time in Gilbert's house. I was determined that Grace and I would be friends until the day they wheeled me into the crematorium perhaps to the accompaniment of The Eagles' "One of Those Nights" playing to mystified mourners. So I saw her occasionally outside of lessons and not only at *The Wanderers* club nights. Most weeks we met for coffee in town or lunch during her mid-day break from her job in *Fenwick's* so we had some time to talk in private.

We were still a million miles from turning the fifties and twenties from Gilbert's safe into bank deposits and it was starting to dawn on me that my initial confidence had been misjudged. I had searched the internet until my brain screamed for mercy and also bought more books that purported to be guides to money laundering. When they arrived through the post, however, they only seemed to deal with people in America and were completely lacking in practical advice. What I wanted was a step-by-step guide as to what to do if you actually had a million in cash but I began to realise that nobody legitimate seemed to have a fucking clue.

For now the money was safe in a furniture warehouse lock-up that I had the bright idea of opening. I had a few boxes and a filing cabinet I needed out of the cottage so

Grace and I took them down to an *Easistore* depot in the Edenbridge industrial estate. We stuffed the money into the filing cabinet and calculated it would be safe there until one of us came up with a sensible plan.

That's not to say we hadn't both had ideas; they just weren't very good ones. I wondered, for example, whether we couldn't take the money to Monte Carlo and see if the casinos were an option worth exploring; could we exchange cash for chips and then get it back later on a debit card? I had to admit that I had never even been in casino in my life so I soon gave up on that one, although Grace pointed out that I could always go up to *The Wealden* to see how things worked. I told her not to be a smart-arse.

One of Grace's ideas seemed to have mileage in it but there wasn't much we could do about it until later in the summer when we were both free. She suggested we take the money to her Greek godfather who owned some hotels and other businesses in Greece and who she was sure would know what to do with the cash. The obvious drawback to the plan was taking the money undetected to Greece. I also wasn't happy about letting him in on our big secret plus the fixer's fee I suspected he would want. After spending holidays with him since she was a toddler Grace was sure she could trust him but I wasn't so keen. Nearly a million quid might easily turn even the wealthiest man's head and who knows who else would have to be let in on the history of the money in order to secure it's laundering. Besides, I really wanted to finish the job myself, so I hoped I could come up with a better plan even though up to now I had drawn a blank.

Talk of Greece reminded me of Renia and our liaison the previous summer. I found myself discussing her with Grace, the first time I had mentioned what had happened to anyone else apart from Chris.

'Why don't you go and find her when we've sorted out the money,' Grace had advised. 'What's the worst that could happen?'

'Okay, let's start with humiliation or heart-break to name but two?'

'At least you'll know. Lots of girls would probably say yes to you – even I succumbed. And don't be put off by the age gap. Less than fifteen years isn't that bad is it? You'll just have to keep fit.'

'Thanks for the advice and the pep-talk. Maybe this summer I'll do something about it.'

24

Some movement in the hall brought me out of my reverie. One or two girls had their hands up for extra paper now and the other two staff were racing each other to provide fresh sheets of A4. Giving out paper is almost the only vaguely interesting thing about invigilating but I was happy to sit up on the stage and let them have all the fun. Lydia was near the front scribbling away, her curly mop hanging down in a dark brown cascade. I caught her eye a few times as she looked up to ponder her next sentence and she gave me a grin. I reckoned I could find room for her on my desert island both for the laughs we would have and the fun I would have looking at her legs. I made a mental note not to bring up the fantasy in a tutorial in case she broke my jaw.

The clock told me I had twenty more minutes to get through before I could escape to the staff room and a cup of tea. The week seemed to be dragging slower than a car pulling a horse-box and it was still only Tuesday. The only thing I had to look forward to today was my gym session with Sasha later on in the evening. This prompted another mind wandering interlude in the direction of a desert island and the possibility of sharing it with my ex lover. Interesting scenarios unfolded as I sat almost comatose in my seat until I dragged myself back to the present and started to examine recent developments with Marc's mistress.

After the scene in the kitchen at Gilbert's I had been seriously concerned about her fate after I had given Gilbert his well-deserved kicking. I watched the local news to no avail and then waited anxiously for the publication of *The*

West Kent News the following Friday to see if it had any reports of burglaries or missing women. As it happened my patience ran out after a couple of days when I thought 'sod it' and rang her.

I made the excuse that I hadn't seen her at the gym lately and wondered if she had settled for a life of leisure. She had laughed and said no, she was actually planning to go that evening. Trying to sound as casual as I could I offered to see her there and treat her to a coffee in the bar afterwards which, to my surprise, she agreed to.

When I came into the gym at seven-thirty she was working hard on the cross-trainer and her figure certainly didn't look too bad; the guy who invented lycra really should have been given some sort of special award for making gym visits more enjoyable. Returning my smile of greeting, her face also appeared clear of any tension or worry so it appeared that I had been fretting for nothing.

I did a weights session, keeping the intensity to a minimum because I didn't want to be dripping with sweat in the bar, and after about forty five minutes I was sat opposite her at a table overlooking the sports hall. Down below through the safety glass I could see about a dozen or so wrinklies were playing badminton very badly.

'So how's life been treating you?' I had enquired. What, or rather who, I really wanted to ask about was Marc Gilbert but I knew that patience was going to be a necessity rather than a virtue if I were to be successful on that score. We chatted like old friends for about ten minutes before I felt able to broach the subject.

'And are you and my best friend Mr Gilbert still an item?' I asked, arranging an innocent smile across my face.

Sasha laughed and rolled her eyes. Her cheeks coloured slightly as well but that was all.

'Yes, just about. He's been very under a lot of pressure lately so things have been a bit hectic. Life is so busy these days.'

I decided to push a bit harder.

'What's he been up to - organising more accidents?'

I said it as teasingly as I could; hoping she wouldn't be offended and relying on my winning smile to keep her sweet. I needn't have worried - for all Sasha's faults she still had her good sense of humour as well as an ability to flirt unsurpassed by all the women I currently knew. Instead of storming out she reached out and administered a playful slap on my hand, her touch reminding me of more intimate moments between us in the past. Maybe it was her way of keeping me in line and it certainly took a few moments for the pleasant warmth of her touch to subside.

'Don't be horrid Neil, Marc isn't like that. His own house was burgled on Friday and he lost a lot of money.'

'God how tragic, I'm not going to be able to sleep tonight.'

'Shut up - I was in the house at the time and I saw one of them. I hope that makes you feel at least a bit guilty!'

'What, you're kidding! Come on tell me the whole story.' I said, sounding as surprised and as interested as I could.

Sasha paused and then ran me through a version of events that tallied pretty much with what I remembered. I was given strict orders not to repeat what she was saying because Gilbert hadn't told the police and he didn't want people knowing any of his business. I nodded knowingly but couldn't help coming to the conclusion that Sasha's mental faculties didn't measure up to her physical gifts - how could she seriously believe that telling the police was a 'waste of time' as Gilbert had said. On the bright side it didn't look as if Grace and I would be ever facing criminal prosecution.

When she came to the part of the tale where I made my entrance I readied as many looks of surprise as I could and used three or four of them in the space of about a minute.

'Marc came rushing into the kitchen shouting his safe had been robbed and had I heard anything. I didn't know what he was talking about - I'd never seen him like that before; he was beside himself.'

'You must have been frightened,' I said, my voice full of bogus concern - I'd worked long enough with women to know how to listen to best effect and this was definitely a complete focus, undivided attention situation. I also wanted to know if she would admit that Gilbert had hit her or whether she was going to gloss over that part of the story.

'Yes I was. Marc can be scary man when he wants to be. Anyway, it's all a bit of a blur but one second I was trying to calm Marc down and the next some bloke dressed totally in black comes in and flattens Marc.'

I furrowed my brow to enhance my surprised expression.

'What!? Are you sure you're not mixing up the evening with a James Bond film. Did Marc put up much of a struggle?'

'He didn't get much of a chance. After couple of seconds he was out cold; then the burglar stops and looks at me.'

I whistled softly and looked sympathetically into her eyes.

'Wow Sasha that must have been a creepy moment. What did you do?'

'Nothing for a second or two because he put a finger to his mouth for me to be quiet and then put his hands together as if he was praying - asking me to not to make a noise. At the time I thought he looked a bit of an idiot. Then I just screamed.'

So I looked like a tit did I? Maybe I should have chosen my outfit more carefully or just let the silly bitch take a beating?

'Sounds like your burglar thought Marc was going to hurt you and stepped in to save you. Why else would he come into the kitchen? Maybe you have a new admirer.'

And maybe I shouldn't have said that. One day I'm going to wise-crack my way into serious trouble. I looked at Sasha for a reaction but she was too busy remembering the details the drama in the kitchen to be distracted by my impetuous remark.

'If he was he didn't hang around to chat me up. He just ran out and then I started to scream.'

'You make men nervous Sasha, I've always said that, especially when you look like you might start screaming. What did he look like or was there a mask?'

'Yes, he was wearing a balaclava - so I won't be picking him out of one of those police line-ups.'

'That would be hard for the police to arrange - them not knowing there was a robbery and all. So Marc has no clues as to the appearance of his burglar - what a bummer.'

Or, from my point of view, great news!

'No, except he was slim and fit looking. Nice eyes as well - come to think of it they were the same colour as yours!'

Fuck. Why do women always have to notice a bloke's eyes - it's as if they all have a Jane Austen gene that kicks in when they're weighing up a man.

Sorry to disappoint you but I was curled up on the sofa last Friday with my inflatable doll practising some chat up lines. You know us maths teachers - girlfriends with pulses are hard to find.'

Sasha laughed.

'Calm down Neil, the thought of you as a burglar is stretching too far into the realms of fantasy.' She sounded almost patronising but I took it on the chin, secure in the knowledge that my plan seemed to have worked, leaving the disposal of the cash as the only remaining job left to do.

'Sorry, it's such an amazing story that's all. Anyway, leaving me out of the list of suspects, has Marc any idea who might have done it?'

'He hasn't a clue I think - except one of the burglars could be a woman according to Mike.'

I had just taken a sip of my coffee and this time it really was an achievement not to choke. Trust me to think I was in the clear only to find a few seconds later that they knew something that could be potentially vital. Would Gilbert extrapolate from this snippet of knowledge to deducing Grace's identity? A sick feeling erupted in my stomach and I had to pause before I could answer in a steady voice.

'A woman! Who's Mike?'

'One of Marc's men. He was down at the main gates when the burglars came out. He nearly got them but there was another guy with a shotgun who gave him the jump.'

'And he says one of them was a woman? What makes him so sure in the dark?'

'Oh he's not one hundred per cent positive. One of them definitely had an Irish accent and he said that there was something about the shape of the other one, even in the dark and wearing black. He only got a glimpse so he could be wrong.'

'Sounds a bit far-fetched to me,' I observed insincerely. 'Anyway, you certainly have had an exciting time. In comparison my life seems pretty mundane to put it mildly.'

'Don't knock boring Neil.' Sasha looked pensively down at the pensioners hitting the shuttles to and fro and then back at me with a resigned look on her face. 'I wouldn't mind a few years of boring but I always seem to pick the wrong sort of men for that, present company excluded of course.'

'Thanks, or are you saying I'm boring? There goes another self-delusion shattered. Maybe I should give up the stamp collecting and take up something a bit more adventurous.'

'Don't worry, you're not boring Neil - you're just, how can I say it, restless maybe? When we went out you were quite entertaining but I never felt you were ever really in the relationship. Perhaps it was too soon after your divorce or there was someone else you weren't telling me about. When Marc came along he seemed to want more.'

I don't know what was more irritating - the fact that I had been so transparent or Sasha's assertion that Gilbert wanted more, when I would have bet my share of his money that he only wanted more or less the same as I had done - a sexy lover who wasn't so emotionally demanding herself. Gilbert was obviously a bloke who collected women with an effectiveness that was in inverse proportion to mine and also seemed to have perfected the trick of appearing sincere to each successive conquest. Maybe that was the dodge I always missed – maintaining a believable amount of earnestness? On the other hand I had been 'quite entertaining' so I tried to let my ego focus on that boost rather than be vexed by the comparison with Gilbert.

'Good old Marc. I must renew my subscription to his fan club.'

I grinned so that Sasha could see I was only pulling her leg.

'You're probably right Sasha,' I continued. 'I only wanted you for your body, although you are fairly entertaining yourself. I've enjoyed tonight - maybe we could do it again and stay in touch via the gym. You never know, one day Marc might dump you and my itchy feet will have gone.'

'Why not,' she said, 'I could do with some encouragement with the weights and you always seem to have interesting training routines.'

So, to my surprise, I gained a training partner. A couple of months later I was still meeting her one evening a week. We usually saw each other on Tuesdays, depending on her job up at *The Wealden* and my friendly summer match commitments with *The Wanderers*. I sorted out some programmes for her so she and we used the hour or so to spot for each other before finishing off with a drink in the bar. It was also extremely convenient to be able to keep a check on anything I could glean about Gilbert and his progress in hunting for his burglars, although I didn't really think Sasha would be privy to any of her boyfriend's shadier activities.

I decided not to alarm Grace by telling her that Gilbert thought a woman was involved in the robbery and as the weeks went by and Sasha had no news about any progress in finding the man in black and his accomplice I didn't see any reason to change that decision. We just carried on with our weekly lessons, both waiting for her exams to be over and the holidays to start.

Suddenly the time was nearing ten past ten so I stood up and strolled across the stage and down the steps to ground level. Lydia glanced at me as I reached the bottom and stuck her tongue out in my direction. I winked at her and continued towards the back doors so that I could quickly slip away when my relief arrived. Amy from the History Department appeared just as I reached the doors so I mouthed 'Thanks' and made my escape.

On the Saturday I had a revision course to run; another way to earn a few extra quid. Ironic really when I had eight hundred or so grand tucked away in a furniture storage unit. I thought Lydia would find it useful and texted her to try and persuade her to come. I needn't have bothered because she replied almost immediately. *Fuck, fuck and triple fuck…I can no way do vectors even if my life depended on it. Shit x. Don't worry*, I replied, *you'll be fine after tomorrow.*

I was pleased she would be there to provide some amusing distractions. I had offered her the day free because I'd taken so much money from her mother for ordinary tuition over the past two years I felt a little guilty. Maybe it was the great legs as well but there you go.

The course went well and we were finished by three. I worked them for an hour at a time with a five or ten minute break between the slots. At lunchtime I went to the Chinese takeaway with Lydia and her friend Kate, another serious smoker who joined us for a puff afterwards in my office.

'Still single?' I asked Lydia.

'Yes thank you,' she stated categorically, 'after the last tosser I think men and I are due a little break from each other. Mind you there are some really gorgeous men at work. Trouble is they're all over forty.'

'What's wrong with that? I asked dryly, 'we're in our prime about then.'

'Sure, sure - had someone in mind did we?' She rolled her eyes and gave me a sarcastic look.

'Only giving an opinion,' I defended myself. 'Wish I could find an eighteen year old who found me sexy.'

'Fishing, fishing. Anyway you couldn't stand the pace so watch your blood pressure.'

'Will you two stop it,' interrupted Kate. 'It's ruining my cigarette.'

'Sorry Kate,' I apologised. 'I'll stick to the maths from now on.'

'Good job, that's what we're paying you for after all!' murmured Lydia, just to wind me up. I laughed and so did Kate even though the real joke had gone over her head.

'All right, all right let's change the subject,' I said, putting my hands up in acknowledgement of defeat. 'Has the Leavers' Ball been organised yet? I haven't heard anything.'

Kate answered after another drag of her cigarette.

'Yeah, it's a week on Friday. You gonna grace us with your presence Dr Mac?'

'I usually put in an appearance to help along the party spirit - show a few moves on the dance floor, check that Mr Hedges behaves himself - that sort of thing.'

Lydia treated me to another scornful laugh.

'More like check out the talent and make an idiot of yourself on the dance-floor. Don't suppose you get out much at your age.'

'Piss off; believe it or not I only go because I think some people might actually appreciate a teacher making an effort. Don't worry though Miss Pain in the Arse, I'll buy you a drink if that's what you're worried about. Anyway, where is it being held?'

'Some place called *The Wealden* something or other,' said Kate. 'It's up near Sevenoaks and pretty posh apparently. Emma and Jenny got a good deal - only twenty five quid a ticket including nibbles.'

'The where - I don't believe it!'

Lydia looked at me with disdain.

'What's the matter - don't tell me you've actually had a night out there already. Which decade was it in?'

'No, never been there - I just happen to know a few people who work there that's all.' I said, belatedly recovering my composure.

For a split second I considered backing out but it was only for a moment - I certainly wasn't missing the leaving do for one of my favourite ever years on the off chance I would run into Gilbert. I supposed that as long as I didn't wear the balaclava and chuck around stolen fifties I would be okay.

25

'Okay, hands up, let's have an answer.'

I took a brief survey.

'Yep, Maddie.'

'Is it minus four?'

'Could be - Holly?'

'Four.'

'Chloe'

'Minus four'

And so on. After a few more 'minus fours' the herd instinct set in and I only got one other 'four', the right answer.

'Well 7S, true to form only two of you are right. Excellent Holly and Zoe, you two clearly weren't influenced by your peanut-brained classmates who were all too busy forgetting…blah, blah.'

I won't go on because I'm aware that reviving memories of maths lessons might be an uncomfortable experience. Suffice it to say that after another example on the board, several more unserious insults and put-downs and I had convinced 7S they were ready to tackle a few equations on their own. I loved 7S and they responded well to my way of creating what I hope was a relaxed and fun atmosphere. Through the years one or two girls have complained but I guess I didn't want my teaching style to be dictated by people whose senses of humour had moved from their brains down to their arses so I never took any notice.

'Right, try and get three done and then come out and I'll mark 'em for you. If you get stuck come on out and I'll give you a hand.'

They settled down to work while I sat down at my desk and started to bring my planner up to date. That is until a tiny little girl with a cheeky smile, big brown eyes and a pony-tail came out and set her exercise book down in front of me. Maddie Smith.

'Doctor Mac, I'm stuck on number two.'

'Are you my little flower, let me ha-.'

Out of the blue I sensed that the class's attention was focused elsewhere. The girls were all looking in the direction of the classroom door which was behind me to my left in the corner of the room. I habitually left it open in the summer to compensate for the lack of air conditioning so if had a visitor they only had to pop their heads around the corner to catch my attention. There were a few giggles and when I looked to see what all the fuss was about Grace was standing smiling broadly in the open doorway. She was wearing jeans, a yellow vest and a Californian tan and looked like she had just come off one of that State's film sets. I felt the waves of admiration and curiosity radiate out from 7S as they took in this stunning vision – what the hell was such a cool girl doing coming to see Dr Mackenzie?!

'Hi Angel, how did it go?'

I admit the 'Angel' was mostly for 7S's benefit – they were as easy to wind-up as a Hitler Youth rally, but Grace didn't seem to mind from the way she continued to stand there looking amused. Maybe it reminded her of lessons with me when she was a Year Seven. I stood up and walked over to her.

'It was fine. Maybe I'll finally get to uni this year.'

'Brilliant. That's you finished with exams isn't it? Are you off to celebrate?'

I took her arm and guided her out of the room into the corridor and away from the straining ears and eyes of the Year Sevens. I gave them a warning look over my shoulder, ignoring the smirks some of the little sods had adopted as facial expressions.

'No, I just came to say goodbye. We're leaving on Thursday.'

'Oh yes, of course. I forgot.'

Grace had told me a few days ago during our last ever tutoring session that she was going to Spain for two weeks with some friends. I had told her I hoped to have thought of some sort of plan for the money by then but she had just pulled my leg about being the world's worst money-launderer.

Grace looked at me and gave me another warm smile. For a stupid moment I thought she was going to cry.

'Neil, look after yourself and thanks for everything.'

She hugged me and I squeezed her back, hard.

'I'll still be here when you get back - unfortunately,' I laughed.

After a few more moments she was gone and I stepped back into the classroom. Holly asked what everybody was dying to know.

'Who was that?'

'Don't be so nosy Holly, you should try and control the fascination you have for my business. You'll turn into a stalker if you're not careful.'

'No I won't,' Holly said indignantly. 'Go on Dr Mac. Who was she?'

'Yeah, tell us,' whined some of the others.

'Alright,' I said. 'If you must know she's my girlfriend.'

The looks and exclamations of disbelief were sadly predictable and it did take a while for me to get them back to work, but overall I thought it made for a memorable lesson.

As it happened that was just about the high point of the week. I would have remained blissfully ignorant of Grace's duplicity if it were not for Rocky and Gere who decided to organise a court for an hour's badminton on the Wednesday. Gere called on Monday evening to invite me along and ask me if I had any shuttles to play with. I said I didn't have any but suggested he ask Grace who I seemed to remember had a stash in the boot of her car.

'You'll have to be quick though, she's flying off to Spain on Thursday and I'm reckoning that with her social life it will be tough to get hold of her.'

'No problemo Slick, I'll call her mobile and get her to leave them at her house. I can swing by on my way home from work tomorrow.'

I met up with Rocky, Gere and Whirler at Edenbridge Leisure Centre at eight. Rocky and I gave the other two a reasonably good hiding but it was hard work and by the end of the hour we were all ready for refreshments. It was a beautiful June evening and we left the cars in the car park of the leisure centre and walked down the high street until we came to a pub with a beer garden out back. Stirling volunteered for the first round and we sat outside in the warm evening air either side of a garden table with integrated bench seats.

'Fuck, I needed that,' I said after my first hefty swig.

Rocky's face was still glowing. 'Four, four Slick; you look like you needed it.'

'At least he's left some in his glass - you've already finished most of yours,' exclaimed Whirler looking at Rocky's glass.

Rocky's round face creased around his goatee. 'Got to replenish lost fluids mate; that was a bit of a frantic session unless you hadn't noticed.'

'Judging by the look of you, you should have ordered a whole bloody keg,' chipped in Gere as he took a dainty sip.

'Come on lads, give him a break. He may be an alcoholic but let's be a little less judgemental.' I pointed out wisely. 'Anyway what's new - I haven't seen you lot since the last match of the season.'

'Yeah, yeah,' said Rocky, slapping his sweaty forehead as if he had just remembered something important. 'What are you doing on Friday the twenty-eighth Slick? It's the league do and we're organising a Men's A table. Gere and thought we should go along and pick up the league winner's cup.'

'Shit, you're joking. I'm out at a leavers' ball that night. Why didn't you tell me earlier? I thought we never bothered going anymore after you and Gere got chucked out of the one, what was it, three years ago?'

'Well, change of plan - plus we haven't actually won anything for three years so the dilemma hasn't actually been there to be considered. Come on fella, this is Men's A that we're talking about. Call me old-fashioned but forget the fucking leavers' thing and show some loyalty.'

'I'd love to but I can't. Where is it anyway, maybe I can come along after I've put in an appearance with the girls.'

I didn't really mean to cut the ball because dividing the evening in half would probably ruin both occasions but it was worth giving the appearance of making an effort. I took another thirst-quenching sip.

'Ever heard of *The Wealden Country Club and Hotel*', said Gere.

'You're joking,' I spluttered, returning most of the lager back into the glass.

'It's the way he tells 'em,' said Whirler, laughing at my discomfort.

'What's the matter Slick,' joined in Rocky. 'Need a straw?'

'Fuck off. No, that's excellent. My do is at *The Wealden* as well so I can kill two birds. I'll be with about a hundred nubile eighteen years olds so maybe you lot will want to join me unless you prefer the league's blue rinse brigade. You never know, they might be pissed enough to be impressed by a trophy.'

That lifted the mood of my three drinking companions. I could see the smiles spreading over their faces as they contemplated a promising night out.

'Genius Slick,' Rocky exclaimed loudly. 'That's a bit of a result. Maybe you can introduce us to some of the young ladies?'

'So you can introduce them to your trophy? I think not. You stand more chance with the league do women anyway – your arses are more compatible.' I said sagely after another mouthful of lager.

'Yeah, it's not a blind school Rocky,' pointed out Stirling even more perceptively. 'Still, it will be nice to see some fit women for a change – especially if they're all like Grace.'

'Steady Tiger, Grace is high class even for my school. Spain doesn't know how lucky it is to be having her for the next few weeks.'

That was the cue for Gere to ruin my evening.

'Spain? When I saw her she was packing her car up – she said she was going with her boyfriend on a trip to France.'

'Bollocks. She told me she was flying to Spain tomorrow. I know I'm getting senile but my geography's not that bad.'

As far as I knew there was no boyfriend either. A doubt crept into the back of my mind for the first time.

'No Slick,' continued Gere, whose face was beginning to betray an irritating smugness. 'I'm telling you sunshine, I saw her gear. Unless *Easyjet* are allowing five pieces of hand luggage as well as a huge fucking suitcase these days she was definitely going by car.'

Excuse me, I wanted to say - Grace and I were close: best-buddies, kindred spirits and all the rest - she wouldn't have lied to me. Still, there didn't seem any point in carrying on the discussion so I relented.

'Okay, maybe I got it wrong. That'll teach me to listen properly when a woman's talking.'

'Four, four,' chipped in Rocky, helpfully. 'Careful Slick, we can't have you actually doing that fella – your reputation will be in pieces. Come on, who wants another?'

With an effort I forgot about Grace for the rest of the time with the others. It would be easy enough to check out Gere's story later and I was pretty sure my faith in Grace would be exonerated. I called her on her mobile when I got home later but I was put through to her voicemail. I didn't bother with a message because I couldn't think of anything to say that didn't sound like I was suspicious.

The next day there was still no response from Grace's mobile when I called, so after school I called in at the furniture lock-up. I let myself in using my code and opened the filing cabinet. It was as empty as a eunuch's underpants. I knew I was being idiotic because I had put the money in the filing cabinet myself but I couldn't help myself checking the rest of the furniture just to make sure the money wasn't anywhere else. When that drew the inevitable blank I accepted defeat.

'Grace, what have you done?' I blurted out feebly.

Outburst over I leant over the filing cabinet in a pose that that to an onlooker might have suggested I was about to be sick into the top open drawer. The truth is I've always had a strong stomach so hurling into a conveniently placed item of furniture has never been my forte even though a fleeting feeling of nausea nudged my senses. After a second or two I slammed the drawer shut petulantly and stood there hands in pockets, shoulders hunched and my mind numb with disbelief.

There seemed to be no doubt – I had been taken for a ride and, to add insult to injury, a nineteen year old girl rather than an experienced grifter had executed the con. Fuck, fuck, fuck – why was I such an idiot? Talk about Amazing Grace – I just hadn't seen this coming; never had an inkling. I would have bet my life on her, still would as a matter of fact, but the truth was I didn't seem to be a very good judge of character where women were concerned. The last two women I had slept with, for example, appeared to have both taken me for a sucker. I had virtually sat in the front row to witness Sasha's exploits with Gilbert and the evidence of the past few minutes wasn't stacking up too well in Grace's favour either.

Believe it or not I had a look through the lock-up one more time before admitting defeat and wandering back to the Mazda. I opened the boot and rummaged in my bag for a cigarette, lit one and slammed the boot lid back down with feeling. I took a deep drag and propped my rear up against the back of the car and looked around. There were only a couple of other guys in the parking lot. They were chatting next to a white van about thirty metres away and were oblivious to me and my misery.

To be absolutely frank, losing nearly a million quid just about beats most things where ruining your day is concerned. I tried hard to remember worse but there seemed to be no doubting that today was definitely top five material. Fuck I hadn't even bought a new shirt with it – hadn't touched it while I tried to think of some way of laundering it. What a sucker!

I finished the cigarette and got into the car and drove home. With an effort I made myself some dinner but only managed to eat half of it. I sat afterwards at the kitchen table with a bottle of red and a cigarette or two for company. The nicotine and the alcohol gradually had the desired effect and sent me into a more philosophical mood. I realised there was no point in getting stressed about something over which I had no control and taking the loss of the money on the chin seemed like the only available option

I couldn't bring myself to hate Grace or wish her ill. She had made the last year more interesting than an Arsenal Premiership-winning season and I had enjoyed every minute.

Marlowe would have never let this happen to him but there you go – that's the difference between an LA detective and a maths teacher! It was *The Big Keep* rather than *The Big Sleep*.

If Grace had succeeded in double-crossing Marlowe I thought his reaction might be the same as mine was becoming. Hell, it was only a million after all – best of luck to the kid; she had balls, metaphorically speaking, and for a while she made me feel like I was a hero in my own personal adventure. It was a neat trick as well telling me she was off to Spain so I wouldn't be alarmed about her departure for a few weeks. Chris had made a few quid too so it wasn't all gloom and doom. Maybe I would let him know what had happened in a few years when I might be able sit down and joke about Grace taking me for a ride. I knew if I told him tonight I wouldn't be able to fool him into believing I was okay.

I didn't want to talk to anyone about Grace or anything else for that matter. What I needed was some time so I could come to terms with what had happened. The last thing I wanted was someone else giving me advice and doubtless telling me what a bitch Grace was. You see, despite all the evidence to the contrary, there was still a part of me that wouldn't believe she had simply taken the money and run. The jury was still out until I called them back in and asked for a verdict. Until then I would wait and see.

26

Almost a week went by and there was no news from Grace - not that I expected there to be any. I distracted myself with school work and spent the weekend with Rachel and Alex.

On Tuesday evening I had my weekly gym session with Sasha to look forward to. It was a hot day and, when I met her in the leisure centre reception at eight, I was pleased to see the warm weather had been kind so far as her outfit was concerned. Instead of the usual three-quarter length leggings she was wearing a pair of intriguingly small white shorts below a marl grey T shirt. After warming up she dispensed with the T shirt and treated me to a bare, toned torso as the matching top to her shorts was little more than a bra. I was going to have to concentrate hard tonight to keep my mind on my lifting technique.

The gym was almost empty apart from a couple of women exercising so slowly on their respective machines that they may as well have been knitting for all the good it was doing them. That meant it was easy to chat as we trained without being conscious of nosy neighbours. And Sasha certainly seemed eager to talk more than usual. If I hadn't known better I might have thought she was flirting with me but I dismissed the idea as wishful thinking and a lack of any bedroom action since the one night aberration with Grace. I succeeded in not looking too obviously at her breasts while she was doing her dumbbell bench presses but it was almost as hard as lifting the ninety kilograms that I had graduated to on my own bench press.

We talked about this and that. I had already told her during our last session that I would be visiting *The Wealden* the following week for the Leavers' Ball and she asked me if I were still going. I admitted it was still the only thing on my social calendar at the moment at which she smiled enigmatically. I thought she was just making conversation but I was to realise later that the smile had more hidden meaning than I could have imagined.

When we were finished and I had pulled my T shirt back on Sasha said 'Come on, let's give the bar a miss. How about a beer at my place, I don't feel like hanging around here any longer?'

The Captain Kirk in my head posted a yellow alert which blinked for a moment but I accepted nevertheless: after all the worst that could happen would probably involve me seeing her naked and that didn't seem like it would be too much of a chore. After all, Grace had run off with the money and Renia was out of reach in Athens so I wasn't exactly being overrun with offers of female company. I might have swapped a night with Sasha for a beer with Renia in *Corelli's* but that particular option wasn't on offer was it?

Within ten minutes I had driven around to Sasha's, parked the car and been shown into the front room and had a beer put in my hand. I sank back into one end of Sasha's largest sofa while she continued to raise my hopes by doing the same at the other end.

'God it's hot,' she sighed, after taking a long swig from her bottle and with a 'hope you don't mind' pulled off her T shirt to reveal the bra pretending to be a work-out top. I couldn't help noticing the imprint of her nipples pressing against the top and the muscles of her upper arms as she removed her T shirt. Steady Mackenzie, she may be as inviting as a United open goal but are you sure you're facing the right way down the pitch?

'Take as much off as you like,' I said emphatically. 'Women normally cover themselves up when I'm around so it'll make a nice change.'

This was too easy. Either women were completely unavailable or they were throwing themselves at you! All right, Sasha was a slut - even if she was gorgeous and reasonably intelligent - but she knew enough about Marc Gilbert to know that playing around behind his back was probably not going to be good for her health insurance premiums. So why was she hitting on me like she hadn't been laid in weeks?

'I think this will do for now,' she said, giving me a look that could have easily pulled me across the sofa like a moth to a candle if I hadn't resisted. With an effort I succeeded in not gripping my can so hard the lager gushed out in a giveaway sign that I was feeling the pressure and attempted to inject some sanity into the conversation. Right now it didn't seem likely that much would be forthcoming from her end of the sofa.

'I don't want to be a kill-joy Sasha but I've a feeling Marc wouldn't be too keen on me being here and you almost wearing your gym kit. Unless that is you've done the intelligent thing at last and dumped the son of a bitch.'

Sasha put her head back and laughed, pushing the fingers of one hand through her black hair. Very sexy.

'Not quite I'm afraid. Marc Gilbert isn't the sort of man you just dump. I only began to realise that recently but his days are numbered, believe me, I just have to do it sensitively shall we say. He's been two-timing me anyway from what I can work out so I doubt if he'll be too upset. I'll have to find another job or course, which is annoying, but I won't be able to carry on working for him.'

I looked at her with an admiring and amused smile on my face. She had it all worked out, no question, but I wondered why she was telling me all this. There didn't seem much I could do to help, if that's what she wanted.

'Okay, so you're going to give him the old heave ho. 'How' is the first word that springs to mind, followed swiftly by 'when'.

'Oh soon; the end of next week - on Friday. I'm supposed to start a two week holiday on the Saturday so that'll make up for the wages he'll probably not pay me when I tell him I'm off.'

I suddenly saw where this was leading. The leavers' ball and badminton league do were both on Friday at *The Wealden* so I was going to be around doubling as a member of the Men's A and teacher from school.

'Hang on Sasha - that's my big night out at *The Wealden*. Surely you aren't planning on employing me as some sort of body-guard when Gilbert goes mental.'

Sasha gave me what was supposed to be a reassuring smile and hitched her legs underneath her bottom so she was kneeling on the sofa facing me. She edged a few inches closer.

'No, not really - I just thought it would be handy to have a friend around after I'd told him. I finish my shift at ten and it would be reassuring to know you are there if I need someone.'

'Couldn't you just phone him? Texting is even more callous. Make the bastard suffer. Tell you what, you call him now and I'll stick around in case he comes over.'

Sasha shook her head again.

'No Neil. I can't do it over the phone. He would come around and things would get ugly. I need to tell him face to face so that he understands it's the end – over, *finito*. Please do me this one favour Neil.'

I let out a long sigh as I digested what she had said. I couldn't very well say 'no' and that wasn't only because of the naked thighs, midriff and shoulders that were filling most of my vision. I liked her and what was the worst that could happen? I really ought to make that my catchphrase. Anyway, if she were planning to walk away from Gilbert I couldn't blame her for making contingency plans.

'Okay, I'll be there if you need me but don't expect any James Bond heroics. Any trouble and I'm dialling 999. And hey, don't go dragging me into any of your reasons for leaving him either - I'm just going to be there by coincidence, okay? '

Sasha smiled and took a small sip of her beer.

'Thanks Neil, I knew you'd help.'

'I'm just a sucker for a semi-naked woman.'

She put her other hand on my leg and leant forward and kissed me briefly on the lips.

'We could forget the semi part if you liked.'

'Is that your way of saying thank-you?'

'The kiss is a little thank-you,' she purred, looking up at me through her eyelashes. I noticed for the first time that her eyes were blue but the smell of her hair brought back several pleasant memories. I lowered my head and kissed her hungrily, meeting her tongue with my own in a little preliminary sparring. It crossed my mind that I really should play a bit harder to get but she tasted so good that I soon forgot to think about everything except my next move. Sasha seemed to be on top of the situation however.

'Take your T shirt off,' she said. 'You look hot. That's right - oh and the vest. I want to examine your chest.'

'Gosh, you're full of gratitude tonight − I didn't know a chest inspection was part of the package.'

Sasha withdrew slightly and cocked her head to one side as she considered my pecs. She shook her head.

'No Neil, I just think decent muscles on a man should be given the attention they deserve. Most women don't let on but we all love a nice set of pecs not to mention buns for that matter. Hold my beer and just lie back a minute will you?'

So I did as I was told as Sasha knelt and ran her hands gently over the muscles of my arms and upper body. I had been turned-on enough by her gym kit but this was almost unbearable.

'You have a very nice way of saying thank-you - I take it this is a 'big' one?' I managed to gasp.

'Yes I owe you,' she said, leaving a nipple so she could speak, 'for being there when I need you on Friday - and a couple of months ago.'

'I'm sorry - a couple of months ago? What did I do then?'

I hope I managed nonchalant but I doubt it. Sasha brought her head up and took the cans and placed them on the floor, leaning over me to put them next to the armrest. The sweet smell of her sweat hit my senses like a narcotic as her breasts brushed against my chest. She leant back, still smiling, and reached up and pulled her top over her head so that I could see them as well. I was searching for a word and 'magnificent' was the only one that seemed to fit the bill.

'It was you in the kitchen.'

Stay cool, focus on those breasts. I looked up at her face and said innocently.

'Me? I think you're mistaking me for someone else. A chef maybe?'

'Am I?' Sasha raised an eyebrow and treating me to a teasing smile, revealing teeth a Hollywood starlet would have killed for. 'Maybe, but right now you're the one who's getting my gratitude. The thought of you robbing Marc is quite a turn-on.'

Then she stood up briefly and let her shorts fall down to her ankles. She kicked them away idly and knelt down again between my legs facing me, giving me a moment to take in that there had been no underwear.

'Why don't all women say 'thank-you' like you?' I murmured, just before she moved her hands to rest on my chest and started kissing me on the mouth. After God knows how long and just before I passed out through oxygen deprivation she drew back and I used the opportunity to pull myself more upright so we were facing each other a few inches apart. I tried hard to look her in the eye.

'Look Sasha, this is fun – you know I don't get out much, but you're making a mistake. I've never even been in Gilbert's kitchen.'

She smiled, showing me the teeth again – the ones she was probably going to eat me with in a few minutes. What a way to go; I just hoped I wasn't going to be too stringy.

'Who said anything about Marc's kitchen Neil? Never mind, I can see you aren't going to admit anything to me. It's lucky for you I like you anyway. You can kiss my tits if you like.'

As conversation stoppers go that had to be my all time favourite so I leant forward and obeyed while trying to keep part of my mind on stand-by to ward off the awkward questions. I worked imaginatively enough to make her groan, which was encouraging, but I couldn't stop her talking completely.

'Aah, that's good. Where was I? Oh yes, the guy in the kitchen. Nice eyes, nice arse. Shouldn't be a problem if he wants a show of gratitude; you know me - I always like to please.'

'Yeah, you do.' I ran my hands down each side of her torso to the firm, narrow waist and her thighs, appreciating the smooth texture and firmness of her skin. 'When was the great revelation about my extra-curricular activities?' I continued, before finding new muscles and contours on her body to admire and investigate.

'About a week ago. I was walking home after our training and it all fell into place. You sometimes used to talk about the Grace girl you tutor. Yes that's good. God Neil, yes that's lovely.'

Sasha's body tensed in appreciation as, more by luck than judgement, I found a particularly sensitive area to caress. I resisted the urge to render her speechless and eased off a little. Obligingly she carried on speaking although I could tell it was a something of an effort.

'Then I remembered you once said you belonged to a karate club when we were seeing each other. Grace obviously hated Marc and I just realised you're such a soft touch and she would have talked you into it. Mike said he thought it was a man and a woman by the gates and I thought 'Yes, Neil and Grace!' Anyway, enough of all that – lie back please.'

I was as aroused as if I had just found Pamela Anderson in my shower so I did as I was told. She manoeuvred herself onto me, one hand on my chest while she reached down with the other to guide me in the right direction.

'God, you appear to have stopped talking.' I gasped, holding her waist gently as she wriggled herself into position.

'I'll just groan now then will I?'

'Sounds good, I'll think I'll join you.'

27

Now the exams were almost over not a lot was happening around school. I only had to invigilate a couple more times in the hall and apart from that I had less than ten hours of teaching a week. This was half of what I had to do for the rest of the year although being at school felt equally as hard as when I was on a full timetable - just one lesson in a day was a real imposition on the admin and report writing I was trying to get done.

I kept my classes hard at it, however. Once you start buggering about and easing off the pace then it becomes even more of a chore to entertain them. I pacified the girls who understandably wanted to be on holiday by letting them leave for lunch five minutes early or letting them talk for the last ten minutes of the lesson if they had worked hard. Educating students is often a question of give and take and teachers need to understand that fifty five minutes of anything, even sex, is usually enough.

Since the previous week, when I had seen more of Sasha than I anticipated, nothing very exciting had happened. She was working over the weekend and still officially Gilbert's girlfriend so I didn't bust a gut trying to see her. I made polite suggestions about meeting up but if I'm honest I was relieved that the logistics didn't work out. Don't get me wrong - I was quite keen to have sex with her but I had a feeling that I was my letting my hormones call the shots again. At least I had enough wit to realise my life was too complicated right now and the last thing I needed was a relationship which had no future beyond an agreeable way of keeping fit.

I was also having more than the odd feeling of trepidation over my promise to Sasha about the coming Friday. The most sensible thing for me to do was to keep off Gilbert's radar but here I was going to *The Wealden* and allowing myself to be involved in a domestic. After we had made love I had continued to laugh off her suggestion that I was the man from Gilbert's kitchen but we both knew that if she shared her idea with him then I could be in for some serious grief. I guessed she had counted on that keeping me onside and in her corner, to mix the metaphors of two sports, when her showdown with Gilbert took place. I kept telling myself that I was worrying about nothing but all the same that didn't stop me from being slightly nervous when the plan popped into my thoughts at unexpected moments.

I met her as usual at the gym on Tuesday; her kids were staying at home so I didn't get another invite back to the sofa. Still, we went for drinks in the bar afterwards where I checked that she was sticking to her plan to dump Gilbert. She said she was and she charmed me into renewing my pledge to be around as we had agreed the previous week.

'I'll be there,' I reassured her. 'But I'm hoping I won't be needed if that's okay – just think of me as your option of last resort. It's my big night out of the year and I'd rather it wasn't spoilt by the sight of my own blood.'

It was my own fault of course - allowing myself to be talked into being part of her strategy. At my age I should have known better than to agree to any requests that are being made by a naked woman unless they are specific to the activity in hand. All right, I wasn't completely blind, I could see she was using me but somehow I wasn't able to resist – heck, she needed a friend and Sasha certainly knew how show her appreciation.

Over two weeks had elapsed and there was still no news from Grace either. I wanted to call Fiona to check on her daughter's whereabouts but I thought it would have looked odd so I remained adrift in a sea of ignorance. As the days went by I began to come to terms with the loss of the money and settle into a more sanguine mood about Grace's behaviour. Life goes on and there was nothing to be achieved by fretting and obsessing about it except perhaps turning into a bitter and twisted old git. It wasn't as if my life was a mess without the money anyway – Rachel and Alex would always be worth more than ten million let alone one million quid, for example, so as the days passed it became easier to keep a healthier sense of perspective.

Despite the evidence to the contrary I still had a feeling in my bones that Grace hadn't double-crossed me in the way that it seemed she had. Her silence was the only thing that made me doubt but I reasoned there could be any number of reasons why she had stayed silent about her plans. Grace wasn't like Sasha, wasn't like most other people I'd met and although nearly everyone lets you down eventually I preferred not to believe that of Grace until I had proof.

Actually I was spending a lot of time thinking. If it wasn't about Grace or Sasha there was also the small matter of my own future that kept nagging away at me. I would sit in my office in free periods fighting my way through mountains of paperwork and spreadsheets asking myself whether I could stand another twenty years of doing a job where at least half of it was pointless and unproductive. There were also the unpleasant parents and the buffoons in senior management who did little else than make teaching more difficult than it was already. No, there had to be more to life than devoting it to paying off a mortgage or securing a comfortable retirement. It was like going on safari in a blindfold – yes you'd been but what the hell was the point?

It dawned on me slowly that I had no mortgage and my parenting duties were no longer a full-time occupation. Then it was obvious - why carry on clinging to a routine I had been increasingly bored with for months? If I wasn't careful I would need a calendar instead of a clock to measure the wasted time. In the end I decided I would leave at Christmas and find something to do that didn't include being stuck in front of a computer screen correlating predicted grades or analysing value-added examination results. Not being told what to do by a moron in senior management would also be a bonus. The tutoring and the money from the house in the divorce settlement meant I had enough in the bank to keep me going for a couple of years; enough time I hoped in which to find a way of life that didn't leave me drained and frustrated on more days in a year than is healthy. An extra four hundred thousand would have come in handy of course but there was no point worrying about that now. It was time for a change before I was too old to have the energy to make it.

Once I had reached that conclusion I began to see everything at work in a new and liberating light. There was now an end in sight and it made even the most mundane chores easier to bear. I realised that I was doing some things for the final time and that brought a smile to my face. Don't get me wrong – for the most part I had enjoyed my experience as a teacher, mainly because, I guess, I got on well with the students and genuinely took pleasure in their company. I had just had my own personal fill of the whole teaching package and needed a fresh challenge.

Upper Sixth Leavers' Day, when it finally arrived on Friday, therefore had an added poignancy for me. Not only had I taught some of the girls for all of their seven years at the school but now it felt a little like it was part of my own goodbye. If anything, I suppose, it diminished my own melancholy at seeing some of them go because I knew I would be joining them soon. A fair number had carried on with A level with me after I had taught them GCSE. That was always gratifying and they had given me lots of fun over the years.

There were the Manchester United supporters Claire and Emma who had taken and given endless leg-pullings. These had sometimes got a bit tense as Claire pointed out in her thank you card. Then there was cute little Sarah who always sat at the front and could leave Lydia and me helpless with laughter with her impersonations; Kate the smoker, who was always ready with a sarcastic but amusing comment; Chloe who could do Decision Maths better than me and the beautiful and brilliant Rebecca whose work was always perfect.

Lydia would be a big miss as well. Her work had never been faultless but I had looked forward to her private lessons as much as those with Grace. I loved her lack of organisation and knock-about humour that sometimes left me helpless with laughter.

Finally, there was the Rose who had made me act in the pantomime over a year ago. She had not done A Level Maths but she had been in my set further down the school with the others. Rose had been a frequent visitor to my office while she was in the Sixth Form to share a joke and help out with departmental admin. She was a born-again Christian but made me laugh like a drain as well and I'm guessing the church could do with more women with her brand of quirky humour. My office was full of pupil memorabilia and a good percentage of it was from Rose over the years: a wig and an "I Love You" mug to name but two. Yes, I would miss her and the others so it was a special Leavers' Day in more ways than one.

As part of the day there were drinks and nibbles at lunchtime in the sixth form centre and all the staff were invited along to mingle with the girls for a last get-together before the leavers' assembly in the afternoon. At the start I was standing with Barry and Anna who, like me, were each holding a glass of white wine.

'Are you two gentlemen going to the ball tonight?' Anna had asked cheerfully.

'Yes Anna, I'll be there, seeing as my social diary is about as empty as a ping pong ball.' I explained. 'What about you Barry, you're not going to chicken out again are you?'

Barry rarely made it back out of the house after a day at work so it was a rhetorical question rather than a genuine inquiry. I suspected that a few whiskies or beers soon had him reaching for the remote.

'No, I'm making a big effort this time. Got the dinner jacket out last night to check it still fits.'

'Did it?' I asked, trying to keep the sound of surprise out of my voice. Heck, Barry was coming out for a drink - was there anything left in the world that I could count on?

'A bit tight around the armpits Dr Mackenzie, thank you, but if I keep the disco moves to a minimum I should be all right.'

'Yes Barry, we don't want any incidents on the dance floor,' laughed Anna, looking mischievously at me. 'Anyway, I'm sure Dr Mackenzie will be providing all the dubious moves.'

'Give me a break Anna. I thought I could rely on you not to buy into all the scurrilous rumours that people spread about me. You should know me well enough by now to realise I'm just a pussy-cat.'

But Anna seemed pleased with herself that she had me on the wrong end of a ribbing for a change and managed to look extremely unconvinced. I was saved from further abuse by a girl asking Barry to write in her yearbook.

'Are you coming?' I asked Anna.

'No, Dr Mac, I've a husband to attend to this evening. Some of us are married you know. Isn't it about time you settled down and started acting your age?'

I knew Anna was joking but I couldn't think of a funny enough reply so I shrugged and said.

'I'm not answering that Mrs Connolly. Come on, let's do some mixing.'

I found Rose and struck up a conversation.

'Feeling emotional about your last day?' I said, tapping her on the shoulder. She glanced around and broke into a wide grin when she saw it was me.

'Not really thanks,' she said, fixing me with her sparkling brown eyes. 'I expect you're going to be missing me though Monsieur.'

'The tears will be flowing Rose but I've still got your mug to remember you by. Are you bringing the boyfriend tonight so I can assess your taste in men?'

'You bet. He's dying to meet Dr Love!'

'Just save a dance for me won't you; something slow to keep him on his toes.'

'You're on,' she said, the smile still wreathed in amusement. 'Will you be wearing the old tux?'

'Of course; I want to look my best. I don't get to dress up very often. What about you, have you bought yourself a new outfit?'

'Sure have and I think you're going to like it.'

'Will I? I'm a bit of a sucker for school uniforms actually.'

Rose laughed loudly.

'Shush Doc, the Head might be listening.'

'Look Rose, do me a favour and don't prompt an association between the Head and school uniforms. I'd prefer to keep my head clear of those sorts of images.'

Then Lydia appeared.

'What are you two finding so funny?' She said, looking at me suspiciously.

'Oh nothing,' I said as seriously as I could. 'We were just talking about school uniform.'

'Oh yeah,' she looked at me knowingly. 'I might have known you couldn't make normal small talk like all the other teachers.'

'It's all right Lyds,' Rose reassured her, a grin still creasing her face. 'He gets bored and likes to spice up the conversation with a few eccentric observations.'

'Probably getting over-excited about tonight I should think,' said Lydia perceptively. 'Hope you're going to buy me a drink after all the money I've given you over the last two years.'

'Only if you promise to get drunk and make a pass at me.'

'Sod off. When I'm that desperate I'll shoot myself.'

'I'll remind you of that during our first kiss.'

Despite herself Lydia smiled while Rose continued with her own giggling. After some more verbal jousting with Lydia I wrote in their year-books and then dealt with the requests of a few others. Then it was time to make our way over to the hall for the assembly. There were a few tears from some as the leavers sang the school song for the last time and then we all trooped out, the tradition over for another year. Only this time it would be my last as well. Afterwards I went up to the staff room for some idle chat, stayed for about half an hour and then headed for home to find my tuxedo.

28

I left Beechwood soon after seven-thirty, my steps to the car lightened by the sense of anticipation of the night ahead. It was lovely summer's evening and I felt relaxed, single and ready for some fun. As I drove over to Sevenoaks I rehearsed my reactions to any possible meetings with Gilbert or Sasha, reminding myself that there was no reason for Gilbert to connect me with the robbery and that I had a perfectly plausible excuse to be at *The Wealden*. All I had to do was keep a low profile while simultaneously having a good time - how hard could that be? 'There you go again Mackenzie,' I told myself,' maybe you should give the chipper optimism a miss until you're safely tucked up in bed later?'

I was a hundred percent sure Marlowe wouldn't have been so infuriatingly optimistic and I had to acknowledge that a guiding principle like "never trust a pretty face" would have been much more apposite for me over the past year. Grace and Sasha had certainly both been full of unwelcome surprises and I hoped Sasha didn't have any further tricks up her sleeve in the next few hours. I doubted it somehow - even if Gilbert threw a hissy fit at being dumped it wasn't really any concern of mine. He didn't seem the type to come over all emotional about a woman anyway unless perhaps that huge ego of his felt sufficiently dented. As long as she didn't involve me in the parting exchanges I should be left in peace to party. So, with the inner debate resolved, I returned my concentration to my driving and looking forward to the evening ahead.

The Wealden Country Club and Hotel was certainly impressive, especially in the warm glow of the evening sunshine. After driving in through the entrance, which consisted of a pair of granite pillars more than three feet wide and twelve high, it was still fifty yards to the hotel along a drive which was bordered at first by thick rhododendron shrubs and then by huge green lawns dotted with trees. Signs directed cars off to the left before the mansion itself was reached into a car park compartmentalised by borders of shrubs and more ornamental trees. I parked the car in a corner bay and then followed more signs along a wide, lightly gravelled path towards the hotel, breathing in the smell of recently cut grass and looking around at the tranquil scene of an English country estate on an exquisite June evening. The path led me back to the main drive and as I approached the hotel I whistled softly in appreciation at the facade of the main building.

There was a large fountain in the middle of an ornamental pond the size of the centre circle at Wembley where the drive ended in a broad swath and then circled the water feature. On the right there was an area for cars where a few Porsches and other flash chariots were parked but apart from that it was an uncluttered and imposing scene. The main door was reached by ascending a generous flight of shallow stone steps flanked by two twenty foot high Doric columns. Just walking up them made me feel important and I found it hard to understand why my ticket had only cost me twenty-five quid. The door itself was a gleaming revolving affair with brass fittings and a doorman dressed in a sober dark blue uniform with a hint of braid was standing outside greeting visitors. He looked at my ticket and gave me directions to the room where the Leavers' Ball was taking place.

Inside the door there was a large reception area dotted about with sofas and other furniture. There was no sign of Sasha but I noticed from a notice and accompanying plan at reception that Rocky's do and the Leaver's Ball were both on the same side of the building which was good news. The casino and restaurant and other facilities such as a gym and sauna were over in another larger wing. As long as our two events weren't segregated it would be possible to socialise with everyone I knew. It also looked like it would be easy to avoid the casino and the other likely places Gilbert would be gracing with his presence.

I walked across reception and found the corridor leading to the ball. The passage was wide, the walls oak-panelled and hung at intervals with old prints showing scenes of the Kent countryside. It took a couple of turns until I found myself in a room from which three other corridors exited. I took the one on the left and after a few yards came to some double doors through which I could see a few familiar figures and hear an Elton John track playing at a reasonable enough volume to tell me that the disco hadn't started yet.

The room was as large as the school hall and had a low stage at the far end but that was where the similarity ended. Chandeliers hung like sparkling alien spacecraft from the high, ornately carved white ceiling and oak panelling continued half way up the walls on three sides. The fourth wall was largely composed of pairs of elegant double doors that were opened outwards to allow access to a garden consisting of a mature, close-cropped lawn, low box hedging and pea shingle paths. There was a bar at the far end next to the stage where a couple of blokes, presumably the disc jockeys for the evening, were chatting and about a dozen large round tables were placed at intervals around the perimeter for people to sit at. The room was fairly empty because most people appeared to be outside in the garden with their drinks. I went over to the bar and got myself a tonic water and ice and then wandered out through the nearest door into the garden.

Barry and Jim, another humanities teacher, were standing together on the grass a few feet away, each with a pint in their hands. I joined them.

'Nice place,' I said, looking around, 'now I know what it feels like to be upper class.'

'We were just saying how pleasant it is,' said Barry, 'an ideal setting for tonight. I'm glad I made the effort.'

'I was right about something else as well,' said Jim, giving us one of his 'I told you so' expressions, which involved a widening of the eyes and a drawing back of the mouth as an old gossip in a sitcom. 'Some of the dresses; Jesus, they don't leave much to the imagination!'

'Yeah, some lucky lads here tonight,' I agreed. 'It seems a bit of a waste when half of them don't look like they'd know what to do with some quality crumpet. Wow, Charlotte's looking good tonight.'

A blonde vision in a long black figure hugging dress walked by us, her low cut top and the thigh-revealing slit in the dress transfixing us momentarily.

'It's alright gentlemen, you can breathe now. Oh, is that dribble on your chin Dr Mac?' Claire Hudson from the history department was suddenly standing next to us grinning. She and a few of the younger teachers were coming tonight but she obviously hadn't found them yet or she wouldn't have been bothering with us.

'Did somebody say something or am I still dreaming?' I said.

'Back to reality I'm afraid,' said Barry chuckling.

'No women tonight then boys?' Claire said looking around.

'No, single for an evening; it's my girlfriend's pole-dancing night but Barry and Jim's women should be over after their mud wrestling tournament,' I explained.

'What a vivid imagination,' said Claire shaking her head. 'For a maths teacher that is.'

'You'd be surprised Claire,' I said sardonically. 'Catch me later and I'll try and impress you some more.'

'I'm not planning on getting that drunk so I doubt it,' said Claire dismissively and waving at some newly arrived young staff, excused herself and departed.

The garden soon filled up with girls and young men dressed in dinner jackets. I stuck with Jim and Barry for a while and then made an effort to mingle more proactively and spotted Lydia and Kate each holding a pint in one hand and a cigarette in the other. I went over and grinned at them.

'Oh God it's you,' grimaced Lydia. 'Look out Kate, there's a pensioner stalking us.'

Kate ignored Lydia's friendly greeting and smiled.

'Hi Dr Mac, very smart. Having a good time?'

'Thanks, you look great yourself. Sorry your stepmother made you bring your ugly sister.'

That forced a reluctant smile to Lydia's face and I spent the next half an hour chatting to them and other girls who came over to us, most of them exhibiting signs of more alcohol consumption than they were used to dealing with. Lydia and Kate had probably seen off more than their fair share as well but I sensed they were girls who could drink Oliver Reed under the table so I wasn't concerned. In fact, I soon realised that I was actually having a good time; *The Wealden* was a lovely setting and I was surrounded by people I liked and had a shared history with. The girls and their boyfriends were charming and the worries I had entertained beforehand faded somewhat.

The music had started up in earnest in the hall by now and waiters had also started to organise the nibbles so I found myself some food and went to find Barry and Jim with my plate. Before I could I was intercepted by Rose and a dark, haired boy who she was dragging behind her by the hand.

'There you are,' she grinned, looking pleased with herself. 'We've been looking for you everywhere. John's been dying to meet you.'

I looked at the pleasant and handsome young man at her side and smiled back.

'Hi, I've heard a lot about you,' I said, shaking his hand. 'You're a lucky man.'

Rose looked both pleased and slightly embarrassed at the realisation I might inadvertently let slip any secrets she had shared with me about John. They were mostly to do with her inability to come to a decision regarding his repeated requests for her to go out with him and I also saw the haunted look sweep across his eyes as I spoke.

'Don't worry, I'm only joking. I never even realised Rose had managed to get a man until today.'

They both laughed and Rose caught my eye with a look that said 'thank you' and after a few more pleasantries and a promise to dance later they disappeared back towards the hall. I turned away to look for Barry and Jim but instead saw Rocky and Gere coming across the grass towards me both looking unusually smart in a couple of blue suits. They were wearing the facial expressions of lottery winners but I guess that is the effect a hundred young women in party dresses often has on ordinary men. Rocky was also carrying a silver cup which I assumed was the Mens' Premier winners' trophy.

'Fucking hell Slick,' Rocky exclaimed, as we shook hands. 'Now I know why you weren't so keen on the league do.'

'Yeah, but I'm afraid it is window shopping only here mate but you're welcome to stay and have an ogle on me.'

'Wotcha sunshine,' cut in Gere. 'Don't mind him. He's only seen women in posh frocks on the telly before.'

'Yeah, it's tragic, but try and keep him under control all the same. I see you picked up the cup – fuck its bigger than I thought it would be.'

Rocky nodded, raising the cup from his side so I had a better view of the inscription of "The Wanderers" for this year.

'Yeah Slick, a few ladies have said that to me in the past, four, four.'

'What, your dick or your arse? Anyway, leaving aside the size of your trophy, I'm glad to see you found me because there's a possibility I might need some moral support tonight.'

Rocky laughed at this and looked at me incredulously.

'I don't like the sound of 'moral' Slick. What did you have in mind - locking you in the toilets to keep you away from all this temptation?'

'No, you idiot - you remember that guy I got you to phone - the one who had taken an irrational dislike to my habit of breathing - well he owns this place.'

It was Gere's turn to look shocked - only this time it was more genuine.

'Not again!! Fuck me sideways - you mean the nutter. The one I told to watch it or he'd be sucking my dick. Thanks Slick, wonderful. What do I do if he comes over for a chat and he has a good memory for voices?'

'Relax mate, why would he want to talk to us? The chances are minuscule and even if he did it was a long time ago and it was over the phone.'

Gere seemed to be convinced and Rocky, as self-centred as always, cheered up at the realisation they would be doing me a favour by hanging around. I sat them down at a wrought-iron garden table so I could finish my food and fill them in on the Sasha situation. They let me say my piece and didn't seem to be too excited by what I had to say.

'Yeah, sounds okay to me Slick,' grinned Rocky. 'You had me worried for a minute.'

'Yeah, I doubt if we'll even see her so just relax and enjoy the evening.' I agreed. 'Anyway, where are Whirler and Rick? I thought they were coming tonight.'

'They'll be over, don't worry. We slipped out after the presentations but they were still hoovering up their puddings,' said Gere in the laconic way he did everything.

'Good, the more the merrier,' I said. 'Come on, let's go the bar and get some drinks. I'm driving but I think I can manage a half without troubling the fuzz.'

'Don't you want your winner's medal Slick? I picked it up for you – it's real quality this year – none of your plastic rubbish.'

'Give it to me later, I need a drink,' I motioned to Rocky who was reaching inside a breast pocket for the latest addition to my pathetically small trophy collection. Rocky shrugged and we set off towards the bar. Rick and Whirler were inside looking for us so I had a more expensive round to pay for than I anticipated. I bought the drinks and then the five of us went back outside and sat around the same table as before. I listened as the others filled me in on what had been happening at the league do and a virtually word for word rendition of Rocky's acceptance speech. Around us the leavers and their friends were cranking up the party mood with a gradual increase in the sound of laughter and the sight of increasingly energetic dancing through the doors into the hall. More girls came over to say hello as inhibitions departed and it wasn't long before my badminton buddies had been coaxed onto the dance floor by a bunch of half-cut floozies. I was designated to keep an eye on the league cup which I perched on the table I seemed to have adopted as a personal base.

The sky was black overhead by now but the garden was atmospherically lit by strategically placed lights in the flowerbeds and trees and I sat for a minute or two enjoying my first cigarette of the evening. I glanced at my watch and saw it was ten thirty already - it looked like I was not going to see Sasha tonight. I stubbed out the cigarette and prepared to wander back into the hall when I spotted Rose coming towards me with her usual amused expression spread across her face.

'Bonjour Doc, all alone?'

I smiled a warm greeting.

'Don't worry about me Rose. I was just about to come over and join in. Where's John?'

'Oh grooving on the dance-floor with some of his mates. I thought I'd come and find Doctor Love. Lydia and Kate are on their way via the bar.'

'Wonderful, I could do with a bit more personal abuse – ah, even better they've found a couple of my badminton buddies. Please don't tell me Lydia has asked to see Rocky's trophy.'

Lydia, Kate, Rocky and Gere were trooping across the grass from the dance laughing and smiling at what I assumed was something Rocky was saying.

'Is this the famous "Mens' A"? At last I can put faces to the names.'

'I only wish it was going to live up to your expectations Rose. Here we go – hang around so I have at least one intelligent person to talk to?'

'No problemo - I wouldn't miss it for the world,' Rose said cheerily, as the other four reached us at the table.

'Hey Slick, great party,' announced Rocky. 'Gere and I were just at the bar and we got talking to these two lovely ladies whom I believe you teach. Have a lager fella.'

Rocky handed me a half in a plastic glass but I was looking at Lydia and Kate.

'What did he call you?'

It was Lydia; eyes wide open and mouth to match. 'You have to be joking – this is too much! Slick – you?!'

She and Kate started to double up with laughter while I gave Rocky a steely stare. He didn't even bother to look sorry for letting my nickname slip out. Rose and Gere were amused as well but the former said rather loyally.

'I think it suits you – not as much as Doctor Love, but it's better than say "Scotty".'

'Thanks Rose. Hey, when you two have got over your seizures why don't you take Frodo and Sam back onto the dance-floor and leave the mature conversation to Rose and I?'

'Only after I've had a fag and taken the piss out of you some more,' gasped Lydia. 'Come on Slick, can I borrow your lighter?'

Just then my mobile rang. As I answered it Rocky and Gere stared at me inquiringly. Gere looked a little nervous and it didn't help when he heard me answer.

'Sasha, hi, how's it going?'

Er, fine I think. I'm in my office now – he's buggered off back to the casino.'

'Great – does that mean you don't need me? How did he take it?'

'Surprisingly well. Look, I still need you to help get all my odds and ends to the car. I should have done it earlier but I kept putting it off – can you pop over. My office is on the first floor above reception – just take the stairs and it's the first door marked private on the left.'

'Sure, how long will it take?'

'Ten minutes max – you're an angel. Thanks.'

'I'll be right there.'

I hung up and looked at Rocky, Gere and Rose who were all waiting patiently. Gere spoke first.

'Well, what's the score? Are you going to need the moral support?'

'I don't think so but I'm not completely convinced. Call me paranoid but "never trust a pretty face" is a catchphrase I think I should have adopted months ago,' I said, dropping my phone back into an inside pocket. I'm a bit nervous about going over to her office on my own, that's all. What do you think?'

'Sounds kosher to me Slick,' said Rocky. 'Why don't you pop over and we'll wait for you here?'

'Which roughly translates to "good luck, you're on your own"? Thanks pal but I think we need a contingency plan. Look, time ten minutes, then call me – if I don't answer I need your help. Think you can handle the responsibility?'

Rose and the other two were listening.

'Mysterious Doc, I like a bit of excitement,' she said, her eyes sparkling at us.

'Amazing Slick, looks like your life isn't as boring as we thought,' added Lydia before stubbing out her cigarette.

'You'd be surprised,' I muttered. 'Look Gere, I don't know what you can come up with but if I don't reappear it's probably because Gilbert's using me for a trampoline so use your imagination.'

'What about me?' complained Rocky.

I looked at him with a puzzled expression.

'I said 'imagination' – I'm guessing the speech has exhausted your supply for the year but feel free to chip in if inspiration strikes.'

'Don't worry Doc, if these two can't think of anything us girls will come up with something.'

'Thanks Rose, but it probably won't come to that. Anyway, hope to see you in ten - I'm off.'

29

I retraced my steps through the hall, squeezing and sidestepping my way across the dance-floor that was now a strobe-lit, ear-splitting obstacle course of gyrating tuxedos and ball gowns. I managed to dodge most of the flailing arms and legs of carousing teenagers and escaped down the oak panelled corridors and finally back to reception. There was a plain brunette manning the desk but I ignored her, taking the nearest flight of stairs as Sasha had instructed. At the top I paused and saw a solid wooden door marked 'Private', which I assumed was the entrance to her office. I knocked twice and turned the handle when I heard her say, 'Come in'.

As soon as I walked in I realised something was wrong. For a start it seemed too big an office for someone of Sasha's part-time status, spacious enough for a desk, a couple of armchairs, a sofa and a large conference table. Sasha wasn't in the process of collecting her belongings either - she was sitting with her legs crossed on the desk in front of me, about ten feet away, holding a drink in her hand. She had on a dark business trouser suit together with a white open-necked blouse; although for a change I wasn't overly concerned with what she was wearing. Instead, the clincher that something more sinister was afoot was hijacking my attention - Marc Gilbert was occupying the leather chair behind the desk. The gravity of my predicament was enhanced by a tough looking guy, also dressed in dinner jacket and bow-tie, who was standing at ease to Gilbert's right.

Sasha didn't smile – she gave me an apologetic, uneasy look as I hesitated and then stopped in mid-stride, lost for words like the victim of a surprise birthday party - except I had a feeling that a loud, 'Surprise!' followed my enthusiastic cheering weren't on the agenda tonight. I turned to make a hasty retreat – my second mistake of the evening. A heavy, who must have been standing sneakily behind the door, hit me very hard on the temple with a punch that sent me staggering back, my senses scrambled by the shock and force of the blow.

I heard Sasha gasp and I raised my hands to ward off the next punch but in the process forgot about the guy next to Gilbert. He must have left Gilbert's side on nimble feet, waited until I spun under the force of the blow and intercepted my trajectory with punch of his own into my guts. I had time to tense my abdominals so it didn't completely wind me but the gasping it induced wasn't entirely theatrical either. I fell on all fours on the floor making a big deal of trying to breathe before I was flattened onto my face, probably by the impact of the sole of a shoe between the shoulder blades. Then I felt myself being pulled up by the arms and dragged across the floor like a Thunderbird puppet whose strings had been cut. My hands were fastened behind me with something that cut into my wrists and I was dumped on the sofa. My back ached, my face stung from the first blow and I was wheezing like an asthmatic but apart from that everything was cool.

I looked at my companions in the room. Only Sasha looked a little concerned but she was resisting any urge to spring to my defence. The two musclemen watched me impassively and Gilbert had an ominous no-nonsense expression on his sun-tanned face.

'Dr Mackenzie we meet again,' said Gilbert. 'I've been meaning to have a word with you about one or two things and tonight seemed like the perfect opportunity.'

If I hadn't been up to my neck in grief I might have laughed at Gilbert's greeting. Was he trying to sound like a Bond villain? If he had actually said, 'We've been expecting you' it would have been perfect.

'A simple invite would have been enough,' I mumbled – the slap on the face seemed to have affected my ability to elucidate my words. 'What do you want – if it's about Sasha we're only good friends.'

Sasha's cheeks reddened and I wondered how much Gilbert knew about the other Tuesday evening.

'It's a bit more than that I'm afraid. I think you may know something about some money of mine that was stolen. Sasha tells me she may have seen you at the scene of the crime.'

'Money? The scene of what crime?' I did my best to be convincing but I had a feeling even a performance worthy of a BAFTA nomination wasn't going to be enough. 'You shouldn't go listening to everything Sasha says – I've found her to be quite unreliable.'

Gilbert's didn't smile. Instead he stood up and came around the desk towards me. I thought he was about to take his turn in the 'let's all slap Mackenzie' fad that seemed to have swept through the office but he stopped a few feet from me. He nodded at one of his helpers who hauled me to my feet by the lapels and punched me in the stomach again. I doubled up and was shoved back on the sofa. It really is difficult to think when all you are concentrating on is trying to get some air back in your lungs so I gave up and settled for groaning. I heard Sasha say 'Marc, do you have to do it this way? Why not give him a chance to talk without all this brute force'. I wanted to say 'here, here' but settled for some more manly moaning.

'I just want Dr Mackenzie to understand the degree of shit he is in,' said Gilbert in a calm, reasonable voice. Then he was talking to me again.

'Look we can do this the easy way or not – it's up to you. So far we've been gentle with you but I'm afraid I'm renowned my for lack of patience so come on – tell me something that I want to hear!'

I could just about breathe again by that time but the thinking was still difficult. I needed to say something that didn't provoke another slapping and also gave Gere and Rocky time to come up with something. Right on cue the mellow rhythm of my mobile ring tone began to play from inside my jacket. One of the heavies took it out and switched it off but at least I knew I wasn't forgotten.

'All right,' I said. 'I get it. You've lost some money and Sasha thinks I'm your man. In my present position I can assure you that I wish I knew where it was but if you beat me all night I still won't be able to tell you. That's because I haven't the faintest fucking idea what money it is you're talking about and how I'm supposed to have stolen it. I'm a teacher for fucks sake – my idea of excitement is staying up to watch Match of the Day. What the hell makes you think I had anything to do with it anyway?'

Gilbert at least had the decency to listen to me but I could tell that he had rehearsed this conversation with me in his head a few times and none of those run-throughs ended after a few minutes with us shaking hands. He had already come to the conclusion that there was enough reason to interrogate me like this and he was going to be very thorough indeed. I guess he had weighed up Grace's involvement with me and what had happened at the car chase. I obviously wasn't an ordinary teacher with a taste for tweed jackets with leather patches at the elbows – I had beaten up Ben and then Gere had called him in the guise of a big shot gangster. No, I was going to have to put up with a lot more than a couple of smacks from his hired help before he was convinced I was kosher. He carried on.

'Don't blame Sasha entirely – I've had a long time to think about this and the more I weighed things up I realised that Grace was the only woman with reason enough and possibly the knowledge of my house to try to rob me. When I checked on her a few days ago I found out she has gone away for an extended break – suspicious in itself don't you think? Then I started thinking about the spot of bother that I had with you a few months ago and I couldn't help thinking you might have the balls to help her. I also knew that Sasha sometimes saw you at her gym so I asked her yesterday if it could have been you in the kitchen of my house on the night I was robbed.'

'Fascinating – you should try for an audition as Columbo. I can just see you in a dirty raincoat.'

This time Gilbert did the slapping – a couple of back of the hand efforts quite popular with, say, Nazis in Indiana Jones movies, but more painful in real life. I was beginning to feel sore and bruised around the mouth not to mention the side of my face, the middle of my back and both wrists. If it carried on like this it would take less time listing the parts that didn't hurt and I prayed Gere and Rocky would do something before even more tender and private regions took the fancy of Gilbert and his two chums.

'When I want a smart-arse answer I'll let you know,' Gilbert said helpfully, stepping back after his exertions.

'Where was I – yes, Sasha. Well she confirmed that it could have been you in the kitchen – same build and I remember she said back on the night it happened that he had unusual hazel-coloured eyes. I can see from here Doctor that even though yours are a little bloodshot that your eyes are hazel.'

'God you're right –it's obvious. Same eye colour and figure – it must have been me!' I managed to spit out sarcastically. 'Come on mate, you're grasping at straws and as I think you know I've an extremely nasty friend who is going to be very upset you're boring me rigid with your fucking monologues. I suggest you let me go now before a few of his boys visit *The Wealden* – it would be very bad for business, not to mention your health.'

It was a reasonable bluff but Gilbert wasn't having it this time. He shook his head and turned to Sasha.

'I think it would be better if you left us now so that Dr Mackenzie and I can carry on talking without the distraction of you in the room. I promise to treat him gently if he doesn't try and bullshit me. Is that fair?'

I would have liked a vote on that one but this was Marc-land so Sasha nodded.

'Okay Marc but please be careful. When will I see you?'

Gilbert smiled with a sincerity that almost made me blink in admiration.

'Why don't you go back to my place? I should only be an hour or so. We can have a drink and I'll let you know how it goes with our guest.'

Sasha nodded and he leant over and kissed her. She smiled and glanced at me with eyes that seemed to say 'sorry' or was it 'you'll be all right. Marc's a good guy really'.

Pass me the sick bucket. How could she be taken in by the smarmy bastard? I was going to get a good kicking, maybe worse, and he had seemed to convince her that he and I would virtually be friends at the end of the night. What the fuck was I going to do? Maybe the mad bastard would kill me whatever I said. Owning up to robbing him seemed a sure fire way to end it all messily while holding out against whatever he had in mind for an interrogation was equally disturbing. Come on Gere get your fucking finger out! Then it dawned on me – what could Gere and Rocky do? Run into the room waving the league cup around as a weapon? That would have been a funny mental image if it wasn't for the fact that I was scared witless.

But I had underestimated Gere. As Sasha slipped down off the desk to leave the sound of a fire-alarm split the relative quiet in the room. There wasn't a bell in the office so the sound was considerably damped but it was still loud enough to be intrusive.

'What the fuck is going on?' snapped Gilbert looking at my two minders. 'Who's set the fucking fire alarm off?'

They both looked as if they would have given a week's wages to know the answer to Gilbert's presumably rhetorical question but, not surprisingly, neither offered any immediate observations. Then one of them touched his ear and seemed to be listening.

'Trouble sir - smashed window at the badminton do and there's some fighting going on.'

'The badminton party?! What's a bunch of pansies like that shower doing kicking off – I would have expected it from a rugby club but badminton. Shit,' cursed Gilbert. 'Sasha, you'll have to stay here while I sort this mess out. Keep your eye on him until I get back.'

She nodded again. Fuck, if she stayed with him much longer she would wear out the neck joint that made saying yes without speaking possible. The three men disappeared out of my line of vision and I heard the door slam. I looked at Sasha who was fiddling with the glass in her hand.

'I take it this doesn't mean you're dumping him,' I said as dryly as I could.

She didn't smile, she just shook her head. 'No Neil, I'm sorry you had to find out this way. I really meant to but he's been so nice this week – a couple of days ago he said he thought we should get married – that kind of threw me. Then he had this idea about you. I tried to put him off but his mind was made up. I told him you would be here tonight so he could ask you for himself. I didn't think there would be any violence.'

I shifted myself into a more upright position.

'What did you think he'd do – ask me politely and show me the door when I denied taking his money? And what do you think he'll do to Grace – pop by her house and invite her out for a McDonalds? Why can't your brain be as cute as your face Sasha? As far as I can tell the next time you see me I might be lying in a crematorium – say hello to my kids won't you?'

Okay, I was laying it on a bit thick but it was the best I could do in the face of blind terror.

'Shut up Neil, I've said I'm sorry. Marc won't kill you – he's just trying to frighten you.'

'Thanks for the reassurance – it'll make the punching easier to bear. I hope you're right because if he does top me you'll know and then you will be the one who has to start worrying about being an accessory to murder. You should have dumped him – there's more chance of a flood in the Sahara than him ever marrying you – can't you see that? You could have anyone you want – don't waste yourself on a bastard like Gilbert.'

That made her swallow the rest of her drink with a gulp. She put the glass down on the desk and stood there, hands on hips, biting her lip. Her brow furrowed with uncertainty and she stared at me as if I had the answer to her dilemma written across my forehead. Sasha looked sexy even when she was dithering like a pensioner at a supermarket checkout but I really needed her to stop thinking and do something to help me. Finally, she walked over to the sofa and sat next to me. The fire alarm was still going so I guessed I had a few minutes longer.

'Stop being so melodramatic,' she said. 'You'll be fine – you heard Marc, he just wants to be sure it wasn't you who stole his money. And don't worry; I know I could never marry him. It was just so unexpected – out of the blue. I always seem to make the wrong decision about men – I even let you slip through my fingers.'

I would have happily throttled her with my own hands if I hadn't been tied – trust a woman to turn a life and death situation into an opportunity for a chat about her love-life -

but I restrained the urge to sob in frustration and forced a smile.

'No, that was a good decision – you're worth much more than what I could offer you Sasha. Maybe we could discuss it later because I think you're forgetting we have a more urgent situation to deal with. Let me go Sasha – you'll regret it for the rest of your life if you don't. Tell him a couple of my mates came in and took me. If you knew the friends involved you'd laugh at the idea of them ever doing anything useful but he won't know and you'll have a clear conscience. In a few minutes Marc and his hired muscle are going to come back in and beat me senseless and then wonder why I can't manage a coherent sentence. There's no way out for me unless you cut whatever's tying my hands.'

Fuck, I'd done it - been Marlowe – okay the speech had started out in Casablanca and Sasha wasn't Silver Wig but the coherent sentence stuff was pretty much perfect *The Big Sleep*. And I could see I was getting to her so I tried to look as sincere as Gilbert had managed a few minutes before and held her stare with my own. I could almost see her mind racing until she looked away biting her lip again and, finally, standing up. She walked back to the desk and rummaged in a drawer until she found some scissors and came back towards me. I tried to struggle to my feet and as I stood up the ringing of the alarm stopped and the room subsided into an ominous silence.

'Hurry Sash-.'

The sound of the handle of the office door turning stopped me in mid-request. Sasha's eyes widened with fear and surprise. Shit and bollocks – now we were both in it up to our necks.

30

'Back off Sasha, he's coming with us.'

It was Gere's voice! I turned my head around towards the door and there he was standing in the doorway with Rose looking over his shoulder. I could have kissed him full on the lips but I didn't want to upset Rose or add to Sasha's confusion.

'It's okay, she was just going to cut me free.' I said as quickly as I could get the words out. 'Come on we haven't got long.'

Gere came into the room and grabbed the scissors out of Sasha's hand. He went behind me and cut through my restraints and then chucked the offending strip of plastic on the floor.

'Are you all right Doc, you look less, er, sartorial than when you left us?' Rose said, looking at my face. She was a couple of shades paler than she had been downstairs and looked uncharacteristically fretful. I shrugged and grinned at her, hoping it would make up for the marks inflicted by Gilbert et al on my complexion..

'I'll be fine Rose. Look Sasha, this could be nasty for you. Maybe you should start screaming. I could give you a slap if it would help.'

I heard Rose murmur 'good idea' to herself but Sasha ignored her and nodded.

'Okay, I suppose I deserve it.'

'Forget it; you can invite me around for a beer sometime. I'll make it as painless as I can.'

A glimmer of a smile played fleetingly across her mouth but it ended abruptly as I slapped her across the face hard enough so that I hoped it would leave a noticeably red cheek without ruining my chances of another beer one day. Then I grabbed Rose's arm and turned for the office door.

'Come on, time to go,' I commanded and the three of us turned and ran. As we reached the top of the stairs Sasha started screaming and I heard Gilbert's voice down in reception. I stopped abruptly with the others just behind me.

'Fuck, looks like we need another way out. We'll skip the stairs and find some other way back to the party,' I whispered.

'The party - don't you mean the car park?' said Gere, sounding understandably confused as he followed me back down the corridor..

'No, I'm not running from Gilbert. I just want to meet up with him in more public surroundings.'

Without waiting for a reply I led them down a few corridors until we found a fire escape and hurtled down it. In a few minutes we had found a way back around to the lawn outside the Leavers Ball.

Just as we ran into the garden the music in the hall started up again to a huge cheer so apparently the fire alert was over and people could carry on enjoying themselves. We stopped next to a table and chairs on the grass and I turned to Gere.

'Was the fire alarm you?' I asked him. I was breathing more heavily than normal after our rapid departure from Gilbert's office but it didn't stop me lighting a cigarette in spite of the head-shaking and tut tutting from Rose.

'No, it was Rose and Lydia's idea,' Gere replied, grinning at her in admiration.

'Hey, that's the benefit of a grammar school education chaps.' Rose beamed proudly. 'Remember all those false alarms at school Doc?'

'Yeah, I do but I never thought I'd be glad to hear one as much as I was tonight. You're brilliant Rose – but what about the fight? I heard one of Gilbert's heavies say there was a punch up and a broken window at the awards dinner.'

'Ah well, we all went back to the dinner. When you didn't answer your mobile Stirling and Rick spotted Eddy and his gang having a bop, took Lydia and Kate onto the dance-floor and started a pushing and shoving match when Lydia made out Eddy had pinched her bum. Everyone had a nose at what was going on and Rocky sneaked outside with a chair and chucked it through some French windows. I don't think anyone saw him. Meanwhile, Rose and I stood by a handy fire bell and smashed the glass and legged it over to reception to find you.'

'Masterful, I hope the Three Musketeers are okay though – oh, oh, speaking of the devil!'

None other than my five co-rescuers appeared from the hall across the garden. Even from a distance their smiles were enough to tell us that the bouncers at the badminton do must have bounced the wrong people. They spotted us and hurried over in our direction.

Rocky stopped in front of me looking like the cat that had had the cream, the fish supper and the Sunday roast leftovers.

'Slick! Safe and sound mate – apart from a few scratches I see. So Gere and Rose found you?'

'Yeah thanks to you lot. How the fuck did you get away with starting a ruck at the awards dinner?'

Rocky laughed and looked triumphantly at the other four.

'Long story but another success for Mens' A I think four, four. In one fell swoop we rescue you and Rick here gets to hit Eddy - next season's game against his lot should be televised by Sky Sports. That'll be a few drinks you'll be owing me you cad!'

'Yeah Slick,' chipped in Lydia, with emphasis on my nickname. 'Come on let's get to the bar and do some ordering.'

I fished in my wallet and took out a twenty.

'All right, here's some money – go and get what you like with Kate and bring back what this lot want.'

'Nice one Slick,' Kate said, snatching the note. 'Come on give us your orders and we'll see you in a minute.'

'I'll come too and find John at the same time,' said Rose. 'He'll be wondering where I've got to.'

That was enough to distract everyone for a moment until the girls were gone. It was Rick who pointed out the obvious.

'Why aren't you on the way home mate, assuming you were in trouble just now and there was a point to us picking a fight with Eddy and his chums?'

'Yeah, good question,' said Rocky, realising the anomaly of my continued presence for the first time.

'Why run?' I said matter of factly as I stubbed out my cigarette on the grass. 'Gilbert can't very well beat me up in front of a hundred guests and I'm sick of the bastard having a go at me. It he wants some action tonight I'm going to give it to him.'

'Er, Slick,' said Rocky slowly. 'Slight problem – what about the dozens of fucking bouncers working tonight to keep annoying people like you in check? Are you mad – there's only so much shit that Mens' A can get you out of.'

'Talking of shit,' said Gere who was standing next to me. 'Some is on its way over as we speak. Don't look now but Sasha and Gilbert are on their way over to shake Slick by the throat for being such a tosser.'

'Wonderful,' groaned Rocky with the smile still fixed like a mask on his face in a pathetic attempt to act normally. 'Right you cads - everyone on your toes.'

I looked to see Sasha walking towards us across the grass from the hall. She didn't look distressed but on the other hand she didn't look like she had just won leading actress at the Oscars either. Gilbert and the two smart enforcers from the office were behind her.

'Fuck, autograph hunters,' I observed. 'When are they going to leave me alone?'

I heard Rocky mutter 'shit' in a stage whisper behind me and to complicate matters Lydia, Rose and Kate appeared out of the hall with a tray of drinks.

Sasha and the three men arrived first. Gilbert came right up to me and said with unconcealed rage.

'You've got a fucking nerve coming back here. If you're trying to take the piss then you're making a big mistake.'

I never could stand someone with an attitude problem making me their target but I resisted the urge to tell him to fuck off. He had the two bouncer buddies standing in suits behind him and I noticed a few more were looking in our direction from the hall.

'I'm sorry, but you're not making a lot of sense.' I said as calmly as I could. 'I'm just here for a night out. Or maybe I should call the police and have you arrested for false imprisonment?'

'Who the fuck's going to listen to you?' He almost spat the words out and his dark eyes glittered with barely disguised rage. 'I could have you arrested for trespassing in my office you twat. No, you're leaving now - but don't think this is over - I'll be seeing you very soon.'

I took a deep breath as I tried to think clearly through the rush of adrenalin that was being chucked into my blood stream. I don't mind admitting I was almost as scared as I was angry but I felt a dangerous bravado lurking somewhere in my guts and a proportionate loosening of my self-control. On the outside I tried to stay cool but inside any lingering characteristics of Phillip Marlowe had been swamped by those of Daffy Duck. I didn't say anything in case it came out as 'you're despicable!'

Then Lydia and the others came up and joined the happy throng. She ignored Gilbert and waltzed up to me.

'Here's your drink. We're assuming the change was a tip Slick so thanks.'

She seemed oblivious of the copious amounts of testosterone around the vicinity and the "exterminate" expression on Gilbert's face as she came between us. Maybe it was deliberate or maybe Lydia really was as insensitive as a brick – either way it didn't impress Gilbert.

'He's not doing any more drinking tonight – he's leaving right now so you can keep the beer for one of your boyfriends,' cut in Gilbert so that Lydia turned towards him. She gave him a dismissive look.

'What's your problem?' she sneered contemptuously. 'We're only having a drink – take a chill pill man.'

Gilbert's face went a disturbing shade of purple despite his perma-tan.

'That's it, escort this twat and the silly bitch from the building; their party's over,' he spat through gritted teeth.

The suit on the right stepped forward and took Lydia's arm while the other came around from behind his boss towards me. Lydia squealed.

'You're hurting me,' she cried melodramatically because even I could see that he wasn't.

But I took it as my cue - this was going to be a Leavers' Ball the Upper Sixth would always remember.

I dropped my shoulders slightly as if in a shrug of resignation as my would-be escort closed to within a foot or so and reached out to take my elbow. He wasn't expecting any resistance - I was just a mouthy teacher and as soft as shite so my next move must have come out of the blue. It was a short right uppercut that moved up under his arms and connected beneath his chin. The impact of knuckle on underside of chin made a dull satisfying sound, and I knew instinctively the fight was effectively over. Accordingly he crumpled to his knees with a comical look of surprise still on his face.

'That's for being so sneaky upstairs?' I said cheerfully, and then brought my knee up straight into his face, pole-axing him backwards onto the grass where he lay still. Another one-liner Marlowe might have been chuffed with – the release of adrenalin had banished Daffy utterly from my mind. Meanwhile, the jaw of the heavy holding Lydia dropped in surprise as this unexpected scenario unfolded.

When he'd gathered himself he let go of her arm and made a lunge at me but it was too late. Rocky, who was standing behind me to my right and obviously getting accustomed to being around while I hit people, deftly took a step forward and delivered a heavy punch into the side of his face. I stepped back and watched in relief as Gere swung a foot satisfyingly into the bloke's side as he staggered from the opposing forces of his own forward momentum and Rocky's punch.

'Just like a badminton match,' Rocky grinned but I turned away and faced Gilbert.

'Who were you calling a twat?' My voice was quiet; it felt like there was ice in my veins. Gilbert recovered his composure a little and managed to say in a voice shaking with emotion.

'You're going to regret this in so many ways you can't imagine you fucking arsehole.'

'Maybe,' I said grimly stepping towards him. 'but short term you should be doing the worrying.'

In the background I heard Lydia shout something like 'Look out there's more coming' but all I wanted was Gilbert's face for a punch bag so I didn't see the scene that was unfolding behind me.

'That's enough Neil, stop it!' Sasha's voice momentarily stalled my progress and I glanced at her.

'Dr M, look o...,' Rose shouted as Gilbert, seizing his opportunity, swung an arm at me. I saw it out of the corner of my eye and I just managed to duck enough to take the blow on the side of the head near the temple – the same place more or less where I had been hit earlier. I staggered back, the renewed pain sending a jolt through my body, but I got my arms up to give myself some protection from Gilbert who had decided to have a go for a quick knockout. I took a few more kicks in the side and thigh as I scrambled to get away from him and then managed to block a huge haymaker of a kick and stood up a few feet from him. All the time he had been going for me he had been commentating on my discomfort with unoriginal word little pictures like 'Take that you cunt', but countless nights sparring in the gyms of Devon and Liverpool gave me the experience to know from the way he was fighting that I could take him if I could manufacture the right position.

I stood up and looked at him - I was through with backing away. I feinted with my left and swung a hefty right cross into his mouth. There was a satisfying squelch as his lip burst and I felt a tooth dislodge. Without pausing, I hit him four or five more times in the face and it was his turn to lurch back with a surprised look in his eyes. I finished off with a straight side-kick to his ear and he fell back on the grass, his head whipping backwards as he hit the turf. As I came up level with his feet he looked up at me with a less arrogant look in his eyes. I let him totter onto his feet because I wanted the satisfaction of knocking him over again but that turned out to be a big mistake. Stepping away from me, his right hand disappeared inside this double-breasted dinner jacket. 'Gun' was all that registered in my mind so, without hesitating, I dived on him reaching for his hand.

I was a fraction too late. As he started to withdraw the weapon he stumbled sideways avoiding my lunge and caught me on the side of the head with it. Despite the adrenalin it hurt like hell and I heard Rose gasp. Not surprisingly, however, my attention was focussed mostly on the gun that was being levelled towards me. Gilbert took a pace backwards out of my reach and looked at me with a vicious look of triumph in his eyes. I thought of diving to avoid the discharging bullets but I also knew that it would be futile and that in a few seconds I could be dead. Rachel and Alex flashed across my mind and also words to the effect of 'Oh God' and 'This is it – being shot by this arsehole – fuck!'

'Look out Marc, behind you, he's got a gun!'

It was Sasha's voice and it sounded convincing enough for Gilbert to fall for it like the proverbial bucket of lead. As he swung around the Men's Premier Cup hit him on the side of the head making it jerk back again and the gun went off in his hand. I saw Rocky stagger back holding his chest and I dived on Gilbert. I got hold of his gun hand with both hands and closed them over the gun and his hand. As we stood wrestling for control of the gun, visible to anyone who was looking, I managed to head butt him in the face while he tried to use his knees and his free hand to loosen my grip. I wasn't having it though; I knew only after a few seconds that I was stronger than him; one of the beauties of badminton is a very strong wrist and a year's wanking can't have hurt either. I forced the gun between us with the barrel against his torso and looked him in the eyes. It was a simple calculation - he had tried to kill me and he had shot Rocky. There would be no rest for me while he was around so I there was only one logical outcome.

'I've just about had it with you, you jumped up son of a bitch,' I breathed, my face an inch from his. Then I squeezed.

I felt heat and a jolt as the gun went off with another almighty explosion of noise. Gilbert's whole body shuddered and I felt his grip on my hand relax. I looked away as the expression in his eyes went from surprise to fear in an instant and I began to feel his weight pressing against me. As he lost the ability to stand, I let him slide slowly onto the grass with the gun still in his hand.

I was suddenly aware of the silence. I looked around and all of the fighting had stopped. Gere and Sasha were kneeling over Rocky who was lying on the grass. Rick was on the phone for an ambulance and Whirler and some teachers were keeping dozens of shocked looking sixth formers at bay. I ran over to Rocky feeling desperate.

'Is he - ?' I began.

Rocky's hands were still holding his chest but he had his eyes open. His face was grimacing in pain.

'No Slick, I'm not dead - no thanks to you - but I am in fucking agony.'

'Thank God, just hang on for the ambulance,' I said, bending over him.

'I'll be fine,' he whispered. 'Look Slick, come down closer, I want to say something.'

I did as I was told and brought my face closer to his. Gere and Sasha leant back to give me some space.

'What is it mate?' I said encouragingly.

'That bullet's ruined your fucking winner's medal,' he said in a normal voice, and with that he raised his head off the grass and sat up.

'You fucking bastard,' was all I could think of to say before I gave the silly sod a hug of relief.

31

For a teacher the last week of the academic year is as blissful a five days as it is possible to imagine at school. The sun is usually shining, there's hardly any work to do or worth doing and soon there will be six weeks of holiday to enjoy. I always prefer the anticipation of a treat to the actual event. Fridays are better than Saturdays and Christmas Eve beats Christmas Day for the same reason. Here I had five lovely days of swanning around school hardly bothering to pretend I was seriously interested in doing anything productive.

I'd done very little for the previous two weeks either. Okay, the few days after the Leavers' Ball had been stressful dealing with the police and trying to avoid the press, but after a week it had more or less died down. Naturally Delores was extremely unimpressed at the reports of my antics. When speculation about Gilbert's seedier side emerged in the papers and I began to metamorphose slowly from hooligan into hero, however, the phone calls became less threatening and more obsequious. She insisted that I take two weeks to get over the whole business and to allow the excitement at school to die down. All of the girls and lads at the ball had left school but there were enough of them with younger sisters to ensure everyone at work was fully apprised of what had happened. This ensured Delores and the staff had to put up with a school-full of over-excited teenage girls on the Monday after the ball and she didn't want me coming back too quickly and provoking another outbreak of barely suppressed hysteria.

The rest of the night after I shot Gilbert is still a blur; there was so much going on and so many emotions to deal with. Until the shot that hit Rocky in the winner's medal had been fired an almighty free-for-all had been going on in the garden. According to Whirler and Rick, at least four more bouncers had arrived to help Gilbert out after Rocky and I had taken care of the advance party. My team would have been in trouble but for the help of half a dozen lads from the boys' school who Lydia and Kate encouraged to lend a hand.

When Rocky went down I remembered afterwards that there had been a lot of screaming but Whirler and Rick said that the fighting had carried on until the second shot – the one that finished off Gilbert. The fists stopped flying when all the pugilists realised it might be more sensible to watch out for flying lead rather than continuing to pursue the admittedly pleasurable and exhilarating experience of being part of a mass brawl.

Sasha had checked Gilbert for signs of life but he was gone. I joined her over by the body and said I was sorry. She showed little emotion – any illusions she might have harboured about Gilbert must have been shattered by his behaviour that evening. I couldn't even bring myself to look at the body more than briefly and I was relieved when we went and sat with the others to wait for the police. Sasha agreed with me that it might be better to attribute Gilbert's behaviour to jealousy in the love department rather than confuse matters with other stuff. Rocky and Gere were happy to go along with that. Then it was questions followed by more questions, first at *The Wealden* and then the police station. They let me go when it became obvious from Sasha's and the others' statements that Gilbert had pulled the gun and I had acted to protect myself. I knew that I could have just taken the gun off Gilbert but I didn't own up to that.

It hit the press and the television news over the weekend. "Badminton Brawl Ends in Shooting", "Sixth Form Prom Shooting", "Teacher Slays Casino Boss" and "Shock Tunbridge Wells School Shooting" and other headlines festooned the front of the papers in the newsagent's in Edenbridge on Sunday. I noticed the fat guy behind the counter give me a strange look along with my change and it didn't end there – in the Co-op a few people just stopped and stared at me when they realised I was the bloke off the television. The police had told me that I had to keep my mouth shut until an inquest was held, so to avoid any visits from the paparazzi I stayed with Gere for a few days. Rocky came around most evenings and we hung out drinking or watching dvds. Rocky also introduced Gere and I to poker and that helped pass the time unexpectedly well. We didn't play for money but the plastic chips in Rocky's poker set provided just as much competitive stimulation. Gere won the most – Rocky's luck seemed to have been mostly used up when he escaped a gunshot wound at *The Wealden* – apparently he was still breathing only because Gilbert's gun was small calibre, otherwise my winner's medal would have had a hole in it rather than deflecting the bullet god knows where. I let him keep the mangled decoration as a memento.

One evening the pair of them had a surprise for me. During a game of poker Rocky let it slip that the pair of them were thinking about starting up a business together. I knew Gere was that way inclined but I couldn't see what Rocky would bring to the party.

'What sort of business?' I asked sceptically.

'You'll never guess Slick. Raise you ten.' Rocky said, his face deadpan. I looked over at Gere for inspiration but he just laughed nervously.

'No fucking idea – landscape gardening maybe. I'm out' I said shrugging my shoulders and putting my cards aside.

'Shall I tell him Gere?' Rocky looked over at Gere who was putting a red plastic counter into the middle to cover Rocky's bid.

'Yeah, go on, he looks like he could do with a laugh.'

I looked questioningly at Rocky.

'Well, go on. I'm all ears.'

'A private detective agency.'

'A private what?!'

'You heard. Me and Underarm are striking out on our own. I have the telecommunication and computing skills while he is the management, computing and suave bastard expert.'

I resisted the urge to take the piss because I suddenly realised that I really didn't know my friends that well – at least as far as their lives outside of badminton and drinking was concerned. If I'm honest I also felt a bit jealous.

'Well I'll be buggered,' I grinned. 'Tell me more.'

And they did. By the time I went to bed that night the jealousy hadn't abated much either - maybe it would be a disaster but neither of them were mugs and the whole idea struck me as incredibly appealing. So I wasn't the only one planning a career change and, strangely, I found Rocky and Gere's plans strengthened me in my own decision to leave my job in a few months.

For the second week I went back to the cottage and tried to make the most of the unexpected leave. I squeezed as much in as I could. I saw Rachel and Alex and also drove down and spent a couple of days with Chris, the only person with whom I could talk completely freely about everything. I had no choice but to tell him about Grace's disappearance with the money as well. I think he was as shocked as I had been even though he had only met her once on the night of the robbery. He offered to give me half of the stash he still had in his loft and I said I'd probably take him up on the offer now I was planning to retire in a few months. For now it could stay with him because I wanted to give Grace a bit longer to justify the faith I had in her.

'But for how long?' Chris had asked with some scepticism. 'It's four or five weeks already. She must have heard about what happened to Gilbert wherever she is. With him dead there's nothing stopping her from contacting you and telling you where she's up to with the money laundering – if that's what she's doing. Maybe you should re-evaluate Neil – she could be gone for years and your money forever.'

I understood what Chris was saying and deep down I was adjusting to the fact that I probably wouldn't see Grace or the money in the foreseeable future, if ever. After all the news coverage I hoped she would make contact but there were no texts or e mails whenever I checked. That money would have come in handy now I was leaving teaching and with Gilbert dead I would have been able to spend it without always looking over my shoulder. It was a bit of a bitch to put it mildly.

So I was almost relieved to come back into school for the final week of term. It stopped me thinking too much about Grace and all the other imponderables in my life. And I enjoyed it – my few remaining classes treated me as if I was Brad Pitt on work experience and I noticed some of the female staff were a little more friendly than normal.

By Thursday I was back in the routine and there was only one more day of term to go. When I went up to the staff room for my cup of tea at Break, Barry was hunched over some marking while Jan, Anna and a few others were fiddling about around the table where I sat down..

'Morning ladies, Mr Jarvis; working hard?' I teased, allowing a tone of incredulity into my voice.

'I suppose you've got about one lesson today Dr Mackenzie, while the rest of us will be actually working,' teased Anna in her melodious South African accent.

'Not even that Anna – free as a bird. Maybe we could go off somewhere?' Today the outlines of her nipples were definitely showing through her white blouse which probably qualified as the only thing of interest in the staff room.

'So how was your date then?' It was Jan directing her gaze at me.

'I beg your pardon…what date - oh, sorry, when did I say I was going on a date?

'Yesterday,' chipped in Anna. 'We know you only do it to wind us up.'

'Who was it anyway,' said Jan, switching to interrogation mode.

'Just another couple of admirers,' I said, yawning. 'Why is it that women are so attracted to celebrities like me? Anyway, I did my best to be entertaining – what about you – fun evening at the bowls club?'

'How rude!' exclaimed Anna. 'Jan he is so rude to you.'

'She knows I'm only joking,' I sighed, ignoring the hurt look Jan was trying to put on.

I had actually been out drinking the night before with Rose and Lydia. Rose had invited herself and Lydia around to my cottage for dinner although we had spent most of the evening in the pub over the road getting mullered. Lydia kept calling me Slick which was amusing at first and gradually became funnier as the evening wore on. They had crashed for the night in my bed while I had been bullied into the single bed in the spare room. I was so drunk I may as well have been lying in the garden and now I felt like I had cement for brains and had eaten a raw hedgehog for breakfast.

'Don't you ever stop Anna?' I said, watching her buggering about with her files on the table. 'It's the end of term remember.'

'I know I'm disorganised Doctor Mackenzie but we can't all be as efficient as you,' she said, looking up at me briefly with those big brown eyes.

'But I'm bored and need someone to flirt with. Barry's not my type so I'm going to sit here and bother you.'

'Charming,' she said. 'You only flirt with me by default!'

'You know it goes deeper than that Anna. You're the breast, I mean best there is out of all the staff.'

'That's almost a compliment I think,' she laughed, and returned to her work.

I turned my attention to Barry.

'Looking forward to Florida - when's the flight?'

'Sunday, quite early. Have you any plans?' he said, looking up from his marking.

'Kefalonia again probably - there's a girl I need to see.'

Barry chuckled.

'After your exploits at the ball I would have thought the ladies would have been queuing up to see you.'

'No chance. It's a pity the Upper Sixth have left; I might have had them throwing their thongs on my desk. Most of the staff haven't been any more friendly either, although that's probably a blessing as they're all totally without sex appeal,' I sighed, looking over at Anna's chest and thinking there was at least one exception to that statement.

Just then the phone on the wall rang. We all looked at it but Anna was the first to move.

'It's all right gentlemen, I'll go. You're obviously so busy you can't possibly be distracted.' She picked up the handset.

'Staff room…yes he is. Right, I'll send him over.' She grinned triumphantly at me.

'It's for you. You're blocking someone in the back car park and they want you to shift your car. I said you'd go over and sort it out.'

'How can I be blocking someone in,' I exclaimed. 'I was one of the first in and at this time of year there's only about three fucking cars there at the best of times! Sod it… Thanks a bunch Anna. I bet it's someone else's.'

I got up and made for the door. I had nothing better to do except flirt with Anna but it was still annoying.

'See you in a minute,' I groaned.

'Have fun!' said Anna, turning back to her filing.

I went downstairs and out onto the quadrangle, crossed it diagonally, skipped down some steps and strode purposefully around the end of the new building to the car park. All I could see as I rounded the corner of the brickwork was my car plus three or four others around it.

The angry and presumably stupid complainant was nowhere to be seen. I looked around waiting for him or her to arrive and it was then I noticed a note tucked underneath one of my windscreen wipers. Cursing under my breath I walked over and snatched out the folded piece of A4 and read the four words written across it in a familiar hand. "Try not to faint!"

I swung around back towards the school building smiling. It was Grace's handwriting and sure enough she was standing there watching me from the corner of the block grinning broadly.

She began to walk towards me but I just ran to her and picked her up and squeezed her tight; I'm not usually given to public displays of emotion but there was no one about and I needed to hold her.

'Dr Mackenzie, put that girl down!' It was Maggie Bishop's voice and I glanced up to see her head and those of what I presumed were her Lower Sixth English class leaning out of some first floor windows.

'Oh it's Grace,' she exclaimed in her precise Oxbridge accent. 'Interesting way you have with old girls Dr Mac – come on girls back to work!' With that the amused expressions above us disappeared back inside.

'Shit, there goes our secret affair,' I grinned. 'How are you? You look great. Why didn't you let me know you were okay?'

'Take me to your office and all will be revealed,' was all she said.

She did look fantastic. Her smooth skin was tanned and glowing and her blonde hair had lightened with the sunshine she must have been seeing a lot of. Her blue eyes sparkled and her figure looked as lithe and athletic as always in the faded jeans and T shirt she had on. Back in my office we sat down, me at my desk and Grace in the easy chair so that I had to swivel ninety degrees in order to face her.

'Come on young lady, it's time to spill the beans. What have you been up to and why the sudden dramatic appearance? I was beginning to give up hope.'

'Oh I would have come back sooner - right after mum told me what had happened to Gilbert - but it takes quite a while to deal with all that money you know. As it is my godfather is still working on my half. He has managed to sort your half out though so I persuaded him to let me give you yours now.'

'My half? You mean you've managed to launder all of the cash? Come on, tell me everything.'

Grace carried on and proceeded to answer all the questions I had spent the last six weeks asking myself. She had taken the ferry across to Calais and then left the car and ridden by train all the way down to Venice. From there it was another ferry to Athens and a bus ride to her godfather's. Travelling like this she had managed to avoid having her bags searched at customs and arrived in Greece with the money safe. There was no boyfriend – only a friend who was hitching a ride and providing company for the journey.

Her godfather had been amazed, to put it mildly, when she explained her predicament but being a true Greek the amazement had been mixed with approval at her daring and bravery. He had immediately set about organising the transformation of bundles of Sterling first into Euros which were then incorporated into bank accounts. As a rich man with a big family and contacts who were similarly engaged in the tourist trade the exchange into Euros was relatively simple even though it required weeks to accomplish. A daily stream of pounds were changed into Euros at all the local and semi-local tourist currency exchange outlets and the Euros were then passed through the accounts of the hotels, restaurants and shops the godfather and his associates owned.

After this Grace was a bit hazy on the details but it seems her godfather used the money to pay off several mortgages, transferred the properties into our names and then bought them back again. That way we would be able to use the sale of a Greek villa as an excuse for the money coming into our accounts. It sounded plausible to me and I assumed our Greek benefactor was an old hand himself at getting around the tax laws of his own country so I was as confident as a man who knew nothing about such things could be in the circumstances.

When Grace had finished explaining everything I gave her my best attempt at a look of respect.

'Wow, all I can say is thank goodness for your godfather and thank God I had such a brilliant accomplice.'

'And this is yours,' she said, reaching into her handbag and passing me a white envelope.

I took it and opened it slowly. A banker's draft for four hundred thousand pounds was inside.

'Grace, you're a genius!' I exclaimed.

She laughed in that soft sexy way.

'You've never said that before.'

'Your maths never merited it but I think this all makes up for that. I can't believe I thought I might never see you again.'

Grace looked at me reproachfully.

'You doubted me Neil? I wanted to tell you but I thought you wouldn't be keen. I just told myself that you knew you could trust me not to steal the money and that I did what I did for a good reason.'

I shrugged. 'On the face of it things didn't look good but no, I never really doubted you. Even if you had double-crossed me I told myself I had a great night with you and I always wanted to remember you like that.'

She blushed just slightly and the corners of her mouth turned up in a conspiratorial smile.

'Yes,' she said, her eyes catching mine for a moment, 'it was fun.'

32

And that's just about it really. By my reckoning I was as rich as I needed to be and with Gilbert dead I couldn't see much of a problem holding onto the money either. Grace would see that Fiona got back her lost investment and use the rest of her share whichever way she chose. Good luck to her – she deserved every penny.

I kept my new found financial independence to myself but it was tough resisting the frequent urges I had to smile even in the most bizarre circumstances. People must have suspected I had a new double-jointed girlfriend or had started wearing marijuana patches. Somehow, in the space of a year, I had gone from bored and burnt-out to smug bastard. All right, the Phillip Marlowe-like situations had been frightening at times but it was better than teaching algebra. In fact, anything seemed better than teaching algebra from where I was standing and I could hardly wait for Christmas when I would say goodbye to school forever.

I never saw Sasha again – she didn't answer my calls and I didn't run into her at the gym again either. I heard a few months later she had married a rich Spaniard who had taken her off to Barcelona. I guess there is a gym somewhere in Catalonia where the men have their workouts enhanced by a goddess in Lycra working out nearby.

Of course it wasn't quite that simple – there was one more thing I had to do before I could properly get on with my own life. Go back to Panos – partly so I could sit in sweaty bars in shorts well away from England and come to terms with having money in the bank, but mostly to see if I could find Renia. There was a month of the holidays free until I was taking Rachel and Alex to a villa in Portugal so I booked a flight to Kefalonia and called Angelos to tell him I was coming. He sent a taxi to the airport to pick me up and the day after the end of term my suitcase and I were sitting with him at a table in his bar by the pool.

'How long do you want to stay?' he asked me.

'A week, maybe two,' I shrugged, 'I'm tired mate, and it's been a tough year for me. Hardly any sex and too many fights - I'm looking for a fit Greek woman who only wants to eat, drink and have sex.'

'*Malakas*,' Angelos scoffed. 'There are no blind Greek women in Panos this summer. You will have to hope some of the English women are desperate - they usually are, ha, ha, ha.'

There was the laugh – Tommy Cooper rides again.

'Thanks for the advice, I'll bear it in mind when I'm shagging my first Greek girlfriend. Anyway, enough of me; how is Panos? Are there any changes since last year?'

There was no point trying to dredge up any sympathy or meaningful conversation with Angelos before midnight on most days so I settled for an information gathering session.'

Angelos gave a hint of a shrug himself and stretched back in his chair with his hands behind his head.

'There are a few more hotels, a few more shops maybe and one or two new *taverna*; not really.'

'And *The Secret Garden*; is it still open?'

He laughed at that one.

'Don't worry, Renia and Petra are still working there - but I think they won't want to see an old man like you very much!'

A very pleasant shiver washed over me making the smile on my face involuntary. Renia was in Panos.

'But I thought Renia was working in Athens now? I hoped someone would give me her address so I could look her up.' I tried to sound casually indifferent.

'She should be but I think she didn't like the job and she comes with her father back to the restaurant for the summer. She is a good worker so they are glad to have her. I think also her boyfriend is a *malakas* and finds a girl with bigger tits so she likes to be away from Athens for a time. Now I think she find another.'

First the good news and then the bad; the boyfriend buggering off is smartly neutralised by a new version; couldn't she have waited a few months? Maybe it would have been better if she were in Athens if only to save me from the sudden mood swings. On the bright side I would at least be seeing her again and, even better, I knew where I stood. When I went back to England I could get on with my life without yearning after her like a love-struck teenager. It also provided the excuse in Panos for feeling masochistically tragic and getting drunk whenever I felt like it. Some childish wallowing in self-pity might be therapeutic, not to mention entertaining for the locals.

A year seemed a long time to wait to see a waitress even if I had been a bit busy being a hero back at home. As relationships went it wasn't hard to admit that this one with Renia was hardly worth the name. I should have woken up to that months ago but I just hadn't got around to it; too busy and, all right, stupid to realise that the odd e mail and a day out a year were hardly the ingredients for a successful love life.

After settling into my room I showered and sat on the veranda in my towel waiting for the time to pass until it would be reasonable to go out for the evening. I wondered what reception I would receive from Renia when I walked into *The Secret Garden*. I guessed she would be a little embarrassed at my appearance but if I was cheerful and nonchalant I hoped we could get back to being friends. In weaker moments back in Beechwood I had indulged myself with the fantasy that I would ask her out. I knew I was never going to move on until I took such a chance but now I was actually in Panos I just couldn't imagine myself ever having the balls - unless there was another fight in the restaurant.

The age gap always bugged me the most. I never understand why wealthy men go for younger wives – it always seemed like inviting pressure and ridicule to me although to be fair I'd never been rich enough to have the option. Nearly fifteen years still sounded a lot, even if Grace had dismissed it - Renia would still be turning heads when I was reduced to gardening as my number one physical activity. To keep up I might have to spend my life in the gym!

On a more positive note I remembered Ranulph Fiennes had trekked across Antarctica when he was fifty-two so maybe I could surprise myself. Then again, how many times would a waiter at a restaurant ogle at my 'daughter' and follow it up by asking her if her father would like a bib with his soup or was she happy feeding him herself. I remembered Mathius making a similar mistake a few years ago with two women he was serving. Rachel, Alex and I heard him ask one of them, 'You are having a good time in Panos with your daughter?' to which the lady in question told him coldly that yes, she and her sister were doing fine. I don't know which was funnier - the shocked look of horror on Mathius' face or the way Rachel nearly choked on a tomato from the Greek salad we were sharing.

As I walked down to the town that evening I wondered what the new the boyfriend was like and pursued those kinds of thoughts until I realised again what I was doing and tried unsuccessfully to snap out of it. It had seemed strange at the time that she hadn't answered my e-mails since before Easter but now I understood why. I had initially put it down to her indifference and now I could congratulate myself on my deductive powers. With all the excitement back in England, I hadn't bothered to e-mail or text her to say I was coming to Panos and to ask whether she would be around. I started a message at Gatwick but 'go to gate 18' had flashed up next to my flight on the departures monitors so I had aborted in irritation and left for the plane. At least she would get a surprise when I walked into the restaurant.

Before going for dinner I avoided Panos's main street which would involve walking past *The Secret Garden* and took a route which brought me out at the tobacco kiosk at the top end of the busy thoroughfare. I bought some cigarettes and then headed down through the couples and families on the crowded street feeling as anxious as if I was visiting The Queen for afternoon tea. As I was passing *Corelli's* the nerves got the better of me and I decided to postpone eating by having a drink and a smoke in the bar first. It was half empty so I chose an empty table near the front and sat down on one of the canvas chairs. A waiter ambled over and I ordered a beer and settled back to observe the people promenading up and down outside. The music from the amplified MTV videos on the screens behind the bar were turned up louder than I would have liked but the sultry evening air and the feeling of freedom evoked by the holiday atmosphere more than compensated for the songs.

After a few minutes my drink arrived and I was just taking my first sip when I felt a hand on my shoulder. I half turned around in my chair to find myself looking up at Renia's smiling face. I must have looked as shocked as if Rocky had just offered himself to me but I smiled instead of reaching for a tazer. I stood up and pulled her into an embrace before stepping back and studying her face.

'Renia, what are you doing here?' I managed to say without letting my voice reach too high a pitch of excitement. 'I mean, why aren't you working?'

'It's my day off and I was talking with friends when I saw you come in,' she continued, still smiling. 'Can I join you?'

'You know you don't have to ask,' I said, as flustered as a TV presenter without an autocue. 'It's really good to see you. I can't believe I didn't spot you when I came in. Can I get you a drink?'

She sat down at right angles to me in the chair on the adjacent side of the table and I ordered her another latte to replace the one she was holding which was nearly finished. She had on her jeans and a high-necked black top which was cut so that if fastened around her neck but left her arms and shoulders bare. She looked sophisticated and even lovelier than I remembered. It crossed my mind as to where her boyfriend was tonight or if he was with the gang she had left to talk to me. Maybe I would be introduced!

'I was sitting over there at the back,' she said, pointing to a table with about four or five dark-haired Greeks sat around it. 'You looked very, how do you say, thoughtful and sad; like you were thinking hard about something.'

'I always look miserable when I'm thinking,' I grinned. 'I was wondering what to say when I saw you at *The Secret Garden*.'

'Did you decide Neil - you can tell me now if you like!' Renia looked at me inquisitively, that familiar amused look still playing across her mouth.

'Er, I don't know, probably something silly like 'I missed you' or, more likely, 'do you have a table for one.''

Her smile spread into a laugh and her eyes flashed pleasantly across the table at me. She had to be a witch because the spell always worked; it had only taken a minute and I wanted to kiss her there and then in front of every holiday maker and Greek in the bar. Fuck the boyfriend and fuck the fifteen years! Regaining my composure I quickly went on.

'Angelos told me you split up with your boyfriend. I am very sorry but why didn't you tell me? I would have come to Greece and cheered you up,' I grinned, trying to keep things light and breezy.

'Thank you,' she said softly and then, after taking a sip of her drink, continued 'but I couldn't e-mail you because I thought perhaps you would think I was, er, mad to tell you I was single. I had a very nice time with you last year but it was only for a day and I thought you would have a girlfriend yourself and think I was, how do you say, desperate?'

I allowed myself a wry smile. The girl I had spent hours thinking about for the last year had been worried I would be nervous about her coming onto me! It wasn't the place to explain the concept of irony to her, however, so I settled for the comforting thought that I had been considered as a potential love interest. I looked at her sitting in her chair and searched for something to say.

'You? Mad? Never – you should definitely have told me. Can you ever imagine me ignoring you? How are you now though Renia? Are you happy?' I tried to sound concerned without overdoing it.

'I am okay working here in Panos. I have many friends. Are you fine too? Do you have a girlfriend now?'

'No, I am still single I am afraid so you should have sent that e mail,' I grinned. 'I have given up on women or, to be more accurate, they appear to have given up on me. For a while I shall stick to my daughters for female company.'

Renia looked sympathetically at me while I searched for some hint of what she was thinking. Then the conversation moved onto our families and her job and how she had hated the firm she had worked for and decided to come to Panos before restarting her career in the autumn. It seemed to me that she had had a bad year but I didn't like to dig too deep during my first conversation with her since last August.

After about fifteen minutes I remembered that she had been with friends.

'Your friends will be missing you Renia. I'd like to stay with you all evening but won't they be cross you have deserted them?'

She looked around in the direction of her friends and waved when she found them looking across at us. We seemed to be the object of a few jokes and mirth on the table and Renia's cheeks coloured in embarrassment. There were two girls and three blokes laughing and smiling knowingly at us and I tried to guess which one was her new boyfriend.

'Do you have someone else now?' I said, still doing my best to be Mr Nonchalant. 'If he is one of those three I hope he knows how lucky he is.'

'No Neil, he is not there. They are laughing because I am talking to a good-looking Englishman. Usually I am not so, er, friendly to tourists.'

'Thanks, but I think you must all need glasses. At least I can relax that your new boyfriend will not around to hit me tonight. He's not planning to phone you unexpectedly is he?'

Renia looked down at the table and then back at me. She was still smiling but she couldn't completely disguise her own slight awkwardness.

'I have no boyfriend Neil - I am single too – I told you a few minutes ago. Perhaps it is you that are mad?'

I couldn't believe my ears - or my luck. I must have misunderstood Angelos. What did he say - 'now I think she find another'- he must have meant she would find another in the future! The bloody Greek *malakas*, why couldn't he get his English grammar right?

'But I thought that...Renia, Angelos told me you were going out with someone new.'

I sank back into the chair and let my head flop back so that I was looking at the ceiling and let out a long sigh of relief and surprise. Renia creased her eyebrows at me but her eyes still twinkled.

'Are you having a heart attack Neil? Are you so surprised that I don't have a boyfriend?'

'No to the first question and yes to the second. If I was one of your friends here in Greece I would ask you out as soon as I knew you were single.'

'Thank you - you are kind to say so,' Renia laughed. 'You always say very nice things to me Neil.'

'It's a gift. Have dinner with me.'

Renia hesitated, as surprised as I was at my proposal.

'Ah…okay I would like to but I will have to tell my friends I will not eat with them.'

I took her back to the place we had eaten last year only this time there were no shock phone calls. Talking to her was as easy as before but I spared her the details of the madness of the last few months. I hoped there would be time enough for that in the future.

It was well after midnight when we left and I walked her back towards her car so she could drive home to her parents' summer rent. The air was still warm even so close to midnight and the insects chirped sporadically from the vegetation. The car was parked in a space down on the road where it went through the pine trees by the beach and even in the moonlight looked as battered as the summer before.

'God it's still working,' I exclaimed when I saw it.

We stopped and Renia reached out and patted the roof of the ancient saloon protectively.

'Don't be mean to my car Neil. It is old like you but very reliable.'

She was looking teasingly up at me, her face pale and lovely in the half-light, and there seemed nothing else to do but kiss her on the lips, gently at first and then more urgently as I felt her arms come up around my neck and her body lean into mine. I had waited a long time to taste and feel her again, but even after twelve months her scent and touch seemed instantly familiar. When we finally paused for breath I heard myself say.

'I'd better warn you I'm probably going to fall in love with you. If it's a problem you can always send me back to England in a couple of weeks.'

Renia drew her head back and fixed me with another coy expression. With mock seriousness she said. 'But what if I fall in love with you and you leave me here with a broken heart? Men are so, how do you say, fickle? Perhaps you only want me for my body.'

I grinned. 'How did you know – I was doing my best to be romantic.'

Her brow wrinkled above the beautiful eyes and in an amused voice she said playfully.

'Ha, ha Neil - it is lucky I know you are crazy for me.'

'You could be right,' I whispered. 'Kiss me again.'

And she did.

Chris grew up in Devon a long time ago. After A levels he went to Liverpool University to study maths and managed to eke out seven years as a student there before the grants ran out. During that time Chris fell in love, married and Katie, the first of his three daughters was born. He taught on The Wirral for four years before heading south to Kent where he continued to teach for twenty two years until he succumbed to the lure of life outside the classroom. During his stint as a teacher in Kent his two other daughters, Sophie and Lucie, were born.

Since the end of his full time teaching career Chris has spread his time between writing, earning a living tutoring maths privately and avoiding men like Marc Gilbert. He lives with his second wife Theresa, near Tenterden in Kent.

Made in the USA
Charleston, SC
07 November 2015